THE IRIS]

First Published in 2000
by Quest Books(NI)
2 Slievenabrock Ave. Newcastle Co. Down N. Ireland BT33 OHZ

Typeset and printed in Northern Ireland by
The Universities Press (Belfast) Limited

A CIP catalogue record of this book is available from
The British Library

ISBN 1 872027 11 3

Front cover by Carousel Design

THE IRISH PILGRIM

BERT SLADER

A Novel

Set in County Donegal in Ireland,
in Paris, Lourdes and the South of France,
and on the ancient pilgrim Road to Santiago in Spain,
in 1950.

With best wishes

Bert

QUEST BOOKS (NI)

For
Eileen, Dion and Jenifer

ACKNOWLEDGEMENTS

Although the characters and story of THE IRISH PILGRIM are fictional, the locations in Donegal, Paris, The South of France, the Pyrenees and on the Road to Santiago are as true to their time, 1950, as memory and research have enabled me to make them.

Anamar's pilgrimage is an actual route with the exception of the first day. Although some of the paths and by-ways of 1950 are now surfaced roads, the mule track across the Mountains of Saleix in the Pyrenees is still as it was at the time of her journey. The route in Spain is now marked by yellow arrows, although this was not the case at the time of this story.

San Juan de La Peña, a monastery in Aragon, carved out of a mountain peak, the monastery of Santo Domingo de Los Silos where the Gregorian Chant is still in use and the village of San Juan de Ortega, St John Amongst the Nettles, all exist and may be visited.

I am indebted to my family and friends for their patience and understanding, to those who have travelled the pilgrim road with me, to everyone who helped me with advice and research and to the staff of the library in Newcastle, County Down for locating the Buck Whaley's Memoirs in the British Museum.

THE AUTHOR

Bert Slader, a former teacher and Deputy Director of the Sports Council for N.Ireland, is now a writer, lecturer and broadcaster.

He has travelled extensively in Europe and Asia, has mountaineered in Arctic Norway, the Alps and the Himalayas, and has led expeditions to the mountains of Iran and the Hindu Kush in Afghanistan. In 1985 he spent five weeks walking alone on the ancient pilgrim route to Santiago de Compostela. Since then he has continued his journey on foot around Spain and Portugal in three further stages, finishing back in the Pyrenees.

His first book, Pilgrims' Footsteps, inspired a ten-day walk to Santiago to raise funds for the multiple-sclerosis charity, MS Ireland. Since then he has led 15 walks for MS Ireland, 10 to Santiago and 5 along the Great Wall of China, in Goa and South Africa.

The second of his five travel books, Beyond the Black Mountain, was filmed for BBC Television. A BBC Radio series was based on his MS Santiago walks and stories of his travels have been broadcast on BBC Radio and RTE.

He was awarded a Waterford Crystal Walker Award for 1997 in respect of his books on walking and his leadership of worldwide fund raising walks for multiple-sclerosis.

His first novel, Belshade, is set in the Blue Stack Mountains in Donegal, Lourdes and the Pyrenees, in the late nineteen-forties.

THE IRISH PILGRIM is a sequel to Belshade set in 1950 in Donegal, Paris, the South of France, the Pyrenees and along the ancient Road to Santiago.

OTHER BOOKS BY THE SAME AUTHOR

Beyond the Black Mountain
A Journey around the Ulster of yesterday

Across the Rivers of Portugal
A journey on foot the length of Portugal

Footsteps in the Hindu Kush
Tales of Bert Slader's travels in Afghanistan

An Echo in Another's Mind
Echoes in the mountains of Ireland, England, Arctic Norway and Iran

Pilgrims' Footsteps Revisited
A new edition of Pilgrims' Footsteps (no longer available) to celebrate the
10th annual walk to Santiago de Compostela for the Multiple Sclerosis
Society of Ireland

QUEST BOOKS (NI)
2 Slievenabrock Ave. Newcastle Co. Down BT33 OHZ
T/N 028 437 23359

CHAPTERS

LOUGH BELSHADE

Donegal wasn't meant to be like this. Where were the showers and the Celtic mists? The clouds were high above the peaks, tiny white puffs, speeding across a sky of palest saxe blue, like swans in flight. The sun's light was far brighter than ever he had thought it would be in Ireland, but then Anamar, his friend from Donegal, the girl who called continuous light rain 'a soft day', she would simply have given him a smile.

'And tell me this now,' she would have said, 'How in God's name would a Yankee ever be able to imagine what it was like in Donegal?'

He hated to be called a Yankee. She knew he was from Louisiana in the Deep South. It was just her gentle way of keeping an American wise-guy in his place, of not allowing him to take himself too seriously.

The rumble of his motor-bike sounded much louder on the hedge-screened mountainy road. The light flickered through the bushes, shadows fluttering against him with a force as strong as a gusting breeze. And then he saw what she called the big lake. It was below him, set into the land like a huge spoonful of water trapped in the palm of a giant's hand. He stopped the bike at a gap in the hedge and cut the engine.

Oh yes, he knew about this lake. It was Lough Eske, with its own narrow road encircling it, clinging to its shores. Lough Eske sparkled like crystal cuts in green glass. The blue of the sky should have been reflected on the lake's surface but the water was in pale shades of Irish green with patches as dark as jade.

He looked up and scanned the hills above the head of the lake. They must be the Blue Stacks, so much smaller than the Pyrenees where he had met Anamar. But here, in their own domain, they were impressive. When they had climbed together on the snow-crusted peaks of the Pyrenees, no wonder she had never allowed any unfair comparison with her beloved hills of Donegal.

And she had no idea he was in Ireland. In his last letter he had explained that the U.S.A's ex-serviceman's training scheme would provide the finance to enable him to continue his education at university. He had omitted to say, however, that he had been offered a place by his first choice, the School of Medicine at Belfast's Queen's University. And here he was in Ireland with his course due to start in six weeks time.

He restarted his motor-bike and continued slowly. The farmhouse and the cottage appeared through a gap in the hedge, high on the slopes above the lake. The scene was exactly as she had described it to him. The back of his scalp tingled. It was a strange feeling, as if he had seen it all before, that he had been here before.

He laughed to himself. Ireland was having an odd effect on him. It must have been Anamar's glorious description of this valley as they had sat outside their tent, pitched at a lake high in Los Encantados, the Enchanted Mountains of the Pyrenees. He remembered his astonishment at this young woman's passion for her own place. Proud as he was of his country, her links with her land were so much more powerful than his own.

At the top of the lane a young woman came out of the house when she heard the sound of the motor-bike and the dog barking.

'You must be Maggie,' he said confidently. Anamar's letters had told him about the sale of the family farm to one of her newly-married friends when her mother died and she had mentioned her own move to what had been her grandmother's cottage in the fields above.

Maggie looked him over. The accent gave him away, so did the motorbike.

'Glory be!' she said as if she was talking to herself. 'I can't believe the sight of my own eyes. You have to be Anamar's soldier boy!'

Maggie shook her head in disbelief, dusted the flour off the front of her apron, clapped her palms together and wiped them on the back of her dress.

'And here's me like Molly from the mountains and the house topsy-turvy. Anamar's not at home.' she said, pointing up at the cottage. 'You'd better come in for a cup of tea.'

She was still talking and he was still smiling as they sat down at the kitchen table. This certainly was the Maggie Anamar had told him about.

'Could you manage one boiled egg or two?' she said, as she put a small pot on the fire, 'I hope that tea's not too strong. My husband says the way I make it you could stand on it.'

'And before you ask, I can tell you Anamar's exact whereabouts, if that's what you want to know. But what's your hurry?' Maggie knew when to be conversational. Anamar might be her friend but she rarely let slip her secrets. This visitor presented an opportunity not to be missed.

'It'll be easy enough for a mountainy man like yourself. She's in the hills just for the day, up at Lough Belshade. She'll have told you all about it in her love letters. That's the lake beside the wee cave where she took herself off to be on her own and then expected her friends to trek up to her every other day laden down with parcels of food, through bogs up to your knees and up a slope like the cliffs of Slieve League.'

Maggie seemed to be able to talk without drawing breath.

'Come on now, soldier boy. She never told us you were this quiet. What about yourself? What have you been up to since you broke her heart in the Pyrenees.'

'I didn't ..... ' He was about to explain that he hadn't broken Anamar's heart. Then he saw Maggie's smile. She hadn't had this much fun for ages.

'I guess I'm a neighbour now.' he said, 'I'll be living in Belfast, attending the university in the Fall. It's only a hundred miles away.'

'Neighbours!' said Maggie, 'Only a hundred miles away! Dear help your wit. It's another country. There's a crowd here who think New York's closer. Anyway, Anamar will be made up when she sees you. You'd better scoot up that hill and catch her otherwise I'll be in trouble. My husband will be back from the town soon and how am I going to explain me entertaining a strange American on a fancy motor-bike while he's been away.'

Maggie poured him another cup of tea, continuing the conversation as if there was no need for him to contribute a single word, telling him the way to Belshade, where to leave the motor-bike, why he needed to keep close to the river, how to find the cave. Later she confided to her friend Rose that she was so nervous she couldn't stop talking,

'He must think I'm the right eejit,' she said to Rose. In the past Rose would have teased her unmercifully, now she felt very protective of Maggie the mother.

'Don't fuss yourself.' she said,'What would he know? Sure he's only a Yankee,' They always called Anamar's friend the Yankee. 'He probably thinks you're a great woman for the chat.'

Still feeling slightly bemused by the encounter with Maggie, the American set out for Lough Belshade. He parked his motor-bike at the grey farm as Maggie had suggested, packed his wet gear and some food into a rucksack and walked up the track. He had bought a map on the way through Enniskillen. At a scale of 1/2 inch to 1 mile, it was hardly ideal for walking but it gave him his bearings.

After half an hour he could see why Maggie had suggested he keep to the river. Although still wet underfoot it was much less boggy near the bank and he made good progress to a small cairn of stones at a river junction. It was steeper now but good walking, taking him into the heart of the hills.

He had never trekked in terrain like this. The going was soft, so springy the bog grass might have been growing on a carpet of turf covering a hidden lake. The river cascaded past him, a torrent raging down between the stones towards Lough Eske. The rock was granite. He stopped and felt the rough, granular surface of a boulder with a climber's hand. The cliffs here might be short of holds but, on a dry day, the rough surface would give a sure grip to hand or boot.

He crested a rise and there it was before him, Lough Belshade, the other lake which Anamar seemed to mention every time she wrote to him. The Blue Stack Mountains really were blue, but there were no vivid colours in this painter's palette. The rock faces were grey, but one wall was a dusky red. The heather's purple was faded, the bog grass bleached straw-yellow, the eroded turf burnt umber.

The lake itself was set into the land, ringed by it, high and low. Its surface fluttered. Little waves chased each other across its width towards the tiny beach at one end where Anamar's cave should be located.

He stood on the height and studied his map, moving along the ridge to extend his view. He searched in his pack for his army field glasses, part of his mind hoping that they weren't there.They were the only item of his personal kit he had kept from his army days and he was still afraid that even this memento would raise his demons.

He had been a young officer in the US Army in World War 2, part of the Allied force called Operation Dragoon. Two months after D-Day, their mission had been an invasion of the Mediterranean coast of France to divert enemy forces from the North.

On that landing he had pitched a reluctant boy-soldier into the heat of battle for the beach. The youngster had wanted to stay on the ship but, as his not-much-older-commander, he had forced him to take to the landing craft at gun-point.

The boy had died where he had first touched the dry sand. He himself had been seriously wounded at the very moment when the battle had been won.

But he had survived and the boy had died. Time and good treatment had restored his body but the wounds of his mind had refused to heal.

'I can mend your broken bones,' the army surgeon had said, 'But only you can mend your mind.'

The therapists had tried to help but he had relived the agony during every waking minute and in the nightmare hours of sleep. Prescribed drugs had merely postponed the torment. Therapy, however prolonged and conscientiously applied, had failed him.

Then he had met Anamar in Lourdes. She was there with a pilgrim group. He had come to Europe, to his beloved Pyrenees to end the misery by taking his own life in the mountains. Before he had left home, he had chosen the peak and the huge cliff which would make it easy.

As he and Anamar had walked and climbed amongst the peaks, the girl from Donegal had saved him. Somehow she had drawn him back from the edge of the abyss. With her he had found a kind of quiet, undemanding friendship which often eludes a lifetime of searching.

During the past year they had been writing to each other and he had mentioned his plans to take up his education again with the help of a grant from the U.S. Government's scheme for the resettlement of GIs. 'Uncle Sam looks after his boys.' he had been told by the resettlement officer, 'You might have been hard to convince when you were a GI but ex-GIs seeking education are VIPs.'

In her turn, Anamar's letters had revealed a serious disagreement with her mother when she had come back from the Pyrenees. She had described how she had stayed in the mountains for a while, living in a cave beside Lough Belshade, supported by visits from her friends. The tale had been told in a series of letters, keeping him in suspense, eventually drawing him into the story when she had recounted to her friends the adventures he and she had shared in the Pyrenees.

If these were 'love letters', as Maggie had described them, it was not because there were affectionate phrases, loving words. But they were the closest contact either had ever experienced. For each of them there was understanding and trust. Neither took anything for granted but both felt able to read beyond the words.

Sometimes he had been worried that his replies would seem dull. But then Anamar was the story teller. In the mountains he had led and she had followed. When they talked, it had always been the other way around. And it had been Anamar who had helped him keep his demons at bay.

He focused his binoculars and scanned the far right-hand end of the lake. The rocks and rough ground ran down to a tiny beach. He was silhouetted against the sky so he let his binoculars hang from the neck strap and waved both arms. There was a movement above a group of boulders. It had to be her. He raised the glasses again and saw a figure. It was Anamar.

At a loping run he left the ridge, crossed the river at its mouth and tackled the rough terrain. Fifteen minutes later he was on another crest and could see her plainly, walking towards him. He waved again and shouted as he would have called to her in the Pyrenees,

'Anamar!.... Anamar!...... Arriba!.............Arriba!!

TO BE A PILGRIM

The figure at the far end of the lake startled Anamar. Last time she had seen someone pacing to and fro on that very crest had been the previous summer when she had been living in the cave on the shore of Lough Belshade. Although she had been in constant contact with home through her many visitors, her father had been the last person she might have expected to come to see her. Then it transpired that he was the bearer of bad news. Her mother had been taken ill, so seriously ill that they feared for her life.

She and her father had returned home together and her mother had died soon afterwards. Although they had only a short time together, mother and daughter had been able to talk to each other for the first time in their lives. After the funeral, bereavement should have bridged the gap between Anamar and her father, instead it had driven them even further apart.

The waving figure on the ridge reawakened those memories, bringing a feeling of foreboding like the sight of the telegram boy riding his bike slowly up the lane at home. Telegram boys were always the bearers of bad news.

The fear brought a wave of sickness. She breathed slowly and deeply and held the nausea at bay. It was too far away to recognise the face but it was a man all right, although not her father, of that she was certain by the way he moved. This was a younger man with a quicker, more agile stride. Suddenly she knew who it was but found it hard to believe the sight of her own eyes. It was the right man but in the wrong mountains, in the wrong country.

It was Hank, her American friend of the Pyrenees. She had left him at a Spanish mountain inn the previous summer. What was he doing here in the hills of Donegal?

Anamar picked up her haversack and walked towards the figure as he disappeared amongst the undulations of the land. When next she saw him he was on a rise, moving quickly, almost running. She could hear his shouts,

'Anamar!.... Anamar!...... Arriba!.............Arriba!!

This was how he would have called to her in the Pyrenees. It was the cry of a Spanish mountaineer encouraging his companions up the steep slope.

When they came close they slowed and almost stopped. It was as if they were both overcome with diffidence. Anamar held out her hands and Hank took them. They stood at arm's length, neither saying a word.

'I guess I've always heard that Ireland is the land of the welcomes. But nobody ever told me about the silent Irish greeting.' Hank was doing his best. When they had been together before, Anamar had always had the first word.

'Well, well, well,' she said slowly. 'The Yankee soldier comes to Donegal. How on earth did you find me?'

She made the next move and they hugged, kissing each other on the cheek. It was the warmest of greetings but not a lover's embrace. It was the greeting of close friends.

Hank had never expected it to be like this. Their time in the Pyrenees had encouraged him to hope for something more. Then he had needed Anamar to make the first moves and where she led, he could follow. She had changed his life. He felt he was a new man now but must still meet Anamar on her own terms.

As they talked he became aware that she had changed too. When first they had met the previous year, he had been in a hopeless state of despair. His physical wounds had healed but the mental trauma had kept him in hospital for months. Eventually he had convinced the doctors that he was on the way to recovery and had discharged himself from their care. They were not to know that he had decided to go to Europe, to the beautiful peaks of his favourite mountains, to take his own life.

And there he had found Anamar. Or rather, she had found him. His medical advisors had focused on his condition, but Anamar, gentle, undemanding, had drawn him out of his depression by interesting him in someone other than himself.

Although she knew of his death wish and without ignoring that confidence, she had managed to concentrate his mind on other things. She had insisted that he take her to see the famous Pyrenees. With her he had walked and climbed amongst his mountains. She would have said that all he needed was 'taking out of himself'. And in her own quiet way she had succeeded where the experts had failed.

Now she seemed stronger, more sure of herself. On their last night together in the Pyrenees they had come very close. But that now seemed so far in the past he might have been mistaken that it had actually happened.

Had it all been a dream with a happy ending as he emerged at last from the tunnel of despair?

Of one thing he was certain. With Anamar he must take nothing for granted.

There was so much to talk about. Hank explained why he was in Ireland and how Maggie had directed him to Lough Belshade. Anamar showed him her sheltered nooks on the slopes above the lake. They saw the cliffs, the little beach, the rocky promontories of the lake where she had spent her time when she came here to stay.

They drank from her stream. They paddled in the shallow water. She took him to the cave, the little cavern under a huge shelter stone. Her father had shown no interest in seeing what it was like but Hank scrambled up to the entrance to look without crawling inside.

On the way back down by the Corabber River they talked, now able to speak to each other far more freely than before. When they reached the gorge where the river cascaded down towards Lough Eske, she showed him the magnificent Doonan Waterfall. He was impressed but stopped himself just in time from mentioning the big falls back home. She laughed, seeming to know what he was thinking.

'Good for you, Yankee-Doodle!' she said mocking his accent, 'My GI Joe didn't tell me that in the U.S. of A. there are bigger waterfalls in people's backyards.'

Hank looked embarrassed.

'Don't worry your wee self,' she said in her own voice. 'You have to think here before you speak. It'll be good practice for living in Belfast. And don't forget. We're allowed to imitate your accent but, for the love of God, don't you try ours.'

When they reached Maggie's house Anamar linked arms with him as they crossed the yard to the door.

Maggie was ready for them. Her husband Tom had looked after the baby while she tidied the kitchen and changed. Hank would have to stay with them in the room she kept ready for her mother-in-law's visits. It would never have done for Anamar to put him up at the cottage. A young man alone for the night with a single girl, the very idea of it.

'They'd have her branded a scarlet woman before the pair of them had finished breakfast,' she told Tom as he patiently rocked the baby, keeping on the right side of his wife as he always did when at home.

Maggie insisted that they stay with her for tea. It was no trouble. She would throw a few more rashers and eggs on the pan. Hank was sure to like the soda bread and the fadge, the thin farls of potato bread fried crisply and a perfect base for an egg.

'Sunny side up or easy-over?' she said to Hank. They all laughed and she was slightly embarrassed. 'But they always say that in the films when the handsome young GI wants his breakfast.'

On the Saturday morning Hank and Anamar walked across the field path to the next farm to see Maureen and her brother Eamon. The two young McGinleys had been Anamar's main support during the time she had spent at Lough Belshade and their mother, Ellie, had been the organiser of the local pilgrimage to Lourdes earlier in the year.

Maureen said little in Hank's presence as if she was shy of the stranger, but was pleased for Anamar that he had come to live in Ireland for a while. She and Eamon had heard more of Anamar's stories of her exploits in the Pyrenees. Although Eamon would never have had the nerve to call Anamar his girl friend, he had been jealous of Hank and the adventures he had shared with her.

Now it was different. He and Hank took to each other right away. Before they parted Hank promised to bring his rock climbing ropes next time he came to Donegal and Eamon agreed to show him a great cliff in the Blue Stacks.

In the afternoon Anamar and Hank drove off on the motor-bike to see Deirdre Ryan, once Anamar's teacher, now her very good friend.

Deirdre was delighted to see them. She had encouraged Anamar to talk about Hank when they had been away. Now she was aware of him being quite different from the impression she had been given. Anamar had described him as quiet and serious, of medium height, slim, intense, looking older than his years and not very quick to appreciate the Irish sense of humour.

Now, meeting him face to face, she could see that he was taller than he looked because of his strong build. He smiled frequently. He was thoughtful for others and courteous in a formal American way, obviously a charming young man. Deirdre approved. She liked her men to be masculine, but not aggressively so. The hearty type always gave her a feeling that the man was not quite as manly as he would like others to believe he was.

This one was much better than expected. She was delighted for Anamar and made a mental note to find out when next he would be visiting Donegal so that she could arrange one of her dinner parties to coincide. New company was always welcome, particularly a presentable young man.

Everyone was up early on the Sunday morning to go to Mass. Tom always took the car and gave a lift to Anamar and the McGinleys. Mr McGinley rarely went to early Mass. He would head off later on his bicycle for the twelve o'clock, but Maureen and Eamon and Ellie were always glad of the ride. The wee car was not designed to take six adults and a baby but it was better than walking.

Tom would stay with the crowd at the church door, holding the baby, totally unconcerned that most of the men thought there must be a serious lack in a man who was happy enough to mind a child that young. Maggie was too sensible to insist on total religious observance from her husband. Mixed marriages were never easy. Tom felt a glow of self-righteousness as the provider of transport to Mass for such a crowd and for looking after the baby. This was as close as he wanted to get to his wife's church.

'You and Eamon can follow us down on the motor-bike.' Maggie said to Hank, assuming he would be going too.

'I guess that's not as easy as it sounds, mam.' Hank said diffidently. 'I'm a Methodist.'

'Holy Mother of God.' Maggie lifted her arms and wailed theatrically . 'To think we had a black-mouth Protestant under the roof for the past two nights and never knew a thing about it.' They all laughed to make sure Hank knew that Maggie was only joking.

'And I suppose I don't count.' said Tom, who sometimes felt they had all taken his conversion to their religion in order to marry Maggie too much for granted.

'Oh you're safe enough now you've turned and just as long as you stick with me and the wee one you'll be all right.' His wife was enjoying herself. 'Come on or we'll all be late. Hank can take Eamon as far as our church and head on into town to join the Methodists. They don't start until later and he can come back here on his own.'

Hank found the Methodist church near the centre of the town. The service was not until eleven so he sat on a low wall and watched the slow Sunday morning flow of people and vehicles through Donegal Town. A tall

man in a dark grey suit with a clerical collar approached him to enquire if
he was a visitor waiting for the church service. They shook hands and
introduced themselves. Hank found the Rev Ferguson very easy to talk to
and told him that he had come to the area to make contact with a friend he
had met in France.

'I left the others at the big Catholic church outside the town.' he said,
'You'll know some of them. They're just back from a pilgrimage to
Lourdes.'

'Ah! Of course. That'll be the group that went with Mrs McGinley and
Father Brogan'. William McClintock Ferguson D.D. smiled. He did indeed
know about the pilgrimage. His friend and member of his church, Dr
Wilson Corr, had been medical officer to the group. Within the
congregation this most unusual circumstance had been a minor sensation.
To calm the ensuing conflict of views the Rev Ferguson had thought it wise
to preach a sermon on pilgrimage shortly before Dr Corr had left with the
group for Lourdes.

As a minister of a church, the clerics of which were usually
evangelical, William Ferguson was one of a small band of scholars and
thinkers. His special interest was the study of Christianity in the languages
of the original texts. His published work had made his name amongst
contemporary theologians but had given him a certain notoriety within his
own church in Ireland. There were those who felt that Dr Ferguson's ideas
went too far in the direction of the doctrines of other churches.

His studies had given him a view of religions where the common
ground seemed greater by far than the exclusive territory. Within
Christianity he regretted the divisions. He was at one with John Wesley,
Anglican rector and founder of the Methodists as a ginger-group within the
church. He disagreed with the followers of Methodism who had ceded from
the Church of England, against Wesley's express wishes, as soon as he died.

Between his church and other faiths, William Ferguson saw bridges
where others saw chasms.

Attendance at Sunday services had greatly improved under his
ministry and church events were much better supported. His congregation
liked him as a minister, admired his preaching style and found him a
caring, helpful man. Some, however, felt he stretched their loyalty from
time to time by inserting into his sermons the little homilies like ,
'According to our creeds, we are all Catholics, members of the world-wide

Christian community, whether we be Methodists, Presbyterians, Anglicans or indeed Roman Catholics.'

The Rev Ferguson took Hank into the vestry room of the church by a side door and made him a cup of tea. It was too good an opportunity to miss. He had nearly an hour before he need ready himself for the service and this pleasant young American was sure to be interesting company.

Hank had been brought up within the Methodist Church in Lafayette, Louisiana. As a young teenager, and no matter how hard he tried, he had found he could not claim the kind of 'born-again' conversion that St. Paul had experienced on the road to Damascus. This concept was so fundamental within his church that he had felt distanced from those who professed to be 'saved'. To him, the evangelicals were claiming that their 'salvation' experience gave them exclusive rights to God's services, that heaven would be reserved only for those who believed as they did.

He had thought that the minister had understood. But when they had tried to talk about it that sincere man had not been able to discuss anything other than the strictly fundamentalist belief and Hank's contact with his church had all but ceased when he went to High School.

As he had drifted away from Methodism, however, he remembered most of the members of that congregation as honourable, decent people, true Christians in the way they treated others, even though he could not share the kernel of their faith.

Here in Donegal, as he talked to the Rev Ferguson, he found him so different to any cleric he had ever met at home or in the army. Others had been good company, intelligent, easy to talk to, but this minister was also at ease with ideas. He was obviously a man of strong convictions and nearly as good a listener as he was a talker.

Hank suddenly found himself recounting the war-time experience which had driven him to the point of suicide and how Anamar had helped him heal his mental anguish. It was so unlike him to speak to a stranger in this way. Apart from the doctors and the therapist who had cared for him after the battle, he had told no one except Anamar about that awful ordeal.

William Ferguson listened. He was well aware that this was no casual disclosure of personal experience. It was a privileged revelation which no longer needed any explanation or advice. All that was required was someone who could hear what was being divulged. As he finished, Hank sat back in his chair and tried to smile.

William Ferguson knew that it was now his turn.

'I don't know Miss Cassidy well.' he said, 'But I've heard she is a remarkable young woman. We have a mutual friend, Deirdre Ryan. She tells me that Anamar was the inspiration behind the recent Parish Pilgrimage to Lourdes.'

He began to talk about pilgrimage and the difficulty some of his congregation had with the very idea of it when they had heard that Dr Corr had decided to go with the group.

'Some of my flock see pilgrimage as an exclusively Roman Catholic rite.' he said, 'They have a picture in their minds of women in black climbing the steps of St. Peter's on their knees, giving alms to the poor as they go. As Methodists they know that only faith will get them to heaven, not suffering, not even good works.

'They see pilgrims flocking to a shrine to pray to statues of Mary the Mother of God or St. Bernadette, the poor peasant girl of Lourdes, when it's a sin to worship idols. Their Protestant faith tells them they have no need of intermediaries, they can pray directly to God, God the Father, God the Son, God the Holy Ghost.'

He paused and Hank smiled.

'So this is the sermon you gave your flock before the others left for Lourdes.' he said with a grin. 'It's always a good idea to tell them what they want to hear first. It sure is the way to get attention.'

They both laughed.

'You make it sound as if I was leading them on.' William Ferguson was enjoying himself.

'But wait for the next bit.' he said, 'I had to pause and grip the pulpit to steady my nerve.

'And what about the famous Protestant dissenter, John Bunyan? I said. I trust you are all familiar with his Pilgrim's Progress.'

Hank could imagine the scene. He had heard his share of spell-binding preachers but this man-of-God and his style were very different.

'As you will be well aware, Methodists love their hymns,' The Rev Ferguson continued, 'So I went straight to the hymn.' He struck a singer's pose but spoke the lines,

'Who would true valour see, let him come hither.' He paused and Hank took up the next line.

'One here would constant be, come wind come weather.' The minister joined him and to their amazement they both found themselves singing loudly in true Methodist style.

'There's no discouragement shall make him once relent,

His first avowed intent .... '

Neither noticed that the door behind them had opened and a distinguished man in a well-cut, Donegal tweed suit was standing in the doorway. He stood mesmerised as they let themselves go on the last line at the tops of their voices.

'............ To be a PILGRIM.'

'Bravo! Bravo!' The man in the doorway called softly.

Hank was slightly embarrassed. It had been a long time since he had been this close to a church and he was only here because the others had expected him to go to his place of worship when they were going to theirs.

The Rev Ferguson was delighted to see the newcomer.

'Well, well, well!' he said happily, 'The good Dr Wilson Corr, the Real Pilgrim himself. And as usual, right on cue.'

DEIRDRE'S DINNER PARTY

Hank came back to Donegal two week-ends later. Wilson Corr had invited him to stay as soon as he heard that he was to be a medical student in Belfast. For Wilson, it was like a wish come true. This young American would be following his own beloved vocation and at Queen's, where he himself had been a student all those years ago. Dr Corr had always felt he should keep himself up-to-date but reading the journals and poring through research papers would never match what he might learn from a bright young man starting from scratch in one of the finest medical schools in Europe.

Hank had already found a part-time job for the summer months as a relief porter at the Royal Victoria Hospital. Shop prices and the cost of his lodgings had made him aware that the training grant from the US Government would enable him to live well in Northern Ireland. But this was a new country and Belfast was a very different city. Working in a hospital as a porter until term started might be a good way to make contact with local people and maybe see how the medical services worked here.

By doing three consecutive night shifts over the previous week-end, Hank had managed a four-day break and drove to Donegal on the Friday morning. He called with Anamar in the afternoon. She was in her kitchen, holding a sheet of note-paper by one corner, as if it was a nasty object. Hank was concerned, thinking it must be some kind of offensive, anonymous letter but Anamar was laughing. It was a laugh without joy, however, almost hysterical.

Hank had never seen her like this. Anamar was always so much in control. Even that night when they had camped high in the Pyrenees in the eye of a fierce thunderstorm, she had been afraid but certainly not terrified.

'I'd better tell you about F.B.O'Boyle,' she said, 'I must have mentioned him in my letters. He's a local man, has a shop in the town selling clothes and dress materials. I used to work for him. It was a grand job while it lasted.'

Hank listened in silence as Anamar recounted F.B.'s involvement in the parish pilgrimage and how he had proposed marriage to her almost as soon as they had arrived in Lourdes.

'It was entirely out-of-the-blue, as if I was the first one he'd ever asked and him well into his forties. He must have been carried away by the excitement of being in Lourdes. We'd hardly ever exchanged a word before except in the course of business or the organising of the pilgrimage. The worst of it was that he couldn't believe I wasn't delighted at such a proposal from a man of his means and position.'

She looked at Hank for support but he was not sure whether he should show concern or laugh.

'I resigned from the job in his shop before he could sack me.' she said, 'And now take a look at this, if you please.'

Hank would have liked to refuse but he read the letter aloud and for some strange reason that seemed to make it easier. It was hand-written on the shop notepaper and Hank started with the impressive title.

O'BOYLE'S HABERDASHERY   DONEGAL TOWN
                                           Sole Proprietor Mr F.B.O'Boyle
Dear Miss Cassidy,

I am writing to you to clear up the little misunderstanding you and I had in Lourdes. I am sure you realise that our pilgrimage, my second visit to the Holy Shrine of Our Lady, was a very moving experience for me spiritually. It should have been a time to concentrate exclusively on the spiritual yet I allowed a temporal matter to intervene. I put my personal hopes before my devotions.

Please accept my apology. With the benefit of hind-sight and although I still believe my proposal was very proper, I am now aware that it was made at the wrong time and in the wrong place.

When we spoke afterwards, you were aware that my forwardness had created an embarrassing situation at the shop. However you saved the situation, if I may say so, at your own expense, by tendering your resignation as my employee.

With mature reflection I now see that it was very wrong of me to allow you to leave your job for my sake. Local trading conditions are improving and the next few years will see a greatly increased number of tourists to our beautiful county.

In dual-harness we achieved a great deal over the past year and I now have a modern business capable of development. We may well have to appoint additional staff.

With all this in mind I would like to offer you the new post of senior assistant in the shop and would be happy to discuss salary with you at your earliest convenience.

Yours very sincerely,
F.B.O'Boyle (Mr)
Sole Proprietor

High Class Clothing Accessories Stylish Tailoring Dressmaking
Dress and Suit Materials Artistic Millinery Modern Designs
Quality and Value Assured

Hank read right through to the end of the last three lines of advertising and shook his head slowly from side to side in disbelief. At home, business letters were short and snappy. He had never seen a letter like this but the style was familiar. His High School studies of English Literature suddenly came to mind. This man O'Boyle's letter was straight out of the previous century. He was about to say so and stopped himself just in time. Would Anamar think he was insinuating that her beloved county was a hundred years behind the times?

Anamar took the letter from him.

'If I'm to head off on my travels again next year,' she said, 'I'll need the money and there aren't many jobs around here. So, like it or lump it, I'll have to take his offer even though it means having old twinkle-toes for a boss again.'

'Twinkle-Toes' was Anamar's secret nick-name for F.B. He always wore highly-polished gentlemen's boots made of the finest leather, black for Sundays and formal occasions and brown for work. When he was talking to customers in the shop he had a habit of rocking backwards and forwards on his heels and toes to the rhythm of a double squeak - high-pitched on the way forward - low-pitched on the way back. Anamar always saw him in her mind's eye as a clock-work toy performing in the toy shop window at Christmas and it helped make working with him bearable.

Hank decided to express his concern even though she might not want him to interfere, but Anamar seemed pleased.

'I wondered when you were going to say something,' she said, 'Now I'm on my own ground you've been singing dumb, giving me the feeling that I'm talking to myself most of the time. Yankees are not supposed to be like that.'

They both began to laugh. For the first time since he had come to Donegal, Hank felt the tension between them ease.

'I reckon you can handle Mr Twinkle-Toes,' he said, 'Way back in the Pyrenees I knew you were some operator but playing at home you're awesome.'

When Deirdre Ryan heard from Dr Corr that Hank was coming for the week-end, she arranged a dinner party for the Saturday. It was one of her greatest pleasures to invite a few of her friends around for a proper evening meal. Wilson Corr was a regular and, as well as Hank and

Anamar, there were to be two other guests, the Rev William Ferguson and his wife May.

Deirdre enjoyed cooking, particularly when she was entertaining. She and Mary Rice, the local girl who was her daily help, spent the afternoon preparing the meal. Once the guests arrived Deirdre wanted to give them her full attention, so everything possible was done beforehand. Mary would have little to do at the last minute but help serve each course as it was required. Deirdre had decided that they would have egg mayonnaise, roast lamb and new potatoes, and for dessert, her own recipe for a baked pineapple pudding.

Deirdre came from County Wexford on the other side of the country and had settled here, teaching junior classes in the local school. Although there were times when she sorely missed the social life of the east of Ireland, she was happy to be living in South Donegal. An unearned income from inheritances supplemented her teacher's salary. It enabled her to own a car, to visit her friends in the East at week-ends, to travel abroad in the long summer school holidays.

Deirdre enjoyed a style of life that many would have envied. She lived in a substantially-built former farmhouse near the main road to Donegal Town. Extensive renovations had made it a comfortable home. What had been the farm kitchen and a downstairs bed-room had been converted into a large, comfortable sitting and dining room with two fireplaces, one at either end, ideal for entertaining. An extension at the back housed a new, modern kitchen, a well-stocked pantry and a laundry room. Upstairs she had her own large bedroom and two guest rooms.

Anamar and Hank were the first to arrive for the dinner party. As soon as he sat down Hank saw the picture. It was a portrait of Anamar, head and shoulders, life-size. The artist had caught the look he had seen on Anamar's face when they first met in the bookshop in Lourdes. But it had not been in the room the last time he had been here.

Deirdre saw his surprise.

'It lives upstairs in my room,' she said, 'But, like the girl herself, it takes pride-of-place on special occasions.'

As they were talking the others arrived. Wilson Corr had brought William and May Ferguson. Even though he was staying with Dr Corr and had met Deirdre and William Ferguson before, Hank felt a stranger in this company. But Deirdre had a special way with her dinner guests. She knew

Anamar would be too quiet if left to herself. Some might think she was shy or aloof but Deirdre knew that Anamar enjoyed good company as much as she did.

It would put Hank at his ease if she could encourage him to talk and when they sat down to dinner she asked him about his adventures in the Pyrenees. She knew the questions because she had heard Anamar tell the stories but Hank seemed reluctant to respond until May Ferguson joined the conversation.

If members of the Reverend Ferguson's congregation thought of his wife at all, it was as a quiet, efficient little person, perfectly suited to be a minister's wife. She organised the women's group, taught in Sunday school, supported her husband in every aspect of church life, could even make a fair attempt at playing the church organ if the regular organist was ill or on holiday.

They knew that their minister was an exceptional man, that they were fortunate to have him as their preacher. They saw him as someone special, charismatic, inspiring enthusiasm, capable of encouraging the young. And, of course, they respected his wife for the dutiful way she sustained her husband.

They were not to know, however, that hard as she worked to encourage this view within the congregation, inside the manse this minister's wife wore the trousers, and not just in a manner of speaking. Although her husband's flock were prepared to accord him a degree of toleration for his religious eccentricity, May would never have tested their forbearance by wearing slacks in public in Donegal. In the privacy of her own home or on holiday in England, almost incognito as it were, it would be a different matter.

Not that May was entirely suited to trousers. She was small and round and so quick on her feet in confined spaces that William often found himself speaking to empty air, as she popped up in front of him to his left when a second before she had been behind him on his right.

May found herself unusually at ease in this company and when Deirdre mentioned the Pyrenees it gave her the opportunity to speak.

'Have you heard of Count Henri Russell?' she said to Hank, 'He's an ancestor of mine. My mother was a Russell from Northern Ireland.'

Hank could hardly believe his ears. Henri Russell, pioneer of climbing in the Pyrenees over a century ago, was one of the few, perhaps the only true hero he had ever had. He knew that Russell's father had been born in Killough in County Down and now he was living nearby in Belfast he hoped to be able to find out more about him.

May was delighted by Hank's enthusiastic response. Deirdre, Wilson and William were all well used to leading the conversation at the beginning of such an evening but were surprised to find they were the audience not the actors. May and Hank had a common interest. They were kindred spirits. When she and William were in company she always played second fiddle. There was no chance that this would happen to-night.

'Did you know Henri went to school in Ireland?' she asked Hank, 'He was a boarder at Clongowes Wood College in County Kildare. His mother was French and they say he was a great man for singing and dancing and playing the fiddle. He must have been some character.'

'Henri was one of the great European mountaineers.' Hank said, 'Climbed in the Alps and then fell in love with the most beautiful mountain in the Pyrenees, Vignemale. Made over thirty ascents of the peak. Constructed caves near its summit. Entertained his guests to dinner on its glacier. Vignemale was Anamar's first ascent of a big mountain.'

Everyone looked at Anamar and she was embarrassed by the attention.

'Oh, I was the innocent,' she said smiling, 'If he'd told me about it before the climb I'd have been terrified.'

Hearing Anamar speak Hank felt himself suddenly at ease. It had been her idea that he should take her to climb a mountain not long after their first meeting and at the very time he had been planning his own death. But on the climb Anamar had tried so hard, had trusted him so implicitly, he had felt the strength of his suicidal depression begin to wane.

'My mother told me that he was born in France.' May continued, 'When his father retired as commander of the Papal Guard he was given a grand estate near Toulouse.'

William Ferguson's mouth was open in unabashed amazement. He and May had been married for twenty-three years and he had never heard her mention that she had a Count Russell as an ancestor.

Mention of Henri Russell's education under the Jesuits at Clongowes Wood College had already made it clear that his mother-in-law's family must, at some stage, have been Roman Catholic. Privately, he would have described the incidence of the mixed marriage in Ireland as, 'generally uncommon but in some regions, extremely rare'. However, unlike many of his fellow Protestants, it was not a circumstance of which he would have strongly disapproved.

His surprise had not been caused by the religion of his wife's forebears. He had never before heard her speak like this in company. At home she could be outspoken but never as animated as this in the presence of friends. It was certainly not the pre-dinner aperitifs. The others had taken whiskey or sherry but neither he nor May had accepted a drink. And, although he was enjoying a glass of wine during dinner, she was keeping to Deirdre's home-made lemonade.

He smiled to himself. This Deirdre Ryan had a special talent for creating congenial company. The diffident person could come out of his or her shell. He had heard Wilson Corr say that it was Deirdre's friendship which had helped Anamar to become the most interesting and enterprising young woman of his acquaintance.

During the main course there were pauses in the conversation. It was understandable. Deirdre's culinary skills were famous, her food required serious attention. The lamb was delicious, roasted with rosemary and garlic and served with mint sauce. The herbs were all from her own garden and the glorious aroma reminded Wilson of wonderful meals in France.

He asked Anamar about her next venture abroad and she began to talk about the plans which had been forming in her mind since she had returned.

'I have the wanderlust again.' she said, 'I can see myself setting out on a long journey, as my mother said before she died - a different style of pilgrimage to the one we made to Lourdes, this time on foot, to somewhere like Rome.' She looked at Deirdre. 'I'll need to read up about the whole idea of pilgrimage.'

Deirdre was smiling. When she and Anamar had ceased to be teacher and pupil and had become friends, she had encouraged Anamar to use the extensive collection of books they called her library. It pleased her now to see her young friend converse so easily in this company.

'I'll have to leave it to next year, of course,' Anamar continued, 'It will give me the chance to earn some money and it looks as if I've got my old job back at F.B.O'Boyle's.'

When the meal was over they went back to the easy chairs and May insisted on helping Mary clear the table.

'Don't get yourselves settled too comfortably,' Deirdre was talking to William and Hank, 'My special envoy to the Methodist Church, Dr Wilson Corr, tells me that you two do a duet. And after what Anamar said to-night about wanting to be a pilgrim again, the least you could do is sing her a hymn to cheer her on her way.'

Hank's head dropped forward and nodded to and fro. He had heard about the Irish ceilidh and the noble call for a song which could not be refused. William Ferguson seldom allowed himself to be talked into something he did not want to do. But how could he refuse Deirdre?

Anamar called for the singers to stand up and perform. May was delighted and clapped her hands like a child at a party. Wilson sat back in his chair trying to stay well in the background.

With a great show of reluctance William stood up and called on Hank to join him. He began to explain the background to the hymn but May stopped him short.

'Come on now,' she said, pretending to be bossy. 'No sermons, sir. Sing us the sacred song.'

William had to start twice. The first time he was far too low. When he began again Hank joined him.

'Who would true valour see......' they sang but it was a plaintive dirge.

May knocked her knuckles on the table top and clapped her hands as she did when conducting her Sunday school choir.

'That won't do at all,' she said, 'We Methodists can do much better than that. Fortissimo! Gentlemen, if you please. Fortissimo!' She raised an arm to beat out the time for her reluctant duetists. Hank closed his eyes. William looked heavenward for inspiration. Together they let it rip.

'Who-oo would true valour see,

Let him come hither! ....'

May rose to beat out the time with one sharp forefinger. Anamar and Deirdre exchanged a look of pure delight. Wilson sank even deeper in his chair. He could hear in his inner ear William's voice, in a rare moment of pique, declaiming. 'hell hath no fury like a preacher suborned'. Mary Rice stood in the doorway scarcely able to believe her eyes. Her friends would have hysterics when she told them about this.

The singers gave their audience one verse only but at full volume. When they had finished William shook hands with Hank and they sat down to loud applause and cheers.

'Bravo! Bravo!' cried Deirdre, 'Your next performance must be in church. Be sure to let us know and we'll be there, even though Anamar and I may have to apply for a special dispensation. And I have another good idea for you, too. Why not a trio? I'm sure Wilson would be delighted to join you. He could hardly restrain himself when you were at full roar.'

They all looked at Wilson and he covered his face with his hands. William pointed a long bony finger at his fellow Methodist.

'Beware the enemy within the gate,' he pronounced like a cleric of the Spanish Inquisition, 'Hank and I may eventually forgive this treachery, but be assured, my one-time friend, we won't forget it.'

Deirdre had never had a dinner party where all the guests had enjoyed themselves so much. May and William Ferguson were a revelation and Hank had really come out of himself. She smiled at Anamar and saw in her the reflection of her own delight. Life should have nights like this.

It was the first of many such parties over the autumn and winter. Hank came to Donegal every other week-end and Deirdre held her dinners once a month. Anamar, Hank and Wilson were the regulars and there were always three or four other guests.

Hank's week-ends in Donegal revolved around Anamar. They went on long walks in the hills and for drives on his motor-bike, exploring the coast. When Wilson took him fishing, she came too. Hank was teaching Eamon McGinley to rock climb and when they went to the sea cliffs or the red wall at Belshade, she sometimes came to watch.

He and Wilson had long conversations at breakfast and when he came back late in the evening they continued into the night. Politics, art, sport, travel, music, local history all had their turn, but they were at their best when medicine was the subject. In a strange way each felt that he was the pupil and the other was the teacher.

F.B.O'Boyle's shop prospered now Anamar was back. The customers returned, but his first new appointment had been unsatisfactory. She had been pleasant and enthusiastic when interviewed by him for the job but had proved to be argumentative and Anamar found her uncooperative when he was not in the shop. Anamar had insisted that the new girl had to go.

F.B. decided that the next time he interviewed, Anamar would be present too. It had not been like this when she had worked here before but now that she had returned it was as if he was no longer totally in charge.

It was a very strange feeling for him to have to consider someone's opinion other than his own, particularly when that someone was a woman. When his mother was alive she had been the boss. He could have done nothing in the shop or out of it without her approval and when she died he had taken on her role.

Was his senior assistant rising above her station? He remembered his letter to her. Had be been too rash in suggesting that they might work in dual harness? Might dual harness become single harness, with him as the horse and her as the coach driver?

F.B. said nothing to Anamar. She was good for the business, of that there could be no doubt. She was training the new assistant as if she had worked in the shop all her life. The shop itself was changing. Anamar had a constant stream of ideas. The window display needed to be modernised. The stock needed to be brought up-to-date. The account books, which he had always kept meticulously, were his pride and joy, but they were not showing the figures in the most helpful way. F.B. made the changes she suggested without demur. Control was slipping through his fingers like the sand on Bundoran Strand.

GRANNY MAC'S GHOST

The autumn was wet, as wet as ever it had been in living memory. There were occasional damp days when the west wind filled the valley with grey mist and a steady drizzle, but more often it rained, big drops splashing down on saturated fields, a quagmire at every gate, water running like streams in the lanes, flooding the road and the lower slopes.

Eamon McGinley was working the family farm almost alone now. His father's rheumatism had slowed him down to an old man's pace, had sapped the strength of his arms, twisted his hands into almost useless lumps. Out of desperation Eamon and Maggie's husband Tom, had taken to working the two farms together. They restricted themselves to sheep and beef cattle and each had one cow and a few hens to keep their families in milk, butter, buttermilk and eggs. Each had his own potato and vegetable patch. It was a hard time, but working together saved both farms.

Eamon could snatch a day off at a weekend when Hank was staying at Dr Corr's and they went rock climbing. It usually rained but Hank never dared to grumble. He had learned that there were certain things in this country about which a stranger must not complain. Had he ever commented on the bad weather Anamar would pretend to take it as an insult to her beloved Donegal. He knew she hated the rain too, but she would be quick to tell him that he was a lucky man to be in the Hills of Donegal and not in some hot, dusty desert in America.

In November Eamon's father went out to see the cattle one morning in the top field. When Eamon went to look for him an hour later he was lying dead in the half-shelter of a stone wall, his clothes soaked and the rain water running down his face. Dr Corr said later that it had been a heart attack. He was sure that death had been immediate and without pain.

Eamon's mother, Ellie, had kept her grief to herself. It was a quiet funeral and if she shed tears, no one was a witness. Her youngest daughter, Maureen, was training to be a nurse in Dublin and began to come home more often to keep her company. Anamar was delighted to see Maureen. She had missed her, the closest friend of her youth, the only one she could talk to about Hank.

Maureen had changed out of all recognition. In Dublin she had a host of girl friends from all over the country and, better than that, as Maggie would have said, she had a steady boy friend. She spoke differently, more quickly, with less of a Donegal accent, teasing Anamar in a way she would never have done before. Her hair was cut short and bobbed, her clothes stylish. To her friends at home she seemed so self-assured, so experienced, so much more worldly-wise, and she had only been away for a few months.

Maureen listened like a big sister as Anamar talked about Hank.

'He's so friendly and attentive but he seems to expect nothing in return.' Anamar told her. 'It's as if he's afraid of overstepping the mark. It's not as if he's shy. But it's strange that we don't seem any closer than we did when I first met him.'

Maureen laughed.

'It's a sight better than having to fend off some of the fly-boys I've met in the city. If you weren't careful they'd be all over you like a measles rash. I have the very idea. My mother intends to invite you for Christmas dinner, so we'll ask him too. It'll give me a chance to talk to him. I'll ask him to come clean about his intentions towards my poor wee innocent friend who's seeing the best weeks of her life slip away waiting for him to make a move.'

'You'll do no such thing.' said Anamar firmly. She was serious. Maureen was enjoying herself too much at her expense. The girl she had grown up with would never have joshed her like this. City life had certainly changed her but not for the worse. She liked the idea of Hank going with her to the McGinley's for Christmas dinner.

It was still raining on Christmas morning. Hank left his motor-bike in Maggie's farmyard and carried Anamar's present under his jacket as he walked up to her cottage. They kissed in the door way and Anamar could see that he had failed to notice the sprig of mistletoe over the lintel. His present was hanging from the hook under the mantle board which her Granny Mac had used for Anamar's own Christmas stocking when she was a child. They opened their gifts in front of the fire.

Hank's was a tailored cotton shirt of the very best quality in stock at the shop. It was from a range supplied by a superior English shirt-maker, only recently available in pale colours. These new shirts made F.B. nervous. As far as he was concerned the only possible colour for a man's shirt was white. To his amazement the new stock had sold well and the shop gained new male customers who previously would have ordered their shirts from Dublin.

Her present from Hank was the book of the film Hamlet. The first section comprised black and white photographs featuring Sir Laurence Olivier as the Prince of Denmark in scenes from the film. Anamar had never had a present like this. She gave him a hug and a kiss.

This time, and although she felt a tension in Hank which she could not explain, it was more than the kiss of good friends. Anamar wondered if the Christmas spirit would help Hank to unwind. At Mass earlier that morning she had found herself praying for him, something which she had only done when they had first met and he had been so chronically depressed.

The rain had eased by the time they walked over to the McGinley's at noon and as the sky cleared it became colder. Ellie and Maureen had been cooking and preparing from early morning but now the work was done. Eamon had the fire going well, adding logs to the turf as he bent below a row of five Christmas cards suspended on a string underneath the mantle-shelf.

Ellie McGinley was pleased that Hank and Anamar were with them for the meal. Since the eldest of her children had left home to find work in England they had seemed such a small family on Christmas Day, and now they were one less. Ellie was sure that no one would have understood her grief for her husband. She had not been able to let her tears flow except when she was alone in the bed which once they had shared.

It had been a steady marriage with few high points, save the births of the children, but there had been very few low points either. Neither of them would ever have been demonstrative in public, nor would they have shown much affection in private either. But Ellie knew that there had been a loving bond between them that many another couple might have envied.

His father had always carved the goose but Eamon was too embarrassed to take on the task this time. He had no idea how to begin. There was nothing for it. Ellie would have to do it herself. There were drumsticks for the girls, huge goose thighs for the men and slices of breast for all. She had almost finished serving the stuffing and gravy when her eyes filled with tears. Carefully she left down the serving spoon on the edge of the big delph platter. She wiped her face with her apron and left the kitchen for the scullery.

Anamar rose with her hand on Maureen's shoulder.

'You go on and make a start while it's hot,' she said quietly, 'I'll see to your mother.'

Ellie only needed a few minutes to come to herself. She took her apron off, dabbed her eyes and put an arm around Anamar's shoulder. When they came back to the table, they were welcomed with smiles and not the slightest reference to what had happened.

Maureen was entertaining the men with a story about a boyfriend who had tried to climb into the nurses' home after a dance. He had made it through a window on the first floor only to find a nun waiting for him. Terrified, he had tried to evade her but she had grabbed him by the jacket. He had managed to escape by wriggling out of it and making off in his shirt sleeves, leaving the nun with the trophy of a coat and the pence for his bus fare in the pocket.

They were all laughing and enjoying themselves so much Ellie found her appetite had returned. The food was a true Christmas feast. Hank joined the fun, telling jokes of his own and asking the others to solve riddles he remembered from the Thanksgiving Day parties of his youth.

Ellie could not help but notice that Hank and Maureen were getting on so well together. Maureen was now a beautiful young woman. The social life in Dublin had made her much more at ease in company, happy to be the centre of attention. Now she could lead the fun. It was obvious that she was flirting with Hank. But it was just the party spirit. Ellie was sure Anamar had nothing to fear.

Suddenly, as if it had been planned beforehand, Anamar and Eamon began to tease Maureen about her smart friends in Dublin. Anamar reminded her of the time she had been showing off by walking along the wall and had fallen off into the dung heap. Eamon asked her what she would do if they found out that her mother kept hens and pigs in the kitchen.

Maureen pretended to hit them both over the head with a Christmas cracker and the others cheered. Ellie was ready to join in the fun.

'Say what you like about that hussy,' she said pointing at her daughter, 'But for the love of God don't be disgracing the whole house and family.'

It was late in the afternoon before they left the table. Ellie put her feet up on the ledge at the side of the fire. The others cleared up, washed the dishes and went out for a walk, following the river up towards the high fields.

They showed Hank the fairy thorn and told him about making a wish while standing inside the bush with its branches holding him like arms. As they went higher the snow began to fall in big wet flakes. Huge clouds gathered from the North-West promising a heavy fall. Hank was due to meet Dr Corr later in the evening at the hotel in the town and Anamar encouraged him to leave on his motor-bike before the snow on the road became too deep.

After tea Maureen and Eamon left Anamar back to her cottage. The snow was plastered against its northern wall but inside it was warm and welcoming. Anamar stirred the banked up fire and it flamed as soon as she added whin roots and dry turf. When her friends had gone she sat for a long time in what had once been Granny's chair with her feet on a warm hearth stone. It was dark outside but Granny Mac had placed the chair here for warmth in the Winter and the view across Lough Eske in the light evenings.

Anamar was very happy to be on her own now. It had been a wonderful day. She banked up the fire again and took a candle into her bedroom. This was a night for an extra blanket and the patch-work quilt, one of her Grannie Mac's most prized possessions. Sleep came as soon as she was between the sheets.

In the middle of the night she wakened with a start. The room was still, silent, so dark she was not able to see the hem of the white sheet folded over the quilt on her bed. But she sensed that she was not alone. She was wide awake now but unafraid, as if there was no need whatsoever for her to feel apprehensive.

She heard a match strike, saw its flame move and listened to the familiar low crackle and splutter as the wick of a candle was lit. The flame glowed brighter and its circle of light revealed the figure of a woman sitting at the end of the bed.

The face was familiar, though Anamar could not put a name to it. The figure was calm, at ease in this room, as if it was as much her room as Anamar's. The candle flame swayed and flickered giving the impression that the images in the mirror on the wall behind the figure were moving.

Anamar tried to speak and failed. The woman smiled a soft, slow smile. Her eyes twinkled and Anamar knew then that it was Grannie Mac.

The grannie she had spent so much time with when she was a child, the story-teller, the seanscealai, who had lived her life to its very end in this cottage and had left it to her beloved granddaughter when she died.

But Anamar had never known Grannie Mac at this age. The woman at the foot of the bed was not much older than herself - but she must be Grannie Mac.

'Don't fret yourself, child dear.' the figure said, 'There's nothing to be afraid of. You and I were friends as well as child and grannie.'

'But your hair was grey, Grannie Mac, and now it's black.' Even in the candle-light the figure's hair was dark, though she could see little streaks of grey.

Grannie Mac laughed and shook gently, enjoying Anamar's astonishment.

'There was a great deal about me you didn't know and I didn't tell you,' she said quietly, 'And more's the pity. But at the time I couldn't tell you the good bits without the bad. And I daren't do that.' She laughed again but stopped suddenly and a look of pain aged her face by twenty years.

Anamar was sitting upright in bed. She wanted to reach out her hand to comfort Grannie Mac, but couldn't move. The figure bowed its head for a moment and when the face was raised again it was smiling softly, as young as it had been when first the candle flickered into light.

'To see you rest so easily here in my bed is a gift beyond price.' she said, 'It's as if my life continues in yours, sharing your joys and sorrows, watching over you as long as you live.'

Anamar thought she might be dreaming and pinched the back of her hand. She felt the pain and was sure this was no dream. She had no sense of fear but there was a greater feeling of excitement in the room.

'You're wondering why I've come to you.' Grannie Mac was leaning towards her, speaking earnestly. 'Do you remember what your mother said when she was dying?'

Anamar nodded. They had lived together like strangers until her mother was on her deathbed. Then, for the first time, they had opened their hearts to each other. Her mother had said that the pilgrimage to Lourdes which she was helping Ellie to organise, would bring a blessing on the whole parish. Anamar had written down the words later that evening. Now she knew them by heart.

'When you come back from Lourdes you'll find you have another pilgrimage in front of you,' her mother had told her, 'It will span countries. There will be rivers and mountains to cross. You'll feel the baking heat, hunger, thirst, fear, doubt and a tiredness you've never known. But before the journey's end, you'll find your reward.'

'That's right,' said Grannie Mac. 'And this pilgrimage should be on your own two feet. You must prepare yourself. The time for your journey has come.'

Grannie Mac pursed her lips and leaned forward to blow out the candle. Anamar saw the red glow and heard the sizzle as wetted fingers quenched the wick completely. She felt for the little battery torch on her bed-side table and switched it on. The room was empty, the door closed as it had been before she went to bed but she could distinctly smell the acrid odour of the quenched wick of a candle.

In the beam of the torch she saw the new candle she had left on the dresser by the door. She got out of bed to look and saw that it had now been used. Little runnels of wax had solidified on its sides. The wick was black and the faintest eddy of grey smoke drifted upwards from its tip.

Anamar lit the candle on her bed-side table and lay still with her eyes open, as if her body was asleep but her mind awake. Grannie Mac had given her another gift, a vision of the future.

She thought of the times they'd had at this cottage. They had often shared this bed and she had always slept soundly. The room was warm and cozy in winter and cool at the height of summer. When Grannie Mac had left the cottage to her, she had put up bookshelves, bought an easy chair and a second-hand table to act as a desk.

Now it was more than a bedroom. It was her sitting-room and study. She smiled to herself. It would never have done to tell anyone that this was how she saw her room. They would have laughed at such pretension.

She blew out the candle and dozed off into a deep sleep. When she wakened the weak winter sunlight lit the room through the open curtains. The fire in the kitchen responded quickly to a good poke and a few broken pieces of turf. She enjoyed poking the fire. At home her mother took offence if anyone else dared use what she called her poker. But here Grannie Mac had taught her the art of tending the turf fire. 'Don't ever jab it with a poker.' Grannie Mac would say, pretending to be so serious. 'It's not a class of a weapon. It's for gently encouraging the fire to do its best.'

She made herself what her mother would have called a decent breakfast. Two rashers and an egg done together in the pan with slices of soda bread fried in hot fat to make them crisp and dry. She suddenly felt the need to tell someone about what had happened during the night. Deirdre Ryan was away for Christmas but she could trust Ellie and Maureen to listen and not to think she had lost the run of herself.

Her Wellington boots slithered along in the wet snow on the path across to the McGinley's. They were not long back from Mass and Eamon was on his way out to see if the sheep were all right in the high field. Ellie had asked Anamar the previous evening if she had wanted a lift to Mass that morning but Anamar had declined. Now she wished she had gone with them.

'I've something to tell you,' she said, 'I'm hoping you won't think I've taken leave of my senses. Last night I wakened up while it was still dark. Although I could see nothing I knew someone was in the room. A match was struck and a candle lit and there was Grannie Mac sitting at the foot of the bed, talking to me as if she'd never been away.'

Ellie said nothing. She lifted the tea-pot and poured the tea. She and Maureen looked at each other in silence. She hoped this new version of her daughter would not try to make fun of what Anamar was saying. But Maureen knew that this was a time to listen.

'I suppose you'll think it was only a dream. But I'm certain it wasn't. And Grannie Mac seemed to know what my mother had said before she died about me setting out on another journey.'

Anamar recalled her grannie's vision of the journey, the heat and the thirst, the mountains and rivers to be crossed, the shadeless plains.

'And where will you go, child-dear?' Ellie asked, after a few moments silence, 'Will you be all on your own? Why do you have to go all by yourself?' Ellie's voice was low, her concern was that of a mother for a daughter, a mother who knows that however strong her own fears, her child has already made up her mind.

'It'll be another pilgrimage,' said Anamar brightly. She felt relieved now that she had spoken out. 'I don't know where I'll be headed or how to find out about pilgrimages but my mind is made up. I'll be going this year, it might be to Rome, or Fatima in Portugal, or even Jerusalem, but I want to walk there, even if it takes me weeks. I'll speak to Deirdre Ryan as soon as she gets back. If she doesn't know, she'll know somebody who does.'

Maureen nodded.

'Now we understand,' she said, 'Now we know why our Anamar, who's supposed to be the cheerful one, has been so down in the dumps. Now we know why you've been so preoccupied. I'm sure your boy-friend will be relieved. You've been so standoffish with him I thought you were losing interest and I was thinking of making up to him myself, just for the rest of the holiday, of course.'

They all laughed. Ellie hugged Anamar. She had been worried about her for months. Whatever had happened that previous night in Anamar's room, it had given her a new strength of purpose. And Ellie knew Anamar well enough to be sure it would carry her anywhere she wanted to go.

As soon as Deirdre returned from holiday, Anamar went to see her one evening to tell her the story of her Christmas night visitation and her decision to go on a pilgrimage that year.

Deirdre sat quite still, listening to every word without a sound or even the slightest movement. Her friendship with Anamar was one of the treasures of her life. She had taught Anamar a great deal but knew she had gained much more than she had given. They were twenty years apart in age but Anamar allowed her to connect with her own youth and with the young people of the day. They could have serious conversations or fun together as if they were of an age.

When Anamar's story was finished Deirdre left all the questions about Grannie Mac unasked for the moment. Anamar needed information about pilgrimages and she knew the very man.

'Have I ever mentioned a distant relation of mine, Father Brian de Courcy?' she said, 'He's in Paris at present, living at the Irish College. It's now run by Polish seminarians but they've given him a home. I called to see him there when I was in Paris last summer. He's writing a book about the great medieval journeys of Christendom. I'll write to him. I know he'll be delighted to help a pilgrim like yourself.'

They decided that if Father Brian was willing to help, Anamar would leave for Paris in April, and spend a week there consulting him. It would give her plenty of time to make arrangements for being away from home for two or thee months.

She told Hank before he went back to Belfast after the holidays. When she mentioned Grannie Mac's visitation he questioned her closely. What was she wearing? How did she speak? Was it the voice of a younger person? Had she not died before Anamar's mother had spoken about

Anamar's next journey? It was as if he felt he should ask the questions but seemed not to need the answers.

For the first time he told her about the nightmares he had experienced after the landing on the beach in the south of France. In some strange way he found it reassuring that Anamar believed her encounter with her grandmother was not a dream.

This was the first time they had been able to talk freely to each other since he had come to Ireland. He stayed a few days longer than intended and they agreed he should come to Donegal every week-end if that was possible. Dr Corr had arranged two rooms for him in his house, like a small, self-contained apartment.

They were very busy on the week-ends which followed. Anamar told him of her plans while they walked the hills and coast-line. Hank shared his mountaineer's experience, talking to her about the best ways to tackle a long walk. They went to Ballyshannon on the motor-bike to buy her walking shoes. In summer Anamar wore light shoes without socks and chose a pair of Clark's sandals with leather uppers and crepe rubber soles. They both reckoned these would be suitable for walking in hot weather in continental Europe.

They designed and made a small rucksack from light-weight, water-proof canvas with pre-stretched leather shoulder straps. They used Ellie's sewing machine for the canvas and sewed the straps on by hand. They were the happiest times they had shared since their climbs in the Pyrenees.

In February she told F.B. O'Boyle in case someone else would mention it first. F.B. stepped back in amazement. His mouth dropped open and he began to rock forwards and backwards on his toes and heels like an agitated child rocking in its pram.

'You mustn't concern yourself about my absence, Mr O'Boyle.' Anamar said briskly. She always addressed him in her most business-like voice. 'I have a ready-made stand-in for the period I'll be away. Mrs McGinley was satisfaction itself when we had her in part-time for the Christmas rush and the January sales. I've taken the liberty of speaking to her. I knew you wouldn't mind. She'd be delighted to hold the fort, as you would say. I wouldn't go if I thought it would be a worry to you. She'll be a safe pair of hands when I'm away.'

F.B. nodded and found himself thanking Anamar. He was confused. How did this young woman come to be making all the decisions? He was still the owner of the shop but what could he say? She was right, of course. And he daren't lose her now. When she had resigned after the visit to Lourdes, business had shown a serious drop. As soon as she had returned it had increased to the point where they now employed another girl. And how could he refuse her anyway? Wasn't she off on another religious pilgrimage? If he stood in her way, it would soon become common knowledge. He could lose his prime position at the altar rails of a Sunday.

'You have a good head for business, Miss Cassidy.' He said, sounding much more pompous than he meant to. 'You always put the best interests of O'Boyle's to the fore. I'm sure your pilgrimage will bring you grace and blessings in abundance. I hope it's not too much to ask that you might remember us in your prayers along the way.'

Anamar smiled sweetly. She had not anticipated any difficulty from F.B. but it was good to have everything arranged so amicably. She liked her job at O'Boyle's and it was reassuring to have it to come back to.

Just before she left at the beginning of May, she received a card from the Reverend and Mrs Ferguson. On one side was a pen drawing of a path winding over a mountain pass with a small figure striding purposefully upwards. On the other, it simply said,

There's no discouragement
Shall make her once relent
Her first avowed intent
To be a PILGRIM

THE DANCING PRIEST IN PARIS

The day of departure was a Saturday at the end of April. Eamon brought the car around to give Anamar a lift to the railway station. His mother and Maureen, who was home for the week-end, came too. When they arrived at the station, the send-off party was already assembling.

Deirdre Ryan and Wilson Corr were talking to William and May Ferguson. Maggie arrived with Tom and their young son. There were a dozen or more from the parish pilgrimage to Lourdes the previous year, mainly women. The exceptions were Danny and Jerome, still as cocky as ever, still in their wheel-chairs. F.B.O'Boyle stood at the back of the group, as if waiting to be invited to join in.

There were hugs and handshakes and suddenly they heard the train, ahead of time, puffing its way slowly towards the station. Danny shouted above the din.

'Hey Anamar, are you not taking anybody with you? Me and Jerome are ready for the road, as usual.'

The noise drowned Anamar's reply. Smoke and steam swirled over the little group. When it cleared, Anamar was surprised to find Father Brogan at her side. He had been very appreciative of what she had done to make the parish pilgrimage to Lourdes a success but there was still a gap between them, which one seemed unwilling and the other unable to cross. They stepped back and he turned away from the crowd. Hidden by his broad back Father Brogan blessed Anamar and her pilgrimage.

The Fergusons had a small paper-back book as a present.

'It's John Bunyan's, The Pilgrim's Progress.' William said diffidently, as if he was uncertain that a tract by a Calvinist preacher was an entirely suitable book for a young Catholic girl setting out on her travels. He smiled, 'And if it adds too much to your burden, I'm sure you'll find a good home for it on your way.'

Anamar boarded the train and let the window down on its leather strap. Deirdre was the last one to hug her before the train pulled out of the station. Anamar stood at the window waving until they were out of sight and then sank back on the seat, feeling uneasy at leaving her friends for so long. It was not that she was unhappy at the prospect of being alone. She was caught between fear of the unknown and the excitement of an adventure. But now it was time to face the journey ahead.

Hank met the train at the Great Northern Station in Belfast in the early afternoon. He slung her rucksack on his shoulder and steered her deftly through the city traffic to the Carlton Café for afternoon tea.

'I've never been here before,' he said, looking happy to see her. 'They tell me this is the best place for someone special.' He lifted the rucksack up into view. It was compact and light. 'I see you've passed the first test. You've kept the baggage down to the very minimum.'

'I had this great teacher,' she said, 'When we were in the Pyrenees he kept telling me that every pound on the back would feel like ten half way up the first mountain.'

Hank smiled. Those days in the mountains with her had been the most important of his life. They had been together again for a few months but, although it had been a happy time, they were only now at ease with each other when it was time to part.

They had tea in china cups and the uniformed waitress brought a silver stand, with sandwiches on the bottom rack and small iced cakes on the top. Anamar was astonished to find that it was Hank who was doing all the talking. Usually she had to begin the conversation and draw him in. This time, he had so much to say. Before, he had been reluctant to talk about himself and it had been left to her to question him about his studies at the University and the family he was staying with in Belfast.

They walked out of town past the University and she heard about his life at home, his time at West Point, his army service. He was revealing more about himself on this one afternoon than in the twelve months which had elapsed since they had met in Lourdes.

They turned into the Botanic Gardens Park to see the Victorian Palm House. Anamar had never expected Belfast to be such an impressive city. On the way out they had passed the devastation of heavy bombing during the war but there were many fine buildings still standing and reconstruction work was underway. Any city would have been proud to have a park like the Botanic Gardens so close to the centre and flanked on one side by the Ulster Museum and on the other by the University.

Hank led the way to the Tropical Ravine hidden behind big bushes. It was another huge glass house but built over a man-made gorge. The entrance door led to a balcony above a cleft with a profusion of tropical plants. There were huge ferns, brilliantly coloured flowers, exotic palms, trees with ripe bananas, oranges and figs, bushes bearing strange fruit Anamar had never seen before.

It was a warm day and inside the humid heat was stifling. Anamar felt uncomfortable but Hank seemed not to notice. To her surprise he began to talk of his feelings for her. Suddenly she was gasping for breath. She wanted to hear what he was saying but desperately needed fresh air.

I'll have to go outside,' she said, 'I can't breathe in this heat.'

Hank took her outside and found a bench where she could sit down. But the moment had gone. And all he could say was, 'Sorry.'

'Sure I'm grand now I'm out in the open,' she said, 'Go on with what you were saying. You were trying to tell me something.'

They were both smiling again but neither could find a way to recapture that moment.

Hank walked her down to the Donegall Quay and the Liverpool boat and was allowed on board for a short while before sailing. Anamar had not been able to book a berth beforehand. They were all reserved. Hank, however, seemed to know the drill. He had a private word with the chief steward. Money changed hands and in a few moments she was stowing her rucksack on a bunk in a two-berth cabin.

They went up on deck and stood at the rail with an arm around each other, holding on tightly, looking across the lough and over the rolling landscape of North Down.

'I'll miss you,' said Hank shyly. 'I'm sure you've guessed that I only came to Ireland to study because of you.' Anamar was smiling to herself. It wasn't much but it was a start.

'All ashore that's going ashore!' A voice called.

They kissed far more passionately than either expected and Hank walked back down the gangway. He stood on the quay waving as the figure on the rails grew smaller and the boat steamed down Belfast Lough. They were both wondering why they found it so hard to be open with each other, why they had wasted so much time by keeping each other at arm's length.

In the late afternoon of the third day of her journey, Anamar's train drew into the Gard du Nord in Paris and Father Brian de Courcy was there to meet her. Deirdre had sent him a telegram. He was easy to recognise and not just

because of his clerical collar. With her description Anamar could have picked
him out in what Deirdre herself might have called, 'a pack of priests'.

'He's smaller than you but twice as wide and three times as deep from
front to back. He has the tiniest feet you ever saw on a man, dancer's feet,
always on the move, steps as light as a feather and him at least fourteen
stone if he's an ounce.'

What was more of a surprise, however, Father Brian was able to pick
her out of the crowd on the platform just as easily. He smiled as if he was
delighted to meet her, laughed when he saw the extent of her luggage was
one small rucksack and took her to a nearby café.

When Anamar tried to thank him he raised a hand.

'Woman dear,' he said patiently, as if she should have known better.
'When our mutual friend, the boul Deirdre Ryan commands, men obey.
And don't tell me you hadn't noticed.' He raised both hands in a theatrical
gesture of concern.

'Glory be! I've only just now thought of it. You've been her acolyte.
She's taught you all her tricks. She's sent you here to check up on me.'

He stood up and danced a few twinkling steps back from the table.
Anamar looked around in embarrassment but no one was paying them the
slightest attention. Father Brian raised both hands in supplication.

'Tell me you're not that sorceress's apprentice,' he pleaded, wringing
his hands. 'Did she let it slip that she gave me the elbow when we were
students? Trampled on my dreams, she did. Left me with the choice of the
French Foreign Legion or the Church.'

Anamar was laughing so much at his antics she had to wipe the tears
from her eyes.

'Don't worry yourself, Father, I'll say nothing about our wee fling
here in Gay Paree. Deirdre's Wicklow crowd might blab but the Donegal
ones can sing dumb when they want to.'

Father Brian sat down and sipped his coffee.

'So it's the Grand Pilgrimage you're after, a journey to the holy of
holies on your own two feet,' he said. Now it was time to talk about her
pilgrimage. 'I hope you won't mind if I ask you why? Is it the young
idealist in you searching for truth and enlightenment? Is it in the hope of
blessings or indulgences?'

He nearly said, 'It couldn't be as a penance for some great sin, now
could it? Not for a well-reared Catholic girl like yourself,' but just managed

to stop himself in time,' That would have been far too familiar a remark to someone he hardly knew. He paused and let himself be serious.

'Maybe it's yourself you're hoping to find along the way.'

He smiled happily. When first Deirdre had written to him about Anamar he had been pleased to help. How could he have refused such a friend? But it had been with a sense of duty. Now he had met Anamar, and although she had hardly said a word, he was looking forward to helping her choose a pilgrimage as much as he would have done had he been going himself. He laughed aloud.

'Forgive me,' he said, 'I'm letting myself get carried away by the excitement of it all. I love the mystical idea of being a pilgrim, the journey of the spirit, the sights and sounds of a strange country, the holy shrines, the camaraderie in the inn at the end of the day But the foot-slogging, now that's a different matter, I don't think I'd be able for it. We'll make a pact. While you are doing your actual pilgrimage, I'll do mine in the abstract.'

Father Brian was just as much at ease, now he was being serious, as he had been earlier when making her laugh. They went by Metro to the Left Bank where he had booked a room for Anamar in the Hotel Select near the Sorbonne. They arranged to meet at twelve noon the next day for lunch and their first discussion. In the afternoon he would take her for a walk in the city and they could continue their talk. They shook hands outside the hotel.

'Don't worry.' His voice was reassuring, 'I won't be quizzing you for motives. You'll tell me when you're ready, if that's what you want. But you can be sure of one thing. To set out, as you intend, is a supreme act of faith and I'll tell you something else, there's always the reward of spiritual grace in some shape or form at the end of a pilgrimage. I'm certain of that. Mind you, it's up to the pilgrim himself to find it.'

He turned and skipped away down the street. For the first time Anamar felt a surge of confidence about her journey. She had yet to decide where she was bound but it was reassuring to have Father Brian as a guide. He might not be going with her but he would be willing her on every step of the way.

Next day they went to a small restaurant in a side street for lunch. The patron welcomed Father Brian as a friend and they were given a table at the window. Anamar took out a note book and pencil to be ready for their talk but food was the first priority for her companion.

'Do you like mussels?' he asked, his eyes pleading with her to say 'Yes'. 'They're a house speciality. You'll love the way he does them.'

The patron himself brought a great bowl of Moules Marinière to the table, with a basket of bread and a carafe of red wine so light in colour it sparkled like ruby glass when he filled their glasses. Father Brian's eyebrows were raised in surprise when he saw that Anamar knew how to manage the mussels, using one as a pair of pincers to eat another and supping the clear soup, in which they had been cooked, with a spoon.

'Don't tell me,' he said, with a sigh of resignation, 'Her ladyship, the lovely Deirdre taught you how eat mussels too. Why did she send you to poor little me when you already know everything?'

The pile of empty mussel shells grew higher and the carafe of wine was replaced.

'It's the only fault here,' said Father Brian apologetically, nodding towards the carafe and conscious that Anamar was only on her second glass, 'The jugs are a wee bit on the small side for two.'

When they had eaten the last mussel and the last crust of bread, Father Brian wiped his chin with his napkin.

'You're spoilt for choice, so you are,' he said, 'There's the three great pilgrimages, Jerusalem, Rome and Santiago in Spain. Chaucer had the Wife of Bath in his Canterbury Tales having been to all three. Now she was a real travelling woman. Knew how to enjoy the journey too. But then that's not the sort of book you're likely to have been allowed to read.'

Anamar said nothing. She took another sip of wine and tried not to give herself away. If he knew she had read The Canterbury Tales, he would start teasing her again.

'What about Rome?' she said quickly.

'Now you're talking,' Father Brian had planned to start with Rome. 'You could follow in the footsteps of one of my great heroes, Hilaire Belloc. He set out from Northern France at the turn of the century and walked the whole way through Switzerland and over the Alps. When his Path to Rome was published, he said that all his other books had been to make money but this one he had written for love. I'm sure you know some of his poetry.'

'I do indeed,' said Anamar, 'When I was in the Pyrenees I think I stayed in the inn he mentions in his poem, Tarantella.'

'Do you remember an inn, Miranda?.....' Father Brian spoke poetry with a voice like an opera tenor. '...... Do you remember an inn? And the tedding and the spreading of the straw for a bedding, And the fleas that tease in the High Pyrenees,'

'And what about the wine that tasted of the tar?' Anamar was not to be outdone. 'I've tasted that vino negro and I'm not sure even you could manage it without a drop of lemonade.'

This was the kind of conversation Father Brian revelled in. He was enjoying himself more than he dared hope.

'Belloc was a great walking man,' he said, 'Often covered long distances on foot. He had four rules for walkers - never fix a time for a journey - take the first part of the day slowly - stick to proper paths -carry as little as possible. When he set out for Rome he had a small bag slung over his shoulder with a piece of bread, half a pound of smoked ham, a sketch-book and a quart of the famous local wine of Brulé.'

Anamar was fascinated. Deirdre had picked the right man.

'Oh, he knew how to enjoy himself too,' Father Brian continued, 'But he was very serious about his religion. Hilaire Belloc was a natural as a pilgrim.

'He made his pilgrim vows before he left for Rome and then found himself breaking all of them with one exception, the promise that he would be present at High Mass in St Peter's that year, on the Feast of St Peter and St Paul.'

Anamar had read Belloc's book on the Pyrenees. She had talked to Deirdre and Hank about his travels and found it hard to see him in the role of pious pilgrim. Father Brian agreed.

'I know what you mean,' he said, 'He could be arrogant and self-important. George Bernard Shaw saw him as a pompous propagandist for Catholicism. Made fun of him and his friend Chesterton by inventing a monstrous beast called the 'Chesterbelloc'. But Hilaire had a feel for the mystical side of the pilgrimage which he seemed to take some trouble to hide.

'It comes out in the Path to Rome when he says at the start of the journey, "It was at the very beginning of June, at evening, but not yet sunset, that I set out from Toul by the Nancy Gate," You can find it too in one of his essays, The Death of Wandering Peter.'

Anamar smiled with pleasure.

'I know it,' she said, 'I have an American friend called Hank. We met in Lourdes and he told me the story. I learned a verse from it when we were walking in Belloc's favourite mountains.'

'And on his arm the stirrup thongs,
And in his gait the narrow seas,
And in his mouth Burgundian songs,
But in his heart the Pyrenees.'

'Bravo! Bravo!' Father Brian rose to his feet and clapped. 'Now you know, whether you go to Rome or not, our mutual friend, the hind quarters of Shaw's monstrous beast, must be your spiritual guide.'

He insisted on paying the bill, arguing that she needed to hold on to her money for the journey. They spent most of the afternoon strolling through the city in the Spring sunshine. They talked about the reasons for making a pilgrimage, the commissioning of a pilgrim at the point of departure, the nature of the pilgrim's devotions along the way, the physical difficulties, the dangers for a twenty-one-year-old girl travelling on her own.

Father Brian mentioned the responsibilities of an independent traveller like herself going on pilgrimage as a member of the Body of Christ.

Put like this, it was a new thought for Anamar. When she had gone with the parish group to Lourdes she had, of course, accepted the ritual of the pilgrimage, but it had been with the same unquestioning observance as the Mass at home. This time she was sure it would be different, there would be another dimension. She had been thinking of this journey as a private venture, personal, independent.

To her great relief, Father Brian seemed to expect no response, as if he understood what was in her mind. Instead, he began to tell her stories about the hilarious adventures of medieval pilgrims.

When they were parting, he asked if she had thought how she would prepare herself spiritually for her pilgrimage. She told him what had happened to Hank in a battle for the beach in the South of France during the war. When the idea of the pilgrimage had come to her, she said, she had felt a need to visit that Mediterranean beach first. It was as if it might help her understand what had happened to Hank and might bridge a gap between them.

'And what better way to prepare for one pilgrimage than by making another.' Father Brian said approvingly. This young woman had the makings of a real pilgrim.

That evening Anamar ate on her own in a small Left Bank restaurant and walked back to her hotel. In a street off the Boulevard Saint-Michel she passed a group of men sitting around a pavement table outside a bar. They were having uproarious fun teasing one of their number, gesticulating wildly, pointing towards him, talking loudly, laughing at him, calling on him to account for himself.

She had almost passed when one of them shouted after her in English.

'Anamar! Anamar! Come back and join us! For pity's sake help me. This crowd have me destroyed.'

It was Father Brian, glass in hand, face flushed ruby red.

Anamar turned back and stopped on the edge of the group. The hilarious clamour hushed. Father Brian rose and presented her to them in French, as an Irish friend of a dear friend. He explained that she had come to Paris to seek his advice before she set out on foot to make a pilgrimage. The group members were impressed. They stood up to shake hands with her and introduce themselves. It was done without haste. Any diversion had to be treated on its merits. They had a long hard session ahead and the night was still young.

The first pair were French. Raoul and Paul jumped to their feet and vied for the honour of welcoming her to the company. They were good-looking young men of her own age standing with arms linked, competing to tell her that Father Brian was such a clever priest but now they had him in their power. They knew his secret. Anamar sat down on a proffered chair wondering why she was not afraid to be amongst these rowdy men.

A huge curly-haired man laughed, leaned across the table and took her hand in two great hairy paws.

'I'm Danny from the County Tipp,' he said, in English but in an accent so strong she had to concentrate to make out what he was saying. 'I'm Brian's minder. I keep him on the straight and narrow in this city of temptation. I paint in my spare time. You know he's lodged at what used to be the Irish College.'

Anamar nodded. Father Brian had been telling her the history of the college. Founded in the 16th century, it had become the most important of the Irish colleges set in Continental Europe at a time when the Catholic Church in Ireland had to train its priests outside the country. The Irish seminarians had left the College during World War 2 and when hostilities were over in 1945, Polish seminarians had been given a short, temporary lease of the property. Five years later they were still in occupation.

'We now reckon,' said Danny with mock seriousness, 'That the Irish hierarchy have sent the boul Brian here to spy out the land. They want the College back. Vlad the Impaler here.' He pointed at a very tall dark-haired man at the back. 'He's one of the Polish mob who don't intend to shift and it's my job to keep our fellow countryman safe from him even if he is an informer.'

'Oh, the shame of it,' wailed Father Brian in French, 'To be called an informer. The most vile insult they could hurl at any Irishman.' He turned to Anamar. 'I appeal to you as a woman and the only sober soul here. Save my good name. If only I wasn't a man of the cloth I would take to fisticuffs.'

Anamar was surprised to find herself not in the least put out by being the centre of attention.

'Don't worry Father,' she said in French, 'We can handle this crowd. If everything else fails you can always ask for a little help from above.'

A chair skraked on the pavement and a tall, dignified man rose theatrically. He was older than the others but moved with an actor's grace. He shook Anamar's hand and embraced her lightly on either cheek.

'My name is Henri, mademoiselle,' he said gently, accenting his words in the way which has made French one of the world's most beautiful languages, 'These Irishmen are teaching us to beat each other with words. You, of course, have no need of a defender but I shall protect the reputation of your clerical friend.

'Much more interesting are your own plans. Father Brian did say you are soon to depart on pilgrimage.'

'That's why I'm here,' Anamar said brightly, keeping to French, 'Father Brian is an authority on religious journeys, or so a mutual friend would have me believe. When his book on the great pilgrimages of the Christian world is published, he'll be rich and famous and we can all claim to have known him when he was but a simple priest.'

The others laughed and Father Brian tried hard to look embarrassed.

'Anamar has already been to Lourdes and to-day we discussed the Road to Rome,' he said, relieved at the change of subject, 'To-morrow we'll look at the long journey across Europe and Asia Minor to the Holy City itself, Jerusalem.'

There was a gasp from Paul.

'But it must be four or five thousand kilometres,' said Raoul, 'It would take months on foot.'

'Of course, but it must be considered.' Father Brian was now in control and in his element. 'With Rome and Santiago, Jerusalem is one of the three Great Pilgrimages of medieval times but then there are other shrines too, Fatima in Portugal, Loreto in Italy ....'

'Hold on a moment,' It was Danny who was interrupting. He reached out an arm towards Anamar. 'Has he mentioned the Irish connection to the Road to Jerusalem.'

Father Brian feigned a grimace and Danny continued.

'There's more than one class of pilgrim,' he said, tapping the side of his nose with a finger, 'Make sure his Reverence tells you the story of the Buck Whaley.'

THE BUCK WHALEY - ANOTHER CLASS OF PILGRIM

Danny rose and steadied himself with a hip jammed against a table,
'Buck Whaley was another class of pilgrim entirely,' he said, as if he'd known the man as a close friend. 'His pilgrimage was to Jerusalem and he did it for a wager. He walked it there and back in less than a year and played hand-ball against the walls of the Holy City. It must have been all of 5,000 miles.' He turned to Anamar.

'You could do a lot worse than follow in the footsteps of an Irish pilgrim. And the Buck is your very man. Mind you he was a Protestant and his oul father was no friend to our Church. Burn-Chapel Whaley they called him in his day. If he'd had his way there would have been nowhere left for our crowd to worship.'

Danny wobbled and sat down heavily, smiling serenely. Henri led the applause and when Anamar rose to leave he kissed her hand.

'Je suis désolé,' he proclaimed in his actor's voice. He wished her well and pointed at Father Brian.

'Listen to every word this friend and man of God speaks but please, chérie, attend only to your own inner voice. Holy wisdom comes from within, not without.'

Anamar smiled. She could imagine the religious arguments which could erupt within this group of friends.

Raoul and Paul sprang forward and held her hands, one on either side.

'Take us with you,' said Paul. 'We need to go on a journey of the spirit. Your strength will protect us.'

'We've been talking about it in whispers,' said Raoul, 'And we've agreed. Take us too!'

Anamar and the others laughed. In the embarrassment of not being taken seriously, the two boys protested their willingness.

'It's not that we want to go,' said Paul, who looked close to tears. 'We need to struggle, to feel the raging thirst of hot plains, to sleep on the hard ground, to walk long hours on bleeding feet, to learn to pray. We need to make a pilgrimage.'

Henri shook his head in comic disbelief. Danny chuckled loudly, struggling to stay on his seat. Father Brian held his sides and roared with laughter. Then suddenly they stopped. The boys were in tears. They were being serious, not play acting as they often did when others were monopolising the conversation.

Anamar had been the first to see that this was not a performance. She put an arm around each boy's shoulder.

'But I don't even know where I'm going yet,' she said softly, 'Father Brian's been telling me about the possibilities. He says it won't be that I will choose a pilgrimage. It will choose me. You can come to see me off when I leave Paris.'

Paul and Raoul dried their tears and went back to their seats. They smiled bravely and waved with the others when Anamar left the little group.

Walking back to the Hotel Select she was elated. Meeting Father Brian like this, so at ease with his friends, talking to them about her intentions, was confirmation that her journey had already begun.

When she met him next day for lunch, Father Brian showed no sign of a hang-over but was anxious to hear what she thought of their chance meeting the previous evening.

'They were an education, Father,' she said happily, 'I can't say I wasn't worried when you gave me a shout and I turned to see them first, but they're a great crowd. I hope you'll let me meet them again.'

'Oh, child dear,' he said, pretending to be serious, 'I'm not so sure about that. There's free-thinkers and heathen and God knows what amongst them. Every evening they set before me such sinful attractions of the flesh as you could never dream of, every class of temptation winking invitations at me like glasses of fine old cognac lined up on a bar counter.'

'You'll be able for them, Father,' Anamar was enjoying the way she could talk to this man. 'Sure didn't you survive the temptations of student life in Dublin and make it into Holy Orders? But tell me more about this character Danny mentioned, the Buck Whaley.'

Father Brian raised a hand to hold her back for a moment so that they could order lunch. They had the dish of the day, Les Trois Saumon, three versions of salmon, smoked, marinaded in oil and herbs and lightly grilled.

'I thought we might start with a light course,' Father Brian was as serious as a French gourmet when it came to selecting what he would eat. 'That will leave room for another speciality of this house as dessert.'

He paused, took a sip of wine and began to tell her about Buck Whaley.

'He was a man of the 18th century, born in Dublin and christened Thomas. His father, old Richard Burn-Chapel Whaley, found him a bit of a handful and sent him to Paris when he was sixteen. The family weren't short of a pound or two and Thomas had an allowance of £7,000 pounds a year - a vast sum in those days.

'His expenses were huge. Gambling was one of his passions. He kept two establishments here in Paris, a town house and a country mansion where friends could come to stay as long as they wished. His tutor could do nothing with him. One night he lost £14,000 in a card game and later, when his banker, Latouche of Dublin, dishonoured the bill, he fled Paris for Ireland.

'When he was nineteen and under age he was a Member of Parliament for Newcastle, County Dublin and, as the occasion required, voted for or against the Union.

'He was a real travelling man, preferring to walk when he was going from town to town looking for a chance to make a good wager. One day when a friend asked him where he was bound for next, and Thomas replied, 'Jerusalem', the first place which had come into his head. Now he was committed to the journey, he took wagers that he would walk to Jerusalem and back in a year, taking sea passage only when necessary and playing hand-ball against the walls of the Holy City when he got there.'

Father Brian sat back in his chair and took a long draught of wine 'just to clean his palate'. He contemplated the Tarte Aux Fraises à la Chantilly which the patron had placed before him in reverential silence. It was a large slice of strawberry tart, glazed, decorated with flamboyant swirls of Chantilly cream and whole strawberries. His tongue slowly moistened his upper lip.

Anamar knew that no words should disturb this sublime moment. She waited while he paid his respects to this splendid example of French culinary art. Eventually his spoon cut a bite-sized portion, his fork added a spiral of cream and he allowed himself to taste it.

When he had finished, he laid down his cutlery and pronounced himself well satisfied with the meal.

'Wherever you go in Ireland, that's the story you'll hear of Buck Whaley. The trouble is, it's only half true. The first part about Paris is accurate enough but the bit about him walking to Jerusalem and back in a year is a total fabrication. The wagers did not require him to walk the whole way and he went by boat as far as possible, then travelled overland by carriage or on horseback.

'It took him ten months. When he came back to Dublin, he brought a document signed by the Guardian and Superior of the Convent of St Mary in Jerusalem as evidence that he'd been to the Holy City. It was an astute move. Such proof meant he had no trouble collecting the £25,000 he was owed in wagers.'

Anamar began to laugh. Back at home she had heard some of the stories about Buck Whaley and his wonderful pilgrimage on foot. But the journey hadn't been for spiritual reasons, it was simply for a bet. Suddenly she could hear her father's voice when he had been to the cattle fair. He had a saying he always used when he was buying beasts and felt he had been cheated by a dealer.

'That one's as big a liar as the Buck Whaley,' he would say through gritted teeth.

'But it wasn't Whaley who was telling the lies,' said Father Brian, 'It's those Irish story-tellers again, making it up as they go along.'

'I suppose I've been sceptical of this amazing hike for years. If you divide the number of days he was supposed to be away into the total length of the land part of the journey, it had to be too much, even for the famous Buck. As well as that, the stories never contained any details of the walk, route, daily distances, places seen, inns where he had sought a bed for the night.

'Only a few months ago I came upon a copy of his memoirs in the library of the British Museum. He had died young and they hadn't been published until a hundred years after his death. In the memoirs he himself made no claim about walking the whole way, neither did he make any mention of playing hand-ball against the walls of the Holy City. In fact he tells a most interesting story of the journey and his account is confirmed by the journal of his companion, Captain Hugh Moore of Mount Panther in Co. Down.

'The trouble is that generations of Irish story-tellers had been telling and retelling the tale, embellishing it as they went along until the man became the myth. Still, he was some travelling man, the Buck Whaley.

'I haven't had the heart to tell Danny the true story but, if you don't mind, I think we'd better look elsewhere for the pilgrim in whose footsteps you should tread.'

Anamar sighed with relief. She had been thinking of a pilgrimage which involved a long walk. But 5,000 miles! There and back? It would take forever.

THE DANCING SUN OR THE SCALLOP SHELL

Anamar and Father Brian left the restaurant and strolled along the boulevard Saint Michel and into the Luxembourg Gardens. The late-Spring sunshine had brought a smile to the face of Paris and, to Anamar's surprise, to the faces of many Parisians as well. City dwellers always seemed so serious, so absorbed in a private world of their own, so separate from the mass of people around them. It was no wonder, she had heard Deirdre Ryan say, that the loneliest one was not the old woman in a cottage in the hills of Donegal but the young one living in a city without friends.

Father Brian suddenly began to talk about pilgrimage in a more serious vein, as if the story of Buck Whaley had emphasised the adventure of the enterprise and diminished the religious observance.

'Oh, the dictionary will tell you glibly that the pilgrimage is any journey taken for nostalgic or sentimental purposes, but we're after something deeper than that. And it's not solely a Christian practice. Hindus, Buddhists, Muslims, Jews, they all go on pilgrimage. In every creed it's an act of practical piety.

'Even Protestants, for dear sake, head off to Jerusalem. Martin Luther wouldn't have approved, but since the last century it seems to be all right. Mind you, the Protestant pilgrim mustn't ask saints for any favours or pray for the dead or slip into any of our Popish practices. When things settle down in the Holy Land they'll be back there in their droves.'

They came out of the Jardin du Luxembourg and walked towards the River Seine. Anamar had not seen this serious side of her companion. It was a different man to the one who had been enjoying himself with his friends the previous evening. Father Brian sighed.

'Pilgrimage is an ancient enterprise of the most powerful, mystical appeal,' he said gently. 'The multitudes are drawn to remote shrines in the hope of miraculous events. They share the ecstasy, not only with those who are present, but with those who made the same journey in the past. The more painful the suffering, the greater the absolution. The more passionate the piety, the greater the atonement. The harder the road, the greater the grace.

'To be a pilgrim is to face the twin demons of self and doubt.'

He sighed again, much more deeply now his own passion had been released.

'Have you ever heard tell of Fatima?' Now, he was speaking directly to Anamar. Before, it was as if he had been thinking aloud.

'That's in Portugal,' Anamar said quickly, 'I heard a wee bit about it when I was in Lourdes last year. It's a Marian shrine like Lourdes but more recent. Our Lady appeared to three young children. Wasn't it during the First World War?'

'That's right,' Father Brian was relieved to have finished sermonising. 'Next year, 1951, is a Holy Year and they're expecting a million people from all over the world to make the pilgrimage.'

When he had been writing about the great religious journeys of the Christian world, Father Brian had found it hard at times to be both chronicler and priest. Often the historical facts were well documented but establishing the Church's stance on the religious significance of a particular shrine could prove more difficult. There were times when he was tempted to feel that the Church exercised its leadership by following a few steps behind its people.

'It happened when Portugal was enduring troubled times. The monarchy was overthrown in 1910. The people had to survive chronic inflation, food shortages, corruption, civil chaos. Portuguese troops fighting on the Allied side in the war suffered great losses on the Western Front. Religion was seen to be allied with the old order in Portugal and was suppressed. Priests were forbidden to preach or wear clerical dress.

'In the month of May in 1917, three young children, two girls and a boy, were looking after sheep near their home village. They began to say the Rosary. There was a sudden flash, like lightning. To their amazement they saw a Lady dressed in white. When their news became local knowledge, the people made fun of them and the priest denounced their vision as the work of the Devil.

'They went back to the same place and the Lady in White appeared again, but only they could see her. The hundreds of people who came with them saw only the sun behaving oddly. And that has happened many times since. A visiting cleric called it the Dancing Sun.

'In some ways it's like the story of the apparitions of Lourdes. As happened there, the Church eventually accepted the children's visions and twenty years ago, the Cult of Our Lady of Fatima was officially approved by the Pope.'

They had reached the River Seine and a sudden shower of rain made them seek shelter in a doorway.

'Fatima became Portugal's national shrine.' Father Brian continued. 'Pilgrims have been making their way there in their tens of thousands ever since. Nowadays, they usually go by train or bus but hordes of Portuguese join great processions on foot, walking for many days to worship at the shrine.

'When Deirdre first wrote to me, I was sure this would be the pilgrimage for you. I could see you falling in with one of those great pilgrim bands, walking with them, staying in the villages, joining their devotions, seeing the miracle of the Dancing Sun.'

'And now you're not so sure.' Anamar said it gently. She could see the flicker of doubt in his face. She could hear it in his voice. She was tempted to ask him for a reason. Did he now see her pilgrimage as a solitary journey? Did he have doubts of his own about the miracle of the Dancing Sun? But now was not the time to ask. If he wanted to tell her, he would do so when he was ready.

'Fatima is in the middle of Portugal.' Father Brian's voice sounded tired. His stride had shortened, his shoulders stooped. He looked older and, in spite of his bulk, more frail. 'If you want to start in France, you'll have to cross the Pyrenees and make your way down through Spain. Pilgrim routes often follow the old Roman roads and there were good roads 2,000 years ago to supply the Roman garrisons in Portugal.'

He was doing his best but, for some reason, talking about Fatima had been exhausting. Anamar saw a café and suggested coffee. Father Brian's face relaxed into a broad smile.

'You've read my mind again,' he said, 'There's something else I need to tell you about Fatima, the Third Secret. I think that's what's bothering me. But let's leave it until another time.'

They sat in comfortable silence under the café's canopy and watched the sun come out before the shower eased. Everything seemed so clean and fresh after the rain. They crossed the river by the Pont des Arts and walked through to the rue de Rivoli beside the Louvre. Father Brian's stride was jaunty again. He pointed out the landmarks. He talked eloquently about the joy of living in Paris. His usual good form was restored.

'Forgive me,' he said, 'These holy journeys mean a lot to me. I've spent so much time with them. It seems important that I give you the right way of each one we mention. When I have personal concerns I feel all my energy draining away.'

Anamar found herself wondering if these concerns had to do with the Third Secret of Our Lady of Fatima. She had to ask. Father Brian shrugged his shoulders and explained that the last part of the children's visions had not become public knowledge.

'Mysteriously, it was written down and sent to Rome eight years ago, with the condition that the sealed envelope must not be opened before the Autumn of this year. Until then we can only speculate about its contents. Some senior clerics believe that the publication of this Third Secret will be exploited by the enemies of the Church and the rumour is that it prophesies the end of the Church as we know it.'

They reached the place du Châtelet. Father Brian danced a pirouette and gestured towards an elegant tower rising high above the buildings. It looked as if it might once have been the tower of a church.

'And here we have the Tour St-Jacques,' he said in the manner of a tour guide. 'For centuries pilgrims have assembled here for the journey to the North-Western corner of Spain. Every one of these pilgrims of St James would be wearing a scallop shell. As their pilgrim badge it would entitle them to special treatment in towns, villages, convents and monasteries along the route. It would enable them to be recognised through France, over the Pyrenees and across the width of Spain to the Holy City of St James, Santiago de Compostela.'

Anamar was startled by a shiver of exhilaration. Later she would say that this was her moment of truth. Father Brian's accounts of the other pilgrimages had been fascinating, but this time it was different. She could see the people assembling here. She could hear the hubbub, she could feel their restlessness to be off, she could share the excitement.

This was the one. But she had not chosen the Road to Santiago. It had chosen her.

She looked at Father Brian and he was smiling broadly.

'I see we've come to the right place,' he said, 'It wouldn't need your gift as a mind-reader to know that you've already heard the call to Santiago. If you like, we can follow in the footsteps of those pilgrims for a mile or so. It will let you get the feel of it.'

They crossed the bridge to the Ile de la Cité and went into the cathedral of Notre Dame. This magnificent house of God was almost empty. A few tourists wandered in pairs, in silent reverence, staying close to each other as if afraid that the mystical power of the place might separate them. Anamar wondered what it would be like if there were great numbers of sightseers. Would the click and flash of cameras and the chatter of the crowd impose an atmosphere of its own?

She and Father Brian sat separately for a little while, each in private prayer. On the way out, Father Brian paused to whisper to Anamar.

'Notre Dame was built on the ruins of a Temple of Diana,' he said, with his eyes twinkling. 'Diana the Huntress.'

Anamar gave him a look. 'Are you trying to tell me that I'll have need of Diana's speed and cunning on this pilgrimage?'

They reached the sunshine again. Father Brian rubbed his chin.

'Maybe so,' he said gently,'She would have made a great guide. But I was thinking of her as the Goddess of Light. Let's hope she shines for you when you need her most.'

They crossed the Pont-au-Double to the Left Bank and wandered through the streets, in and out of churches. Anamar drifted along as if in a dream, hardly appearing to notice when he pointed to a bas-relief showing a pilgrim with his staff or a scallop shell on a wall.

Around a corner they entered the rue St-Jacques and Anamar found herself jolted from her day dream as if someone had shaken her by the shoulders. Since they had left the Tour St-Jacques her mind had been back in a past century as part of a pilgrim band. Now she was in the present again, actually taking her first steps on the Road to Santiago.

'Not just yet,' She was amazed to hear herself say it aloud, although it was barely audible. 'Hold on, Anamar. You have another place to go before you set out on this road.'

'Well said,' Father Brian had heard every word and knew exactly what she meant. 'You have that Mediterranean beach to visit. But first you have to endure a wee bit more of my harangue before I dare let you set out on this particular pilgrimage.'

They both laughed and turned towards each other to shake hands. Oblivious of people passing on the street around them, Father Brian held one of Anamar's hands in both of his and blessed her and her pilgrimage to Santiago.

They walked along the Rue St-Jacques for half an hour before going their separate ways. To-morrow at lunch, he could tell her about Santiago. Each, in her or his own way, had talked enough, had thought enough about pilgrimage for one day. He wanted to do his notes before their next meeting. She needed time on her own to come to terms with the decision.

Anamar knew nothing about the history of the Road of St James, except that it was an ancient pilgrimage to a Holy City in Northern Spain. But everything had changed at the Tour St-Jacques. Before, she had been a traveller searching for a journey. Now she was a pilgrim preparing for a pilgrimage.

The rest of the afternoon and evening passed agreeably. Once Father Brian had told her about the Way of St James, she would leave for the South of France. She would visit Hank's beach, the Plage de la Pampleonne, walk on its sand, paddle in the sea, and then, duty done, she would be free to set out for Santiago.

Next day Father Brian arrived early at the restaurant and arranged for a larger table. His notes and maps were spread out already on either side of his place setting, but Anamar knew him well enough by now to be sure that the discussions would have to await their turn. Food would be the first priority.

They ordered cruditées, thinly sliced raw vegetables with mayonnaise. Father Brian had snails in garlic. Anamar flinched at the very sight of them but, when she tasted one from his plate, was amazed to find it delicious. The main course was Sole Meunière and the patron brought to the table a large platter with two exquisite fish. Father Brian toasted Anamar with his glass of wine and served the sole with the skill of the expert.

'Let's take the story of St James first.'

It was obvious that he intended to be very businesslike.

'In the sixth and seventh centuries there was a tradition in the Church that St James the Greater had preached in Spain during his lifetime. In the Acts of the Apostles we learn that he was put to death on the orders of King Herod, who wanted to please the Jews. According to the tradition, his disciples then rescued his body from the dogs outside the walls of Jerusalem and sailed with it to the North-Western coast of Spain.

'They buried him where the oxen pulling the cart stopped. Centuries later the tomb had to be concealed with rocks and bushes when the Visigoths and the Moors invaded Northern Spain. It lay forgotten for hundreds of years until the ninth century, when it was rediscovered by a hermit.

'The local bishop declared it the Tomb of St James and Pope Leo 3rd had it proclaimed throughout the Christian world. Soon it became a place of pilgrimage and the first notable band of foreign pilgrims came from France in the tenth century, led by a bishop from Gascony.'

Father Brian reached a particularly succulent part of the sole and he paused to allow himself to enjoy it in silence before he continued.

'The French pilgrims established a route across Northern Spain. It was really the old Roman road, still in use a thousand years after it had been constructed but no longer maintained to their high standards.'

He produced a map of France and Spain and marked four lines in red. They showed the ancient roads from Paris in the North, Vézelay and Le Puys in Central France and Arles in the South. Three of the roads merged before they reached the Pyrenees and the fourth from Arles, which crossed the mountains by a different pass, joined them just after Pamplona.

'There they are,' said Father Brian, 'The Four Great Roads to Santiago. Once they reached Spain and became one, it was called the Camino Francés, the Road of the Franks, or the foreigners.

'But how do you know so much about the actual route?' Anamar was so excited she had to reach out and touch the map, tracing the route over the Pyrenees with her finger.

Father Brian smiled broadly. He had cleaned his plate with a piece of bread as a gesture of respect to the juices of the Sole Meunière and nodded to acknowledge that Anamar had asked exactly the right question.

'Chapter and verse,' he said grandly, 'We have chapter and verse. In the middle of the twelfth century a French cleric called Aimery Picaud edited a book about the Camino de Santiago, the Codex Calixtinus, astutely called after the Pope of the day, in the certain knowledge that its title would ensure it could not be ignored.

'One of the volumes is called the Pilgrim Guide and it gives details of routes, hazards, places to stay, comments about the water and the wine and descriptions of the people and customs of the lands passed through.

'When you come back I'll be very interested to hear your impressions. I have a feeling some things won't have changed much over the past eight hundred years. I've seen a copy of the Codex Calixtinus in the Vatican Library. It was probably the world's first tourist guide.'

Their meal was over but they sat on, Anamar asking the questions, Father Brian answering them as best he could. She wanted to know how to find the way or somewhere to stay, whether the local people would recognise her as a pilgrim, whether anyone would speak French. Father Brian allowed himself a look of concern.

'You'll have to learn as you go,' he said seriously, 'Once you cross the Pyrenees you'll have to pick up enough Spanish to get by. But I have a suggestion, and it's not just to ensure you don't forget your devotions. Go to see the priest when you stop for the night in a village. He'll keep you right. He'll know his duty to a pilgrim. And, of course, he'll tell you the time of evening Mass!'

They laughed and Anamar wagged a finger at him as if she was surprised that he might doubt her piety.

'I had to mention Mass,' he said with a smile, 'An old priest I used to know was fond of saying that we Irish would eat the altar rails at home but once away, we soon lose the appetite.'

He gave Anamar the map and a more detailed list of towns and villages from the Codex.

'It might seem as if I've been very helpful but it's very little for such a long way. It's five hundred miles still to go once you've reached Spain. You'll have to be very careful. A girl travelling on her own just doesn't know who to trust, even when someone seems helpful.'

But Anamar was not going to let anything spoil the moment. She poured each of them a little more wine from the carafe and toasted Father Brian, thanking him for all his help.

'I knew all along that Deirdre Ryan would never have sent me here unless she was certain you'd be a star turn,' she said happily. 'I must write to her. She'll be dying to hear how we've been getting on.'

That evening Father Brian and Danny arranged a lift for Anamar all the way to a small town near St Tropez in the South of France, leaving in two days time. They called at her hotel to tell her the news and to invite her to have dinner with them and their friends on the evening before she left.

Anamar had never felt so purposeful in all her life. Before she went to bed, she wrote to Deirdre, Hank and Maureen. She told each of them what had happened and outlined her immediate plans.

On her last night in Paris, Father Brian and Danny called for her at the Hotel Select and walked her to the restaurant. Their table seemed to take up almost half the dining room and it was laid and ready.

The others were already there, talking loudly to each other, arguing about where they would sit. Henri took charge. He insisted that Anamar and Father Brian sit at either end, Raoul and Paul on one side and Danny and himself on the other.

Anamar began to laugh, remembering the hilarity of her first meeting with these men and now seeing them neatly arranged around a table and on their best behaviour.

'I'm greatly honoured,' she said happily, 'This must be a special occasion indeed to have transformed the rough crew I met the other evening into such civilised companions.'

The menu had been chosen previously by Father Brian and Henri and they announced that each course would remain a secret until served. The wonderful smell gave the first dish away as the patron appeared with a huge tureen. A whisper passed around the table, 'Soup de Poisson.'

'You're right of course, but this Is the famous Bouillabaisse,' said Henri with a wave of an arm towards Anamar, 'In the hope that when you reach the Mediterranean, you will order this supreme fish soup of the Azure Sea and think of us.'

The conversation was mainly in French, particularly when the men were talking seriously about food and wine. Anamar expected Father Brian and Henri to be experts but was amazed to find that Paul and Raoul were also knowledgeable. Danny was the only one not prepared to allow his eating to be inhibited by too much talk about the cuisine. He winked at Anamar.

'If we were at home now in an hotel in the County Tipp, everyone would think it very queer to hear these fellows talking so much about the grub and the grog instead of eating and drinking.'

The main course was Coquilles St Jacques and Henri directed the patron to set the huge serving dish of scallops in a cream and white wine sauce in front of Anamar. Father Brian rose from his chair.

'Every pilgrim to Santiago needs a scallop shell as the badge which shows that he or she is on the Camino, the Road of St James. We ask you to take yours first. The shells will serve us too, as pilgrims on life's journey, and greatly in need of all the help we can get.'

Father Brian had been very quiet but when the first two courses were over he told the others a little of the history and the route of the Road to Santiago. Then he raised a hand and asked a question.

'Anamar and I have been talking for days. Now you can help us. Suppose you felt called on a pilgrimage, what manner of pilgrim would you be?'

The conversation stopped for a moment. There were smiles and a few nervous laughs. In this company, when someone raised a question, it would be met head on with a clever response or derision. But on this occasion they all knew that Father Brian required a serious answer.

Henri was the first to respond.

'I suppose it falls to me, as the one true unbeliever in this company, to speak with the voice of reason. You may all feel bound by the duties of your faith but I agree with our friend Sartre. He argues that each man must have the freedom to make his own choice.'

'Or woman,' said Anamar very quietly, just loud enough for all to hear.

Henri's eyes twinkled. This girl had spirit. He inclined his head towards her in acknowledgement.

'Of course, mademoiselle, of course!' he said graciously. 'But if I felt called to make such a journey I would trust my own instincts. I would feel no compulsion to observe the rituals, no need to seek grace through self-imposed hardship. I would follow my own star.'

'But where would you go? Who would be your companion?' It was Paul who surprised even himself by interrupting Henri and addressing Anamar. He needed to know the answers to both questions. Although he had accepted that she would be travelling on her own, she must be an exception. He could only conceive a journey like this in the company of others.

Henri smiled the smile of a man at ease with himself.

'I am sure,' he said quietly, 'The only way for me, like Anamar, would be alone. My reasons would be different but we would both need solitude. Had I companions they would surely deflect me from my own quest.'

Raoul agreed and angered Paul, who felt himself insulted that his friend could contemplate such a venture without him. They turned to face each other and began to argue, Raoul shaking a fore-finger in his friend's face and jumping to his feet. Paul cowered back as if in fear of a blow. But the anger had gone from Raoul's face. In its place was a smile of exhilaration. He held out his hands to his friend.

'Words have always been our enemy,' he said taking hold of Paul's hands, 'We are doers, not talkers. We have the courage to follow the beat of a different drum. We are adventurers. We should walk with Anamar for a few days, if she will allow us. We could be company for her when she crosses the Pyrenees into Spain. The Sorbonne will have closed for the summer by the time she starts her journey. It would be the adventure of a life-time.'

Father Brian began to clap. It seemed such a helpful idea, a real gesture of friendship. Anamar smiled and joined in the applause.

'Why not?' she said cheerily. 'Once I decide my starting point I'll be able to write to tell you where and when we can meet.' She shook hands with the two boys. 'So that's the deal, then. We'll cross the big hills together.'

'Bravo! Bravo!' Paul was so excited he was out of his seat, shaking hands with all of them. 'The Three Musketeers will conquer the Pyrenees!'

The dessert arrived and created a natural pause in the pilgrimage discussions. The patron himself placed a large silver salver in the middle of the table. On it was a wonderful pyramid of profiteroles. It brought a gasp of appreciation from the diners. The balls of choux pastry were smothered in chocolate sauce, each oozing cream.

Anamar was served first and took only one. It was delicious. She had a second and wondered if she should try another.

There was a hint of panic at the table. The pyramid was being dismantled at an alarming rate. The patron, however, had been standing by, watching the demolition of his art with pleasure. He had a waiter take away the first salver and put a second in its place. An air of calm descended on the table. Anamar decided in favour of 'just one more'.

It took Father Brian a little longer to reach the moment of ample sufficiency.

'It must be my turn,' he said, returning to the question he had posed about how each might see himself as a pilgrim.

'As you all know,' he said jovially, 'Even I have my pretensions. It ill-befits a man of the cloth, but there you are, I'm nothing if not honest with my friends.'

'I would see myself as the travelling scholar, the Oxford Cleric in Chaucer's Canterbury Tales, who spent his all "on learning or another book".'

'An elegant choice, if I may say so,' said Henri, 'But what about Danny? He's usually the one with most to say.'

Danny's cheeks were red and puffed as if he were in distress. He had never enjoyed an evening more. The food and wine were superb. All his life he had yearned for company like this. Best of all, this young woman had drawn every one of them into her pilgrimage.

He felt deeply moved but, as others talked, his past life had come to haunt him in stark flashes, of opportunities missed, mistakes made, good advice ignored, friends let down. He thought of the home he could not wait to leave and, only later, had realised that he loved dearly. It was the sins of omission which distressed him most, the failures by default.

He began to cry, without sound or movement, except to screw the thumb and fingers of one hand into his eyes to try to stem the tears.

'I would make the most unworthy pilgrim of all. I would need to take the pilgrim's vow, to hear Mass daily, to observe the rituals, to make my devotions, to do my penance through suffering, to pray that my contrition would be enough ....' He looked far older than his years.

'All her adult life my mother intended to go to Lourdes but, what with one thing and another, she never got around to it. When she was dying I knew she wanted to ask me to make the pilgrimage for her, to entreat the Holy Mother to intercede for her, but couldn't find it in her heart to ask me. She could never load her duties into the creel on someone else's back.'

He wiped his face with his napkin and sat back in his chair. There was a silence which no one seemed to want to break. Then Father Brian, the man whose calling it was to speak when others lacked the word, asked Danny if he would sing for them. It was a shrewd move. Danny could never resist the noble call.

'I daren't trust myself to sing an Irish song,' he said, 'I might lose the run of myself and never make it to the end. So here goes with a Scottish one .....

'Will you go lassie go and we'll all go together,
Through the wild mountain thyme and along the blooming heather,
Will you go lassie go?'

Danny sang softly, gently, in a light tenor voice that seemed so strange in such a big, rough man. The diners at other tables paused and turned towards him. The patron brought the kitchen staff to let them hear. Anamar felt herself deeply affected. He was singing about her and her home. He had drawn them all into his song. This was the way her Granny Mac used to tell her stories, as if the words were inside the heads of her audience and she was only bringing them into mind.

Danny sang the last line with his eyes closed and every note hanging in the air.

'Will you go lassie go?'

There was loud applause and cries of 'Bravo!' and Danny sat down smiling shyly. A neighbouring table sent over a bottle of fine white wine. His good spirits were quickly restored and there were toasts to Anamar, to the Road of St James, to Ireland, to France, to present company, to their fellow-diners.

Anamar took care to make each toast a sip rather than a draught of wine. These men were much more used to the juice of the grape than she was.

The men had clubbed together to buy Anamar a gift. Father Brian produced a silver cross on a silver chain and passed it to Paul and Raoul to present to Anamar. Together they placed the chain around her neck. It was done without a word. As she sat down again, she held the cross in the fingers of her left hand as if in reassurance that all this was happening to her.

No one thought to ask her what kind of pilgrim she might be. There was no need. For Henri the unbeliever, for Paul and Raoul the adventurers, for Danny the lapsed and troubled soul, for Father Brian the friend and priest, for all of them, Anamar was the real pilgrim.

BEWARE OF ROGER THE ENGLISHMAN

Danny and Father Brian called at the hotel next morning and took Anamar to Les Halles, the market area. The others were already there as arranged, waiting for them in a side street beside a large, ancient truck. Each one had a note of his address to give to Anamar. Danny opened the driver's door and climbed up on the step to lean into the cab. His bulk filled the opening. He was obviously giving the driver instructions.

Father Brian began to talk to Anamar about the importance of keeping a record of her journey.

'You must keep a note of the places you visit, with dates. When you go to Mass ask the priest to sign and date your record. You'll need it when you reach Santiago. It will allow you to claim the certificate which shows that you've made a proper pilgrimage.'

He took Anamar to one side, speaking to her now not as a friend but as a priest.

'The certificate is called a Compostellana. It's a record of your pilgrimage, but it's also a plenary indulgence, offering substantial remission from Purgatory.'

Anamar saw his face set in such an intense expression she could hardly believe her eyes. Could this be the same man who had laughed and joked with her, who had enjoyed his food and wine so much at their working lunches, who had danced so nimbly with her through the streets of the city, who had been the soul of bonhomie in the company of his friends?

As he blessed her, she realised that it was his prayer too. He was willing her a safe passage, to be able for the rigours of the road, to find grace and joy at journey's end.

Henri gave her a Michelin road map of the whole country and a large screw-topped bottle of water. He shook hands with her and kissed her on both cheeks. Paul and Raoul were distressed but they had a gift too. It was a brown paper bag with fresh rolls, a piece of cheese and some paté wrapped in grease-proof paper.

When Danny shook her hand, it was lost to view inside his great paw and he placed another paw on top in a gesture as eloquent as any kiss.

Father Brian helped her into the passenger side of the lorry's cab and passed up her rucksack. He too, shook her hand, this time as a friend again. The driver and his helper were small men who looked like brothers, dark-haired, dressed in the faded-blue trousers and tunics of the French working man. They nodded in greeting, the driver reaching across his helper to shake her hand.

Sitting on the outside, Anamar was surprised to find that there was plenty of room on the bench seat of the cab. The helper sat back from her as if he was afraid they might touch. He took Anamar's rucksack from her knees and set it on the seat between them to be sure.

Danny's grinning, bearded face appeared at the open window on the driver's side.

'Aren't you the great Donegal woman,' he said, nodding his head in admiration, 'You'll skim through France, over the Pyrenees and across Spain like Genghis Khan and it'll be God help any man, peasant, nobleman or cleric who tries to divert you from your way.'

He turned his head to fix the driver and his helper with a stare of such menace that it frightened Anamar as well as the men. Danny nodded his head forward in a gesture which gave the driver permission to leave and the lorry's engine rumbled into life. He stepped down from the running board and blew her a kiss.

The lorry rolled forward and Anamar knelt on the seat with her head and shoulders out of the window to wave. They all looked so sorry to see her go. Father Brian and Henri each held a hand aloft. Paul held on to Raoul with one hand and waved with the other. Danny's both arms were swinging above his head as if signalling a message. The driver swung the steering wheel and they were gone.

For half an hour no one spoke in the cab and Anamar was glad of the peace. There was so much to think about. Once again, parting had been hard. It had to happen but it disturbed her to see them so sad. She had felt a similar conflict of emotions as the train pulled out of the station in Donegal Town. It had been difficult then to leave her friends. They had been sorry to see her go but all had been cheerful, trying to make it easy for her.

Leaving Hank, as her boat sailed from Belfast's docks had been much more confusing. The sensation of loss at parting was much deeper and far harder to understand because neither she nor Hank had been able to speak about how they felt for each other. But that parting too, had to happen. Now she was off on another stage.

A stream of young people walked the pavement, heading out of the city. They carried haversacks, rucksacks and blanket rolls, Their thumbs were raised, all trying to hitch a lift. There were so many it might have been a crowd going to a football match. Anamar had heard that hitch-hiking had become popular in France since the war. Father Brian had told her that the French government was so concerned it was considering a ban which would allow only foreigners or service personnel to hitch lifts.

Suddenly the lorry stopped and the helper climbed over the driver and jumped down on his side. He came around to the pavement and wrote a figure on the pavement in chalk. The driver leaned across her and shouted, 'Aix-en-Provence', at the young people below.

The helper was soon surrounded by a mob. They were bargaining with him for the price of the lift but he shook his head and pointed to the figure on the pavement. They could take it or leave it but that was the price. Some drifted away but about a dozen stayed and began to pay their fares.

Anamar worked it out that they were being charged the equivalent of about twenty-one shillings. It seemed a lot but it was much cheaper than the train fare and she thought it unlikely that there would be any free lifts on this particular road. She was amazed at the number of passengers the helper had accepted. Danny had told her that the lorry had brought peaches from the South and was returning with a load of empty boxes. But if the back was full of boxes where would the passengers sit?

Eventually she discovered the driver's name. He was Jean Marc and his helper was Bibi. Bibi said nothing. He was small and slightly built. He sat with his body very still, turning his head quickly from side to side. His eyes darted from her to Jean Marc and back, watching them both. It was another hour before Anamar realised that Bibi was deaf and was trying to read their lips.

The driver stopped every two hours or so to allow the passengers to answer the call of nature. The girls went behind into the bushes but the men had no thought of seeking cover. They simply stood with their backs to the road and relieved themselves. Anamar had seen this performance when she had been to France before but it was still an astonishing sight. Back home in Donegal it would have caused accidents as passing drivers struggled to believe the audacity of such a wanton act. The Guards would have had them up on a charge of indecent exposure.

The hours and kilometres passed and Anamar followed the journey on her map. When she felt hungry and opened her brown paper bag, Jean Marc and Bibi were very reluctant to share, accepting only a little bread and cheese.

By late afternoon they were beyond Chalon and heading for Lyon. The driver pulled into a parking space at a small road-side restaurant and announced that this was a one hour stop for a meal. The passengers headed for the dining room but Jean Marc, Bibi and Anamar were taken into a small room beside the kitchen and served almost immediately.

A basket of bread, a jug of wine and a large casserole were placed in the middle of their table. The two men could hardly wait until Anamar had served herself. They devoured the pork and bean stew like starving wolves. The bread basket was emptied and replenished every few minutes. Large slices of an apricot and peach tart were followed by second helpings, then coffee. For two such small men their appetites were prodigious.

Eventually they sat back in their chairs and rested. Jean Marc began to respond to Anamar's attempts to start a conversation. Bibi smiled shyly and did a trick with a napkin and a fork. He could make the fork disappear and reappear at will. His gestures invited Anamar to guess where the fork was hidden and, to his delight, he had to unveil each hiding place with a flourish.

As they left, there was no bill for the meal, only handshakes and thanks from the patron. Anamar guessed that this was the reward for bringing custom to his restaurant.

Back on the road the light faded quickly and the lorry rumbled on. Anamar slept in snatches.

It was still dark when she wakened, shaking with the chill of the night. The day had been hot but the cab was draughty and now bitterly cold. She opened her rucksack, found her spare blouse and sweater and put them on. Her cape was at the bottom of the bag and she took it out too.

Even though it was dark in the cab, she felt self-conscious as she struggled into her clothes but, with her legs tucked underneath her on the seat, with the hood over her head and the cape wrapped tightly around her, it kept the draughts at bay. She couldn't see his face but she was sure Bibi was laughing. The shivering stopped and as she warmed she went back to sleep.

The lorry stopped with a jolt and Anamar felt she was suffocating. She must have slept for hours and now the sun was baking hot. Jean Marc and Bibi were laughing loudly as she struggled out of the cape and the spare clothes. They climbed down from the lorry and she could hear Jean Marc telling the passengers it was journey's end, that they had reached Aix-en-Provence.

By the time Anamar climbed down to stretch her legs, the passengers had gone. She stepped up on the foot rung at the back of the lorry to see how they had managed. The peach boxes had been piled five or six deep, crushed down by body weight, then piled high again, leaving a space which hardly seemed big enough to let twelve people stand, never mind sit down. Anamar smiled to herself. The close contact should have helped keep them warm.

She went with Jean Marc and Bibi to a café for breakfast and Jean Marc explained that they still had one hundred kilometres to go to their home village near St Tropez.

Jean Marc's face showed the tiredness of the journey. His sun-browned skin had taken on the pallor of extreme fatigue. He drove on, more cautiously than before as if he realised the risks of exhaustion.

Beyond Toulon they reached the outskirts of a village and Jean Marc pulled into a yard beside a large shed.

'This is it,' he said, 'Alban-les-Saintes'.

Anamar offered to pay for the lift but he and Bibi laughed.

'Thank your friend, Danny,' Jean Marc said wearily, 'And tell him we obeyed orders.' He shook hands with her and went to sleep on the bench seat of the cab as soon as she climbed down.

Bibi gestured to Anamar to follow him and took her to a house on the main street with a sign above the door, Auberge de Jeunesse. The door was open and Anamar saw two people at the far end of the hallway, arguing fiercely, the man shaking his arms in frustration, the woman poking him in the chest with her forefinger.

He was a handsome man in his early thirties, fair-haired and of average height. He was losing the argument. The girl was younger, with long dark hair and a beautiful face and figure. She was dressed in dark blue with a tight shirt and the shortest shorts Anamar had ever seen.

Anamar turned to thank Bibi and say 'Good bye' but he had gone. When she looked back the girl was walking towards her with her hand out.

'Welcome to our little hostel,' she said in English with an American accent. As she shook hands she smiled broadly. 'I am Yvette, the leader of the village group which runs this hostel. I guess you are English and the English are always welcome here.'

Anamar was taken aback. Why did Yvette think she was English? It must be her clothes. Later Yvette would tell her that only an English girl would be eccentric enough to travel alone so far from home.

'I'm not English,' Anamar said quickly and then was embarrassed in case it sounded as if she was protesting too forcefully. 'I'm Irish and I was hoping I could stay for the night. I'm not a member of any Youth Hostel Association.'

Yvette laughed. She explained that theirs was not an official hostel, anyone could stay here. She gave Anamar a mug of coffee.

'Beware of Roger, the Englishman,' she said loudly, as if she was hoping that Roger was listening behind the door. Anamar guessed he had been the man in the hall when she arrived, 'He thinks he is so attractive that we women will all fall at his feet. You will meet Stephan, the warden of the hostel. He is a dull peasant but he hates Roger. He will be your protector.'

'MY GI NEVER CAME BACK'

Stephan followed Yvette as she showed Anamar to the dormitory upstairs. It was a spacious room, bright and airy, with four sets of double bunks arranged around the walls. Anamar picked an upper bunk near the window. There were clothes on some of the others but this one and the one below appeared to be free. Stephan gave her a blanket and a pillow and when he discovered that she had no sheet sleeping bag, he went off to find one.

While he was away, two French boys came into the room, greeted the girls and sat down on a lower bunk at the other side of the room. Anamar had been thinking that she was in the female dormitory. Obviously not, the sleeping arrangements here were communal!

Yvette saw the look of shock on Anamar's face and began to laugh.

'This is France, chérie,' she said, 'How do you say it in English? .....
Anything goes.'

At home Anamar had heard that youth hostellers were a friendly crowd, but being expected to sleep in a mixed dormitory was a welcome she could never have anticipated. This would make a great story back home. Deirdre Ryan, the experienced traveller, would take it in her stride, but Maggie and Maureen would be astounded.

She was sure that she was going to enjoy her stay here. Yvette was already helpful and had told her it was less than an hour by bus to St Tropez.

When she had settled in, she went into the village to buy some food for her evening meal. As she reached the main street she was aware that someone was following her. It was Roger. She stopped and waited while he sauntered confidently towards her.

'Sure aren't you the lovely colleen from the Emerald Isle,' he said with a charming smile and in an imitation of an Irish accent so awful, Anamar cringed.

She looked at him without showing the slightest interest.

'Is that a fact?' she said, allowing only her eyes to show her annoyance.

He stepped back as if she had slapped his face. The smile and the confidence vanished, replaced by a look, not of fear, but of failure. He stuttered before the words would come.

'I'm sorry,' he said at last, his face pale with strain, 'I'm desperate. I've no money - no money at all - not enough for one cup of coffee. I haven't eaten for two days, that's what the row was about. Yvette lets me stay at the hostel for nothing but she was telling me that if I don't stop begging food from the hostellers she'll put me out.'

He looked so much smaller and older.

'You're my only hope,' he said quickly, in case she would speak, 'Yvette likes you, she admires the way you're travelling around on your own. And I'm not begging. Just give me a chance to buy your food. I know the farmers around here and the drivers who take the produce to the markets. I guarantee I'll buy enough to feed the both of us for less than you would pay for yourself.'

Anamar had expected a very different proposal. This man was at his wit's end. He must be starving. Whatever dignity he had before was now gone. He was pleading with her.

'Let me buy your food for this evening as a trial. Give me the money you were going to spend. I won't cheat you. I daren't. Yvette would kill me. There's a side to her you haven't seen - like a wild cat when she's angry. She survived the war here and not by hiding away until it was over. God help the man who crosses her.'

Anamar suddenly changed her mind and gave him a few francs for the food. Until he mentioned his fear of Yvette she had no intention of giving him anything. Now she felt she had nothing to lose. If he cheated her he would have two women to deal with, not one.

He scurried off like a frightened urchin and Anamar strolled the length of the village. There were a few food shops, a hardware store and a small café with tables on the pavement. At the far end was a church and a tiny notice board showing that evening Mass was at six o'clock. When Anamar had been away from Donegal before she had attended Mass far less regularly than she would have done at home. Now she decided that, while she was here, she would try to make it to church every evening.

On the way back she sat down at a pavement table outside the café and ordered coffee. The sun was hot but her seat was in the shade. She stretched her legs and sat back in comfort, in spite of the rickety chair. After the long journey, it was blissful just to be here. She even had someone to do the shopping. Surely Roger could be made to feel he had to do the cooking too. Would that be taking advantage of his misfortune? But why not? Deirdre would have said he was the type of man to be kept under your thumb. Anyway, she was enjoying herself here. It was like being on holiday.

She met Yvette back at the hostel and began to tell her about her encounter with Roger and the deal she had done with him. Yvette shook her head in disbelief and then began to laugh.

'We women are all the same,' she said, her American accent becoming more pronounced, 'Wherever we come from, we all have a soft place in our hearts for the loser. We think we can change him, cure him by threats or kindness. It never works.

'When Roger came here first I looked after him. But he was a poor lover, not worth the trouble, not worth the cost of the food.

'Keep him at a distance. Keep him out of your bed. Use him as your servant. Make him do the shopping. Insist that he does the cooking. Show him no kindness. Give him the hard word.'

She was still laughing as she took Anamar's arm and led her through to sit in the little garden. The girls were finding it easy to talk about themselves. Yvette said that she worked as a free-lance hairdresser and manicurist, visiting clients in their own homes. She also contributed local news items to a weekly newspaper in Toulon. Anamar told her about her life in Donegal and her work in F.B.O'Boyle's dress shop.

When they came into the kitchen at the end of the afternoon, Roger had arrived back from his shopping expedition. He still looked nervous. Without speaking, he pointed to a peach box on the table.

Yvette and Anamar began to unpack the food. There were onions, garlic bulbs and huge tomatoes, a small bottle of olive oil, a larger, unlabelled bottle of wine, six eggs carefully wrapped in newspaper, two lemons, a small packet of coffee and a large stick of bread.

In a newspaper parcel were four fish the size of decent trout, which Yvette called sardines, although they were far bigger than the only sardines Anamar had ever seen, which were tinned. At the bottom of the box there must have been twenty peaches. Roger offered the change from the money Anamar had given him and she put it back in her purse.

'The peaches are a present from Jean Marc,' Roger said quickly. He had no intention of being caught out in any kind of deception.

'Well done,' said Anamar, 'You have been busy.'

Yvette grimaced. Even though she was impressed, she made no effort to say so. Anamar smiled.

'You've made a grand start,' she said to Roger, 'I suppose you can't wait now for us to leave the kitchen so you can get on with your cooking. Would seven o'clock be OK? I'm just off to Mass and I should be back by then.'

The two girls left the kitchen as fast as they could manage. Once out of ear-shot, they began to laugh, clutching each other for support, the tears streaming down their faces.

When they recovered, Anamar asked Yvette if she wanted to go with her to Mass.

'No! No thank-you chérie,' she said, trying not to start laughing again, 'Better you go alone and pray for both of us.'

When Anamar returned she could smell the fish cooking. Some new hostellers had arrived but Roger had commandeered the best table and was ready to serve.

He pointed to a seat and Anamar took her place. The table had been laid as carefully as Roger could manage. There was a bowl of tomato salad, bread on a bread board with a bread knife, a jug of water and the bottle of wine. Anamar poured herself a glass of wine. Roger served the fish and placed a dish of fried onions on the table.

She began to wonder why she was enjoying herself so much? It was not as if she liked Roger. She was sure he needed to be watched closely as Yvette had warned. It was not as if she was looking forward to his company during the meal. But, although he was trying so hard, it was not to impress her with a view to close friendship. She was quite sure of that. He was starving and she was his only hope. He had looked ill-at-ease working in the kitchen but he was doing his utmost not to spoil this chance.

He sat down and looked at her anxiously.

'Is it OK?' he said, watching her try the tomato salad.

He had sliced the tomatoes, used a sprinkling of olive oil and seasoned them with salt and pepper.

'And where did you get the salt and pepper?' Anamar kept a straight face and looked at him directly. 'I didn't see either amongst your shopping.'

'They were on one of the shelves and .....' Anamar cut him off.

'So you just helped yourself,' she said severely, 'I hope you're not going to treat my stuff in the same way. Still, the tomato salad's not too bad, less salt and more pepper would make all the difference.'

Roger ate quickly, trying to talk to Anamar between mouthfuls of fish. Although she appeared to be showing no interest he was determined that she should hear his story.

'I was in the army,' he said quietly and clearly, as if reporting to a superior officer. 'Served in North Africa and Italy. 'De-mobilized earlier this year and couldn't find a job. Took the boat to France on the 1st of March. Intended to stay for six months. Hoped to get work picking grapes.'

Anamar looked up from her food.

Picking grapes in the Spring? It was unbelievable. Surely even a townie would know that grapes could not be harvested until the Autumn.

'OK! OK! I know what you're thinking,' Roger said wearily, 'My ex-army mates said that I could make money at the grapes but nobody told me when. Anyway, I went to France and the £20 pounds I had left from my de-mob gratuity only lasted to the end of the month. When I arrived here I had nothing left. Yvette let me stay for a week.

'Then I tried hitching to Switzerland. There was no work there either. I had to sell a half litre of blood to get some cash. Now I'm back here but Yvette doesn't want to know and Stephan thinks I'm after his job. Even he despises me. I've had no regular food for weeks.'

Roger spoke matter-of-factly, without self pity, as if it was important that Anamar understood. He took a tattered photograph from his shirt pocket and passed it over. It showed a scene of a film set, with men in the uniforms of Greek soldiers. Roger was addressing them from the steps of a Temple. Instead of a helmet, he wore a crown.

'Before the war I was an actor,' he said grandly, 'That's me playing the King of Thebes.'

Anamar gave no indication of being impressed. The fish were over-cooked, fried in the pan for far too long. She had managed to eat one but the other had been watching her with a reproachful eye, daring her to eat it. It was a pity, she thought, that sardines had to be cooked whole. It meant that they still looked like a real fish on the plate rather than food.

She looked up.

'Would you fancy another sardine, Your Majesty?' she said.

If she was going to insist that he did the cooking, she would have to teach him a few of the basics and supervise him closely.

Roger accepted the sardine with not the slightest sign of polite reluctance. She decided to say nothing about his cooking. It was one thing to be unkind about his tomato salad but to have criticised the fish when he was obviously trying so hard, would have been cruel.

Yvette arrived and she and Anamar had coffee in the garden while Roger washed up.

'I need not have worried, chérie,' Yvette's eyes were twinkling, her hands raised in congratulation. 'On the outside you seem so gentle and kind but inside ....' She began to laugh loudly. 'But inside you are like me. Roger is now your slave and not because he adores you. He is afraid. You have him in your power. With men like him, it is the only way!'

The other hostellers were all inside and the two girls had the garden to themselves. Yvette asked Anamar why she was here, why she had come to the South of France.

Anamar told her Hank's story of Operation Dragoon and the landing of the American troops on the beach at St Tropez. She was describing his traumatic experience when she noticed that Yvette had become quiet and very still, There was a pause and Yvette said quietly,

'I remember those days too, chérie. I knew some of those GIs. I got to know one of them very well. I was young, very, very young. When they left I was sure my John would return. I wrote to him three times but he never replied. My GI never came back.'

Anamar took her hand.

'When I go to the beach to-morrow, will you come with me?'

Yvette nodded. For the first time since she and Anamar had met, her self-assurance had gone. She looked vulnerable and held on tightly to Anamar's hand. They sat in silence. In Mediterranean France there was no gradual fading of the evening light. Darkness fell like a stage curtain and suddenly it was night. They moved closer to the door and sat in the light from the back porch.

Yvette brought a radio to the doorstep. It was tuned to AFN, the American Forces Network. Fats Waller was singing, 'My very good friend the milkman says .....' and Anamar smiled. She squeezed Yvette's hand. Her mother had hated what she called 'that jazz rubbish' but when she and her father had gone to bed, Anamar would have listened to AFN with the sound turned down low.

Joe Loss and his Band played 'In The Mood', 'The Ink Spots' sang 'Why do you whisper green grass ...' The music was bringing Anamar closer to home than she had felt since she had left for Paris. Then the disc jockey played her favourite, 'So tired of dreaming of you ..... and the brass section sighed, almost sobbed. 'So tired of waiting for you .... ' Then she realised that Yvette was crying.

She turned the radio down and talked about her adventures in Paris. She mentioned Father Brian and the way he had helped plan her pilgrimage. She recounted the hilarious evenings she had shared with him and his friends in Paris, standing up to act the parts, Father Brian the erudite, convivial priest, who danced his way through the streets of the city on their walks, the urbane, man-of-the-world Henri, the sensitive soul-mates Raoul and Paul, and, of course, Danny, fearsome or gentle as required, the giant of a painter.

She talked about finding the Tour St Jacques and her decision to do the pilgrimage to Santiago. Stephan suddenly appeared in the porch as if he had been hiding in the shadows. He was a small, strongly built man in his twenties, shaven-headed, of sallow complexion. He was staring at Anamar.

'I know about St Jacques,' he said excitedly in French, 'The Seigneur of my home village in Ariège told me the story. He is a true pilgrim. He walked from Lourdes to Santiago before the war. You must go to see him before you start.'

It was not a suggestion. Stephan was appealing to her. Yvette looked thoughtfully at Anamar, then nodded in agreement. They had been talking in English and she went back to that language.

'He's right.' she said, 'The peasant pretends not to know any English but he's been listening to us. He is brighter than he looks. He understands every word. Your dancing priest has given you inspiration for your pilgrimage but now you need real information about the journey. This Seigneur could be your gift from St James.' She laughed.

'If you can handle Roger the film star, you need have no fears about a French Seigneur from the wilds of the Pyrenees.'

Anamar knew they were both right. Yvette arranged to let Stephan have the key of her office the next morning, so that he could use the hostel telephone when they went off by bus to St Tropez.

The two girls hardly spoke during the forty-minute bus journey. Yvette took Anamar's arm. It went beyond the reassuring touch of a friend's hand. They had only known each other for less than two days but already shared an intimacy which only exists between close friends.

Yvette was so poised and sophisticated. Not only was she very beautiful but she had a sense of style which meant that anything she wore looked smart. Anamar smiled to herself, thinking of the sensation Yvette's short, dark-blue shorts and tightly fitting blouse would make in Donegal Town of a Saturday afternoon. Their backgrounds and experience of life were so different but the bond between them made her feel less anxious on what she thought might prove a difficult visit to Hank's beach.

The harbour at St Tropez was stunningly beautiful in the morning sunshine. The sea sparkled. There were huge white-hulled yachts and motor cruisers moored on the quay-side. Little gangways spanned the gap between ship and shore. Suntanned sailors and their guests passed from the luxury of their floating homes into the very heart of the simple town.

The quay was backed by a row of little shops, many with stalls outside, draped with the most attractive holiday clothes Anamar had ever seen.

The beautiful boat people went barefoot on shore, the girls in shorts even shorter than Yvette's. They strode purposefully on dry land as if in a hurry to get back to their paradise afloat.

Yvette and Anamar walked out of the town and hitched a lift with a farmer in a small, decrepit truck. He left them at the end of a lane with a sign which said, Plage de la Pampleonne. Anamar caught her breath. This is it, she thought, the very place.

The beach was vast, miles of golden sand, almost deserted except for a tiny camp site at the end of the sandy lane and two beach bars a little farther along to their left.

Each of the girls wandered off on her own, without a word. The sun was so hot Anamar tied a cotton scarf over her head and walked slowly. Yvette seemed not to notice the heat. She strode towards the sea, her eyes fixed on a point beyond the gentle waves.

They came together again at the edge of the water and took their shoes off to wade into the sea. The beach shelved gently and Anamar tucked her skirt up into her knickers. When the water was almost at knee height, the little waves lapping against their legs, they held hands and Yvette spoke so quietly Anamar barely heard the words,

'I was fifteen years old.'

It jolted Anamar out of her own reverie. Her thoughts had been so focused on Hank, Yvette's reason for being here had slipped from her mind.

She suddenly realised that if Yvette had been fifteen years old at the time of the landings in 1944, they were the same age, both born in 1929. It was such a surprise. She had assumed Yvette was years older.

'I had a baby,' Yvette said, quietly, 'My GI John never knew he was the father of a baby boy. I couldn't tell him in my letters. They took the child away from me shortly after he was born.' There was a long pause. 'Some day I'll find him.' She tried to smile. 'My pilgrimage will be to find my son.'

Anamar wished she could find words to help. She put an arm around Yvette's shoulders and held on until she felt the tension ease in her friend. Suddenly she saw Yvette as Madam Butterfly. Deirdre Ryan had often played the opera records on her gramophone. She said a silent prayer that Yvette's story would have a happier ending.

They turned towards the shore, looking at the land of France the way their men would have seen it, as their landing craft hit the sand and they jumped into the shallow water to run ashore.

Yvette's shoulders were slumped forwards, her head in her chest. She seemed overcome with sadness and Anamar took her arm for support. Yvette raised her head and her body straightened.

'The past is over, chérie,' she said, as much to herself as to Anamar. 'Your GI returned to you in Ireland. Don't forget to go back to him.'

They walked slowly towards the shore and the sand was so hot Anamar felt she was walking on burning embers. She hopped from foot to foot but Yvette walked slowly on as if unaware of the pain.

The sun baked the beach and Anamar began to feel faint as she had done in the Tropical Ravine in Belfast's Botanic Gardens. Then an on-shore breeze made the great heat bearable. They put on their shoes and walked towards the beach bar.

All Anamar's thoughts were for Yvette. She tried to think of her friend's anguish for the loss of both her baby and her lover and found that beyond comprehension.

She thought of Hank, feeling closer to him than ever before. It was as if coming to this beach had enabled her to understand his torment here. Feeling the sand under her feet and the water lapping around her ankles, seeing this huge stretch of sea-shore, had been enough.

The bar was a rickety construction of poles and reeds but it had an ice box. They sat in the shade and spoke their order in unison as if they had been rehearsing it, 'Coca Cola, s'il vous plait'. They looked at each other and began to laugh.

'At least they left us a drink as a memento,' said Yvette, still trying to smile. 'It is a pity they're not here, they would have paid the bill.'

The girls hitched a lift back to St Tropez and Yvette insisted that Anamar buy a pair of shorts. She knew the stall holder and a price was whispered which was less than half that marked on the make-shift label. They were the same dark blue as Yvette's but slightly longer. Anamar tried them on behind a canvas screen. They were a perfect fit.

'Hey! Hey!' Yvette called to her, 'Lucky you weren't around when the GIs were here. We French girls would have had no chance.'

Stephan was waiting for them at the bus stop in St Alban-les-Saintes. He was hopping up and down with excitement.

'I talked to the Seigneur,' he shouted in French before the girls could descend from the bus. 'He wants you to come to stay in his village, Mont L'ours-les-Cascades. He wants to meet the Irish pilgrim. The Road of St James is his life's work. He will tell you the way. He will make you maps. He has lived in England and speaks English very well.'

He shook hands with Anamar and on the way back to the hostel explained that he could arrange a lift with a lorry driver from the same company as Jean Marc. It would take Anamar to Toulouse and the Seigneur had offered to meet her there and drive her to Mont L'ours.

Roger was hard at work preparing the evening meal. Anamar had told him that Yvette would be eating with them and he looked up nervously as they entered the kitchen.

'I hope you like rabbit,' he said and whistled in relief when they smiled. 'Stephan gave it to me to cook for you. He snares them and sells them to the butcher. He showed me how to prepare it in a stew with onions and garlic. Doesn't it smells wonderful?'

Anamar asked Stephan to join them but, although he looked pleased to be asked, she failed to persuade him. During the meal Roger let the girls talk without interruption. They all liked the stew and he finished it off by wiping the pot clean with big chunks of bread.

Having talked it over with Yvette, Anamar decided that she would go to stay with the Seigneur in two days time. Stephan was asked to confirm the arrangements and went to Yvette's room to make the telephone call. Roger asked no questions but was plainly disappointed that Anamar was not staying longer. Yvette gave Anamar a knowing look when she saw the expression on Roger's face.

'Don't worry,' Anamar said to her coquettishly, 'It's only cupboard love. You'll soon have him all to yourself again.'

She and Yvette walked up the street to the café to discuss what they should do about Roger. She had guessed that there would be a British Consulate in Marseilles. Deirdre Ryan had told her that British Consulates would pay for the repatriation of one of their own nationals who had lost his money. An emergency travel document could be issued and the person's passport retained until the cost of the repatriation was reimbursed back.

Yvette could hardly contain her excitement. She gave Anamar a hug.

'You are brilliant, chérie, a genius sent to rid me of this man.' She laughed and clapped her hands. 'After you leave, I will take him to Marseilles and hand him over to his Consulate. I will make him their problem.'

When they returned to the hostel and told Roger, he was as pleased as a child with a birthday present. For the first time Anamar saw him happy. He began to admire her shorts.

'They're very smart,' he said enviously, 'In England they're all down to the knees. They make me look like a midget. That length would suit me perfectly. The producers always say I have toga legs.'

The girls began to laugh. Anamar had never heard a man admit he was vain but then this was Roger the film star.

'In the morning, soldier boy,' she said confidently, 'We will make you a pair of the smartest shorts you've ever seen. And better than that, it'll only take us ten minutes!'

Even Yvette looked puzzled. But Anamar winked at her,

'Leave it to me, chérie,' she said, imitating Yvette's accent when she spoke in English, 'All will be revealed in the morning.'

After breakfast next day she placed a chair in the middle of the common room and insisted that Roger stand on it. Yvette drew up an easy chair and sat down to watch the performance. Anamar gave Roger her full attention.

'In order to create, we must make sacrifices,' she said, imitating the grand tone which Deirdre Ryan sometimes affected, 'Are you prepared to lose these trousers to gain a pair of shorts?' She pointed at the sand-coloured cotton slacks which he was wearing.

'Of course,' said Roger eagerly, 'I have another pair like these in my suitcase. They were part of my desert uniform and I was allowed to keep them when I was de-mobbed.' He began to unbutton the trousers in order to take them off.

Yvette whistled and clapped loudly.

'Hold on a minute,' said Anamar, theatrically raising one hand in horror, 'We may be in France but where I come from a man should only drop his trousers in front of his wife and even then she is expected to turn her back so he's not embarrassed.'

Yvette laughed and Anamar produced a large pair of scissors from behind her back. Roger shuffled nervously on the chair and nearly fell off as Anamar approached, brandishing the scissors. Yvette's shouts of encouragement and shrieks of laughter brought the other hostellers to the doorway.

'Easy, easy,' said Anamar sweetly, patting Roger's knee, 'I'm only going to cut the bottoms off.'

She made a nick just above the knee and slit the trouser right around the leg.

'Could you not make them a bit shorter? asked Roger timidly.

Anamar looked around to the audience.

'So now he's an expert on tailoring,' she said wearily, 'Should I give him big slits up the sides so he can be really daring.'

Yvette was sobbing with laughter. She pointed at Roger but could not manage to speak. In seconds Anamar had cut off the second leg at the same height and rolled up the bottoms of the shorts in two neat rolls to mid-thigh length.

'No need for hems, soldier boy,' she said, 'Roll them down a turn for formal occasions and up one for casual. Believe me, rolled shorts will be the next fashion.'

The girls watched as Roger jumped off the chair and strutted around the room in his new shorts. He was delighted with them and thrilled to have an audience. He rolled them up another turn and posed, he glided sideways and twirled like a dancer.

Suddenly he stopped to thank Anamar and stepped across to the other hostellers to let them see the finished job.

Yvette went off to a wealthy client who needed her hair done urgently and Anamar spent most of the morning writing letters. She told Father Brian about her plans and asked him to pass the letter around their Parisien friends. She regaled Deirdre with the story of Roger, the film star and his shortie shorts.

Her letter to Hank took much longer.

3 June 1950
Alban-les-Saintes

Dear Hank,

As you can see from the enclosed postcard I am in the South of France. I'm staying at a great youth hostel in a village near Toulon and have made friends with Yvette, who is the leader of the local group which runs the hostel.

I miss you. When you came to Donegal I must have become used to you being around at the week-ends. When we said 'Good-bye' at Belfast docks I didn't realise I would miss you so much. I really do miss you.

Yvette and I went to St Tropez yesterday and when we came to the beach, there was the name you used to talk about on a wooden board, Plage de la Pampleonne. I walked on the sand and paddled in the shallow water. When I turned to come back, I imagined the fierce noise and smoke and the terrible smell of the battle and thought of you and your comrades. It must have been terrifying, truly awful.

All I could feel was the sun baking down. All I could hear was the lapping of the water around my ankles and the calling of the crickets, they really do make a racket, don't they? And all I could smell was the beautiful scent of mimosa.

But wading back to shore I think I began to understand what you had been through. Without any more discussion or you answering any more questions, I think I understand.

Yvette had a bad time too. She fell in love with one of the GIs but when his unit left the area she never heard from him again.

Through the hostel I've made contact with a man who walked to Santiago before the war. I'm going to see him to-morrow and he will tell me about the route and make me a map I can follow. Just as well you taught me about maps last year in the Pyrenees!

I'll keep you posted.

Your apprentice Pyrenean mountain goat and aspirant pilgrim,
Anamar

In the afternoon she walked out into the countryside and found a path which led through a wood to a small river. There were no rushes to be found so she twisted stalks of corn together in the traditional Irish way to make a St Brigid's cross. This one was for Yvette, who went to church no longer. She made another for Stephan who probably still did go to church when he returned to his home village. Back at the hostel she sat in the garden under the shade of a tree and listened to the crickets.

That evening they had sardines again. To Anamar's surprise she heard that Stephan would join them. Yvette smiled,

'I gave him no choice,' she said, 'I simply told him that he would eat with us. These men must do as they are told.'

Stephan had been in charge of the food and this time the sardines were cooked to perfection. As a second course, Yvette produced an open peach tart, glazed and glistening through the pastry lattice on top. Roger had little to say and Stephan spoke not at all. The girls talked as if they were alone and agreed to keep in touch with each other.

When the meal was over they walked to the café on the main street and drank white wine. Anamar found herself speaking about her feelings for Hank more openly than she had ever done before. It was such a pity she and Yvette had to part so soon. Yvette promised that she would come to Donegal the following year. She would start saving right away and Anamar was certain they would meet again.

Next morning she was up at five to walk to the lorry park. To her amazement Stephan and Roger came to see her off as well as Yvette. Roger was wearing his shorts and strode along in front. When they reached the lorry park Anamar presented Yvette and Stephan with their straw crosses.

'In Ireland it's usually made of rushes,' she said, 'It's the cross of St Brigid. She was known as a great healer. Put it up on the wall of your room and it will bring a blessing to the whole house.'

The driver and his helper were waiting. Anamar shook hands with Roger and Stephan, hugged Yvette, and they were on their way. It was three hundred miles to Toulouse.

The two men talked together during the journey, ignoring Anamar. She dozed for most of the way but when they reached the outskirts of the city she sat up. The lorry stopped in the market area and Anamar saw a low-slung, black car with a long bonnet. It fitted Stephan's description. Standing in the shade beside it was a well-dressed gentleman, distinguished, at ease with himself.

Anamar had no doubts. This must be the Seigneur.

RAMÓN THE SEIGNEUR

Anamar climbed down from the lorry and walked towards the man standing beside the car.

'You must be the Seigneur,' she said brightly, 'It's very good of you to help me. I hope I won't be an imposition.'

The man smiled and made a little bow.

'My dear young lady,' he said as they shook hands. 'Not only is it a privilege to offer hospitality to a Santiago pilgrim, to me it is also a most pleasant duty'.

Stephan had said that the Seigneur spoke English well, but Anamar was still surprised by his command of the language.

He introduced himself as Ramón Mont L'ours Barriano and, when she responded with her own name, she said,

'Please call me Anamar, everyone does.'

'And if I am to call you Anamar,' the Seigneur said firmly, 'You must call me Ramón. We pilgrims must not stand on ceremony.'

They both smiled and Anamar was relieved to find this man so easy to talk to. Stephan was so much in awe of him she had expected him to be very reserved.

Travelling in the car was luxurious after the long lorry journey and Anamar was content to sit back and listen to Ramón. He spoke quietly, without haste, as if he felt he should tell her about himself to put her at her ease.

'I live alone,' he said and then quickly added, 'With a house-keeper and two servant girls. It will be easier for them if you refer to me as Monsieur Barriano when you speak to them and I will call you Mademoiselle Anamar.' He looked a little embarrassed to be saying this but Anamar was pleased that he was able to speak to her so freely.

The journey took over two hours and Anamar encouraged him to talk about his life.

'I was born in Spain, in Navarre, my father and mother still live there on his family's estate. She is French and I live in what was her home village. It takes its name from her family, Mont L'ours. I'd better tell you why I became a pilgrim to Santiago and how I came to live here.

85

'In 1931, when I was sixteen, the anti-monarchist party in Spain won the local elections so convincingly that the King abdicated. With many of my school friends I was attracted by socialism at the time. My father was a Carlist, a member of the right-wing Catholic Party, strongly opposed to communism and socialism.

'He encouraged me to go to England to get me away from my socialist friends. When I was nineteen I went to Durham University to study European History. I spent two wonderful years there.

'In 1936, the socialist and communist parties united as the Republican Popular Front and won the election. The Nationalists encouraged strikes and civil disobedience. The fascist Falangists fermented trouble. In July, General Franco, the commander of the army garrison in Morocco, rebelled and joined forces with the Falangists and the Carlists as leader of the Nationalists. The civil war ensued and my father called me home.'

Ramón paused, glancing at Anamar to see if he was holding her interest. 'Did they teach you about the Spanish Civil War in school?' he asked.

'It was mentioned,' said Anamar, 'But only just. In Ireland we're preoccupied with our own past. But a friend, who used to be my teacher, told me about the Irish Brigade led by General Eoin O'Duffy.

'According to her, most of the foreigners who joined in the Spanish Civil War were in the International Brigade, on the side of the Republicans. But in Ireland many people saw the Republicans as communist and anti-Catholic and the Irish Brigade fought for Franco's Nationalists. O'Duffy's Irish fascists called themselves the Blue Shirts. My friend said that O'Duffy was such a poor leader, his brigade suffered heavy casualties, some inflicted by their own side. They didn't stay too long in Spain.'

Ramón managed a smile.

'I remember them too,' he said slowly, 'I fought on the same side. All my sympathies were for the socialists but my father's Carlists and the Falangists were allies and family honour meant that I, too, joined the Nationalist army.'

Ramón's face was pale. He spoke quietly as if, having come this far, he needed to continue.

'It was a ferocious and bloody war,' he said wearily, 'Both sides were guilty of acts of the most barbaric cruelty. And afterwards the reprisals were horrific. All war is abhorrent but civil war is the most violent and evil of all.

'When it finished in 1939, my side had won but, for me, there was no sense of triumph, only relief that it was over, then desolation. I left the army with the guilt of all the deaths on my conscience.

'When I came home I told my parents that I had decided to make the pilgrimage to Santiago in atonement. My father could not understand my motive but my mother prayed for me. She asked me to start from Lourdes so that I could pay her respects to Our Lady of Lourdes before I left for Santiago. One week later I was on my way.'

Anamar was moved beyond words. The quietness in the car as they drove was like the silence of private prayer. She had only just met Ramón and she was certain that he was not the kind of man who talked about himself to strangers.

After ten minutes or so she said,

'Thank you,' and glanced across to see him smile again.

In his own village Ramón Mont L'ours Barriano was a popular but slightly remote figure, interested in local life but not entering into it, although he fully accepted his role as leader. He owned most of the village and vast tracts of the surrounding lands. His farm manager, his foresters, the keeper of his vineyard and all who worked for him were expected to do their best at all times without him having to interfere.

He was respected as a strict but fair man, capable of understanding his workers' misfortunes and responding sympathetically. In the short time they had been together, Anamar had seen him smile more often than the villagers might have done in three months.

They were in the Pyrenean foothills now and Anamar could see the shapes of high peaks in the background reaching up to touch the clouds. The little country road wound its way down through a shaded ravine. The Seigneur handled the car with the skill of an expert. He had been driving fast on the better roads but now he slowed as if expecting farm traffic around any corner. They emerged from the gorge into a narrow valley and the brilliant sunlight. Suddenly the car turned sharply right, crossed a hump-backed bridge and stopped.

In front of them was a large open area, dirt surfaced, too irregular to be called a square. An ancient church with a Romanesque facade stood at the right-hand end. Facing the bridge were dwellings of different sizes, built in some distant age in the Pyrenean mountain style. Some were in much better repair than others, most were two-storeyed with a wooden balcony on the first floor under the eaves for storing wood and fodder.

There was a blacksmith's, a bakery, a shop with a post office sign. On the left, set well back, was a larger house, in the same style as the others but on a much grander scale. At the corner of the South side a huge vine climbed over the balcony to the roof. In summer it would provide the most welcome shade. The front balcony had a row of pots of red geraniums in full flower.

On a hillside behind the house was a vineyard, the vines in neat rows and beyond, wooded hills. Above the church the river flowed down from the gorge, flanked on the same side by a cliff as high as a mountain. A magnificent waterfall tumbled down in three great cascades, one below the other.

'Mont L'ours-les-Cascades.' Ramón could not keep the tone of pride from his voice. He drove across to the big house and parked behind it.

They were met at the door by a tall, elderly lady dressed in black who was introduced as Madame Mons. She shook hands with Anamar, welcomed her formally but without warmth and showed her to her room. It was situated at the back on the first floor. The view was down the valley to where it opened out into a narrow plain below the vines and cultivated fields, orchards and grazing cattle.

The walls and ceiling of the room were wood panelled, the floor polished wood, with rugs. It was so well-furnished and comfortable, such a contrast to the hostel in Alban. Madame Mons gave her towels before she left and said they would eat at eight.

The sun was low, shining directly on the balcony as Anamar opened the glazed door and stepped out. There were piles of wood on either side but enough room for two chairs. She held the balcony rail and was suddenly aware that she was looking West. If she started her pilgrimage from here, this would be the direction she would take.

Until this moment the journey had been something exciting which would happen in the future, now she was almost ready to go and the exhilaration was overwhelming. For a few moments she stood staring at the distant skyline, its high peaks miles beyond the little valley, behind range after range of wooded hills.

The deep clang of cow bells broke the spell and she turned to unpack her rucksack. Madam Mons knocked and entered with the two servant girls each carrying a bucket of water, one hot, the other cold, each covered with a white cloth. The girls mixed the water in a large delph bowl on the marble wash stand until they felt it was at the right temperature. Madam Mons assured herself that it was satisfactory and they left Anamar to her toilette.

Dinner was served on a large polished table in the main downstairs room. It was a spacious apartment, wood panelled like her bedroom with a large stone fireplace and leather chairs.

There were brass paraffin lamps with tall glass globes, hunting trophies on the walls, a wood-mounted, coloured globe of the world with brass fittings, a glass-fronted cabinet with fossils, mineral crystals and unusual rocks. On the walls there were bright, modern paintings and old prints, ancient maps mounted and framed. On one wall was a locked gun rack with shotguns and rifles.

Three places had been laid and Madame Mons sat down to eat with Anamar and the Seigneur when she had finished supervising the girls in the kitchen. The bread board was beside her place and she carved thick slices to fill the basket as required. The wine was in a beautiful glass jug, with a silver lid, like Deirdre Ryan's claret jug.

During the soup course Ramón spoke in French so that he could include Madame Mons in the conversation.

Now they were eating together, the housekeeper was a little more friendly than she had been when they had arrived. She indicated that she had heard about Anamar's intended pilgrimage and was impressed. For years she had hoped to make her own pilgrimage to Lourdes, she said, but the right opportunity had never appeared.

On first meeting Anamar her manner had been as cool and formal as it always was on the rare occasions when the Seigneur had female visitors. It was not jealousy, nor would she have taken the liberty of being possessive. Madame Mons might be an employee but she saw herself as protector not protected.

As she served an aromatic game pie from a large casserole, Ramón excused himself to her and spoke to Anamar in English.

'We must make the best use of your time here,' he said and consulted a note book. 'I suggest that we meet at eight-thirty each morning after breakfast and spend at least an hour and a half planning your route. After a break, I could teach you some Spanish from eleven until twelve noon.'

He paused to see if she was in agreement. 'Your afternoons would then be free, I am sure you will want to go walking and, when you wish, I will accompany you. Before and after dinner there will also be time to talk.'

It was all so clear and helpful, Anamar wondered why she felt a little uneasy. It was like being back at school. When she was in the senior class the Principal, Master Robson, was a Scot who had lived for years in Donegal. He could be an inspirational teacher but he believed that Irish youngsters required rigid order, stringent discipline, strict adherence to the daily timetable and the school bell.

Monsieur Barriano's approach seemed so different from the fun she had shared with Father Brian.

Then she saw a look of concern on his face as if he felt he was being too dictatorial and realised that Ramón was a very shy man who was trying very hard to help her. She smiled broadly.

'What a wonderful programme,' she said enthusiastically, 'I only hope I'm not taking up too much of your time.'

Madame Mons nodded to the girls. They cleared away the used plates and brought in a large board with three rounds of cheese.

That night Anamar slept as deeply in the big feather bed as she did at home in her little cottage in Donegal. She wakened early and pulled back the curtains to reassure herself that she really was in Mont L'ours. As she stood there, the picture of the valley below unfolded at first light.

She heard a noise below the balcony and rose to see Madame Mons leaving the house by the back door. It was twenty minutes past seven by her watch. Mass must be at seven thirty. She dressed quickly, let herself out the same way and arrived at the church as Mass began.

There were less than a dozen people in the church and when Mass was over Anamar let the others leave first. Madame Mons nodded curtly but hurried back to the house without speaking. The priest stopped Anamar at the door and shook her hand,

'You must be the Irish pilgrim,' he said in French, with a smile, 'Your fame has arrived before you.'

There was no sign of Ramón at breakfast. At eight-thirty Madam Mons led Anamar upstairs and knocked on the door of his room. It was large and comfortably furnished in the same style as the main room on the ground floor, the whole space brightly lit by the sun's early rays from the East. Ramón had obviously breakfasted at a small table on the balcony and Madame Mons took his tray. He showed Anamar to an easy chair near the window and sat down on another, facing her.

In businesslike fashion he quickly established what Father Brian had told her about the origins of the Pilgrimage to Santiago, given her a list of the main towns along the route in Spain, advised her of the religious duties of the pilgrim, and discussed the difficulties facing a young woman making such a journey.

They moved to a table and he placed a map in front of them. It was hand-drawn on good-quality paper using a fine mapping pen and coloured inks, black, red, green and royal blue. It startled Anamar. This was exactly the same type of map which Master Robson used to draw when she was at school, only his were in coloured chalks on the black-board. Hank would have been thrilled to see it. He loved maps.

'It's beautiful,' she said, 'It's a wonderful map. That broken red line must be the route.'

Ramón was embarrassed.

'It's for you,' he said gently, 'It will take you beyond the frontier with Spain into Aragon and there are two more to guide you across Spain to Santiago. When I came to live here after my own pilgrimage I decided to draw these maps in case I ever went again.'

Anamar was so excited she could hardly speak. Ramón began to talk about the detail of the route. The efficient, businesslike expert had gone, in his place was a man of passion, guiding a student along the Way of St James.

Together they followed the broken red line from Mont L'ours-les-Cascades through villages, towns, valleys and forests, over hills and mountains to the point where she would cross the Pyrenees.

Anamar told Ramón about the offer Paul and Raoul had made to accompany her over the mountains into Spain and he thought this a very sensible idea.

They talked about the terrain, the distances between villages, the best places to find a room. If she was to start from Mont L'ours he reckoned it would take her two weeks to reach Luz-St-Sauveur, a small mountain town in the valley of the Gave river. This route would lead to Gavarnie and the Pyrenean pass she would have to cross into Spain.

Ramón suggested that she stay with him for five more days to complete the planning of her route and make her preparations. It sounded just right to Anamar. It would give her time to write to her friends and make arrangements with Raoul and Paul about where and when they would meet.

She looked at her watch and held it to her ear to check that it was ticking properly. Surely it could not be right. It was ten o'clock and she said the time aloud. They had been talking for an hour and a half.

Ramón smiled,

'What a beautiful watch,' he said, 'On your journey to Santiago you will find a dramatic change in your perception of time. It will fly or stand still at will, totally outside your control.'

One of the girls arrived with coffee and they moved back to the easy chairs with a view up the valley.

Anamar took the watch off her wrist and reached it to Ramón. It was her turn to tell a story.

'It was a present from my Granny Mac,' she said, and could feel the warmth of her friendship with her grandmother, whose cottage was now her home.

'She paid for it by rearing turkeys from a clutch of eggs left to her by an old dealing man called Malachy Rice. Malachy was reputed to have a fortune hidden away in his cottage but when he died there was nothing of value except the turkey eggs. Granny Mac looked after Malachy at the end of his life and his brother gave her his only legacy, the clutch of eggs.'

Ramón turned the watch over and read the inscription aloud.

'To Anamar. From Granny Mac and Malachy Rice,' He looked at Anamar again and gave her back the watch. 'A beautiful golden memento and with a value to you, beyond price.'

Anamar was about to tell him of her encounter with Granny Mac's ghost before she had left home, but she hesitated, unsure that she knew Ramón well enough yet.

'My granny knew I would make this pilgrimage. She told me I'd feel baking heat, hunger and thirst, fear and doubt, and a tiredness I've never felt before and she promised me I'd find my reward before the journey's end.'

Ramón stared at her intently.

'Your grandmother was a woman of great perception,' he said after a long pause, 'She could see the pilgrim in you and her faith will prove to be justified.'

Ramón suggested a short walk around the village. He greeted everyone by name and it was easy to see that he was well respected. They met the priest as he came out of the shop. Ramón introduced him as, 'Monsieur le Curé, Père Jean Marriot'.

'Merci monsieur,' the curé said to Ramón, 'But I have already met the Irish Pilgrim.' He turned to Anamar, 'You are in good hands, mademoiselle, the Seigneur and I are old friends. We have our differences about religion but he is a true pilgrim of St Jacques.'

Ramón was a little embarrassed and Anamar found herself enjoying his discomfiture. As they walked away she whispered,

'You must tell me about these differences with the curé, monsieur, it is always interesting when priest and squire differ.' She glanced at Ramón and he was smiling broadly, almost laughing. He was beginning to relax with her. It was easy to see he was enjoying having her as a guest. She decided that before she left, she would have to make him laugh aloud.They went back to his room and began the Spanish lesson. Ramón loved the language of his birth and had clearly given a good deal of thought to what he would try to teach her.

He started with the special sounds of Spanish, explaining that all the vowels were single sounds and that, with the exception of 'h', there were no silent letters. He said that, like French, the Spanish words must not be pronounced as they would be in English but in their own accent.

Anamar produced the notebook Henri had given her when she was leaving Paris and took down the words for 'please' and 'thank-you', how to ask the way, or the time of Mass, how to find a meal or a room for the night. She learned the difference in the phrases for 'good afternoon' and 'good night'.

She found herself enjoying the sound of Spanish but knew she would need to do her home-work. Ramón would expect her to spend some time revising and was sure to start the next day with a test.

After lunch she went on her own to see the waterfall that gave the village part of its name. About a quarter of a mile behind the church was a steep escarpment. Anamar looked up to its crest and saw the full flow of a stream falling vertically, spray flying in the breeze. The water dropped free in three great cascades, one below the other, dashing off the ledges which separated them and cutting a channel through the valley floor to pour into the main river.

She crossed a footbridge and climbed on a good path beside the falls. At the top of the first cascade she could look down on the village laid out at her feet like a relief map. There were steps fashioned in the rock on the next, much steeper section of the track. At the top of the second cascade the way was blocked by a cliff and there were stepping stones leading to the other side of the falls.

Anamar was enjoying the climb and followed the trail to the top. There it opened out into a small grassy alp and behind, a dense forest led to rocky peaks hidden from below.

The view was breathtaking. To her left the valley narrowed to a gorge, hemmed in by steep cliffs. The village seemed so small. To her right the river flowed down through farmland and Ramón's vineyards. She looked ahead and the skyline to the South was the snow and rock peaks of the High Pyrenees.

She sat down as near the edge of the cliff as she dared and hugged her legs with her chin on her knees. This was a place she would love to share with Hank, and Deirdre too. It was their kind of country.

Much later she descended the path and followed a faint side track at the head of the second cascade. It led behind a rocky mound to a natural hollow, almost overhung by the cliff. There were four caves and the ruins of tiny buildings with rock walls and the remnants of sod roofs. Grazing animals had ensured that the site was not overgrown. At one time this must have been a little settlement.

She heard a noise and looked behind to see Ramón standing on the track. He waved his long staff.

'I followed you up by the waterfall to assure myself you were safe,' he said, 'And now I know you are familiar with mountain tracks. I hope you don't mind.' He pointed to the ruins. 'I see you've discovered our little secret.'

On the way down he told her about the Cagot families who had lived in the settlement two hundred years ago.

'The history books tell us little about the Cagots but in the village we have our own stories,' he said when they paused at the top of the lowest of the cascades.

'They were a mysterious people, small in stature, strange looking to others. Some said they were the descendants of the Visigoths. They were not allowed to enter churches nor were they allowed to marry outside their own people. They could not own land, live in the centre of a town or village, go barefoot, touch food in the market or enter a mill.

'Cagots were exempt from taxes and military duty. Many became skilled craftsmen and builders. All had to wear a mark like a crow's foot on their clothing.

'When they want to insult us, the people from neighbouring villages call us, "Cagots", and when they are really angry with us they call our village "Mont L'ours-les-Cagots".'

'We try to keep the story from visitors but now you know our secret.'

Anamar knew how proud he was of his village and its people. She smiled,

'Where I live in Donegal it's the same. Sure aren't there name-callers everywhere!'

Suddenly she remembered Stephan, the warden of the hostel at Alban-les-Saintes and the man who had directed her to Ramón. Could he have been descended from the Cagots?

When they arrived back at the house, Anamar excused herself and went up to her room to write letters.

The most urgent was to Paul and Raoul to arrange to meet them. That afternoon she had decided that when she reached Luz-St-Sauveur, she would make a detour from her route and go North to Lourdes. Near the bridge outside the Grotto Domain she remembered a small hotel called St Jacques. She would stay there, it would be easy for the boys to find it.

She wrote to Deirdre and Hank, telling them about the Seigneur and his village. She also wrote to Father Brian, knowing he would pass on the news to his friends, and to Maureen, adding a paragraph for Ellie to tell her she was going back to Lourdes. She took a lamp up to her room after dinner and finished the letters.

Before she went to bed, Anamar turned out the paraffin lamp and sat on the balcony looking down the valley. The cow bells clanged more quietly now as if the darkness muffled their sound. The warmth of the evening air allowed her to rest and think about the day. She had heard so much from Ramón, learned so much from him, seen so much from the top of the escarpment, but it was all clear in her mind.

When she went back inside and lay down in the soft bed, sleep came before she could even wish for it.

CAGOTS AND CATHARS

Anamar was up early to go to Mass. When she was ready to leave her room she happened to catch sight of her reflection in the full-length mirror on the inside of a wardrobe door. It was the first time she had seen herself since she had left home and she was amazed at the change.

Her face, arms and legs were tanned. Her hair was shorter, with much more body to it, and had been more easily managed since Yvette had cut and restyled it. She felt healthy. There was no doubt that thinking she looked well was a great boost to the confidence.

After breakfast Madame Mons conducted her up to Ramón's room again. He was still at breakfast on the balcony and Anamar joined him for coffee. They discussed what she would wear on the journey and the kit she would carry. Anamar suggested that they should go for a walk that afternoon. She would dress as if she were setting out for Santiago and carry her rucksack packed for that day.

Ramón thought this an excellent idea and began to explain that Spain was an exceedingly conservative country, inferring it was crucial that she should dress accordingly.

'The French and the British laugh at the old-fashioned ways of the Spanish,' he said seriously, 'Even in Catholic Ireland our standards would seem to be unhealthily prudish. In Spain, shorts are not permitted away from a beach, even for men. Cameras must not be used at a swimming pool. Popular magazines with glamour pictures of girls are seen as pornographic and are confiscated at the frontier.'

He was so uncomfortable Anamar felt sorry for him.

'I hope you do not mind a man advising you what to wear,' he said self-consciously, 'But it will be easier for you if your skirt is well below the knee and you wear a shirt with long sleeves and a high collar.'

Anamar nodded in agreement and they moved inside to the table and the maps.

For an hour they pored over the route, from the frontier with Spain in the mountains, down to the River Aragón and towards the province of Navarre. Ramón might live in France and see it as his home but his passion was for the country of his birth. The further they travelled together on the maps, the less detail he gave, knowing that by this stage Anamar would be attuned to the journey. But when they came near the village of his birth he tried to keep the emotion from his voice and concentrate on her pilgrimage. He stopped and looked directly at Anamar.

'Will you call with my father and mother?' He was asking a favour. 'They would be interested to meet you. I could write to tell them. My father is Spanish first and Catholic second but yours is a Spanish journey and will be close to his heart. My mother is a devout Catholic and she will see you as making a double pilgrimage to the shrines of the Holy Mother of God in Lourdes and to His Apostle James at Santiago.'

'Of course I will,' she said, 'And no doubt they'll be interested to hear about you from a stranger. Don't worry, I'll try not to embarrass you while I'm there by telling them wild tales about our escapades in Mont L'ours-les-Cagots!'

Ramón smiled. She was teasing him with the name of the village. At first he had been uncomfortable with her sense of fun at his expense, now he was enjoying it.

Before the end of the session he helped her put together a small First Aid kit. He produced an army field dressing, a strong bandage for a strained knee or ankle, a small flat tin of antiseptic cream, cotton wool and a packet of tablets for treating water to make it safe to drink. He had asked Madame Mons to make a linen wallet to hold the kit. It had two ribbons to tie around it and was exactly the right size. Anamar held it in her hand. It was so light and compact.

Madame Mons arrived with the coffee and Anamar showed her the First Aid kit, now carefully packed and tied in its linen wallet. For the first time the housekeeper gave her a smile. She was not a woman whose suspicions were easily allayed but this young woman was earning her confidence.

When they met again for the Spanish lesson, Anamar's fears were justified. Ramón questioned her closely on the sounds and phrases they had covered the previous day. He was as sharp and strict as Master Robson. This was Ramón the martinet again. The slightest error was corrected, every word and intonation was carefully scrutinised. Anamar found herself fussed and confused. She made mistakes even when she knew the right answers.

Suddenly Ramón seemed to realise that he was making it much more difficult.

'You must forgive me,' he said, 'There is so much I would like us to cover and so little time, and I have such an affection for my mother tongue. You probably feel the same about Irish but I think you would teach it differently.'

He began to talk knowledgeably about Irish language and culture, aware of the great oral tradition of story telling which had such a powerful influence on Irish writers in English.

Anamar knew he was trying to put her at her ease after the interrogation and let him talk. When they went back to Spanish she learned to count to fifty, how to buy food in a shop, order a meal, ask for the bill, reckon in Spanish currency. She made notes and promised herself she would spend more time at her home-work that evening.

After lunch she went up to her room to get ready for the walk. She packed her rucksack with care and left to one side the items she would not want to take with her. They would have to be posted home. She waited until she heard Ramón go out by the back door and saw him in his knee breeches and boots carrying his long stick.

Madame Mons was with him, holding a small parcel. This must be the food she would carry to represent the weight of provisions she would have on her journey. She hurried downstairs and stepped out of the back door.

Madame Mons lurched back a step and gasped, with her hand over her mouth,

'Mon Dieu, Mon Dieu! Quel spectacle!' She was horrified.

Ramón's mouth was open, his face as pale as it could be under his countryman's tan. He held up his hands to say something but failed to speak.

Anamar had emerged in her short shorts with the sleeves of her blouse rolled up as far as they would go and the top two buttons of her blouse undone. She kept a straight face and snapped the fingers of one hand as if she had forgotten something.

'You did say I was to dress as I would do for the pilgrimage,' she said to Ramón, 'Of course you did. And here's silly me in my best St Tropez outfit.'

She turned, went back up to her room and reemerged in less than a minute, this time in her light cotton skirt below the knee, her sleeves rolled down and buttoned at the wrist, her blouse fastened to the neck and wearing sandals without socks.

Madame Mons closed her eyes in relief and shook her head from side to side muttering again, this time about 'Les Irlandaises'.

Ramón found himself gesturing at Anamar and smiling. Then he began to chuckle and stood pointing, shaking with laughter and relief, still unable to speak a word.

Anamar kept her straight face.

'Is it all right? she asked with a great show of concern, 'Will I do as a pilgrim?'

Madame Mons was staring at the Seigneur. She had known him for ten years but she had never seen him laugh like this. And now he had started it seemed as if he was unable to stop.

He was still chortling away to himself, shaking his head, holding his sides. He began to rub the sides of his head just above his ears.

'This is too much laughing,' he managed to say, 'I have cramp in the muscles of my head.'

Madame Mons began to smile too and touched Anamar's arm with a friendly pat from one hand, as she gave her the parcel of food. She waited and waved as they set off past the church, heading up the valley towards the gorge.

It was a wonderful walk, following a track on the right bank of the river with the road on the other side. Like Hank, Ramón was an expert guide but he was much more communicative, pointing out the best pools for fishing, finding uncommon plants hiding behind stones, looking for rock crystals, identifying birds and butterflies, examining the strata of the rocks on the cliffs of the gorge.

After two hours Ramón dropped back to let Anamar know she was walking too quickly and she had to stop to wait for him. They climbed a cleft in the rock wall and came out above the cliffs. Turning back, they used an animal path through the forest and reached the small plateau above the waterfall. Ramón named the high peaks to the South and they saw the mountains of Saleix to the West which Anamar would have to cross on her second day.

Anamar's rucksack had been comfortable on her back but although it did not feel too heavy, she had been aware of its weight on the climb up from the gorge. It would not do to try to carry more on her long journey.

She emptied the rucksack and set out the contents on the grass to let Ramón see what she proposed to carry.

The packet of food contained bread, cheese, garlic sausage and two apples. There was her light woollen sweater, a spare blouse, underclothes, the ex-army water-bottle and poncho cape she had bought at home, a pair of socks in case the sandals chafed her feet, a tiny brass compass, a notebook and pencil, a piece of soap and a tooth brush, each wrapped in grease-proof paper, a tiny towel, a small torch and the First Aid kit.

Ramón nodded approvingly.

'You will need a little oil or cream to rub on your skin at the end of the day,' he said thoughtfully, 'And a sharp knife and, of course, your maps. We may think of something else before you leave but you have the essentials, anything else can be bought along the way.'

Anamar showed him the secret pocket she had made in her skirt. It was on the inside of the waist band, with a flap which could be kept closed with press studs. In it she would carry all her money except the little she needed to have in her purse.

Ramón was impressed.

Descending by the path beside the cascades, they visited the ruined settlement of the Cagots again and sat down, separated by the width of the site. Anamar tried to imagine what it would have been like here two hundred years ago.

Ramón had been sitting by the caves in silence. When they rose to go he spoke as if he had been considering whether or not he should ask the question,

'May I walk with you on the first day of your pilgrimage? I would not be there to act as your guide or to burden you with my company. It would be a great privilege to share a few steps of your journey.'

Anamar smiled,

'Of course,' she said without a pause, 'You can help me set the right pace. My friend Hank would agree that I walk too quickly. He says that if I start fast, I'll never get to the end.'

Before dinner that evening, Anamar made sure to revise the Spanish phrases, repeating the words aloud, trying to ape his accent. She enjoyed the sound of the language, it had a rhythm and cadence unlike Irish or French or any version of English she had ever heard.

As Madame Mons served the grilled trout, Ramón told her about Anamar's pilgrimage and mentioned that she would be visiting Lourdes on the way. When she had finished serving, Madame Mons placed a hand on Anamar's arm and smiled. She was thinking of the pilgrimage to Lourdes she must make soon. She had been putting it off for years. It would have to be this year. She would speak to the priest. He would know of a pilgrimage group she could join.

After dinner one of the girls took the glasses and the wine jug upstairs to the balcony of Ramón's room and he and Anamar sat in wicker easy chairs looking out over the village and the church to the dark chasm of the gorge.

Ramón encouraged Anamar to talk about life in Donegal. He had never been to Ireland but two of his friends at Durham had been Irish.

'They wanted me to visit their country and tour the whole coastline with them,' he said wistfully, 'But when I had to go home to fight in the Civil War we lost touch.'

'You've no excuse now,' said Anamar firmly, 'You've been helping me plan my journey here. It will be my turn to help you plan your visit to my country.'

They were back at work next morning at eight thirty to cover the next stage to the city of Leon. This time Ramón mentioned only the villages and towns in which she might find somewhere to stay and the number of kilometres between. He quoted from his notes and Anamar took down the names and distances, checking the locations on the map.

They took coffee earlier than usual and Ramón talked about the history of the pilgrimage. He mentioned the Templar Knights and the way they had protected the pilgrims from robbers and land owners seeking to impose exorbitant tolls.

He described the band of medieval pilgrims, perhaps as many as sixty of them assembling in a town, the rich and the poor, the devout, those convicted of crimes but permitted to make the pilgrimage in expiation, those who were there to enjoy the journey or to make money from their fellow pilgrims. They would be accompanied by guides, guards and minstrels, and encouraged by the Church through the holy orders of monks and nuns.

'There would have been robbers who joined the pilgrim band,' he said, 'Stealing from them as they travelled. They were the infamous "coquillards".'

He remembered the feeling of welcome he had experienced on his own pilgrimage, the gifts of food, water and wine from villagers who had little to give but who wanted to show their approval of those who wore the scallop shell.

Suddenly his tone changed.

'Have you heard of the Cathars? he said seriously, 'Sometimes called the Albigensians.'

'I have indeed,' said Anamar, 'My friend Deirdre and I visited the cathedral at Albi last year on our way home from Lourdes. Deirdre told me that they were a sect which had been suppressed by the Church six hundred years ago.'

Ramón was impressed,

'They were strong in this area before the massacres,' he said gravely. 'Some villagers were spared when they confessed and recanted. Others were burned alive.'

'Deirdre seemed to think that one of their heresies concerned the practice of allowing women to be elders within the sect.' Anamar remembered Deirdre's scathing criticism of the male hierarchy of her own Church.

'Your friend was right,' said Ramón, 'The sect was popular because the elders, who were called parfaits, were so helpful to the people. Some priests were happy to see them do their good work, others were jealous of their popularity. A Holy Crusade was mounted against them and tens of thousands were killed. The Inquisition accused the Cathars of the most terrible heresies, so much so, it is difficult now to be sure what they did believe. The villagers in Mont L'ours-les-Cascades forsook the Cathar ways at the time of the Inquisition, but the stories are still part of our history.

'One that may interest you tells how the Cathar parfaits from here fled the Crusader soldiers by setting out on the pilgrimage to Santiago, hoping not to be noticed amongst the pilgrims. They were pursued, but eluded capture by hiding in the mountains of Saleix which you will cross on your second day. They never returned here but the news came back that they were preaching to the pilgrims and making converts to Catharism along the Road to Santiago.'

Ramón and Anamar had spent so much time talking at their coffee break that they were late starting the Spanish lesson but, having done her homework, Anamar found the session much more enjoyable. Ramón gave her lists of phrases and words to learn and seemed pleased with her progress.

That afternoon she climbed up past the cascades and wandered in the forests beyond. She met no one and found the silence cleared her mind.

Ever since she had decided to go on pilgrimage, she had experienced moments of doubt. Even when she was in Paris with Father Brian, uncertainty had briefly slipped into her mind. It had been hardest when she had been with Yvette in Alban-les-Saintes. She had enjoyed her new friend's company and living with her in the warmth and ambience of the Mediterranean coast had been idyllic. She had been sorely tempted to stay longer.

But the call of the Road of St James had dragged her away and these few days in Mont L'ours with Ramón had been inspirational. The doubts were gone. She could hardly wait to get started.

That evening at dinner, Madame Mons was less reserved and joined in the conversation. She had made an omelette filled with potatoes, onions and peppers and said with a smile that this was not a recipe which the Seigneur had brought with him when he came to live here from Spain. Spanish dishes were part of the traditional cuisine in this part of France and this was one of his favourites.

That night Anamar found it hard to get to sleep. She dressed and sat out on the balcony, watching the stars. The sky was so clear here, the constellations of stars so easy to identify. The cool atmosphere after the heat of the day and the air of calm in the valley eventually allowed her to rest and unwind. One more day and she would be on her way.

Her last full day at Mont L'ours started as usual. Ramón quickly covered the rest of the journey, pausing only to allow her to take note of the places and distances. When he was speaking of her arrival in Santiago, he was evasive, as if he was unwilling to anticipate her own first impressions.

Then he produced a book from his bookshelves by the Irish writer Kate O'Brien. She described the streets of Santiago as 'full of sudden light' and contrasted their dark, grey, granite structures with the buff-coloured sandstone of the Cathedral, 'the most beautiful building I have ever seen'.

It was enough. They closed their notebooks, Ramón gave her the three maps and a light oilskin wallet to keep them dry. They shook hands.

'My work is done,' he said and looked sorry, now that she was free to go.

'And mine is about to begin.' Anamar's tone was hopeful rather than confident. She was about to undertake the most difficult venture of her entire life and she was feeling nervous.

After coffee, Ramón led her across the village to the church. Although the rest of the building was more recent, the archway at the front was Romanesque. In a dark corner he pointed to the inside of the curve of the arch above head height. Anamar had to wait for a moment for her eyes to adjust to the shadow and then saw a faded painting on the plaster.

It was the remnant of a fresco depicting a figure in medieval dress, carrying a stick and a gourd. There was a scallop shell on his hat and two more at chest height on his robe. One leg and foot had flaked away but there was a sandal on the other foot. Underneath, the legend said, 'St Jac ....' the rest of the name had gone.

Anamar stepped back with a little gasp.

'You didn't tell me ....'. Her voice was shaking. She looked at Ramón in disbelief.

He raised his hands by way of apology.

'I couldn't show it to you when you came here,' he said, 'There is more to see and I felt I must talk to you first so that you would understand.'

He pointed to a symbol cut deeply into the stone. It was in the shape of a crow's foot.

'The Cagots were here too and left their mark.' He crouched down and shone the torch at the foot of the arch. There was another symbol deeply etched into the stone, this time it was a fish. 'Even the experts agree, these are both authentic Cagot marks.'

He took Anamar into the graveyard behind the church and to the furthest corner where the grave stones were ancient. Three of them were small circular stones, two with a splayed cross and the third with a stone mason's hammer carved on the face. All were chipped, as if they had been vandalised.

'And these are our Cathar grave stones,' he said, unable to keep the pride from his voice. 'I had to wait until you heard our history before I could show you our ancient connection with both the despised Cagots and the once revered Cathars.'

Anamar was deeply moved and sat down on a grassy bank to stare at the stones. When she had visited an ancient site at home in Donegal, she had often sensed a strange, confusing awareness that it was a heritage beyond the Christian tradition. Here in Mont L'ours, amongst the symbols of the Cagots and the Cathars, it was equally bewildering. Were these cultures, too, as her Scottish teacher, Master Robson, would have said, 'outwith the Christian tradition'?.

She went back to the house and sat with Madame Mons in the kitchen, drinking a tisane. She smiled to herself. Just two days before, this could not have happened. Madam Mons said that she had made another of the Seigneur's favourite dishes for dinner, Cassoulet. So that was the wonderful cooking smell which had drawn her into the kitchen.

Madame Mons told her how it was prepared with duck, garlic sausage, white beans, mutton and onions. Cassoulet was the most famous dish in this part of France, she said, but made in their own special way here in Mont L'ours.

The two servant girls had been working outside, but when they entered the room and saw Anamar they immediately withdrew. It annoyed Anamar that she had not been able to make contact with the girls. They were about her own age, sturdily-built, with coarse features and large red hands. Try as she might, she had failed to exchange even a few words with them. Anamar turned back to Madame Mons and her tea.

Later she followed the river down the valley and sat on a rock at its edge. Drops of water thrown on the warm stones encouraged the butterflies to settle.

Suddenly she realised that to-morrow would not be the start of her pilgrimage. It had begun weeks before, on the morning she had left her own cottage in Donegal. Going to Paris had been necessary. The visit to the beach at St Tropez had allowed her to fulfil a promise to herself. Her stay here with Ramón had helped her prepare. To-morrow the walking stage would begin.

That evening the priest, Père Marriot, had been invited to dinner. He was a cheerful, elderly man, energetic in a restless way which often seemed out of place in the village. He could hardly wait to tell Ramón the news. A young hunter had shot a bear in a forest nearby.

Ramón was enraged. He rocked to and fro in his chair in silence. Sallow patches appeared on his cheeks, his whole body rigid. Anamar had never seen a man so angry. Suddenly he excused himself and left the room to telephone the police.

The curé explained to Anamar that, although the Seigneur was a keen hunter, he believed there was a danger that the bears might not survive much longer in this part of the Pyrenees. His views were well known and he expected them to be respected by everyone in the area.

When Ramón returned he was much calmer. He had spoken to the police. The bear had been shot in one of his forests and he intended to take a private prosecution against the hunter. He had already spoken to his lawyer who had pointed out that it would allow them to publicise the plight of the bear. He looked at Anamar.

'You will have noticed that the bear is part of the name of the village and of my own name,' he said, 'We have a legend here which says that if the bears die out, the village and my family will die too.'

All four of them made a great effort to put the incident behind them and by the time the girls brought in the Cassoulet they were in good spirits. On previous evenings Ramón would drink no more than two or three glasses and Madame Mons would scarcely finish one. But to-night there was an air of celebration. No one was counting.

Remembering that she was walking the next morning, Anamar began to drink more water. Hank always said that mountaineers needed to drink at least one glass of water for every glass of wine!

Ramón told a humorous tale about a monk and a rabbi, in the course of which the rabbi triumphed in a scriptural argument. The curé retaliated by calling Ramón, 'Monsieur le Cagot'. It was all in fun and yet another side of the Seigneur which Anamar was seeing for the first time.

Before she left for bed, Madame Mons rose and fetched a black lace scarf from a side table as a present for Anamar. It would be light, easy to carry and very suitable for attending Mass in Spain. From the pocket of her dress she produced a Rosary. The beads were of a dark red wood, carved and polished. The room seemed so quiet for a few moments after the hilarity as she gave the Rosary to Anamar and asked the priest to bless it.

Anamar went up to her room and returned with the copy of Pilgrim's Progress in one hand and the other hand behind her back. She presented the book to both Ramón and Père Marriot and told them, with a smile, how she had been given it by the Rev William McClintock Ferguson, a Methodist minister. From behind her back she produced for Madame Mons a little posy of flowers she had gathered that afternoon by the river. Madame Mons was unused to shedding tears but she shed them now. She was moved by this kind gesture from a girl on the brink of a momentous journey. But the tears were for her own youth, too.

The bed was so comfortable it was strange for Anamar not to be able to sleep. She lit the lamp, as Deirdre would have advised in the circumstances, and sat up. When she was younger they had written Limericks for each other and now one was composing itself in her head. She reached for her note-book and pencil.

Ramón and the Curé, they say,
Both lovers of food, in their way,
When they sat down to dine,
Madame Mons she did shine
With her dish of the day, Cassoulet.

It took only five minutes and she smiled when it was finished. It might not have been one of her best but Deirdre would have laughed anyway, just to encourage her. She put the lamp out and, still smiling, fell asleep immediately.

At Mass in the morning the priest mentioned her pilgrimage and the few people present waited for her to go up to the altar rails first. Ramón appeared for breakfast downstairs and when it was over they took their packed rucksacks outside.

He was wearing boots and climbing breeches, with a shirt and a wide-brimmed felt hat. He had two long staffs, one of which he gave to Anamar. She was wearing sandals without socks, her long cotton skirt, a blouse with long sleeves and a straw hat with a brim. She had attached the scallop shell from the restaurant in Paris to the lid of her rucksack.

Madame Mons and the priest were there to see them off. The villagers began to assemble, the two servant girls at the back. There must have been nearly twenty of them. The priest said a blessing and a prayer. They shook hands with everyone present and turned to set off.

After twenty yards or so they looked around and the people were waving. It was a moving moment for Anamar and for Ramón, too. It was a tribute to them both. At last, at long last, the talking was over, the walking was underway.

THE FIRST DAY

The path led to the river, skirting Ramón's tidy vineyards on the slope. The meadows hummed with insects, huge bells on broad leather collars clanged loudly as the cattle moved lazily to find fresh pasture.

They looked back three times and the people were still there, still waving. Madam Mons held a bright scarf above them all. Anamar shook her stick and waved her free arm. Ramón looked slightly awkward but eventually lifted his stick in formal salute.

The sun was behind them, already warmer than on previous days, although it was early. It was pleasant to reach the forest, still cool, the leaf-cushioned track easy on the feet.

At first they talked to each other with hardly a pause. There was so much on their minds which could only be discussed now they were on the move. Suddenly, the conversation ceased as if, at exactly the same moment, they had both said everything which needed to be said.

Ramón was making sure Anamar knew that she was setting the pace and finding the way. The time passed so quickly she forgot to pause for a rest until they had been going for nearly two hours. They exchanged a look when eventually she suggested a stop and sat on a bank above the river to drink from their water bottles. Half an hour later they passed through a small, eerily silent village and crossed the river by a stone bridge. The one man they met saluted Ramón courteously but didn't speak.

Beyond the village they heard a rumble of thunder and big black clouds came rushing towards them from the West. As the first drops fell they scrambled to don their water-proof capes. Anamar's was an ex-army model which hung loosely, with gaps at the sides. She needed Ramón's help to arrange it properly. His was much lighter, like a cycling cape with a hood and had thumb tabs inside to hold it down.

The rain splattered on the ground, the big drops making the dust on the road jump. But the sun was still shining from a cloudless patch of sky and Anamar laughed at the incongruity of walking in bright sunshine with the raindrops bouncing off their capes. When the shower became a deluge they decided to stop and stood in the shelter of an over-hanging bush, well away from trees. The thunderstorm came nearer and they held the capes out from their sides to let the water run off without soaking their feet and ankles.

Then, as quickly as it had come, the storm was gone and they had missed the worst of it. The sun's light was so bright it hurt their eyes. Its heat made the water vapour rise like a miniature cloud at ground level. They splashed each other with drops of water like children, as they shook their capes. Ramón was smiling, beginning to enjoy himself. By lunchtime the ground had dried and the sun was so hot they had to seek the shelter of a big tree to have their break.

In the afternoon, without either making the suggestion, they walked separately, Ramón some fifty yards behind. Anamar enjoyed the time on her own but was beginning to feel weary in the heat. She stopped every hour for a break and Ramón came to join her, understanding how she felt but saying nothing. Her shoulders were sore and her felt feet very, very tired. It was not that her sandals were hurting her, or that she had blisters. Her feet, legs and shoulders were exhausted. Eventually she told Ramón and then felt irritated when he explained that, as she was not used to carrying a rucksack for such a distance, her body was protesting.

She knew he was right but it was annoying to hear him say so. He might have all the answers, but it was no help to hear him put the blame on her carefully packed rucksack. She had no choice. That particular pilgrim's burden would have to be carried the whole way to Santiago! However, it was good to have someone with whom she could be angry. She gritted her teeth and tramped on.

In the heat of the afternoon, and through a daze of tiredness, she looked up from the ground directly in front of her feet and saw a village ahead. It was built into the land below a range of hills that appeared to block their route completely. These must be the Mountains of Saleix. Ramón had assured her that there was a way through the peaks, but it was certainly not obvious from here. It was five in the afternoon and they had been walking, with only brief pauses, since they had left Mont L'ours eight hours before. Anamar was sure they must have covered twenty miles, but decided not to ask Ramón in case she would be disappointed when he told her it was less.

There was no hotel or bar in the village of Vicdessos and no sign of a shop, but Ramón had made arrangements by telephone for them to stay in a private house. It was an oddly-shaped building, constructed to fit into an angle of the street. Anamar's tiny room was triangular with just enough space for a bed and a dresser. She filled an enamel bowl with cold water from a huge jug and bathed her feet.

It was bliss. She lay back across the bed with her legs hanging over the edge and her feet in the bowl. The first day's walk was over. Would the ache in her shoulders ever ease? She wiggled her toes and splashed the water like a child.

Towards the end of the walk she had refrained from mentioned her sore shoulders again, or the stinging pain of tiredness in her feet, or the growing weariness of the last few hours. Ramón must have known, of course, but to have admitted her tiredness would have sounded as if she wanted sympathy and, of that, she had no need whatsoever!

Deirdre Ryan would have said, 'Better to suffer in silence than tell the world your woes, child dear. If you look for sympathy, all you'll get is pity'. Anamar smiled to herself, Deirdre would have understood.

She dried her feet, especially between her toes, massaged her arches and ankles and put on her thin cotton socks with the sandals. Her feet were refreshed and to her amazement the socks made the sandals feel like new shoes.

She went to Mass at seven and was amazed to see Ramón in the church. It had been obvious that he was friendly with the curé in Mont L'ours but this was the first time she had seen him in church. She wished she knew him well enough to ask why she hadn't seen him go to Mass in his home village.

The evening meal was pilgrim fare which would have pleased even Belloc on his travels. A substantial soup was followed by a chicken casserole, cheese, fruit and wine, presented without ceremony by the woman of the house as if she provided such food every day of her life.

During the day Ramón had made a list of last-minute suggestions as they occurred to him and ticked each off once it had been discussed. He insisted that before they parted they would swop capes. His was lighter and much more easily put on than her own.

Anamar was not surprised, but was finding it difficult to thank him properly.

'You've thought of everything.'

'Would it were so, ma brave.' He smiled seriously. 'The experienced traveller knows that he must not fail by default in his preparations. But he is also aware that, no matter how carefully he readies himself, he will never allow for every eventuality.'

In the morning they left early and Ramón walked with Anamar up a rough, unsurfaced road to the tiny hamlet of Saleix on the lower slopes of the mountain range. One of his men would be coming for him in his car before noon so he had plenty of time to see her properly on her way. Anamar was so excited at the prospect of going on alone, she spoke to the villagers and hardly noticed their surprise.

The dwellings were at different levels, some hidden by trees and bushes, some surrounded by a profusion of brilliantly coloured flowers There were bright blooms in make-shift containers on window-sills, planted beside front doors, an abundance of blossoms hanging from pots. Anamar would remember this place as the village of the flowers.

They came around a high hedge and found themselves in front of the church. It was neither old nor beautiful. It looked uncared-for, taken-for-granted. The door was closed and locked and they stepped back to view the simple arch around its entrance.

Ramón noticed it first but said nothing, then Anamar saw it above the door, carved in plaster, its paint faded and flaking. There was no possibility of doubt. It was a scallop shell, the badge of her pilgrimage. She gave a little cry of joy. Here it was, one day's journey from the fresco on the church arch at Mont L'ours-les-Cascades. Her scalp tingled with excitement. It was one thing to have sat down with Ramón to discuss the pilgrimage, but now she was travelling the ancient pilgrims' way. It was as if this little symbol had been placed here to tell here she was on the authentic road of St James.

She looked at Ramón and he smiled. This was as far as he would go. They shook hands and he produced a small silver scallop shell from his pocket.

'It's to go on the chain with your cross,' he said shyly, 'It's to keep you on the real road.'

Anamar gave him a bear hug and they kissed on both cheeks. Her next step would begin her solitary journey. It was all she could do to give him a brave smile but she managed it. For some strange reason it was proving harder to leave him than it was to face the long journey by herself. She looked away and headed up the steep track into the mountains of Saleix.

At the first bend she stopped to look back and he was standing in the same place, a forlorn, dejected figure. She raised her stick and shook it in a gesture of exultation. She would not disappoint him. She would revel in this journey.

There was a moment's pause, then Ramón waved his arms.

'Arriba! Arriba!,' he shouted, 'He shook his stick as if this was a gesture he had used all his life.

The track was hemmed in by bushes and trees, so dense and luxuriant they threatened to overwhelm it. Anamar could see no further than the next bend. She reached an old wall and realised that she was passing through the ruins of a village engulfed by the woodland and its undergrowth. There were traces of more than a dozen dwellings, set closely together, some quite large, all now being reclaimed by nature. But for the path-side wall she might have missed them entirely.

A snake slithered across the track, as startled as she was. It must have been a foot and a half long and a truly astonishing sight for someone from Ireland where St Patrick had banished snakes all those centuries ago. There were yew trees around a single ruin and in her mind's eye Anamar could see the hamlet in its heyday. Why, she wondered, had this dwelling been so placed at a distance from the others?

The track was steep and the going much harder than the previous day. Maybe she was walking too quickly. She slowed her pace and that was better. Her reverie was broken suddenly by a cuckoo's clear, shrill call, echoing within itself. Above all the woodland noises it was a nostalgic sound from home, of late spring days at Lough Eske, the cries always from the same clump of trees near her cottage.

The track rose, steeper still, until she emerged from the depths of the forest unto the open mountain. A sheer cliff rose to her right, guarding the north flank of a gorge ahead, cut deeply into the mountains. Anamar guessed she had climbed hundreds of feet and was now high enough to reach into the heart of these hills.

A stone-built shepherd's refuge, strategically placed on a grassy alp below the mouth of the gorge, was a good place to stop for a rest. She had made good progress from the village below and, having been hemmed in by the forest thickets for so long, it was a relief to have a view of what lay ahead.

She sat in the shade with her back against the wall of the refuge and her legs stretched out full length in front of her. The water in her water bottle was tepid but she drank deeply. It would be easy to refill from a stream. The biscuits Madame Mons had packed for her were delicious. Her eyes closed and she almost dozed. In such a comfortable resting place it was reassuring to find that, although she had been so tired yesterday, she had recovered well with a good night's rest.

She sat up, thinking of walking on, and heard a loud noise in the bushes. It came from the edge of the forest a hundred yards back. Leafy branches moved as if inadvertently brushed by a man or beast. She felt her chest tight with fear. She jumped to her feet, staring intently at the exact spot. But all was quiet, the leaves were still.

Since she had left Ramón at the village of Saleix, she had passed only ruins of habitations. She had met no one, had neither seen nor heard anything except the snake, the cuckoo and a few distant rustles of birds or tiny animals amongst the trees.

Slow, deep breaths helped to quell the anxiety. It must have been a big animal, maybe a deer, startled by her presence, she decided. Maybe it was just her imagination, prompted by being alone in this remote place. She quickly repacked her rucksack and started off along the path which led into the gorge, telling herself that she must not allow her mind to play tricks. There was a long way to go and many out-of-the-way locations to be traversed in the next few weeks. It would be very different from the previous day with Ramón. She would need to become used to solitary travel.

The path through the gorge lay beside the river. It was less steep than before, easier to keep up a good pace. She tried to think of Hank and how he would have enjoyed this terrain. Next time she wrote to him, she would tell him the story of being stalked by the phantom of the forest and how she had escaped into the canyon. Writing to Deirdre, she had better tell a different tale. It would be best not to mention the phantom, even in jest, it would only worry her.

She came out of the upper end of the gorge panting for breath. It was time to slow down again. She was now in a high open valley, surrounded by steep cliffs and peaks, its lower exit guarded by the gorge. Ahead, on the skyline, was the ridge she would have to cross. But that was hours away and looked very high. She would need to walk steadily, to stop rushing away from the phantom of the forest.

The pass marked on Ramón's map, the Port de Saleix, was not immediately obvious but she checked and felt sure she was on the right way through these mountains.

Although it would mean a late stop for lunch, she decided to keep going, with only short breaks, until she reached the ridge itself and had climbed at least part of the way to its crest.

Even in the hottest part of the day it was hard to keep reminding herself of Ramón's advice to go slowly but the fear of what was behind her was still driving her on. The path led her well above the river now, skirting cliffs to her right. Below, beside the river she could see small stone cabins and a few cows but no herdsmen. The refuges looked ancient but were obviously kept in repair.

High in the valley now, she stopped and steeled herself to look back. She carefully scanned the slopes down to the mouth of the gorge, No one was following. There was no sign of human life in the whole of this huge enclosed valley.

It was now well after two o'clock and a relief to stop for a decent break and something to eat. A grassy ledge more than half way up the slope to the ridge was an ideal place to rest and she made herself comfortable.

A huge bird circled overhead, its wings stretched to single feathered tips, its white head and neck tucked into the base of its wings. It must be a griffon vulture, scouring the valley for suitable pickings. Anamar smiled to herself. It was an impressive presence, intimidating, but not so frightening as the phantom of the forest.

'No doubt he's eyeing me up, wondering whether I'd make a good meal.' Anamar was talking to herself but not yet speaking the words aloud. On this journey there would be plenty of time for conversations in her head with herself and her friends.

And as the big bird swooped nearer she could hear Deirdre saying, 'For pity's sake woman show him one of your arms. He won't hang around once he sees it. There's more beef on a wooden crutch.'

The excitement of finding the way made sure it was a short stop. A faint path led to the ridge but it was so steep and rocky she had to use her hands to scramble up. Head down to be sure of her footholds. A simple slip here would mean a long fall. Willing herself not to go too quickly, she steadily climbed upwards. Then the slope eased and she raised her eyes.

She was on the very crest of the ridge. Below, on the other side, a village lay beside the river. It must be to be her resting place for the night, Aulus-les-Bains.

But before she continued, Anamar needed one more sight of the way she had come. She recrossed the pass and sat down to look back towards the East. Perched on the ridge, she was on the outer rim of the Mountains of Saleix. Beyond the range to the South were the highest peaks of the Pyrenees and one so much higher than all the rest. It was a massif with a number of summits, rather than a single mountain. It must be Maladetta, the highest peak in the whole range.

Looking down, Anamar followed the faint line which traced the route she had been climbing all day. There it was laid out in front of her like a huge map - the ascent through the woods above Saleix in the far distance, the gorge which led to this huge valley at her feet.

On the way up it had seemed so remote and forbidding, a wild and barren place of stones, rocky outcrops and cliffs, jagged peaks behind. So scary when she had heard the rustle in the bushes below the gorge. But later, it was frightening in a different way because this terrain was so vast and distant from the world she knew.

Now, that part of her journey was behind her and she felt proud to have managed it on her own. Looking back, it no longer seemed so formidable, so hostile. These hills were part of her life now. Back home she would talk about them with the same kind of possessive pride she had for her own Blue Stack Mountains in Donegal.

She crossed the crest again and felt euphoric on the descent. There had been two paths at the pass. The one on the left had seemed more direct but the other on the right had looked more used and in her present mood the choice had been easy. It led her down in great sweeping zig—zags towards the wood and the village on the river.

Aulus-les-Bains, in the late afternoon, was a splendid village which seemed to be in two distinct parts. Near the river there were large houses and hotels, some reached by footbridges across the water. Many looked in need of repair and decoration but they were in the grand style, representing the elegance of the past.

She remembered Ramón telling her that the village had been a spa since Roman times and at the height of its popularity in the 19th century. Before the first world war thousands of 'curistes' had flocked here to take the waters but during the second world war the spa and its hotels had fallen into a deep sleep. When peace came, Aulus had forgotten to waken.

The main part of the village was on the hillside above the river and Anamar found a room above a small café mentioned in Ramón's notes.

The church was above the highest part of the village and she was early for evening Mass. The building was unimpressive from the outside, just another old church, but inside there was light and airy space and a strangely familiar feeling. She blessed herself, genuflected in front of the altar and allowed herself to pause from the motion of her pilgrimage in readiness for the stillness of the Mass.

A white pulpit with a white canopy, both ornately embellished with gold paint in some distant age, hung high on one wall. Wooden stairs led to a balcony at the back, lit by a circular stained-glass window. A brightly-decorated plaster figure of Joan of Arc guarded the interior. Then, around the corner to the nave, Anamar was surprised by another statue attached to the wall. She sat down on the nearest pew and stared in disbelief.

The name plate said, 'St Roch', and the saint held up the skirt of his brown robe to show a painted wound on his left thigh. At his feet the figure of a tiny hound dog, with a small loaf of bread in its mouth, looked up to him with the intensity of devotion which only a dog can manage. St Roch carried a staff with a gourd tied near its top. But it was his clothing which gave him away. He wore a big hat with a silver scallop shell and four more silver scallop shells on the cloak all glinting in the light. On his left breast was the bright red sword of St James in his role as slayer of the Moors. It was the garb of the Santiago pilgrim in medieval times.

Anamar had heard the story of St Roch from Ramón but he hadn't told her she would find his statue here.

St Roch was a French cleric born in Montpellier in the South of France at the end of the 13th century. While on pilgrimage he had come upon a terrible plague and, through caring for others, had caught the disease himself. When he became too ill to look after his own needs, a dog had brought him food and had remained with him during his travels. The wound on his thigh was a plague bulbo.

As the centuries passed after his death, Roch had become the favourite saint of French pilgrims, and because the Road to Santiago had become the most popular pilgrimage, his statues usually wore the emblems of the Santiago pilgrim.

Ramón had enjoyed telling the story to Anamar and had smiled broadly.

'What intrigues me most of all,' he had said, 'St Roch made his pilgrimage to Rome, he never went to Santiago!'

Anamar smiled at the statue and sat back, pretending to herself that St Roch was taking her under his notice. But wasn't it typical of Ramón to let her find it by herself, knowing that it would provide all the reassurance she needed at the end of her first day on her own. Ramón knew when to tell her what she needed to know and when to keep a secret. That was his way.

She had just begun to pray for a safe journey when she realised that this church had brought her back to the rote and rhythm of her faith. Once habit and repetition had dictated the nature of her observance. But far from home the routine and ritual of religious practice in Donegal had begun to slip away. Neither her time at Belshade nor this journey had eroded her faith but it had dramatically changed how she complied with her devotions.

Staring at the statue, Anamar fell into a day-dreaming daze as if mesmerised by St Roch. Visions of the journey to come slipped unbidden into her mind - scenes of dim churches with the scallop motif on the altar rails - pilgrim statues in dark corners - her attention drawn to them by sudden shafts of light or murmurs of sound, as if her shadow was making sure she missed nothing. Suddenly the door clanked open and she was roused by the priest coming in to prepare for Mass.

When she lay down in her narrow bed to sleep she became aware of the gentle chime of sheep bells, a lighter, less sonorous clang than the cow-bells earlier in the day. This new sound had been with her since the descent to the village. She would remember Aulus-les-Bains for its sheep bells and St Roch.

In spite of the strenuous trek across the mountains, Anamar was up early on the morning of the third day before anyone else was astir. She had paid the previous evening and been shown how to let herself out. It was hard to start without even a cup of tea but she was hopeful breakfast would come later.

It was a dull day, cloudy, threatening rain, time to put on the waterproof cape and be prepared. The village was still beautiful down by the river, even in such dismal weather and her spirits soared when she found a café open for the early risers.

Her route followed the river on a winding, unsurfaced country road, less strenuous walking than the previous day. It had been twenty-five kilometres, according to Ramón's notes, but it had taken over eight hours because of the mountainous terrain. To-day's stint would be nearly as long but much easier walking.

The road followed the river and Anamar watched chestnut-brown horses with blond manes pause as they grazed. The rain ceased and she was glad of the shade of a wooded stretch. A narrow gorge led to a small village and on its outskirts a sign on a stone wall said 'Maison de Retrait'. There were big pillars at the gateway and a courtyard in front of the building. Wooden balconies faced the road. The place was well cared for but there was no sign of any residents. Were they all at their prayers?

In the early afternoon she reached the village of Oust and its beautiful church of golden stone. She turned towards Seix. It seemed like back-tracking but this was the route according to Ramón's map. Even before she entered the village her mind was made up. This was the friendliest place so far. Everyone had smiled as they passed on the road in. As soon as she stopped in the square villagers came across to speak to her, making her feel welcome.

The houses looked very old, timber-framed, with over-hanging roofs and wooden balconies. When she asked about a place to stay she was directed to the greengrocer's on the other side of the square. Ten minutes later she was standing at the window of her room above the shop looking out at the life of the village below. It was a cheerful scene, busy, businesslike.

Anamar could hardly believe that she was enjoying herself so much. She sat at the one table outside a café, in the shade of a tree, treating herself to a coffee. The church was across the square but she decided against going inside. That could wait until evening Mass. When the time came she was late, but so was almost everyone else. As she took her seat she looked up and there it was, beside the rétable, another painted plaster statue of a pilgrim with staff and scallop shell. This time the legend said, 'St Jacques'.

Ramón might have told her. He should have said something about keeping a look-out for these symbols of the pilgrimage. She would have missed this one and the one of St Roch at Aulus-les-Bains had she not gone to Mass in either place.

Before she went to bed she sat at the open window of her room looking out over the village square and the river. She could hear murmurs of conversation as people passed below. Then she was aware of the smell of a peculiar type of tobacco smoke. She hated the acrid odour of the kind of cigarette most Frenchmen seemed to smoke. But this was a lighter, sweeter smell and vaguely familiar. It was pipe smoke but not the foul reek of men's pipes at home.

Then she remembered. Some evenings at Mont L'ours Ramón had smoked a pipe as they sat on the balcony after dinner. She had commented on the pleasant smell and he had explained that he smoked rarely and only a tobacco called Balkan Sobrani.

She looked out of the window and there were men in the street. But the light was poor and it was so hard to be sure which one was smoking. Ramón was too much in her thoughts, she would have to learn to manage without him.

Next morning she made good time on a flat road in a fertile valley. In the heat of the day there was good shade. The road took her under an arch of rock when a buttress tried to block the way. She saw a single pear tree in a field and reasoned that it must crop exceptionally well to have been left when other trees had obviously been cleared to free the land for grazing.

As she walked she found herself holding conversations inside her head with people she knew. It was like day-dreaming but much more real. Her friends, particularly Deirdre, Hank, Yvette and Ramón would understand. They would have been the companions of her choice had she not decided to travel alone. Each would have been at his or her best, in different circumstances.

Hank would have revelled in the stretch over the mountains. Ramón would have been delighted to see her discover for herself the statue of the pilgrim, St Roch. Deirdre would have appreciated the moment of truth, setting out from Mont L'ours-les-Cascades with the good wishes of the villagers. Yvette would have loved the time to talk. She would have enjoyed the fun and helped her to see the bright side when the going was hard.

How would they have reacted to the rustling in the bushes on the second day? Hank would have stayed calm and gone to investigate. Deirdre would have held her nerve, sat tight and waited. Ramón would have convinced her it was nothing to be alarmed about. He would have made one of his serious jokes to help reassure her. Yvette would have leapt to her feet, yelling at the top of her voice and the pair of them would have legged it up the gorge as if the hounds of hell were after them!

She had forgotten that this was another relatively short day when the outskirts of St Girons appeared in the middle distance. At the end of a stage it was great to feel in such good form. Four days on the road and here she was feeling she could have walked much further had she needed to. But then Ramón had been adamant. 'After the first two days, go gently for a week and walk yourself into the journey.' He was right, of course. But then he was right so often it could become a little irritating.

MADAM CELESTINE

Madam Celestine D'Abrat was painting her nails when she heard the footsteps on the stairs. She loved this room on the first floor at the head of the spiral staircase. A sign said that it was the reception for the hotel and also the office but, best of all, it was her own private sitting-room. The ground floor was a bar and restaurant, no longer under her control, but the next two floors were hers, and the hotel had its own entrance, elegantly sign-posted at street level.

Sometimes guests would complain that the noise of feet on the wooden stairs kept them awake at night, but Madam D'Abrat had resisted the temptation to deaden the noise by laying a carpet. It was not a question of her being unwilling to spend the money, you should understand, but it was possible to tell so much from the footsteps on the stairs. They heralded the confident, introduced the hesitant, betrayed the furtive. They were her first contact with new arrivals. At any time of the day or night, they allowed her to tell the mood and condition of her guests. A woman in her position needed to know her customers.

But on this day the footsteps were distinctly different - a firm but light-footed tread, brisk without being in a hurry, not one of her usual clients. It had to be a woman, young, careful, physically confident and strong. Unlike many confident women, however, the step was unaggressive, gentle even. It was the gait of a walker, not a lady of fashion, the tread of a climber not a marcher.

The door opened and Madam D'Abrat smiled, apparently in welcome, but in reality, in self-congratulation. She had got it right again. The young woman was above average height, good-looking without being beautiful and with the fresh complexion of the outdoors. She was simply dressed, wearing strong leather sandals without socks, carrying a mountain walker's stick and having a small knapsack on her back.

Madam D'Abrat took an instant liking to this young woman, allocated her the best available room in the house and, to her own amazement, heard herself offering half board at terms reserved only for her most favoured regulars.

Anamar enjoyed wandering around St Girons in the late afternoon. It was a proper town with interesting shops and a number of bars and cafes on both sides of the river, linked by an impressive old bridge. The sound of water falling over the weir drew her across to a labyrinth of alleyways, streets and little squares. At this time of the day It was hot and humid and she was pleased to have no further to go. Ramón had been vague about St Girons except to say that it would be a good place to spend the night.

Madam D'Abrat's hotel had no dining of its own and there was an arrangement whereby her patrons could have breakfast and dinner in the restaurant on the ground floor. After Mass Anamar was hungry and went into the bar. Madam D'Abrat was already seated at a table, as if waiting for her to arrive.

'Sit with me, chérie,' she said with a smile, 'You must tell me about yourself. A guest like you has never climbed my stairs and I confess I am intrigued. You are a Woman of Mystery.

Anamar looked blankly at Madam D'Abrat. At home, an hotelier might be as inquisitive as this lady, but never so blatantly obvious. She felt her face redden and almost stammered in reply.

'I'm from Ireland. I'm following the Road of St James to Santiago in Spain. I've been walking for four days. Last night I stayed in Seix ......'

'And you've walked from there to-day.' Madam D'Abrat interrupted, eyebrows registering theatrical amazement. In spite of initiating the conversation, she was as surprised as Anamar that it was taking place. She reached across and gently placed a carefully manicured hand on Anamar's arm. On each of her long fingers there was at least one ring. Her nails were long and painted scarlet.

'You and I are free spirits,' she said quietly, 'Neither of us needs a man to lead us by the nose. We can find our own way through the world.' It had been a long time since she had felt so comfortable in the company of another woman. 'We must be friends. I know from the hotel register that you are Anamar. I am Celestine.'

They shook hands. Celestine recommended the fish soup and the Cassoulet and while they waited for the food to be served, they sat talking as easily to each other as if they had been friends for years.

The hotel was a family business passed on to Celestine. She had worked in Toulouse in a jewellery shop and the social life of the city had been wonderful but she had returned home to keep the hotel open during the war.

When the food arrived, Celestine poured the red wine, they touched glasses and wished each other well. It was easy to understand Celestine. Her voice was husky but she spoke French delightfully, as if she loved the language, enjoying the effect of her words like an actor in a play.

During the meal Anamar found herself talking freely about her pilgrimage, the visit to Paris to meet Father Brian, her journey to the Mediterranean and the story of the four days walking to St Girons. When she mentioned Ramón, Celestine could not contain herself.

'Ramón Mont L'ours Barriano! Oh! La, La! You have met the serious Seigneur, the love of my life all those years ago in Toulouse when we were young. You haven't stolen his heart?' She sighed. 'I never managed to find it, much less steal it. Is he still in love with his books, his studies, his precious research?'

Anamar laughed and told her how helpful Ramón had been with information and advice about the Road of St James, how he had dictated notes and had given her maps, how he had accompanied her on the first day.

'Oh that's the serious Seigneur, chérie.' Celestine gestured with her hands in supplication. 'The mystic. The philosopher. But did you fall in love with him?'

Anamar blushed and put her hand in front of her face to hide her embarrassment.

'It wasn't like that at all we were ....' Then she realised that Celestine was having fun with her. They were both laughing now, and Celestine proposed the toast 'Don Ramón, the Serious Seigneur.'

Later Celestine sipped her wine and watched Anamar as she talked. She was captivated by this young woman who was trying so hard to speak French well, and for once found herself without envy for the youth and beauty of a female companion.

She could recognise the spirit that had drawn Anamar into this adventure, a journey of the body and the soul. When she had been Anamar's age she would never have considered such a thing, but now she could comprehend. She could see that Anamar was enjoying telling her tale, needing to share her experiences with someone who could understand.

Suddenly she stood up, excused herself, and went to the bar to make a telephone call. She returned in a few minutes.

'Come! Come! My precious friend, my pilgrim. I have someone else I want you to meet.'

She led the way to a bar at the other end of the town. As they entered, she was greeted by a bellow from the patron. He was a large man with forearms as massive as a wrestler's and covered with thick golden hair. He was neatly dressed and, although it was late in the day, his white shirt and blue and white striped apron were unsoiled. In spite of his bulk he darted around from behind the bar and kissed Celestine loudly on both cheeks.

'This is my dear friend and would-be lover, Clement.' Celestine sounded as if she didn't believe a word she was saying, 'Once he led us along the righteous path to Heaven, now he is the devil's coachman driving us down the road to Hell.'

Clement roared with laughter, took Anamar's hand gently in his great fist and kissed it lightly.

'There is no one so vulnerable to the taunts of his friends as the unfrocked priest. You must be Anamar, the Irish Pilgrim on the Road of St Jacques. When Celestine rang she said you were a woman of spirit. She didn't tell me you were so beautiful.'

Celestine gave his wrist a little slap.

'Behave yourself. It's past the pilgrim's bed-time, but she had planned to travel West to-morrow without visiting the pilgrim treasures of St Lizier and I knew she must meet you.'

They sat down at a table in a corner and listened as Clement talked about the traces of the pilgrimage to be found in two neighbouring villages, St-Lizier and Montjoie. Anamar was spellbound. They were not marked on Ramón's map. He had never even mentioned their names.

As they walked back to the hotel, Celestine suddenly suggested that they should explore the villages together the next day. Anamar could spend another night In St Girons.

Anamar was finding it hard not to take too much pleasure from the fact that Ramón had failed by default. Now her unlikely mentors were Celestine and Clement. Had Ramón been with her, he would have been mortified and, she had to admit, she would have enjoyed his discomfort.

Next morning they left the hotel at ten and stepped out on the road to St-Lizier. Anamar wore her usual walking clothes, the cotton shirt and skirt and leather sandals. She brought her rucksack and staff as a matter of course.

Celestine had dressed as if for a day at the market. Her light cotton trousers were saxe blue and her blouse a lighter shade with small white spots. She wore a magnificent straw hat with a huge brim trimmed with a blue and white ribbon tied in a bow. On her feet were her comfortable lace-up shoes, like low boots, the ones she always wore when she knew she would be on her feet all day. She carried a straw basket with a beautiful chiffon scarf of palest powder blue tied to one of the handles.

It was a short walk beside the river on a narrow country road. The only traffic was horse-drawn and Anamar guessed that the main road must be on the other side of the river. They were greeted by carters and men on horseback on the way to St Girons. Anamar answered a stream of questions from Celestine on how she managed with so few clothes, how she found the way, how she intended to cross the Pyrenees, how long the whole journey would take, how she would cope with being on her own.

They entered St-Lizier and, once inside the walls, Anamar thought it must be the most picturesque village she had ever seen. The arcaded streets were cobbled, the houses wood framed and plastered, the roofs red-tiled. Clement had told them that there had been a Roman settlement here. They saw the magnificently turretted bishop's palace and found the plaque he had mentioned on one of the houses in the place des Etendes. It had an impressive carving of a scallop shell and recalled that a certain Antoine Lassalle had made the pilgrimage to Santiago in 1655.

There were two cathedrals. Notre-dame-de-Sède had the better view but, once their eyes had become used to the dim light, the interior of the Cathedral de Saint-Lizier was splendid. Clement had complained that some of the restoration work had been poorly done. The 12th Century frescoes were being allowed to fade away but Anamar saw only the perfections. The Romanesque two-storeyed cloister was magnificent. She was awed by the centuries of worship represented in this Hotel-Dieu. At last she recognised the true significance of travelling in the footsteps of pilgrims who had been passing through places like St-Lizier for a thousand years.

Celestine had left Anamar to her meditation and returned with a priest, a quiet, serious man who seemed uneasy in the presence of two women. He took them to an ante-room to show them ancient books in his care and as they talked his shyness faded. He explained that a confraternity of the friends of St Jacques had been formed in the village in the 16th

Century. The books contained lists of local people who had made the pilgrimage in the 16th, 17th and 18th centuries. They had gone on foot or on horseback, as independent travellers or in groups. Each name was noted with the pilgrim's occupation, joiner, verger, notary, canon, carpenter, nobleman, weaver, student, shoemaker.

When they left St-Lizier and walked in silence towards Montjoie, Anamar had so much on her mind. The evidence of the pilgrimage had been all around them in the village. Reading about the occupations of these local people of centuries past, who had set out from here to go to Santiago, had been the highlight. They made the history real. They had created the statues, carved the plaques and scallop shells, named the streets after St Jacques. They would be her guides.

Celestine was smiling broadly. She was delighted that this visit had worked out so well. Anamar deserved the best help she and Clement had to give.

They saw no one on the road to Montjoie and before they reached the village she led the way into a field and sat down in the shade of a tree. Now Anamar saw the purpose of the basket. It contained the picnic. Celestine spread out a checked cloth and unpacked. There was a bottle of water and a half-bottle of wine, a baguette, two big tomatoes, a small bottle of oil and vinegar, paté, thin slices of ham and two pastry horns filled with crème pâtisserie.

She took Anamar's hands.

'This is the happiest day I've had since I left Toulouse.' She looked as if she might shed a tear. 'I've been to St-Lizier many times but never saw its pilgrim treasures until to-day.'

Without prompting, she began to talk about her time in Toulouse. Life had been exciting there, but when she had married the much-older owner of the jewellery shop, she had felt her freedom restricted. When he died in 1940 she discovered, to her amazement, that he had left large debts and the shop had to be sold. Instead of being left a widow with means, she needed to find another job. She moved from Toulouse to St Girons without a backward look but feeling she had left her youth behind. Since then she had tried to build a new life as an independent woman, free from ties, making her own decisions.

Anamar smiled.

'I know how you feel. In Ireland people would say, "Celestine is her own woman," and I'm sure they say that about me too.'

After the meal they leaned back against the tree and talked quietly, as if they had been friends for years. Montjoie was not far and they entered through the ancient walls in mid-afternoon. The fortified church had three towers, of which the centre one was much the highest. The two lower towers had bells under their arches. The roofs were tiled like St-Lizier, the streets cobbled, even the inner square of the village was fortified.

But there was no sign of life, not even a stray cat amongst the stones. Anamar and Celestine wandered around like two actors on the set of a medieval play, their performance finished but unable to leave the stage.

It took nearly an hour to walk back to St Girons and Anamar went to her room to write up her notes. She needed time on her own to think about the day. She washed her underclothes and her walking shirt and hung them on hangers in front of the open window. She was no longer irritated by Ramón's failure to tell her about St-Lizier. Perhaps it had been deliberate, to encourage her to find things out for herself.

At dinner in the bar Celestine was in yet another outfit, white blouse and trousers with a black waistcoat embroidered with gold thread. She was radiant with happiness.

'What a day! My legs feel like lead. My feet ache. But I am so happy.' She was pouring wine for both of them. 'Who here would believe that Celestine D'Abrat has been a pilgrim for a day? Who would believe she has visited two cathedrals in one morning, when she hasn't been inside a church since last Christmas?'

'I felt so happy in St-Lizier, so excited to be following the pilgrim trail. I still feel elated.' She shook her head gently, as if to bring herself back to her senses. 'I haven't believed in God for years. I go to Mass at Christmas but I've no time for priests and religion. Now you're leading me back, like a lost sheep to the fold.'

It was Anamar's turn to be puzzled. Was Celestine serious? Or was she still making fun of her? Was there something that she should be saying? Before she could speak Celestine smiled and raised her hands, palms upwards in a gesture of supplication.

'I should have known,' she said archly, 'The church has sent an innocent to bring back a lost soul. But I'm up to your tricks. It'll take more than Saint Jacques and Sister Anamar to get me back on my knees again.'

This was more like it. Anamar knew where she was, when Celestine was like this.

'Hold on, woman dear! Hold on!,' she said, laughing, 'It wasn't me who suggested the trip to St-Lizier. It wasn't me who insisted that you come too.'

Celestine's hands were raised again, this time palms downwards.

'I know! I know!' she cried dramatically, 'I was carried away. Once upon a time it would have taken a young man to get me so excited. Now all I need is the sight of a stone scallop shell on an ancient wall and I'm in a religious frenzy.'

She paused and pointed a long scarlet fingernail at Anamar.

'But what about you, chérie. It's easy to see that I need an act of contrition. What's a beautiful young girl like you doing on a pilgrimage? You haven't sinned enough to warrant such penance. For me it would be different. I'd need to walk half-way around the world and back to expiate my sins.

'You should be enjoying yourself, making men fall in love with you, having a good time at parties and dances.' She took Anamar's face in her hands.

'You have wonderful skin, my girl, even though you don't protect it from the weather. You have a fine figure, good legs, your own teeth. She put a finger and thumb to her mouth pretending her own were false. You have your own hair. She placed her hands on the sides of her head and moved her hair as if straightening a wig.'

Anamar was laughing so much her sides were sore. This was the way to go on a pilgrimage. She had been too serious about her journey. There were times when the pilgrim needed good company, a friend who would make her laugh when she was too solemn, who would pull her leg when she was too earnest.

It was a joyous evening, uproariously irreverent when Clement joined them later. As Anamar climbed the wooden staircase to her room, she realised that she had not been to Mass on either of the evenings she had been in St Girons. Meeting the lapsed Celestine and Clement, the unfrocked priest, had allowed her to experience what the too serious pilgrim was certain to miss.

She lay on her back on the comfortable bed, the wine singing pleasantly in her head, and resolved that if she made it to Santiago, she would make sure St James was aware of the help she had been given by Celestine and Clement.

Next morning, Celestine was not feeling at her best, but she was up at her usual time. She knew that, in spite of the late night, Anamar would be early on the way.

'Speak quietly, Chérie,' she said, as if every word was painful to hear, 'Your precious St Jacques has taken offence at my feeble efforts to weaken your pilgrim resolve and has given me the worst hang-over I've had for years.'

Anamar was not surprised. She had been amazed to see how much wine and cognac Celestine had been able to drink without appearing drunk. She herself had wakened with a strange, dry taste in her mouth and feeling very thirsty. But it would not do to admit her condition, even to Celestine.

'You must not blame St Jacques,' she said primly, Imitating Deirdre Ryan, 'Monsieur Vin Rouge is the more likely culprit. I'm sure I've told you that Ramón says........'

But Celestine had her hands over her ears.

'Spare me the advice of the Don Ramón, the Serious Seigneur, chérie,' she said wearily, ' There was a time when I had to listen and always failed to hear.'

They drank large glasses of cold, freshly-pressed orange juice, sipped coffee and ate croissants. It was a complete cure. Even Celestine was feeling better. She walked with Anamar to the edge of the town and wished her well. They hugged each other and kissed on both cheeks. For Anamar this was the third difficult parting. She set out feeling depressed but more determined than ever to follow the pilgrim road.

When it was over, she would come back to St Girons to see Celestine.

THE PHANTOM STALKER

It had rained during the night and the road was awash with wet cow dung and horse manure. Anamar splashed through the mire, her feet and sandals soaked, the mud between her toes, yellow japs splattering up her lower leg and the bottom of her skirt.

After two and a half hours' walking without a break, the narrow country road led to a sign for the village of Audressein. It was on the other side of the river and so off the route, but Anamar knew where she was going. She crossed the bridge and made her way to the church. Ramón had said that it must not be missed. It was by the river, surmounted by the now familiar three towers, set above two arches with bells, one much larger than the other. Between the roof of the church and the bell arches was the neat addition of a steeply-roofed balcony with a wooden balustrade and a clock. At ground level little statues had been defaced by breaking off their noses.

But it was the frescoes under the three arches of the church's cobbled porch which Ramón had wanted her to see. The best preserved featured a troubadour, others were faded and peeling, but the one she had come to see was of St Jacques wearing a scallop shell in his hat and carrying a huge pilgrim's staff.

Anamar's mood of depression lifted like the morning mist from Lough Eske. It was time to wash her feet in the river and allow herself the luxury of a long rest.

In the late afternoon she passed through the big village of St Lary and climbed steadily towards the Col d'Aspet. She was wishing she had chosen an earlier stopping place when she came upon the tiny hamlet of Portet d'Aspet. These might be the foothills of the Pyrenees but, on foot, were real mountain country. It was a pleasant surprise to find a comfortable room at a farmhouse on the edge of the village. A good meal and bed at nine o'clock allowed her to be on the road again much earlier than on any day so far.

On the way through the village she passed the church. It was still locked. Mass was not until eight-thirty, her devotions would have to wait. Then she noticed the name, 'St Roch'. It must be a pilgrim church. There was sure to be a statue of St Roch inside but there was no one about to ask.

At the head of the pass a sign said '1069 metres', far higher than the mountain tops at home. The view was spectacular. On the other side of the pass, the ground fell away much more steeply into a narrow, wooded gorge. The road zig-zagged, doubling back on itself as it led the way downwards in a series of tight hairpin bends. The day was fine and warm, without a breath of wind.

As Anamar strode downhill she heard the tramp of footsteps on the road above. She stopped to listen and scan the slope. There was a movement amongst the trees. The noise ceased but when she started again the footsteps followed a few moments later, stopping each time she paused.

Was it the echo of her own steps? Sound could play tricks in a gorge like this. While she had been in St Girons she had forgotten about the phantom of the forest. Now, on her own, it was easy to believe that someone was following her again. She called out three times but the only reply was the echo of her own voice.

Once she had started to climb to the Col on the previous day, there had been hardly any traffic. But on this morning nothing at all passed in either direction. The trees clung to the sides of the gorge. The road was narrow, poorly surfaced, showing signs in places of having been avalanched at the end of the winter. There were neither dwellings, nor any sign of human activity. Since the stage across the Mountains of Saleix, this was the most lonely stretch of route so far.

She stepped it out on the way down, walking faster than usual, conscious that it would be more tiring but anxious to get away from this valley.

The map showed that she had to make a left turn towards St Beat but when she reached the sign post the road which branched off was so narrow and rough she hesitated. It was like a cart track through the hills at home. She consulted Ramón's instructions again. This had to be it. If the previous section had seemed remote, she now felt she was climbing into isolation.

It was not Anamar's intention to walk so quickly, but fear drove her on, winding up the pace as she climbed. The path twisted and turned up the slope. Her breathing quickened from a complete breath every four paces, to one every second step. This was as hard as running or climbing a steep slope at altitude. She willed herself to slow down. Neither Ramón nor Hank would ever have allowed her to go at this speed.

There was nothing for it but to grind on up to the pass. The slower pace helped her breathing, She had now found a climbing rhythm which she could keep going, no matter how high the pass.

There was no spot-height on Ramón's map but the little sign at the Col de Mente said, 1349 metres. She tried to do the calculation in her head. Three times 1349, plus one twentieth .... Anyway it was over 4000 feet! This route was proving to be one high pass after another, even before she reached the big one over the crest and into Spain.

She had to stop at the Col, and not just to catch her breath. The view on either side of the ridge was magnificent, a great panorama of mountain terrain, stunning rock formations, deep, thickly-wooded valleys, sharp rock and snow peaks above. It was even more spectacular than either of the previous passes. For the first time since she had heard the footsteps behind her, Anamar felt the fear subside. There was no one on the track below, no sound of the tramp of feet, no sign of the Phantom Stalker.

She could now appreciate the beauty of the forest through which she had been climbing. There were ancient woodlands with a great variety of trees. Over the past few days she had been making a list of the trees - mountain pines, silver firs, oaks, sycamores, silver birch, willow, beech and chestnut. Even as she had trudged anxiously upwards to this col, she had been conscious of the huge forested areas of France and now was suddenly aware of how little woodland had been left uncleared in her home county, Donegal.

St Beat had an impressive church perched on a hill above the town, with a square tower and a bell tower, but there was no time for a visit. She travelled on past a cement works on the outskirts. Maranic, when she reached it, was bright and interesting, in total contrast to the dullness of the route which led to it.

A sign in the window of a house said simply, 'Chambres' and Anamar was shown upstairs to a tiny room by an almost silent woman who became friendly and welcoming as soon as Anamar asked about the time of evening Mass.

Having paid when she had arrived, Anamar let herself out of the house at seven o'clock before anyone was about. A long, lush valley led directly South towards the mountains. There were neat homesteads amongst the farmland and woods. The pleasant road followed the river. Passing drivers waved to the lone walker. Anamar felt they were cheering her on her way.

Four hours later, on nothing more than water and a few biscuits, she reached the outskirts of Bagnères de Luchon and decided that she deserved a treat.

She loved the spacious elegance of this spa town. It had a air of refinement, the grandeur of a place sure of its eminent position. She knew it would be expensive but Anamar sat down at a pavement table outside a grand café. So far on the journey she had spent less than she and Ramón had budgeted. St Girons had been easily the best value, but then she had Celestine to make sure she had the best fare for the least cost. French women seemed to have a talent for finding real bargains.

The waiter was at her side as soon as she sat down. It was ten-thirty in the morning but he was dressed in white shirt, black bow-tie. black waistcoat and trousers.

She ordered coffee and two croissants with butter and peach jam. This was sheer luxury. She stretched her legs out below the table and looked up at the snow-capped summits. It was sunny but not hot. The residents and visitors of Luchon strolled by as if their town was the centre of the world.

Deirdre Ryan had told her about walking holidays here with her father. Hank had quoted Hilaire Belloc writing about Luchon at the end of the 19th century, 'It (Luchon) has the character and great luxury of one of the main towns of France'. Fifty years later, and in spite of two wars, it was still thriving, still charming, still confident of its place as one of the most famous spas in Europe. Anamar made a promise to herself that someday she would come back here on holiday.

The croissants were delicious, the buttery pastry flaking in her hands, the jam oozing out over her fingers. She had to lick them clean when the waiter was inside. It would never had done to wipe the worst of it off on the starched napkin.

After the worry of the previous day her spirits were restored. The road to the West and Arreau led through a line of little villages in a high valley. Ramón's notes recommended that she stay in the first of these, St Aventin. It was a steady climb, but when she reached the village she could see that Ramón was right again.

It was a most interesting little place, set into a slope so steep it clung to the mountainside, straddling the road without using any land for building which could have been used for cultivation. The church was on the hillside above and most of the houses below the road. The roofs were tiled with much smaller tiles than were used further East. Nearly all the houses had tiny dormers which seemed like pigeon coops, although other birds were using them as well.

There was no sign of an inn or a bar. As Anamar looked around the village she met two young girls. They might have been twins, about twelve years old, dressed identically in dark blue cardigans and skirts with pale blue aprons tied around their waists. They wore wooden clogs, which were much better in the mud than Anamar's sandals. She asked them where she might find a room for the night and told them she was on the way to Spain.

They took her to their home, one on each side, holding her hands. In a few minutes they had become her friends. Their mother smiled when she saw the three of them and heard that Anamar was a pilgrim. She had no spare room but the girls could share a bed for the night and free the other one for Anamar.

She could hardly believe her luck. Everywhere she went she seemed to have not the slightest trouble finding accommodation and here she was immediately accepted as part of the family. There were three older children, all boys under twenty and shy in Anamar's presence. They seemed to spend all their time outside the house, constantly busy with farm chores.

The girls were called Marie and Jeanne and were cousins of the same age. Marie's father and mother had been killed by the Germans during the war and she had been adopted by her aunt. Jeanne's father had been killed at the same time but Anamar asked no questions about the circumstances.

Jeanne and Marie went with her to see the church before evening Mass. Although it was ancient, Anamar could see that there had been some restoration. The carved figures around the walls looked very old, some had been defaced. A panel showed bunches of grapes, another animals. There was one of the Madonna and child with both noses broken. Others were scenes packed with people. There was a portrayal of a mighty battle, but the most impressive was of a troubadour playing a lute. His face, too, was disfigured.

The tower had pillared windows and there were more fine carvings under the porch. A twisted pattern in stone was sculpted in a design which might have been Celtic or Moorish. Was the latter a clue as to why the figures had been defaced? The girls showed her two more stone figures near the road and they were the most badly mutilated of all.

The girls' mother met them at Mass and they walked back to the house together. Anamar felt at home in the farmhouse. This was the French version of the country life into which she had been born and raised in Ireland. But she had been away from home for so long she was aware now of the farm smells. To some city people they might have been overpowering stinks but farm people were as comfortable with the smell of hay, sheep, horses and cows as town gardeners were of flowers and shrubs or their pets.

The evening meal was a substantial soup with huge loaves of bread and a round of their own cheese on a platter. Anamar felt privileged to be sharing the food around the table, with this family, in this house. Much as she had enjoyed the luxurious treat of petit déjeuner in Bagnères de Luchon just a few hours walk down the road, this was her choice of a place to stay, a proper pilgrim's lodging.

The boys went back to the outside work and Anamar sat with the girls and their mother around the open fire. She made animal shadows with her hands on the whitewashed wall. She showed them the 'Cat's Cradle', twisting string around her fingers and pulling it free with one neat tug. She taught them a little rhyme in English, illustrated by hand actions,

> 'This is the church, and this is the steeple,
> Open the doors and here are the people!'

They sang for her, songs she had never heard before. They all joined in for,

> 'Frère Jacques, Frère Jacques,
> Dormez-vous, dormez-vous,
> Sonnez les matins, Sonnez les matins,
> Ding! dang! dong! Ding! dang! dong!'

At home 'Frère Jacques' was always sung as a round, but Anamar didn't know the French word. She explained how it worked as best she could. She led the way herself, followed by Marie, Jeanne and their mother. The first attempt ended in giggles and laughter, as did the second. Then Anamar switched the order, starting with mother, then the girls, with herself coming in last. It worked and they clapped themselves loudly at the end.

Later in bed, the girls wanted to keep Anamar talking, asking questions about her home and her work, about her pilgrimage and what she intended to do when it was over. Eventually they promised to go to sleep if she told them a story. That was easy. She told them about the parish pilgrimage from Donegal to Lourdes. To amuse them she mentioned her proposal of marriage from her much-older shopkeeper boss, who thought all he had to do was ask and she would gratefully accept. They began to giggle so much she was afraid she would never get them to settle.

Breakfast at seven was simply bread and hot milk, but Anamar felt she had been treated like royalty in this house. When she tried to pay, the girls' mother refused to accept anything. This seemed so unfair that, when the girls left her up to the road, she gave them exactly what she had paid for a night's stay and dinner at Celestine's in St Girons. The girls ran home with the money. As Anamar looked back, the mother was up at the road, shaking her fist but only in fun. The smile on her face told a different story.

It had rained heavily during the night and the road was muddy. Anamar stepped carefully in her sandals. She was well used to them by now. Earlier her feet had felt tender towards the end of a day but now the skin was so tough she felt she could have gone bare-footed once off the surfaced roads.

The sky was clear, but it was eight-thirty before the sun rose high enough to breast the ridge and flood the valley with light. The map showed she was approaching a line of tiny villages. Garin was the first, then Cathervielle with a small church and an elegant eight-sided spire. Farmers were at work in the fields. The houses were all old, chalet-style, with steep, slated roofs. Portet de Luchon's rugged church was bigger, with another fine eight-sided spire, another monument to religious fervour in the past.

The valley opened out on the way to the pass, no fear here of someone trying to follow her without being seen. The view of the high peaks to the South was even more impressive as she climbed higher. The sign at the Col de Peyresourde said, '1569 metres'. Time for a longer rest than usual.

On the descent there were horses grazing free and a fence made of rock slates. Set back from the road was a group of beehives, perhaps three dozen of them, there to take advantage of the mountain flowers. Looking down she thought she could see Arreau, then she realised that it must be another village not even on her route. It was still a long way to go to Arreau.

She reached it during the afternoon. Once it had been capital of the area and Ramón thought it one of the most beautiful small towns in the Pyrenees. The houses were stone built, half timbered with steep neatly-slated roofs. There were creeper covered walls and balconies draped with flowers in profusion. Arreau had been built at the confluence of three rivers rushing down from the peaks above. Anamar smiled to herself. At home in Ireland this would have been called 'the Meeting of the Waters'. But the roads met here too. Arreau was well placed for travellers and market business.

It was a relief to reach this pleasant place not too tired. Having been on her own since early morning, it was good to be amongst friendly people. But was it all going too well. At a time like this her mother would have been at her most wary. 'You're happy now,' she would have said, 'But mark my words, there'll be tears before bed-time'. Anamar smiled to herself. Her mother's cup was always half empty, never half full.

In a side street she saw a sign in the window of a house which said, 'Chambres a Louer'. A well-dressed woman in her forties opened the door and examined Anamar from head to toe before asking her what she wanted. A thin grin flitted briefly across her face, as if there was a joke which Anamar would not understand.

'I don't take foreigners,' she said loudly, and closed the door in Anamar's face. It was a few moments before she recovered from the shock of such an abrupt dismissal. Then she saw the woman watching her from behind a curtain and moved quickly away.

She found a small hotel a little further down the street and asked a shy young man behind the bar counter about a room for the night. Without a word he took a key from a rack and showed her to a spacious first-floor room overlooking the river. When she asked the price, he wrote it down on a pad and suddenly she realised that the boy must be dumb. It was as cheap as St Girons and she almost sighed aloud with relief. Even though Ramón had helped her work out a budget for the trip, she had been worried about having enough money. Spain was sure to be cheap but costs were a concern in France.

She was carrying most of her money in large notes tucked into the secret pocket on the inside of the waist of her walking skirt. It was time to change another note. She would have to wait until the banks opened before she could leave Arreau in the morning.

Since the walk began she had been neglecting Ramón's suggestion that she rest in bed for a little while at the end of each day. It was only when she lay down and let herself feel the tiredness that she realised she must try to do this more often. After an hour, she rose, refreshed, and had coffee in the bar. Her first impressions had been right. In spite of her earlier rejection, people in Arreau were friendly.

It was a great pleasure to wander around, crossing the bridges, finding her own way to the church. The massive iron-studded door of the porch of the Chapelle Saint-Exupère was open, but a locked iron grill barred the way into the church itself. When her eyes became used to the light it was possible to see the inter-woven arches of the nave and the splendid paintings on its ceiling. The walls were decorated with a Templar-cross motif but the most dramatic adornment of all was the painting of saints and angels on the ceiling of the porch.

Evening Mass was in the town's other church, Notre-Dame, and Anamar was surprised to see the very small number attending. After dinner she went back to Saint-Exupère. The porch was still open. She grasped the iron bars and stared into the semi-darkness.

For some bizarre reason it felt as if she was inside, looking out through the bars which were keeping her imprisoned. Was this what it was like to be in jail? Did nuns sometimes feel like this in a closed convent? Why did the Church have to segregate itself from the world? What strange power forced the Church to keep itself so inaccessible?

The images tumbled through her mind, making nonsense of her questions. She tried and found she couldn't let go of the bars. It was at that moment she smelt the tobacco smoke again, the Balkan Sobrani. She released her grip on the bars and turned but there was no one there. The smell must have wafted in from the street. Outside there were dozens of passers-by but, as far as she could see, no man with a pipe.

Anamar found it hard to settle in bed that night. She sat up and turned on the light to finish her notes. Each time she thought she had put the Phantom Stalker out of her mind, something would happen which would bring back the fright she'd had on that first day on her own. She set the notebook on the table, turned off the light and decided that if there was a stalker, she would make a plan which would shake him off, once and for all.

POUDRI

Anamar heard the rain lashing against the window before she was properly awake. Then she remembered that she would have to wait until a bank was open before she could leave Arreau and let herself relax full length in the bed. An opportunity to have a lie-in must not be missed and it was bliss. This was the tenth day of her pilgrimage and such a pleasure to take a break from her routine of 'up early, away before seven'. She listened to the rain beating down and smiled; last night she had heard two local people agreeing that Arreau was one of the driest places in France!

By the time the bank opened, the rain was over and the streets were nearly dry. It was a steep climb out of the village and up to the pass, the Col d'Aspin, nearly as high as the Peyresourde the previous day. The countryside was so fresh and clean, the air so invigorating. The sunlight glinted on the leaves and sparkled in little puddles at the side of the road.

She looked for spiders' webs, as she always did at this time of the morning. Usually the roadside bushes and banks were covered with the elegant, geometric, gossamer-thread patterns, minute drops of dew sparkling on the strands. They would be hard to best as examples of nature's art. But not to-day. No doubt all swept away by the storm, unless, of course, the spiders had known of the coming storm last night and decided not to bother.

The road snaked upwards in great sinuous curves and Anamar thought of the racing cyclists grinding their way up these passes on the Tour de France. Hank had seen Pyrenean stages of the race before the war. He had told her about the fanatical support of the huge crowd of spectators, who would paint the names of their favourite riders on the road, on the way up to the passes. They would line the route at the col, roaring encouragement, handing out newspapers for the riders to stuff inside their shirts, to help keep the wind off on the descent. It was hard to imagine the pageant of the race on her lone trek, with not a sign of another human being, but the courage of the riders strengthened her own resolve. If they could do it on bikes, she could surely manage it on her own two feet.

There were sheep and cattle on the high pastures, pretending not to notice her. The horses were obviously aware of her presence, some pulling away to put distance between her and them, others ambling slowly towards her, as if enjoying the company. The descent was nothing like as steep and was marked by a series of wayside statues of Christ on the Cross.

By mid-afternoon she had decided how she might shake off her phantom stalker. She would spend the night in the village of Ste-Marie de Campan and make it known that she intended to stay the next night in La Mongie. It was an obvious place to stop on the way up to the Col du Tourmalet, nearly two thousand feet higher than any of the passes she had climbed since Aulus-les-Bains.

Arriving in La Mongie, she would find a room and go to bed for an hour, pretending that she was staying here. She would explain to her host what she was doing, asking him to tell anyone who enquired, that she had gone to bed early and would not be leaving until late next morning. She would then pay for the room and leave by the back door in the evening. It would take over an hour to make the steep climb to the pass where she knew there was an inn. She would eat and sleep there, leaving very early to make the long trek down the valley to Luz-St-Sauveur. Since Ramón had left her on her own, she had been too easy to follow. By the time her stalker discovered that the bird had flown, she would be long gone.

On the way into Ste-Marie she passed a small chapel dedicated to St Roch, yet another pilgrim shrine along the way. Ste-Marie de Campan was tiny. Plaques on the wall of the church listed the dead of the two World Wars. In 1914-18, thirty-eight men from the area had been killed and in 1939-45, only three. She remembered Hank telling her that over six million French people had been killed or wounded in the First World War.

Then she spotted a simple water fountain of cut stone. It was dated 1856 and, above its two small pipes, was the pilgrims' emblem again, the scallop shell. The inn was opposite the church and quite busy. Anamar had spotted its attic room with two wooden dormer windows, neatly fret-worked, brightly painted in red and blue. To her delight, the woman showed her upstairs and lifted the latch to that very room. It was as if her cheerful mood had earned her this perfect place to spend the night.

Next morning, it was a leisurely start through meadows. There was time to linger by the river, to listen to the birds, to look for butterflies. The traffic on the road was mainly horse-drawn carts driving to and from

Campan. She exchanged waves and greetings with the farmers. In contrast to the previous solitary days, it was almost like having company as she walked.

The road steepened out of the meadows and there were waterfalls on the way up. She was able to see a long way back towards the village and in the distance spotted a tiny figure, walking quickly, carrying a stick. It was probably a man, although it was hard to be sure, it was so far away. Anamar was surprised she was not afraid that it might be the stalker. If it was, she had a surprise for him.

She arrived at La Mongie and took a room at the tiny inn at the upper edge of the village. When she told the innkeeper and his wife of her suspicion they wanted to telephone the police Then she explained her plan to leave him behind and they laughed, assuring her of their co-operation.

After an hour's rest in bed, Anamar had a light meal of soup, bread and cured ham and sat talking to her hosts until evening. Before she left, the innkeeper went out for a few minutes and returned with the news that there was a second walker staying in the village, a man of middle-age, dark-haired, keeping his distance, speaking only when spoken to.

Anamar paid the bill and slipped out of the back door of the inn. She followed a farm track up the valley for half an hour before taking to the road. It was still light and she was able to see the route twisting up towards the pass, hidden in thick mist. It was hard going but the brief stay at La Mongie had refreshed her.

She marvelled at the skill of those who had built this road. There had been a track across this col for hundreds of years. It curved upwards, lifting the traveller from one level to another as easily as possible, making use of the hollows and ramps of the slope, taking the line of least resistance. The modern road builders would simply have followed the faultless line of the ancient path.

The carriageway was clear of snow but there were big patches across the mountainside. She walked up into dense mist and had to keep to the road. Suddenly she came out above the white vapour and could see that it was low cloud which now filled the whole valley, hiding La Mongie and the forests below. The light was fading and she was almost surrounded by big mountains. There were eight of them to her left. Before, she had seen them from afar, now she was amongst the High Pyrenees.

There was much more snow when she reached the Col du Tourmalet but the pass was clear, the light just good enough to read the altitude sign. It said '2115 metres', nearly six and a half thousand feet, more than twice as high as the mountains of Donegal. The inn at the crest of the col was closed, but some way down on the other side, the lights were on in a bar and there were two cars parked in front of it.

Anamar opened the heavy door and stepped into a room lit by oil lamps, which was both bar and dining room. There was a log fire at one end and, directly in front of it, a group of four men and four women were being served dinner by a burly man wearing a white apron and a chef's hat. All the heads turned towards Anamar, amazed to see her arrive at this time of the night. The chatter ceased. The guests watched in silence as the man in the chef's hat set down his serving platter and greeted her.

'Welcome to Chez Poudri,' he said quietly, 'What can we do for you?'

His accent was unfamiliar and Anamar had to strain to make out what he was saying. She explained that she had walked from Campan that day and was going on to Luz-St-Sauveur in the morning. He showed her upstairs to a simple room and suggested that she come down right away to eat. Anamar hung her rucksack on the hook behind the door to keep it out of reach of mice, and sat down on the edge of the bed. Her stalker would never find her here.

When she came downstairs, the group of guests called her to the table, shifting noisily to make room. They were all about her own age, friendly, talking loudly, sometimes three or four of them at the same time. One of the men filled her soup bowl from a huge tureen and another poured her a tumbler-full of red wine. They introduced themselves in hilarious fashion, with Anamar not sure whether she was hearing their real names or nick-names or joke names just invented for the evening.

The man in the chef's hat grilled the lamb chops on a grid over embers raked to the front of the fire. By the time they were served, Anamar was in conversation with the girl sitting directly opposite, who seemed to be called Fi-Fi. As the two of them talked, others began to listen and Anamar found herself telling them where she was from and why she was in France. She mentioned her stay in Paris, her trip to the South and her time at Ramón's village. The man in the chef's hat drew up a chair and joined them. She talked about her pilgrimage walk so far and they listened in silence, except for a few respectful questions and gasps of astonishment. She made no mention, however, of her stalker.

Suddenly she began to feel embarrassed by the deferential way they were responding to her and tried to change the subject. She asked them where they were from and what they were doing here. They all lived in Bordeaux and were on a touring holiday in the Pyrenees. They had motored over some of the passes she had crossed on foot and were eating here before driving down to Luz-St-Sauveur where they had booked rooms for the night.

The man in the chef's hat willingly refilled the wine bottles before they were empty. It was only a few steps to the barrel in the corner, but the trek to the kitchen for supplies of cheese, bread and water for the table was beginning to tell. He refreshed himself with deep draughts of wine. He set his hat at a jaunty angle, traded insults with the men, flirted with the girls, smiled winningly at Anamar, grabbed Fi-Fi around the waist when she knocked his hat off.

The conversation rose to a roar. A haunting song from one of the men silenced the clamour for a few moments. Three of the girls began to pirouette in a solemn dance, the rhythm set by clapping hands, and a space was cleared to let them all join in. It was easy, compared to Irish dancing. A slow step followed by a skip and a hop on the turn was the basic movement and Anamar was soon as proficient as any of them.

Another of the men rose to do his party piece. Anamar recognised it immediately. It was an impression of Monsieur Hulot, the creation of the French actor Jacques Tati. She had seen one of his films in Ballyshannon with Deirdre.

Like Tati, the man was tall and thin and wore a smart pullover and jacket, his trousers at half-mast, a tweed hat on his head. A slim, elegant, unlit pipe, like Hulot's, clamped between his teeth, waved like a conductor's baton. He postured and strutted around with Hulot's stiff-legged walk, doffing his hat to the ladies. He crawled around on his hands and knees apparently searching for some minute item lost on the floor. He found it impossible to sit on a chair without falling off, involving them all in hilarious confusion, as they had to move seats to let him find one he could stay on.

But in spite of her elation at the great night's craic, Anamar was not at ease. Once the group left, she would be on her own here with a man she had just met. Someone suggested that it was time to go, but it was half an hour later before they all began to move. Fi-Fi followed the man in the chef's hat into the kitchen, carrying some of the dishes. A quarter of an hour later, as the others were already going out through the door, they emerged, flushed and giggling. The man in the chef's hat strutted around like a rooster with something to crow about. Fi-Fi wagged a finger at Anamar, obviously seeing a look on her new friend's face of which Anamar was unaware. The two girls embraced,

'You'll be all right with him,' Fi-Fi said, with a wink and a nod towards the sweating patron, 'He'll attend to all your needs!'

She laughed loudly and Anamar blushed, her mind confused as Fi-Fi linked her arm to the door. The cars took off, wheels spurting gravel. In seconds their lights were gone and and the sound of their engines a faint rumble from the road below. Anamar went inside and closed the door. The man in the chef's hat removed it and held it in front of himself like a trophy. His head was bald in the shape of a monk's tonsure. Little beads of perspiration, in tight clusters, glistened on his scalp. He was sitting to one side of the fire. Anamar sat down on the bench at the other side and began to tell him how much she had enjoyed meeting the group. He wasn't listening.

'Call me Poudri,' he said, interrupting, 'I live here by myself and you travel alone. We should be friends.' He walked across to her and held out a hand.

Anamar folded her arms and looked at the fire. He sat down beside her and touched her hair lightly with the back of his fingers.

'Don't be afraid,' he said quietly, 'I will protect you in this lonely place.'

Anamar sensed that he was about to put an arm around her shoulders and, as she stood up, the arm encircled her hips. She turned away from it and Poudri almost fell off the bench as his hug missed its mark.

'I think I should pay you now,' she said firmly, 'I intend to leave at six in the morning and won't need breakfast. You'll be able to sleep late.'

Poudri pretended not to understand.

'But you are my guest,' he said, 'You are on a pilgrimage. Why should I charge you for food and lodging. You are my beautiful Irish pilgrim. Have some more wine.'

Anamar had to take the glass in case he spilt it on her clothes and then stepped back out of reach. She hadn't drunk as much as Fi-Fi or the others but the five or six glasses she'd had were much more than usual and certainly enough for one night. She saw the official tariff sheet on the wall and left exactly the amount shown for one night's demi-pension on the table in front of him.

'Bonsoir Monsieur Poudri,' she said trying not to sound annoyed, 'I'm going to bed.'

There was an oil lamp on a window ledge and she took it to light the way, climbing the stairs without hurry in case it gave the impression that she was rushing away. There was a window ledge beside her room and she set the lamp on it to have both hands free to open the door.

Bending to pick it up again, a body hurtled against her from behind. An arm was flung around her neck, a knee pressed hard into the small of her back. She clawed at the arm, choking for breath. Then she found a power she never knew she had. Weeks later she described it to Deirdre Ryan as a blinding mist of rage before her eyes.

She grabbed the man's free arm with both hands and smashed it against the edge of the window ledge. The sound of flesh on stone was a sickening thud. There was a scream of pain and rage. Hot blood fell on her sandal. The forearm around her neck released its grip and she turned to see Poudri reeling against the wall, clutching his bleeding arm, shouting obscenities.

Inside the room she locked the door and pulled the chest of drawers and the bed against it. Her rucksack was still unpacked, hanging on its hook. Moving quietly, she lifted it down, slipped her arms through its straps, grabbed her stick and opened the window which looked out to one side of the inn.

The sky was clear, a moon in its third quarter lit the road and the mountain side and glistened on big patches of snow. There was a lean-to shed directly below the window and she threw her stick to the ground beyond it.

As she began to ease herself out of the window, backwards, feet first, she heard Poudri's footsteps pounding on the stairs. He began to batter the door with what sounded like a sledge hammer. She slid down the sloping roof of the shed, dropped to the ground and retrieved her stick. Running down the road, she heard the crash of splintering wood and, seconds later, she turned to see Poudri's face at the window, his one good arm shaking an axe at her.

Anamar slowed her run to a trot. Tucking the stick under her arm, she slipped her thumbs through the straps of her rucksack to stop it bumping on her back. There was not the slightest doubt that she could out-run the portly Poudri down this road. When there were sports at home, only Eamon could run faster. At harvest time and lifting potatoes in the Autumn, she could work as hard and as long as any of the boys.

Then she remembered seeing an old truck around the other side of the house when she had arrived. Poudri had transport. It would be better to leave the road soon and take to the mountainside.

It only took a moment to stop and find the little torch in her rucksack. Ramón's map clearly showed, that although the road went down the left hand side of the valley, her route branched off it and followed a track on the other side of the river.

As she reached the track she saw the lights of a vehicle coming down from the pass. A big rock gave her cover and she watched as the truck roared past the track turn-off without a pause.

The moon's light enabled Anamar to see the road and the main features of the mountainside but it was not bright enough to allow her to run on rough ground. She avoided the banks of snow and a shallow ford led across the river. The sandals gave her a good footing on the gravel bed. The water was icy but it washed Poudri's blood from her foot. Instead of following the path downstream on the other side, she turned right and climbed to a vantage point where she could conceal herself behind a group of big boulders.

In a few minutes the lights of the truck reappeared, coming up the valley. Poudri had realised the she must have left the road for the track. The truck wheeled off the road when it reached the junction and lumbered down towards the river as far as it was possible to drive.

The engine spluttered and stopped. Poudri climbed down from the cab and crossed the river on foot, carrying something in one hand. It looked like a thick staff. Then she saw the moonlight flash on metal. It must be a gun, probably the hunting rifle from the wall above the fireplace at the inn.

Poudri climbed on a rock and looked down the valley. He started downhill keeping to the track, rushing for a few strides, then having to stop in case he tripped. After ten minutes he had disappeared in the half-light.

Anamar's feet were numb with cold. She shivered with fear and the chill of the night air. She slipped on her spare shirt and her sweater. Her feet and sandals were still wet from the river crossing, so she dried them with her towel and put them on again with her socks. Pulling her cape over her head and tucking it around her legs kept the heat in. There was no way of telling how long she would have to stay here but this was a comfortable spot. There was good cover, too, and an excellent view down the valley.

She thought about the stalker and found herself smiling at her efforts to out-wit him. But suppose he meant her no harm. Maybe he was her guardian angel, looking after her along the way. And now he was tucked up in his bed at La Mongie, thinking she was safely asleep in the same village. Nobody would believe her if she ever made it back home. She could hear her friends laughing and Maggie would lead the teasing,

'And there you were perched out on the mountainside at midnight, with all your belongings in a wee bag on your back, trying to escape a maniac in a chef's hat carrying a hunting rifle,' she would be saying, 'But sure you've always had a talent for hair-brained adventures. What about the time you headed off into the mountains and lived in a cave for a month at Lough Belshade? When you headed off on the parish pilgrimage to Lourdes, there was your fancy man, F.B. O'Boyle, who thought all he had to do was offer you the ring and you'd jump at the chance to marry him? You must have given him some sort of encouragement.

'What about the time you had to sit out a thunderstorm in a wee tent on the top of the Pyrenees and nobody to hold your hand but your ex-GI, Hank? And when he came all the way to Donegal to be with you, the first thing you did was to head off on another daft pilgrimage nobody has ever heard of. Oh you have a talent for the peculiar, all right. Nobody could ever accuse our Anamar of doing the sensible thing.'

At home there was nothing like this atmosphere of the still night in high mountains. The terrain of snow and rock seemed to have absorbed all sound. The silence was so profound, the air so cold, the moonlight so silvern, they disoriented the senses. All previous experience was challenged, all perception changed. It was as if Anamar was a natural element of this habitat, closer to the sky, breathing pure air, her body vitalised by the cold, her mind exhilarated by the adventure.

A noise behind her head set her heart racing but it was a small deer, probably the Pyrenean chamois, crunching across a snowfield about a hundred yards away. Two more came out of the darkness and filed unto the white apron like a stage. Then a group of about a dozen appeared and the fawns amongst them began to play chasing games, dashing up and down the snow just for the fun of it.

Suddenly they all stopped, heads turned in the same direction. Something below had startled them, neither heard nor seen by Anamar. In seconds they were gone, darting uphill into the darkness.

Although she was not able to see him, Anamar knew it must be Poudri, returning from his search. Then she heard him muttering loudly to himself, his voice carrying towards her on a light breeze. She sat very still, her gaze fixed on the track. When he appeared, it was the glint of the moonlight on the gun barrel again which drew her eye to the figure clumping along beside the river.

He crossed the ford without a glance towards her lair, climbed into the truck and reversed it slowly back up to the road. Well over an hour had passed since Anamar had taken refuge behind the boulder and when she stood up she was stiff and cold. She kept the cape on. There was no heat in the garment itself but it kept the cold air off the upper part of her body. Her eyes were now well used to the light and she made good time on the descent.

She saw the ruins of an ancient settlement. The cabins were roofed with sods and the stone walls of the two corrals were so high she guessed they must have been to protect the animals rather than keep them penned in. Poudri's footsteps in the snow led down to the river and it looked as though he had crossed it to search the ruins.

Flowing down the steep slope to her right and into the river there were tributary streams to be forded and she took off her socks at the first. Further on there was the roar of rushing water and, cresting a low ridge, she found the way barred by a mountain torrent. It had cut deeply into the mountainside and was in shadow. It was very hard to see the stepping stones which led to the path on the other side. Anamar took out the torch again, careful to keep it pointing downwards. The stick was a great help, but there were a few anxious moments before she reached the other side. It would not do to fall in and get her clothes wet at this stage of the night.

The next torrent was even more intimidating. Some way off she could hear the crash of water falling through rocks. These streams must be fed by the snow on hidden mountains far above. Anamar could see a jagged skyline of the dark peaks to her left but the slope on her side of the river was so steep the water seemed to be cascading down from the sky.

It had cut a deep cleft into the hillside and the place where the path led to a ford was in darkest shadow. The light of the torch revealed no stepping stones. Using the stick it appeared to be knee deep. She remembered Hank saying that it was not the depth of the raging stream which was dangerous, but the force of the water.

She took off her cape and packed it in her rucksack. The torch had a lanyard. She hung it around her neck, switched it on and gripped the stick with both hands. Hank's instructions were to use the staff on the downside, to move it only when both feet were securely positioned, to step forward only when the staff was firmly planted. She kept her sandals on and tucked her skirt up inside her knickers. The way they used to at home when they were children playing on the beach at Bundoran.

The water was as cold as a glacier stream. It rushed against her legs, foaming up her thighs with a force she had to fight against with all her might. It was one step at a time. The torch light flickered around her legs. Her right foot banged against a hidden rock and she would have been down but for the staff.

Half-way across she had to pause, staff and both feet planted, to gather her strength. The power of the torrent was at its greatest here. She moved with tiny steps, lurching from one to the next. It needed her full concentration. Drive the staff into the stream bed, take one step, then another, move the stick again but only when both feet felt secure. She rushed the last bit and a slip as a stone moved made her stagger, but she was close enough to the bank to fall forward on to it. The torch banged on the ground. She almost dropped the stick into the water but she had made it.

It was time to fill her water bottle, put the cape on again and rest in a sheltered hollow, cradling her legs with her arms. There was no feeling in her feet as she dried them and tried to put on her socks. She hugged each foot in turn against her thigh to warm it and dried the inside of her sandals. It had been a hard crossing and she said a prayer that it might be the last along this route.

A dog barked on the other side of the valley. The sound of cow bells clanging quietly led her down to silent cabins, all on the low side of the track. They were built into the hillside with stone walls, huge, heavy slates on the roofs, solid wooden doors. The upper storey, usually the hay loft, was accessible from the track but the living quarters were in the lower storey and reached from below.

There were mules and goats in the fields as well as cows and, farther on, one of the cabins looked abandoned. Its door was open, as was the hay loft. Anamar suddenly felt tired and thirsty. She drank deeply from her water bottle, made a bed in the hay and allowed herself to doze for half an hour before continuing the descent.

It was lighter now and a good wooden bridge led to the silent village of Barèges. It was obviously both ski resort and spa from the signs, but all was shuttered and barred. Anamar walked down the middle of the street, stepping quietly so that no one would be disturbed. She kept to the road and half an hour later was startled by the sound of a vehicle coming behind her. She pushed herself into a bush at the roadside and watched. It was a small dark blue van and, if the driver saw her, he gave no indication.

Over an hour later dawn was breaking and Anamar walked into Luz-St-Sauveur. A sign post, pointing the way she had come, indicated that it was thirty-seven kilometres to Ste-Marie de Campan.

Even in the early morning light, Luz looked an interesting town. Ramón had told her that its fortified church was one of the wonders of her pilgrimage. Although it was only half past six, it was open already, presumably for early Mass. The way in was through a tower in its outer wall and by the main door of the church itself.

Anamar sat down in a pew and laid her rucksack on the bench beside her. This was another haven, warm and welcoming, even the wooden seats were comfortable. She was aware of the presence of God in this place. In other churches on the journey she had been sincere in her worship but doubted that now. Had she merely been going through the motions? Solely concerned with the rituals of her devotions? And was it not the unthinking rote and rhyme of religion which caused her most concern with her faith? Father Brian had made a point of telling her that pilgrims could find themselves so intent on making their pilgrimage, they neglected their devotions to Our Lord.

She stretched out her legs, dozed for a few moments and suddenly jerked awake, trembling violently. Her legs shook. Her body shuddered. Try as she might, the quivering continued, almost out of control. The door behind her opened and a priest rushed to her aid.

'Please don't worry,' she was able to say, 'I had an accident earlier and this must be delayed-action shock.'

He brought her a glass of water and asked no questions. In minutes the shaking stopped, leaving her exhausted. She thanked the priest and he directed her to a café nearby. With a large café crème and crusty slices of fresh bread on the table, she felt much better. Mass would have to wait to much later in the day.

Thus far she had been travelling West. Now having reached Luz, her route turned south to take her over the main range of the Pyrenees into Spain. Her plan, however, was to make a detour by bus to the north, to Lourdes, where Raoul and Paul from Paris should be coming to meet her. They had offered to accompany her over the Pyrenees and should be arriving in Lourdes the next day. Together they would return to Luz by bus and join the route there on foot.

The nine A.M. bus was half full and Anamar slipped in and out of sleep as it trundled down the valley. When it reached Lourdes she walked to the bridge at the entrance to the Domain of the Grotto and found the Hotel St Jacques beside it. Once booked in, she went to bed right away, wakened in time for Mass and a meal in the early evening, and went back to bed again, to sleep the sleep of the truly tired.

LOURDES

Anamar wakened with the sun's rays lighting her room. She stretched full length in the bed and felt good. Poudri's attack and her night flight down the valley might have happened in the distant past. Only her feet felt sore. Walking in wet sandals had chafed the skin on the top of each foot. She shook powder into the socks and put them on. They would give the feet a chance to recover. To-morrow the socks would need to be washed!

In need of a breath of fresh air, she came downstairs and went outside into the sunshine. Two bearded men were standing beside a wall, arguing loudly, gesturing, unaware that they were being watched. They were dressed in dark brown cloaks and knee breeches with large felt hats. The only modern touch was their walking boots. Each held a staff at least a foot taller than himself and shook it in his companion's face.

Anamar smiled in amusement at the comical sight of these figures in ancient costume, bickering in public. Were they supposed to be advertising a medieval play? Were they part of a pageant? Then she saw the scallop shells on their hats. They were dressed as pilgrims, as Santiago pilgrims. They saw her watching and one of them left his stick against the wall and and ran towards her, arms outstretched, shouting in French,

'Anamar! Anamar! Here we are! It's your brother pilgrims, ready for the road.'

He grabbed her in a hug. His hat fell off. It was Raoul. Raoul in a beard. Anamar stepped back from him, speechless, hoping it was just a bad dream. The other figure joined them. It must be Paul behind a huge, black beard. They held her hands and danced in front of her. She tried to speak,

'Just a minute boys. Hold on. Give me a chance.' In the confusion she was unaware she was speaking in English.

Then the words came, and in a flow of French she never knew she had. Here they were, before their very first steps on the pilgrimage, and they were making a show of her. Had they no idea what she was trying to do? That this was a journey of the spirit? This French farce was making a fool of her. She felt sick with rage.

Anamar had never been so angry in her whole life. Her face was flushed. She stamped her foot. She shook her fist in their faces. She told them that she had not spent the past twelve days crossing the mountain passes on her own two feet to be insulted by this charade.

The boys reeled back in the face of her fury. They tried to apologise but Anamar shook her head. She was not listening, she told them. They would be wasting their time with excuses. They could go where they liked as long as they got out of her sight. They could take themselves back to Paris. She would cross the high pass into Spain on her own.

Paul began to cry. There was something ludicrous about a bearded man in tears that almost made Anamar laugh in derision. He began to pull off the moustache, then the sideburns and finally the huge black bush that covered his chin. Anamar knew then that it was the false beards which had made her so angry. It had to be the lowest moment of the whole journey.

When Poudri had attacked her, her blood was up. At no time did she feel that he would catch her. This was much worse. The boys had no idea why she was on the pilgrimage. To them it was all a joke. She had taken them into her confidence in Paris and they were making an eedjit of her. Friends of Father Brian should have known better than this.

She turned away and climbed the stone steps to the bridge. The Domain of Our Lady was quiet at this time of the morning and she walked through to the Grotto. Beyond the baths, she sat down on a grass bank near the statue of St Margaret, Queen and Patroness of Scotland, and looked out over the river.

It was hard to be angry here. Maybe the boys were right. The Road to Santiago was just a pageant for people playing at being pilgrims and she wasn't even in traditional dress. On her own, doubts had been easily dispelled. When Celestine had challenged her, she had done so without diminishing her quest. When Father Brian and Ramón had questioned her resolve, they had done so as friends.

But this was different. Was it worth going on? It would be easy to take a train back to Alban-les-Saintes for the summer. Yvette would be delighted to see her. She could help out at the hostel, But what about Father Brian and Ramón? They had given her their time. They believed she would do it. What about her promise to herself and the memory of her Granny Mac? Had she not resolved to be a pilgrim before she left Ireland, before she knew anything about the Road to Santiago?

Hunger took her out of the Domain and back across the bridge. Paul and Raoul were packing their luggage on their bicycles outside the hotel. There was no sign of the staffs or the costumes. She stopped and leaned against the parapet. The bikes each had a tiny motor fixed over the back wheel to make it easier to pedal, but it was five or six hundred miles from Paris. It must have taken them four or five days to travel here.

She went down the steps and walked towards them. Paul turned away when he saw her, hiding his face. She guessed he was still trying to hold back the tears. Raoul went into the hotel and returned with a package wrapped in brown paper.

'We were going to leave some things we brought for you for the climb over the Pyrenees.' He gave her the parcel, 'Don't worry, it's not another pilgrim costume.'

He held it while she undid the wrapper. There was a pair of walking boots, with thick socks, woollen gloves and hat, and a proper mountaineer's anorak like Hank's.

'It was too much to carry on the bicycles,' said Paul, still trying not to cry, 'We sent it by post with our cloaks and hats.'

Anamar turned away for a moment. Her eyes were pricking. If she had been too hard on them, she now found it impossible to say anything that would make it easier. However, they had demonstrated their friendship by coming here and bringing her kit for crossing the high pass. She put an arm around each of them,

'All right,' she said, 'I'll give you one more chance. Come on and I'll treat you to breakfast. I'm starving.'

During the day they followed her everywhere she went, first to buy a small glass bottle with a good stopper, then to fill it with water at the Grotto. Paul found a priest to bless it. When she visited Ramón's parents this would be her gift to his mother.

Paul was interested in ancient fortifications and delighted to hear they were going to Lourdes' Castle, set on a rocky height above the town. But this was not a tourist trip. Ramón had strongly advised Anamar to make the visit.

At the top of the castle, to one side of a spacious courtyard, was the Chapelle Notre Dame du Chateau, built at the end of the 17th century. As soon as she stepped through the door Anamar saw the statue. It was another ornate plaster figure, embellished in gold, dressed in typical pilgrim style with a long staff and a gourd. Although the shells were no longer in place, there were distinct outlines of three scallop shells side by side on the upturned brim of the hat. Underneath, the legend said, St Jacques de Pelerin.

Anamar was elated. This was why Ramón had insisted she go to see the castle. It was another link in the chain of clues leading her on. In a strange way, it made the antics of Raoul and Paul no longer offensive.

Back at the hotel the boys unpacked their bicycles and, before they were stored in the basement of the hotel, Anamar insisted that she would have a ride. Raoul started the little motor for her and the bike shot off like a runaway colt. She clung on to the handle-bars. The boys stood on the bridge and watched her hurtling down the street towards them on the first circuit, still not in full control.

Next time she appeared, it was from the opposite direction and there was much more traffic. But the bike could go where cars, buses and horse-drawn carriages could not. She sped through tiny gaps, mounted the pavement, dodged around pedestrians, nearly ran over Raoul's feet, narrowly missed a souvenir stand. People were looking at them.

As she passed on the next lap the boys howled at her to stop, afraid she would crash, but the only response was a cheery wave and a dramatic wobble, caused by one-handed steering. It took her directly across the road on a charmed path through the traffic and down a side street. Two laps later she came into view with both legs off the pedals, sticking straight out from the sides of the bike, demonstrating that she was not doing the work. Two more laps and the test ride was over. As she dismounted, Anamar announced that when she went home after the pilgrimage, her first purchase would be 'a wee motor for the back wheel of her bike'.

If the boys thought that lending her the bike for this escapade would restore them to Anamar's favour, they were mistaken. She told them that they were going to evening Mass with her and they made a great show of willingness which all three of them knew was entirely bogus.

Later they ate in a small restaurant in the upper town, and only interrupted Anamar with respectful questions when she was telling them about her journey so far. They listened in silence when they heard how she had outwitted the phantom stalker, just at the time when she needed him to protect her from Poudri. The story was told in such a matter-of-fact way, neither of them knew whether to laugh or be angry for her. And Anamar was of no help to them at all.

After dark, they joined the evening candle-light procession through the Domain of Our Lady. Paul and Raoul had ceased to attend any form of religious observance when they became students, but they took part in the ceremony as if they had never been away. They held their candles high. They joined the singing at the tops of their voices, feeling they were meant to be part of this throng.

On the way back to the hotel the boys were very quiet, still chastened, still wary of this fearsome Irish girl. Next morning, going to Luz by bus, Raoul sat beside her and Paul was in the seat behind with the rucksacks, his head peeping over the backs of their seats, determined not to be left out of the conversation.

Although Anamar was allowed to take her stick on to the bus, the driver had insisted that the boys' big staffs should be stowed in the luggage compartment. In their excitement they forgot to collect them when they alighted at Luz and Anamar waited for a few moments until the bus was about to move off, before reminding them. They dropped their rucksacks and scurried back, waving and shouting to the driver. To their great relief, Anamar was laughing when they returned.

'I could take you nowhere,' she said, 'I'd need to lead the both of you on ropes with bull rings through your noses.'

The boys laughed, still not really sure that it was permitted. They were neatly dressed in shorts, short-sleeved shirts and walking boots. The extra gear they had brought for Anamar had been packed, at their insistence, in their large rucksacks, but when Anamar hefted one to feel its weight, it was nothing like as heavy as it looked.

There was, however, further evidence of the thaw. She took them to see the fortified church of Saint-André in the centre of Luz, her church, her refuge after her night flight from the inn at Tourmalet, her haven. Had they but known, her willingness to share this sacred place with them signified that she had forgiven their antics in Lourdes. Her closest friends would have known, however, that although she might be prepared to forgive that lapse, to forget it was another matter entirely.

Paul could hardly contain himself. Saint-André was part of his university course at the Sorbonne. He maintained that it was the best preserved fortified church in France. The Knights Templar had built it in the 12th century, when they were the protectors of pilgrims on the road to Santiago. The order had been suppressed in 1314 and the Knights of St

John of Jerusalem had taken it over removing all trace of the Templars who had once been their brothers in Christ.

He took on the role of tour guide, pointing out the deep wooden balcony at the back, its weight supported by two iron pillars. He showed them the intricate carving and gilding of the pulpit, attached high on a side wall. He explained the significance of the brilliant paintings behind the altar.

Anamar looked up to examine a roof arch. Footsteps on the staircase caught her attention and she saw that Raoul had climbed the narrow steps to the pulpit. He had just begun to act the part of a fearsome priest in full flow when he saw the look on her face. He paused, put his hands together in prayer and genuflected towards the altar. Anamar smiled weakly. As they left the building Paul pointed out the narrow doorway, used only by what he called 'the accursed race', the Cagots.

Outside in the square, they were finding it hard to see the church in its entirety because of the surrounding buildings. A woman called to them from the doorway of a hotel on the south side.

'You are following Le Chemin du St Jacques?' She made the question sound like an answer and shook their hands. When the boys queried how she knew, she pointed to the scallop shells attached to the backs of their rucksacks..

'You carry the badge of the pilgrim.'

The boys were so proud of themselves. They had yet to take the first step along the road and already they had been recognised as pilgrims. For Anamar, it was another moment of pure joy, like her first sighting of a pilgrim statue in the church at Aulus-les-Bains. But since she and Ramón had set out on the first day, no one had mentioned the significance of her shell.

The woman took them upstairs to a front bed-room. No wonder the hotel was called after the ramparts. It overlooked the castellated walls, the church itself, the bell tower, the keep which guarded the entrance gate with its vertical openings for dropping stones or boiling oil on attackers. From here it looked smaller, more compact, but undoubtedly a formidable fortress. Paul was so busy with his sketch book he had to suspend his lecture on the history of the church.

Pigeons flew in and out of the higher windows. Paul looked up from his pad and reminded them that there had been traces of a wooden gallery inside the church, just below these windows, showing that archers and musketeers would have used them at times of attack.

The woman introduced herself as Madame Fleurie and invited them to have some soup with her before they left. It was a simple hotel and the dining room was furnished with bare wooden tables and chairs. The walls were completely covered with a magnificent mural which stretched from one wall to the next and right around the room.

Deirdre Ryan's artist friend might have called the style 'naive' but, taken literally, that would have done less than justice to the bold colours and the dramatic scenes depicted.

A girl with a pitcher on her head descended steps from a house. A river flowed down through a bridge in a rocky valley, fed by high snow-capped peaks which ringed a glacier. A shepherd standing on a prominent rock watched his flock. Figures in traditional costume were depicted outside their cottages on a day when no work was being done.

But most startling of all was the painting with the church of Saint-André as the centre-piece. The nearby houses were half-timbered with wooden balconies in typical French Pyrenean style. The church was seen from street level, a bastion below high peaks, at the heart of the village. It was little different from its present state but able to be shown at its best.

Madame Fleurie served the soup with bread and a glass of wine and took great delight in their appreciation of the mural. Later, Anamar would be cross with herself for not asking about the origins of the painting. When had it been done? Who was the painter? Was he famous? Why was it here in this house?

Madame Fleurie came with them out of the Luz part of the town as far as the marble bridge over the river Gave. A narrow gorge led south towards Gavarnie and although the main road was on the east side of the river, she recommended that they cross to the west side and walk through the Saint-Sauveur quarter of the town.

Before they parted, Madame Fleurie turned to the boys and gestured to them to stop. With a sideways look at Anamar she told them that they must not wear shorts in Spain, not even in the mountains. The boys laughed, unimpressed, it would be just another opportunity to show that they dressed as they pleased. Madame Fleurie was incensed by the insensitivity of the young.

'In Spain, shorts are permitted only on the beach.' she said angrily, 'Dressed as you are, you will be arrested by the frontier guards as soon as you descend to their post on the Spanish side.'

Then another thought crossed her mind and she smiled serenely,

'They will search your bags for magazines with pictures of nude girls,' she said, 'And nude boys!' she added, with a wink at Anamar.

She stood waving as they climbed the road towards the first of a row of once elegant hotels and Anamar wondered what Madame Fleurie was thinking. She seemed so reluctant to part from them. In a few minutes she had become their friend. She seemed so interested in the Road of St James. Would she have liked to walk a part of the way with them? Should she have asked her to come as far as Gavarnie, the last village before the pass to Spain?

It was obvious that Saint-Sauveur was a health spa and nearly every building, apart from the spa itself, was an hotel. A few had been recently painted, others had little to offer except evidence of a glorious past. Anamar and the boys strolled by, watched with interest by those who were here for the cure. Beyond the buildings there was a rocky area with woodland and a wild flower garden. A little sign said, 'Le Jardin Anglais'. The road turned left and crossed the deep gorge of the Gave on a spectacular stone bridge, high above the water.

Raoul knew its history and, to her amazement, Anamar found herself allowing him to persuade her to go back to one of the hotels and have a coffee. A detour from the route was one thing but this was backtracking! The boys obviously intended to enjoy the walk and were going to see that she did too. It was only twenty kilometres to Gavarnie, Raoul said, and four hours walking would take them there.

The boys had been competing for Anamar's attention since the previous evening and it was now Raoul's turn. He knew about Saint-Sauveur and its bridge. As a young man his father had worked in one of the hotels here. This was one of the most famous spas in France. It had been popular since the beginning of the 18th century. Napoléon the Third was a frequent visitor, his father had said, when he was telling him the story of the bridge.

Some years before, Napoléon's mother, Hortense, had come to stay in the area and had been seduced by her coachman when on a visit to Gavarnie. Court gossip had it, of course, that Hortense had been the seducer. The child was born in Saint-Sauveur and, in his turn, became Napoléon. The building of the bridge had been ordered by the Emperor to commemorate his birth here.

It was a magnificent construction, a single, semi-circular span of stone, over twenty metres in diameter, across the ravine, sixty-five metres above the river Gave. In its day, it was a sensation, one of the wonders of the Pyrenees.

Paul was laughing behind his hand. Deirdre Ryan would have called it 'sniggering' and would have disapproved. Raoul paused in his story.

'He saw it on the plaque above the bridge.' Paul said accusingly. 'He thought I didn't see him reading it. He's making the rest up.'

Raoul was very angry.

'Of course I saw the plaque.' he said, 'But my father did work here and he told me the story of Napoléon's mother.' He walked out of the café in case he lost his temper in front of Anamar, and waited outside.

Anamar finished her coffee in silence, secretly hoping that the boys had stopped speaking to each other. Maybe they would give her head peace on the way to Gavarnie.

It was uphill but easy walking. The narrow road followed the gorge. In places it went through tunnels and along a ledge which had been drilled and blasted out of the mountainside above the river. There were huge waterfalls dropping into the Gave. Thickets of trees grew on terrain which seemed too steep and too stony to allow any vegetation to survive.

After two hours of silent walking the gorge opened out into a broader area and they reached the village of Gèdre. Raoul's face lit up in a huge smile. Far to the South, just visible between the lower mountains, he saw the wall of high, snow-capped peaks, broken by the famous Brèche de Roland. He took hold of Anamar's arm to get her attention. He grabbed Paul by the shoulders and pointed him towards the view. All was forgiven. The boys hugged each other in delight.

Above Gèdre the route wound up the ravine past a glorious cascade, the highest yet. They kept to the verge as a steady stream of buses brought the day-trippers from Gavarnie back to Lourdes. The road here threaded its way through the debris of eons of avalanched rock and crossed a river by a white marble bridge below the village.

It was a place where even the most urgent of walkers would have to stop to look at the view. But Anamar turned away from the rugged skyline.

Her eye caught sight of a bronze figure in a niche in the rock. It was a statue of Count Henri Russell, the son of a French mother and a father from County Down and the distant relative of May Ferguson, the Methodist minister's wife in Donegal. This was the man Hank claimed had been the greatest pioneer of mountaineering in the Pyrenees.

Anamar had been here before. Two years ago, when she had first met Hank in Lourdes, he had brought her here on his motor-bike to climb a big mountain. She would never forget the ascent of Vignemale, according to Hank, one of the classic peaks of the Pyrenees and his favourite peak. They had climbed the beautiful valley which now lay to the right and camped for the night on a high ridge. When she returned home she must remember to tell May that her family name was still honoured in Gavarnie.

Before dawn next morning, they had set out for the summit. At the snout of the glacier Hank had tied them both to a climbing rope, kicked and cut steps with his ice axe in the frozen snow. When they reached the top it was a true summit, a space just big enough for the two of them amongst the jagged rocks with what seemed like the whole world below their feet.

It had been a long, hard day but Anamar had never known such exhilaration nor such tiredness. Hank had been in the grip of suicidal depression since the battle for the beach at St Tropez but sharing this ascent with her had drawn him back from the edge of the abyss.

Earlier in the day she had listened to Paul and Raoul demonstrating their knowledge, now it was her turn. The boys were spellbound when she told them about the climb. She spared them no detail of the difficulties. Of course, they had heard of Vignemale. They had friends who had taken them rock climbing on a cliff near Fontainbleu. But this was real mountaineering. Anamar was a mountaineer!

Had they looked her directly in the eyes, they would have seen that she was smiling. When first she had talked to them in Paris about crossing the Pyrenees, she had been aware that they saw themselves acting as guides to an inexperienced girl over a difficult pass. The ascent of Vignemale had changed all that. She was now the leader.

Gavarnie was at its best at this time of the day. The day-trippers had arrived by bus in the morning, to shop or eat or sit around and watch the other trippers. On foot, on horseback or astride a mule, many would have made the journey up the valley to see the famous Cirque de Gavarnie. It was worth the trip. The awesome ring of snow-capped cliffs above a glacier was split by a stunning waterfall, The Grande Cascade, the longest waterfall in Europe.

By the time they arrived, the crowds were melting away at the end of the afternoon The horses were walking back unattended to their stables or paddocks for their evening feed. Gavarnie had become a most pleasant place to spend an evening.

Most of the guide books were scathingly critical of Gavarnie, its trippers and horses, and, of course, the horse dung on the streets. Anamar smiled when she thought of how their comments angered Hank. He liked the village. Everyone had a right to come to admire the view, to breathe the mountain air. Only a townie would mind the manure. And Hank was also aware how important tourists had been to the local economy over the past two hundred years.

At the gîte d'étape, Anamar and the boys were allocated a room with two bunks and a single bed. They bought some food for the next day, went to Mass at six o'clock and found another fine plaster statue of a pilgrim in the church. This time it had the legend, 'Saint Jacques de Compostelle'. They were still on the pilgrim road. In the evening they had a cheerful meal of soup, mutton stew and custard tart and were in bed and asleep by ten.

THE AMBUSH AT THE PYRENEAN PASS

Anamar was wakened by the boys talking in stage whispers. They were still in their bunks, hoping that she would hear and respond. Her torch allowed her to look at her watch. It was just after five o'clock and still dark. She turned over noisily to let them know she was not yet ready to get up and pulled the coverlet over the one ear which was not sound-proofed by the pillow. At six she could stick it no longer and willed herself to get up and dress.

The boys hopped out of their bunks and began to pack. Anamar's first words were to warn them not to make too much noise, and not to put their boots on until they were leaving. They had paid the night before and slipped out of the gîte d'étape before half past six.

A good path led them out of the village, above and veering away from the main track up the valley to the Cirque. The air was cold. It was still and quiet, as if the whole valley was waiting patiently for the light of dawn. Paul rushed ahead like a youngster on a treasure hunt, and Raoul went after him with a look of apology to Anamar.

Beyond the woods, Paul suddenly stopped and stood stock still, waving gently to the others to join him. Ahead, just below where the path crossed the crest of a low ridge, were five little creatures, bigger than hares, bulkier than rabbits. The boys looked at Anamar. They had never seen animals like this before.

'Marmots.' Anamar was enjoying being knowledgeable. The French always gave the impression of being so expert about everything. 'In French it's m-a-r-m-o-t-t-e,' she added quietly, spelling the word letter by letter. 'They live in colonies, usually one acts as look-out, sitting upright like a little bear, ready to squeak loudly at any sign of danger.'

As if on cue, one of the marmots let out a series of shrill squeaks and they all scurried off to their burrow.

The sun had still not risen above the the high skyline when they reached the crest of the ridge and the path turned West. It was the perfect vantage point to see the Cirque - just far enough back to see the semi-circle of sheer black cliffs, surmounted by jagged rock and snow peaks, and split by the Grande Cascade with the glacier at its foot.

They stopped and stared. It might be a long day ahead, but they had started early. Anamar had no intention of being rushed. She decided it was time for breakfast. Paul lit the small paraffin stove and heated water in an aluminium dixie. Raoul sliced the cheese and yesterday's bread.

They sat silently, in a line facing the Cirque and ate goat's cheese, bread and honey. There was coffee for the boys and tea for Anamar. For a few moments she let herself think about the hard travelling to come. When the boys returned to France, there would be long, lonely days, times of doubt and despondency. But this was an instant of pure bliss. She was surprised that it was so difficult for her to acknowledge to herself that the experience was being enhanced because the boys were here. She could share the grandeur, the excitement, the significance of what she was trying to do.

After more than two hours steady climbing, the path zig-zagged up a scree slope. There was snow lying and the boys were beginning to labour under their big rucksacks. Anamar called a halt. Her aim was to reach the high pass before noon and by Ramón's map they were ahead of schedule. They had another stop at a small stone built cabin. It must be the refuge that gave this valley its name, Valée du Cabin des Soldats, but there were no soldiers using it on this day. The door was open and it was clean inside, probably now used by mountaineers and hunters as a shelter in bad weather.

Without explaining that she thought they needed a good rest, Anamar insisted on a much longer stop here. The boys had been finding the climbing strenuous and there was a long way to go. The sun had now risen above the cliffs and they sat in its warmth, backs against the wall of the cabin, watching marmots at the far side of the valley. They talked about what it would have been like here during the war. It was certain that German soldiers would have guarded this pass. The woman at the gîte had told them that, in spite of the guards, escaping Allied prisoners-of-war had been guided across to Spain by members of the maquis resistance.

Anamar saw the tiny figure first, miles away down the valley but following their route. Paul noticed her staring and saw the figure, too. He jumped to his feet and pointed for Raoul's benefit. But his friend dragged him down again.

'We should turn away,' he said quickly, 'If it is the phantom stalker, we don't want him to know we've seen him. I have an idea.'

He suggested that they have a long stop for lunch on the other side of the pass, set up an ambush and wait for the stalker. Anamar thought he was joking but Paul was enthusiastically in favour.

As they headed upwards again Anamar found herself agreeing with Raoul's plan. If this was indeed the shadow, he had been following her for two weeks. In a few days the boys would be going home and she would be on her own again. She decided to stay out of the ambush herself but let the boys get on with it.

High above to the South, there were two distinct clefts at the top of the sheer face which buttressed this end of the Cirque de Gavarnie. This was the frontier ridge and the clefts were dramatic vertical cuts, as if they had been made to allow passage through an otherwise impenetrable rock wall. Hank had told her about the Brèche de Roland and now the boys insisted on a stop to hear the story.

Anamar explained that the cleft to the right is known as the False Brèche. It leads the unwary climber into serious difficulty. The cleft to the left, the true Brèche de Roland, is a hundred metres high and over fifty metres wide. On the French side it is reached by a steep snow slope and gives direct access to Spain on a true mountaineering route which leads to the magnificent canyon of Ordesa.

Paul and Raoul knew of the 11th century French lyrical poem, the Chanson de Roland based on the story of the Emperor Charlemagne's retreat across the Pyrenees after the sacking of Pamplona. His rear guard, under the command of his nephew, Count Roland, was massacred by the Basques in revenge for the raid. Legend has it that, to keep it from the enemy, Roland tried to break his magic sword, Durandal, by striking it on the rock of this ridge.

'Count Roland smites upon the marble stone;' as the song of Roland records.

The Brèche was formed by the blow and the sword rebounded from the rock, unbroken. It survived the battle. But, like most of his men, Roland himself died of his wounds.

Paul had been taking the lead in relating the tale but Raoul could not resist confronting the myth with the history. There had been a mighty battle, he said, but it had taken place at Roncesvalles in 778, over a hundred kilometres to the West, not here in the Cirque.

On the last stage up to the pass the snow was deep and concealed the path. At the col, the frozen crust broke with each step and Anamar was glad the boys had brought her boots and climbers' socks. The air was still. It was over seven thousand feet high but, without a wind, the conditions were perfect for walking.

This was the pass the French called the Port de Boucharo. On Ramón's map the name was in Spanish, Puerto de Bujaruelo.

It was another emotional moment for the boys. They had never been this high, never climbed in snow, never been in real mountains. And here they were standing on the actual frontier between their own country and the unknown Spain.

They looked back down the valley of the cabin of the soldiers. Raoul thought he saw the figure of the stalker amongst the rocks but could not be sure. On either side of the pass the rocks reared up above them. To the South, it looked as if they were almost as high as the rim of the Cirque. But there was yet another dramatic view at their feet when they crossed the pass and looked down to Spain.

The ground fell away so steeply that the bottom part was hidden by the convex slope. It joined a deep, broad valley from the West. The vista beyond was a vast panorama of peaks, many snow-capped, drawn together in close array like her own Blue Stacks, but on a gigantic scale. The mountains reached back in the dim distance to a skyline of palest blue. This was the huge terrain of Spain. Somehow the ancient road would take her through it, like the pilgrims of old, to plains, tablelands, across other unknown ranges, to the city of the Apostle, Santiago.

At this frontier, a new journey had just begun.

The descent, however, was much steeper than the ascent. Neither Paul nor Raoul could see a way down. It looked too difficult in the snow, too dangerous. They glanced at Anamar and she was smiling. She could see a route. Instead of going directly down, they would traverse to the left, using their sticks for stability. The leader would kick steps in the snow. On the steepest part, they would zig-zag downwards, taking it in turns to do the work at the front.

Paul asked them to wait for a moment and darted back across the crest. A wind from high above blew down through the pass. The sky darkened as big clouds obscured the sun. Within seconds, it was a very different day. Paul came rushing back, slithering in the snow.

'It's a man.' he said, gasping for breath, 'He's walking quickly, but still a long, way behind.'

Anamar led off on the traverse, cautioning the boys to step carefully, telling them not to move the stick and a foot at the same time. As he followed, Raoul quickly found a rhythm. But, trying to go too fast for himself, Paul slipped and slid in the steps of the others. Anamar stopped and asked Raoul to lead. She put Paul between them where she could watch him and insisted that he go slowly.

By the third leg of the zig-zags Paul felt he had mastered the technique and was pleased that Anamar was behind, so that she could see how well he was doing. Raoul was enjoying the leading. He kicked and stamped good steps and kept his concentration. Soon Paul wanted to change places with him and, reluctantly, Anamar agreed.

There was an immediate improvement in the way Paul moved. He was less awkward, taking more care with every step and beginning to go more quickly. With fifty feet to go to a snow bowl, Paul slipped.

He fell face down on the icy slope and tumbled head over heels. His stick flew from his hand, spinning end over end and impaled itself like a javelin in a bank of snow. He yelled loudly, gathering speed like a sledge, scrabbling at the snow with his hands.

Anamar and Raoul could do nothing but stand and watch. With a swish like a skier on a fast run and a muffled thud, Paul slid into a deep drift at the bottom of the slope. Slowly he picked himself up. He was plastered with snow but none the worse.

He shook himself like a dog and sprayed the others with small melting particles. Anamar shook her head, still amazed at his capacity to be totally predictable.

'Time for lunch.' she said, 'We'd better keep our strength up in case Paul wants to have another go at the Cresta Run.'

A little further on, there was a stony area with large rocks and a stream flowing out from below the snow. They sat down behind a huge boulder and leaned back against a smaller one. There was shelter here from the gusts of wind, and all the cover they needed to keep watch up the mountain towards the pass.

Paul lit the paraffin stove and its muted roar was a comforting whisper of civilisation in this wilderness. There was the goat's cheese again, garlic sausage, a packet of dates and, of course, the bread and honey.

Raoul thought he saw something move high on the face to the right of the pass. As they all stared, a herd of deer began to descend a snow slope. Paul counted thirty-three of them. They continued slowly, dropping down towards the river.

'They're called isards.' Anamar was smiling to herself at how easily she had become the expert on the fauna of the Pyrenees.

'They're the Pyrenean version of the Alpine chamois. Hunters kill so many there are far fewer than there used to be. We're lucky to be down wind. If we're quiet they could come quite close'

The isards hopped and trotted, working their way down to the river. About a third of them were young and played together, chasing one another, skittering across the patches of snow, just the way they had done that night near Tourmalet.

As they came closer, they looked so sure-footed, so lithe, so quick across the rough ground. The tips of their small horns curved backwards. They were the beautiful creatures of this wilderness. Anamar wondered how someone could shoot such an animal, just to have the head stuffed and stuck on a wall at home. This was the place to see them, to share their hills. They were the living part of this fastness of rock and snow.

The boys said nothing. They were bewitched by the scene. Paul kept touching Anamar's arm lightly when he wanted to tell her something, but daren't speak.

Suddenly the isards turned and fled up the slope. Their leaps and bounds took them through the rocks and over the snow at a speed which seemed incredible to the human animals watching below. In a few seconds they had reached a gap in a cliff, then appeared above it, racing for the top of the ridge. Something had startled them.

For a few minutes neither Anamar nor the boys could see the reason. Then Paul spotted a figure above. It was a man descending directly from the pass. Not for him the traverse and the zig-zags to make the steep angle easier. He plunged straight down the slope, using his heels to make steps and his long stick as a third leg, descending rocks and snow with equal agility. Without appearing to be in a hurry, he was moving quickly, covering the ground far faster than they had done. In a few minutes he would have caught up with them.

They ducked behind the big boulder and Raoul put his finger to his lips. He readied himself where the edge of the boulder met the path. They heard the crunch of his boots on the snow, then the rattle of his steps on the stones of the bare track. He was singing quietly to himself. Anamar thought it was in Spanish. His steps, punctuated by the clatter of his big staff, came nearer.

She sat back against the rock. This was one for the heroes.

'Attention Monsieur!' Raoul leaped out from behind the rock to block the man's passage. He held out his arms as if to stop a herd of cattle and shook his stick like he had done with Paul in Lourdes.

'Who are you? Why are you here?'

He grabbed at the man's shoulder with his free hand and they spun around. The man's anorak hood was up and his back towards the others. Paul was not sure what he should be doing. The man knocked Raoul's arm away and found himself grabbed around the waist from behind. Paul had launched himself into the fray. They tumbled over and the hood fell back.

It was Ramón. The Phantom Stalker was Ramón Mont L'ours Barriano, the Seigneur.

Anamar jumped to her feet and ran to help him. Her face was scarlet with embarrassment. She found herself saying,

'I'm sorry. I'm sorry. I'm so sorry Ramón. I had no idea. The boys were only trying to help me. Please forgive us.'

She sat Ramón down with his back to the rock and told Paul to light the stove. For the first time she looked Ramón directly in the eye and he was smiling. He began to laugh, self-consciously at first. Then he shook his head in disbelief and laughed louder. He laughed until the tears came. It was infectious. Paul started to giggle, then Raoul began to chuckle too. Soon the three of them were snorting and cackling. Eventually even Anamar found she had to join them.

'Thanks be to God for small mercies,' she whispered to herself and thought, 'Ramón is taking it so well. I've never been so embarrassed in my whole life. Deirdre Ryan will have a field day when she hears this one.'

When the coffee was ready, Paul and Raoul had to share, as they had only brought three mugs with them. Anamar tried to explain the reason for the ambush but Ramón waved her efforts away.

'I am the one who needs to apologise. When I was talking to you about the pilgrimage in Mont L'ours, I was not just your adviser, I was trying to encourage you, to inspire your journey. Then I began to feel I was responsible for you. By the time you were ready to start, I was so concerned I could hardly sleep at night.'

He was speaking in English and although the boys were looking puzzled, Anamar decided to leave the translation until later. Ramón's voice was low. He seemed angry with himself for causing her such distress.

'I was much more worried about you being on your own than I dared show. I decided to follow you for the first day on your own across the mountains. Then I thought I would continue for a few days and found I couldn't stop. I was drawn onwards. I had no idea you were aware of what I was doing.'

Anamar took his hand and held it for a few moments.

'Now you're here,' she said cheerfully, ' You might as well make yourself useful. You can act as guide and interpreter for the next few days - that's if you are not in a hurry back.'

Ramón shook hands with the boys and embraced Anamar, kissing her on both cheeks.

'I would like nothing better than to walk with you for a few days,' he said, visibly moved by the invitation. 'It would make me very happy.'

The track dropped steeply down to a gorge, then opened out and they could see a tiny hamlet below on the far side of the river. The houses were stone built, in a little cluster, one much bigger than the others. There was the ruin of a church and a humped-back stone bridge at the foot of their track.

'Bujaruelo,' said Ramón, emphasising the pronunciation. Anamar found her self repeating the word to get the sounds right. After the refined elegance of French, Spanish had a power and grandeur of its own.

Raoul and Paul led the way. As they crossed the bridge, two armed frontier guards emerged from a stone hut and barred their way. Voices were raised, the guards were shouting, grabbing at the boys' rucksacks. Paul and Raoul were protesting loudly. Ramón ran on ahead of Anamar. As he reached the guards, he took his passport from his pocket and gave it to them.

It took a few seconds for them to read the document. They looked at each other and their manner changed immediately. They pulled the hems of their rumpled tunics down to smarten their appearance. They stood to attention and saluted.

Indicating Anamar with a slight nod of his head, Ramón introduced her in the manner of a Spanish grandee.

'My friend is an Irish pilgrim bound for Santiago. I am accompanying her as far as Jaca.'

The guards bowed to Anamar and she wondered what information in Ramón's passport had caused such a transformation.

'I wish you a safe journey, senorita,' one said respectfully and stamped the four passports without any further questions.

As they left, one of the guards said,

'Por favor, Senorita, will you say a prayer for us at the tomb of the Apostle?'

Anamar smiled and gave them her note book and a pencil so they could write down their names.

The largest house in the hamlet of Bujaruelo was a simple inn and, as she entered the main room, Anamar had a strange sensation of stepping back in time. A huge log fire burned in a fireplace designed for cooking as well as warmth. There were blackened pots and pans. Cured hams, garlic bulbs and onions hung from the rafters on hooks. A large wine barrel with a spigot was cradled in a frame. A second smaller barrel stood on a bench. The bare wooden tables were roughly made, but looked as if they had survived hard usage.

A woman, who did not speak a word but obviously understood Ramón's requests, served soup from a pot on the fire with hunks of bread. She drew them glasses of red wine from the cask. The soup was delicious but the wine smelt of the tarred barrel. The boys turned up their noses as they sipped at this uncivilised brew. Ramón smiled when he saw that Anamar knew how to drink it, in draughts with the food, without ceremony.

Before they left, Ramón had a glass of brandy from the smaller cask and knocked it back in celebration, like a man returning home after a long absence. The food and wine cost so little, Anamar was certain a mistake had been made.

'This is Spain,' Ramón said with affection. 'To travel simply in this country we need not be wealthy.'

They walked down a good track, in places cut into the sheer rock of a gorge. There were pine trees, bushes like the whin, others like the blackthorn with white flowers tinged with pink. The river was a torrent, cascading over huge boulders, spray flying on to the path. They came to a narrow ravine where waterfalls fell free for hundreds of feet from a cliff edge high above and out of sight. Further on there was a luxuriant growth - white thorn, birch, yew, elder, cowslips, saxifrage and tiny succulents amongst the stones at the side of the track.

Two hours later they met a broader valley where their route turned to the South. Although the high peaks were now behind them they were still amongst the mountains. A path beside a torrent brought them to Torla, a village set tightly into the hillside. Ramón obviously knew where he was going - through a narrow street, into an alleyway, across a tiny square.

A gateway led to the overgrown courtyard of a large, rambling, stone-built manor house, a coat-of-arms carved in the stone above the door. Ramón called it the casa senorial. It seemed as if it had been here for centuries. There was no sign of any kind but it proved to be an inn and Ramón had arranged rooms for them in a few minutes, singles for Anamar and himself, a double for the boys.

Dinner was not until ten. It was still a wonder to Anamar that continentals ate so late in the evening. In France it might be eight but obviously, by Spanish standards, that would seem early. They rested and went down early for Mass. The boys would have liked to explore the bars of Torla but thought they had better not offend Anamar. Irish people were much more devoted to church observance than the French, they reckoned. It was easier to tag along with her and Ramón than say that they had other plans. They could visit the bars on their way back.

The church was built on the steepest part of the slope to overlook the whole valley. From the narrow balcony outside its door Ramón pointed back towards the peaks and showed them the magnificent Valle de Ordesa.

It had been designated a National Park at the end of World War 1, he told them proudly, speaking in French for the benefit of the boys. The canyon's walls, buttressed by rocky outcrops, were almost a thousand metres high, falling sheer to the valley below. Behind, were the snow-capped backs of the peaks they had seen from France, which formed the Cirque de Gavarnie. Now the canyon was a wild life sanctuary, there were ibex, the Pyrenean chamois, known in Spanish as the sarrio, the wild mountain goat, the capra, maybe even bears.

Lammergyers rose on currents of hot air, carrying animal bones to drop on the rocks from a great height, so that they might feed on the bone marrow. There were golden eagles, Egyptian vultures, falcons, capercailles, griffon vultures and a great variety of trees and flowering mountain plants. It was as awesome, as breathtaking as the Cirque de Gavarnie.

The boys were fascinated. When they left Anamar and were returning home, they would visit the Canyon of Ordesa as well as the bars of Torla.

Back at the inn for dinner, they were shown into the dining room. Four young girls were standing in the doorway to the kitchen, chittering like sparrows in a hedge. They smiled when they saw Anamar but as Ramón and the boys came into view, the girls squealed and fled into the kitchen.

A wonderful carved wooden wardrobe formed one wall of the room. Ramón had heard it was six hundred years old. He drew their attention to the faded, flaking murals on the walls. They were famous throughout the region, he said, but it was obvious that no one in the village knew what could be done to preserve them. As the old plaster on the walls crumbled away they were falling to the floor as dust. In total contrast, the floor itself was of beautiful black stone tiles, scrubbed and polished until they shone.

They had starched white napkins and tablecloth but the other tables were bare wood. Their glasses and cutlery were of the finest quality. The wine was served in a beautiful pottery jug, the bread in a woven basket lined with a crisp white napkin. It was obvious that they were honoured quests.

It was so different from the meal at the inn near the frontier, but Anamar was aware of the same eerie sense of having stepped back again in time. If her own Donegal had seemed years behind Dublin and Paris, this was like the previous century. She had a strange feeling, too, that she had been here before. Deirdre Ryan had often talked of reincarnation and they had teased each other about who or what they had been in a previous life.

Deirdre had maintained that Anamar had been a feisty nun, shifted from convent to convent, where each Mother Superior had tried in vain to bring her under control. Anamar had got her own back by pretending she had dreamt that Deirdre had been a Crusader's wife who, tired of waiting for his return, had run off with a handsome young troubadour who had come to the castle with a band of minstrels.

But behind the fun, they had both admitted to experiences which had undermined their natural scepticism of reincarnation. Although they did not believe it, neither did they disbelieve it.

Deirdre was interested in Buddhism. She had trekked with her father in the Ladakh Province of Northern India before the war, close to the border with Tibet. Without being able to pin it down to a specific revelation or vision, she had an affinity to this Himalayan wilderness - the sights and sounds of the temples, the prayer flags on a pass, the chanting monks with bells and censers, horns booming out across the valleys.

It had not been a surprise to find the welcome in this remote corner of the world, the brightly coloured, embroidered, decorated clothes of the women, the chattering life and smells of the villages. Without a common language, the local people and she seemed to understand each other. It was as if she knew this hidden land.

When Anamar heard the story, she remembered a dream she had had years before Deirdre had mentioned reincarnation. It had been a flash in an otherwise dreamless night's sleep. She was riding a huge black mule with silver-buckled harness, dressed in a dark blue woollen cloak with a hood and leather boots. The small party with her were all mounted and they were on an ancient track through wooded hills on a moonlit night. Around her the voices spoke an unfamiliar language which, without recognising a word of it she sensed was Spanish. Each time Ramón spoke to her in his mother tongue, the dream would flash again in her mind's eye.

It was all so vivid but she had told no one at the time. Her mother would have scolded her for imagining such stupidities. Her friends would have laughed at her. She had never mentioned it to anyone until she and Deirdre had reached a stage in their friendship when they had been able to confide in each other.

Anamar had been sitting relaxed and silent, deep in her reverie. Then Raoul put a hand on her arm and offered to fill her bowl with soup from the great earthenware dish in the middle of the table. She laughed in embarrassment and excused herself.

'It was the fresh air and the exercise,' she said happily, in French, ' I've been day-dreaming. Maybe some day, when I know you all much better, I'll tell you about my day-dream.'

Ramón told them that the soup was Porru Saladu, made with salt-cod, leeks and potatoes. Anamar could tell he was pleased with the way they were being received at this inn. He was a proud man who had found it hard to make excuses for their reception at the border. This was the Spain he would want them to see.

The soup would have been Hank's perfect dish for walkers, appetising, filling, replenishing all the liquid and salts they had lost on the journey. The boys had second helpings. It was followed by a huge plate of thin slices of different types of garlic sausage, Ramón called them chorizo, with cured ham and the most delicious mayonnaise Anamar had ever tasted. Ramón saw her enjoyment.

'Ali-oli,' he said, delighted with the meal. 'It's the special garlic mayonnaise of the Spanish Pyrenees. You will find it goes well with the next course, Cabrito Asado.'

It he had told her that this was roasted goat before she had tasted the meat, Anamar might have declined to try it, but it was even better than her favourite, roast lamb. The final course was an almond tart, dusted with white icing sugar.

'The Basques claim this as their own special tart,' he said to Anamar, 'But when you reach the end of your journey you will find it decorated with the sword of St James and called Tarta de Santiago.'

Although Ramón referred to the boys by name, they called him Monsieur but they were no longer over-awed by his presence. The wine was giving them confidence. Now they had ceased to be completely engrossed with each other, they were excellent company. Ramón encouraged them to talk about their student escapades and, in return, he told them stories of Mont L'ours les Cascades and the Cathars.

Anamar smiled to herself. She could see the boys keeping in touch with Ramón, going to see him in Mont L'ours, visiting the Cathar sites.

They had a late start next morning and walked down the valley beside the river. Ramón had recommended a very short day after the long hard trek over the mountains. It had rained during the night and was sunny and warm, the air fresh, the leaves still sparkling with droplets of water.

The track was the ancient road, paved in parts, with occasional standing stones to mark the way in bad weather. Broto was a small lively village, just one street astride the river, but it had benefited by the establishment of the National Park of Ordesa much more than Torla. There were a few small hotels, cafés and restaurants and Ramón had them booked into their rooms in a few minutes.

The boys would be parting from Anamar the next day to return to France and were reluctant to leave her side that afternoon. It had been agreed that Ramón would stay with her for a few days more.

That evening the meal was good but lacked the atmosphere and old-world style of the previous day. The boys were subdued. Neither ate very much. It seemed as though they were dreading the journey back on their own. Anamar encouraged Ramón to talk about the Ordesa Canyon and he did his best, but the boys were only listening out of respect. They went for a walk down by the river and met Ramón and Anamar again at ten for a drink.

In the bar Ramón ordered Calisay, a Spanish liqueur and each made a little speech. Anamar thanked the men for their company across the pass in the high Pyrenees. Paul looked at Raoul and urged him to speak next. Though he started well, with a salute to Le Chemin de St Jacques, words failed Raoul and Paul took over. He told them that the past three days had been the happiest days of his life.

Ramón proposed a toast,

'To the Irish pilgrim who changed our lives.'

The boys rose to join him, raised their glasses to Anamar and drank the sweet liqueur in one draught. The spirits soared. The conversation was as animated as it had been when Anamar had first met the boys in Paris. They were eventually ushered out at midnight by the smiling owner.

They met again at breakfast and the boys watched as Anamar and Ramón headed westwards up a long valley. They were waving when the others looked around. Anamar thought they seemed so young and vulnerable.

She and Ramón walked on all morning with hardly a word between them. It was good to have him with her. She felt so much at ease in his company. He was happy too. She could see it in his face and in the smile he gave her when she looked across to see how he was going.

The track was good, the day warm. Without rushing, they were covering the ground quickly. Anamar found the boys coming back into her mind. They were obviously intimate friends, probably in love with each other and she had never met a pair of men so open about this kind of relationship. Yet they were her friends too. At home, most men would have been uncomfortable in their company. She had never heard anyone talk about love for someone of the same sex, except for occasional warnings from the priest at Mass.

Did women ever feel like this for other women? Next time she had the opportunity, she must talk to Deirdre Ryan about it.

They spent the night at a tiny inn in the village of Biescas, where the villagers were so reserved with the strangers that even Ramón failed to have a conversation with any of them.

The next day was longer, well over thirty kilometres on poor roads. It was warm early and soon they were walking in the hottest conditions Anamar had ever experienced. They had to stop often to rest and drink water, to refill the bottles where there was a well or a fountain. Anamar soaked her scarf and put it over her head and neck. As the water evaporated there was a wonderful cooling effect. Ramón seemed little affected by the heat, but it helped when he said that it was an unusually hot day for early June in this part of Spain.

Anamar hardly noticed the small dwellings, the horse and mule-drawn traffic, the baked earth of the land, the snow-capped peaks far to their right. It was easily the hardest day so far. It raised a doubt in her mind that she could do this journey. She swayed and staggered for a few steps. Ramón took her arm and led her gently to the shade of a single tree, just off the road. She felt light-headed, slightly sick in her stomach.

Ramón sat her down with her back against the tree, soaked her scarf with water from his bottle, fanned her with his hat, talked to her quietly. He squeezed water from his own scarf to drip on her legs and wet her wrists. Her mother would have called it 'a wee turn'. After a short time she began to feel a little better.

Ramón stopped a man driving a horse and cart but Anamar shook her head at the prospect of a lift. She would be all right in a few minutes, she said. The carter pointed to a building in the distance. It was a road-side bar, he said.

When she felt a little better Ramón suggested that they walk as far as the bar and rest there until the intense heat began to wane.

After a doze in a comfortable chair, followed by even more cool drinks and a cup of coffee, they set off again. Only five kilometres to go and Anamar felt much better.

An hour later and they had arrived. It was no longer hot but the sun lit Jaca's houses and cathedral in the soft, early-evening light of inland Spain. The houses looked old. A broad boulevard led them in past a sunken circular fort on one side and the town on the other. Where the boulevard met the Calle Major, the Café de Somport on a raised terrace, commanded the prime position. Ramón had been here may times, he said happily. In his mountaineering days, Jaca and the Café de Somport had felt like the centre of the world.

SAN JUAN DE LA PEÑA

They sat on the terrace of the Café de Somport and drank café con leche, watching the people passing to and fro. There were workmen and children returning home from school, local women laden with shopping, well-dressed ladies strolling, farming families in for the day. Jaca seemed like a small city rather than a town but there were more soldiers on the streets than civilians.

It was a garrison town, Ramón explained, near the border and Generalissimo Franco took the defence of Spain's frontiers seriously. The 16th century citadel, built in a star shape, surrounded by a deep ditch, was the only one of its kind left in Spain still used as a military fortress.

They could see down the Calle Major. The off-duty soldiers were in twos or threes, talking loudly, but there were larger, noisier groups of eight or ten. When two parties met there was shouting, cheering, pushing. Anamar said nothing but she could see that single girls crossed the street to avoid the soldiers. One girl was joined from behind by two soldiers, one on each side, and she darted into the nearest shop to escape their attentions.

On her own Anamar would have felt uneasy here, having Ramón as company did have its advantages. Her smile turned to laughter when he lit his pipe. It was that sweet tobacco smell again, the Balkan Sobrani. She had to explain her mirth by telling him of the times on her own in Seix and Arreau, when she had smelt the distinctive pipe smoke and had felt she was being trailed by the phantom stalker.

Ramón tapped the stem of his pipe against his teeth in embarrassment and smiled too. He was happy here and Anamar found him such good company, attentive when she needed support, silent when she wanted to be quiet, ready to talk when she required conversation.

The man she had met as the Seigneur of Mont L'ours-les-Cascades had been so interesting, so helpful and hospitable but Ramón the walker, the pilgrim, was a different man. Then she had been his student, now he treated her as an equal. As their friendship had grown so had her own self-respect. At home in Ireland men were not always very comfortable with independent women. It was one of Deirdre Ryan's grumbles. The typical Irishman, she would have said, egged on by his mother and abetted by the Catholic Church, thinks a woman's place is in his shadow.

When she had first met Hank, he had become her mountain guide, teaching her the lore of the hills. She knew she had helped to drag him from the depths of his suicidal despair by encouraging him to take her on the walks and climbs but he had never told her directly that she had been a help.

On their last night together in the Pyrenees he had become the only man who had ever shared her bed but that had seemed to close more doors than it had opened. Later, when he came to Donegal to find her, it had been easy to renew their friendship, but it had been at arms' length. She was sure he was fond of her but, in Ireland, he had treated her as the leader and himself as the follower, unable, or unwilling as yet, to tell her anything about his feelings.

When she had told him about the pilgrimage he had been encouraging, but it was the helpfulness of a friend, not a lover. And for her part, she had found it easy to talk to him about the practicalities of the journey but impossible to confide her deepest thoughts to him. It was as if there was a bond which gave them the responsibilities of friendship but allowed neither the rights of intimacy.

Since they had parted when she boarded the Liverpool boat, she had written every week or so but the only time she had felt really close to him had been when she visited the beach near St Tropez with Yvette.

Now she had Ramón as a companion, older than Hank, much older than herself. At first she had thought him too intense, too serious, interested only in his research. But that had been his natural reserve. She smiled to herself. Deirdre would have wagged a finger and teased her unmercifully had she been here.

'Just you be careful of that old world charm, m'girl,' she could hear her saying, 'Next thing you know you'll be joining the ranks of the hopelessly infatuated.'

They found rooms in a small hotel on the edge of the town and decided to stay two nights. Anamar was tired and went to bed early. After a deep, dreamless sleep she was up before Ramón, ready to see Jaca. It was so unlike the French towns she had visited. The sense of stepping back in time was here, too, as it had been in Torla, but the powerful military presence added another, more threatening dimension.

They saw the citadel, without daring to go too close. The alleyways were littered with animal droppings and some of the houses were dilapitated but there were also fine dwellings with magnificent family crests carved in stone. There were wrought iron balconies, elegantly worked portals, window boxes and hanging baskets with a profusion of beautiful blooms.

Ramón explained that, in the 2nd century B.C, the Romans had built a settlement here called Iacca. Early in the 8th century A.D. the Moors had captured the town but, after a fierce battle nearby, it had been retaken. Most of the conquering army had been local women and Jaca became the capital of the Kingdom of Aragon.

The cathedral was hemmed in by a maze of streets. When it had been rebuilt in the 11th century, it was the first Romanesque structure in Spain and pilgrims had spread its influence along the Camino de Santiago. Inside, the building was huge. She genuflected and sat down on her own. Without feeling at home in this place, she was sure she should be here. She prayed for her friends and family, for the souls of her mother and Granny Mac, for Ramón, for all those who had helped her on the way, for a safe journey to Santiago. She rose, lit a candle on one of the side stands and said the prayers again.

Half an hour later her eyes had become accustomed to the light and she met Ramón under the statue of the Santiago pilgrim. He said nothing, but smiled when he saw the serious look on her face. Across the street there was a café under the arcades and they sat down at a pavement table, still silent. It was very reassuring for Anamar that there were times when she and Ramón did not need to talk to each other.

The cathedral was the hub of the town. The streets around it bustled with business. But although there was a market a short distance away, their table under the arcades was a haven. The customers were well-to-do ladies of the town, businessmen in suits, army officers. The coffee was excellent. Anamar and Ramón had honey and almond pastries which would have graced a French pâtisserie. For Anamar, it was like a holiday from the walk, like the morning she had gone into Luchon for coffee.

In the afternoon she made up her notes, wrote letters to Deirdre, and Hank and had a siesta. She went out to buy stamps and postcards to send to Maureen, Yvette, Celestine, Father Brian and the boys. It was nearly three weeks since she had set out on her pilgrimage. Time to keep them all up to date.

That evening they went out to eat at eight and the streets of the town were crowded. It seemed now as if the whole garrison was on a night out. The bars were packed with soldiers and women, the noise of the talking and singing spilling out on to the streets. The cafés were closed. There were bands of soldiers roaming from bar to bar. Ramón laughed as he guided her to a small restaurant in a side street.

'Wine and women,' he said indulgently, 'And sometimes song. That's the way of the soldier. There was a time when I was one of them. And I was stationed here, too, like the Roman legionnaires and the Moorish warriors in their day.'

'I suppose there are some bars here you'd better not take me into,' said Anamar, 'It might be too much of a shock if the resident ladies of the night welcomed you back with open arms.' They both laughed, Anamar because he looked so happy and Ramón, because she felt able to make fun of him like this.

Ramón was in the mood to talk. He spoke about her pilgrimage and the sense of privilege he felt at being asked to help. He tried to apologise again for following her.

He ordered more wine and began to speak of his time in England. He told her about the girl he had befriended at Durham University when he was twenty, who, unknown to him, when he was called home to fight in the Civil War, was bearing his child. He had only found out about the pregnancy through a fellow student, when mother and child had both died during the premature birth.

Back in Spain, he had found any kind of close relationship very hard. The Civil War had made his life even more difficult. Although he had been on the winning side, when the war ended he had been racked by guilt. His pilgrimage to Santiago had helped, but it was only when he had moved to France to take over his mother's family property, that he had begun to find life bearable. He had developed the estate with its village, forests, grazing and vineyards. The people, the mountains, the river, the local history and traditions which were his heritage, became his life.

His pilgrimage had encouraged him to take a much deeper interest in the Camino de Santiago. He had travelled to monasteries and university libraries. He had revelled in the study of the Cathars, the Cagots, the legends of the Holy Grail. He had found the strength within himself to live life to the full.

And then there had been the telephone call from Stephan which had brought her to his home. Her presence had given him a happiness he had never known. Suddenly he stopped talking, as if he had said too much.

But there seemed to be no necessity for Anamar to say anything. When she had met him first, she had been impressed by his English but now the words came so easily to him. He began to talk again, of his childhood on his father's estate, of his inner thoughts, his explanations of the legends of his village, his views on religion and the occult. He needed only the gentlest encouragement to continue.

It was a magical tour of the world of his spirit, as if it was a tale he had never told before. At times it was eerily close to her own unspoken thoughts on belief. It was indiscreet, even a little frightening as he searched for the words to speak his truth. It was as if he was telling her that their friendship was the most important of his life.

Then he sat back in his chair, sipped his wine. Anamar reached across the table and put a hand on his arm. She thanked him. No one had ever spoken to her like this before, she said. No one had been so trusting, so open. She would remember this evening on the long, lonely days ahead.

She smiled. The owner of the restaurant was hovering with the bill, not wanting to interrupt.

'We'll go Dutch on this one,' she said happily, 'I can't have you paying when you've been entertaining me all night.'

Next morning they were on the road at seven, walking due West. The traffic was heavy at that time of the day, army lorries, marching soldiers, laden mules, carts drawn by donkeys and horses.They passed an army training camp where officers were schooling horses over fences. Their men were struggling to complete an obstacle course, carrying the disassembled parts of a field gun.

After an hour they turned South on a good track and reached the village of Atares another hour later. They turned towards a huge escarpment, densely wooded, perhaps fifteen hundred feet high, without any sign of a track, or a feasible way up, on any part of it. Ramón led the way directly towards the foot of the slope on a narrow path. Anamar had never seen him so excited.

The rough mule track was hard to follow. It twisted in and out of dry wadis, forded streams, wound its way between the pines. Ramón led the way up the rocky slope. Every few moments he would look back to see how she was doing. They climbed in silence, both going well within themselves. The slope steepened and Ramón called a halt. The heat was rising, reflected from the stones and the baked earth.

'This is one of the ancient roads of Aragon,' he said, 'It was in use long before the Romans built their fort at Jaca. The Moors destroyed a religious community here in the 10th century and twenty-five years later King Sancho began to rebuild San Juan de la Peña. When the pilgrimage to Santiago started a thousand years ago, and although it made their journey longer, no self-respecting pilgrim would have missed the visit to St John of the Mountain.'

They climbed onwards, only able to make out the next few feet of the track. They were now at the base of the steepest part of the escarpment and it towered above their heads. Huge lammergeier vultures circled above their heads. They were near enough to see the pinkish-gold breast and the wedge tail. But it was the vast wing span, often as much as three metres, which was terrifying when they came close. In spite of her experience on the big mountains of the Pyrenees, Anamar was intimidated. This was wild and remote country.

When they had been going for four hours Ramón called another rest. There was partial shade from bushes and they were both glad of the break. Anamar drank deeply from her water bottle and ate some bread, cheese and chocolate.

Although it was just as hot as the day they had walked into Jaca, the air was fresh on a gentle breeze and she felt she was coping with the heat much better here.

Below them the ground dropped steeply. It was hard to make out the line of their ascent but easy to see the village and the road from Jaca. From their perch high on this slope, it was as wild and remote as the mountains of Saleix.

When they started the next stage it was immediately obvious how they would manage this slope which had looked sheer from below. The ancient road, still a narrow mule track, zig-zagged upwards, making the best use of the variations in the terrain. They were in the shade of trees now and the steady pace kept them going well. After yet one more false summit, they were suddenly out on a rocky knoll at the very crest of the slope.

Ramón was delighted with the ascent. He shook Anamar's hand as if they had climbed a big mountain. In the far distance the skyline was the great snow summits of the High Pyrenees. Ramón named some of the peaks. It was not possible to see the exact route they had taken over the mountains but he pointed to the area where they had crossed. Anamar could hardly believe her eyes. Three weeks ago she had started her travels on foot on the far side of these peaks, now they looked so far behind. Suddenly she was aware of the vast scale of her journey. But she was making progress - with a little help from her friend, of course!

Further on, another path crossed theirs to form a crossroads.

'Los Quatros Caminos,' Ramón said as if thinking aloud, 'When we visit San Juan de la Peña we will need to come back here for the descent to the village where we will spend the night.'

They emerged from their track through the bushes under a massive overhang of red ochre-streaked rock and the entrance to the monastery of San Juan de la Peña carved at the base of a ledge. It had been tunnelled deep into the mountain. Only the outer wall, the gate house and cloister were to be seen, tucked tightly under this great protuberance of the cliff.

Ramón explained that when King Sancho re-established San Juan de la Peña it quickly became the spiritual centre for the kingdom of Aragon. It was endowed with relics and huge sums of money. The Roman liturgy was used rather than the Mozarabic. It remained one of the most important monasteries in Spain until a fire in the 17th century caused its closure.

More recently, it was taken over by the state and became a National Monument, open to public view but no longer a religious building. They rested on a seat outside the door until a guardian came and collected a small admission fee. There was no one else about so he acted as their guide.

Ramón wanted to see the whole monastery, but after a short time in the depths of the mountain Anamar was tired. She sat on a stone under the great overhang, resting in the cloisters. They were in the process of being restored, although no one was working at them on this afternoon. In contrast to the carvings in the cathedral at Jaca, the cloisters here were embellished by the most beautifully executed figures and biblical groups Anamar had ever seen.

The guide showed her Adam ploughing with two oxen, Eve spinning, Cain and Abel offering a lamb and a sheaf of wheat as sacrifices, the Nativity, the adoration of the Magi, Joseph setting out like a pilgrim.

It was a magical place.These sculptures were truly glorious representations of the Christian belief in stone. The most fascinating of all was a sturdy figure of Adam covering his nakedness with one hand across his chest and the other holding a large fig leaf across his crotch. Anamar smiled, the sublime and the droll in one splendidly carved stone.

The guardian replenished their water bottles and wished them well. The valley was ringed with steep cliffs and the last leg of the day's journey was by the Monks' Path, a steep route down the rocks and scree to a village fifteen hundred feet below the escarpment.

A narrow ledge around a cliff led down to the steepest section. The sky darkened. A vivid flash of lightning and a roll of thunder announced the arrival of the storm. As they stopped to put on their waterproof capes, there were three more brilliant flashes quickly followed by bangs like exploding bombs. The rain fell in a deluge. Anamar pointed to sheltered a ledge below an overhang on a cliff but Ramón shook his head.

'Lightning strikes are much more frequent there, than in the open.' he said, 'The mouth of a cave is worst of all. It's like sitting in the gap of a giant spark plug. We have two choices, to keep going down the path, or to sit out in the open and wait until the storm passes.'

'Let's go,' said Anamar, 'Sitting here, I'd feel like a blindfolded prisoner, waiting for the firing squad.'

The stones of the scree were wet and Ramón kept looking at Anamar's feet to see if she was slipping, but the crepe rubber soles of her sandals were gripping well. She was able to keep up the good pace. The thunder and lightning were now like a barrage of gunfire, each salvo's roars and rumbles split by vivid bolts of fire. Then the flash and bang were simultaneous. The eye of the storm seemed trapped in their precipice-ringed valley.

Anamar saw a lightning strike hit a ridge and run along its crest. They both looked up at the same moment as a ball-shaped flash hit a high rock and ran like a thin stream of molten lava over its edge. Its sound was an almighty thunderclap which shook the valley walls and echoed around them, now on one side, then on the other.

They stopped and stood like statues, held by the storm. The rain eased and immediately turned to hail, big hailstones the size of marbles tumbling down with increasing intensity. The white balls bounced off their capes with a force they could feel, covering the scree with a frozen carpet. They trudged down, crunching at every step. Anamar's bare toes were freezing in the sandals. She was glad now they had kept moving. Surely they must reach the village soon.

She caught sight of a smile on Ramón's face. He knew she was going well. Thunderstorms were common in the Pyrenees, he said, but he had never been out in one like this. Anamar said nothing. She and Hank had survived a lightning strike on their tent in the Pyrenees two years ago, but this was not the time for a story.

A glimpse of the village emerged below. It seemed to be tucked in under the steep slope but not too far now. Ramón strode on ahead and where the path turned left, he hopped up on a boulder and waited for her. She laughed at the sight of him in his big hat and boots, the hailstones bouncing off his cape and it held out with one arm like a fallen angel's wing. With the other arm he shook his stick at the storm and roared back at the heavens,

'This is my kind of country! And yours, my Irish Pilgrim! Welcome to the Camino in Aragon!'

In the midst of the cold, the wet and the fear of the storm, Anamar found herself laughing. What was he like perched up on that rock? He could have been one of the Valkyries, choosing a hero destined for death in battle and ready to carry him off to the mead and ale of Valhalla. She was glad she was not a man. The best of them were always ready to be heroes.

The hail turned to sleet, then rain, as their path reached the village. The lane was flooded ankle deep, and they sloshed their way to a flight of stone steps which led to the inn. Outside the door, a quick swish with one hand pulled Anamar's cape over her head. She shook the worst of the wet off over the rail and over Ramón and pushed open the door. The inn at Santa Cruz de los Seros was another haven, this time from the storm.

The main room took up the whole of the ground floor. There were hooks for their capes, bare wooden tables and benches, a bar at one end and a huge open fire with the hearth at waist height. The comfort of the log fire drew them as much as its heat. A young woman came down a grand set of stone steps from the first floor. Anamar took her sandals off, dried her feet and warmed them, 'not too close to the fire', she could hear her mother say, 'you'll get chilblains and measly legs and they'll be agony'.

The rooms were tiny, partitioned sections of a bigger apartment. Anamar's had a little balcony which looked over the village and the church which gave its name to the village, Santa Cruz de los Seros. When the rain stopped, doors and windows opened and the village came to life. The evening meal was simple, bread, wine and small, succulent lamb chops grilled on the open fire by a young man who might have been the girl's husband. It was obvious now why the hearth was at waist height.

They ate the chops with their fingers, wiping up the juices with chunks of bread. The young man brought them another bowl of chops with no more fuss than refilling their wine jug from the barrel. Anamar lost count of the number she had eaten. The bones on the sides of their plates were picked clean. Her own tally was seven. It would have been too embarrassing to count Ramón's but his pile was even bigger than hers.

They drew their chairs up to the fire and Ramón ordered the Calisay liqueur again. His toast was the climb to San Juan de la Peña and the descent through the inferno on the Monks' Path. They could laugh about it now and Anamar could hear herself telling the story to Maureen, Maggie and Eamon at home.

Ramón began to tell her about the Holy Grail and its link to San Juan de la Peña. In the early days of the Church, according to local tradition, Pope Sixtus the 2nd was condemned to death by the Romans. Before he was killed, he entrusted the Chalice, which had been used by our Lord at the Last Supper, to St Laurence, a Spaniard from Huesca. Sixtus predicted that Laurence would be martyred within three days of his own death, and had instructed him to give the Chalice and all the other church relics and treasures to the poor.

Laurence entrusted the Chalice to a fellow countryman to take back home to Huesca. It remained there until the Moors attacked the town in the 8th century. When the Bishop of Huesca fled, he took the Chalice with him to San Juan de la Peña. For centuries the beautiful, blood red chalice of translucent quartz remained in the monastery of San Juan and was used by the abbots when they celebrated Mass.

In the 14th century the Chalice was reclaimed by the Pope and given to King Martin el Humano at Saragossa. A hundred years later it was bestowed upon the cathedral at Valencia, where it remains to this day.

During the six hundred glorious years when it was at San Juan, many people believed that the Holy Chalice of the Last Supper was also used by Joseph of Arimathea to collect the blood of Jesus on the Cross. Thus, here at San Juan, the legend of the Holy Grail had originated and had led to the cult of mystical chivalry personified by Sir Percival and his son Lohengrin.

Anamar listened in dazed silence. Deirdre had often spoken of the legend of King Arthur and his Knights of the Round Table, one of whom,

Sir Percival, had won the right to see the Holy Grail. But King Arthur's court had been based at Avalon in England. Deirdre had mentioned, too, a story, spread throughout Europe by troubadours, that the Holy Grail was hidden in a mountain cave in the Pyrenees. Deirdre would be fascinated to hear this tale from Aragon.

The innkeepers had gone to bed, but Ramón kept the fire going. They sat on, as if neither of them could end this glorious evening which had followed such an unforgettable day.

Ramón seemed so happy. He had certainly enjoyed staying in Jaca but, once he was on the move, he came to life. Even when they faced the storm, he was in his element. She was going to miss him when the time came for him to leave.

The rain had stopped during the night but the grass and bushes were wet and the path muddy when they set out next morning. Anamar had expected to be jaded after the hard day, but both of them were feeling fine. On a good path with no long climbs, they reached the road and followed it to Puente la Reina de Jaca. Anamar had been confused about the name of this village. She had thought Puente la Reina was two or more days away. It was easily explained. The Queen of Navarre had built two bridges. This was just the first of them.

It was a tiny hamlet and the Queen's bridge had long since been replaced. This was the main road from Pamplona to Jaca. They ate well in a roadside bar and had a long rest. There was still five hours walking ahead.

Ramón showed Anamar on the map that there were two traditional pilgrim routes for the next stretch, one on either side of the River Aragon. He had chosen the one on the southern side and they made good progress in the afternoon.

Their route followed tracks and unsurfaced roads, passing through farming country, forests, scrub land, market gardens and a few tiny hamlets. Ramón stopped to show Anamar a short stretch of paved Roman road. The rest of it had been dug up for building stone, he explained. They came out of woodland to be confronted by a huge fortification like a castle keep. It was both lookout tower and citadel, part of the walled village of Ruesta, perched on the hillside, overlooking the vast plain of the River Aragon. On the other side of the valley there was another similar tower, in another fortified village on top of a hill.

They had walked, by Ramón's reckoning, thirty-three or thirty-four kilometres, well over twenty miles. He was at some pains to explain to Anamar that, when she was on her own, she should not try to do this far in a day, unless she had no choice. In this case, Ruesta was the only village in this area with somewhere to stay.

It was an ancient inn, small and dilapidated, but Anamar's room was clean and the bed comfortable. For dinner there was soup, chicken and an array of vegetables that a city hotel would have been proud to offer. Ramón looked depressed when they were served.

'This valley is famous for its market gardening,' he said ruefully, 'But there are plans to build a huge reservoir here within the next ten years, to be called Mar del Pirineo, the Pyrenean Sea. It will be a wonderful achievement. It will provide water and electricity. There will be boating and a camping site for the tourists but this village and the one on the other side called Tiermas will have lost their fertile land and their livelihoods. Both will die.

Next morning the route of the old Roman road took them across the hills, through forests and scrub land, with superb views of this fertile valley of the Aragon. Anamar could imagine it when the dam was built and the Pyrenean Sea formed. It would be a most magnificent prospect. But there could be no progress without a cost, as Master Robson, one of her teachers used to say. He would have shared Ramón's sadness. She pictured abandoned farms and villages at home, where the people had left in famine times when the potato crop had failed. This dam would change everything.

Before noon they came out on an upland area of flat rocks, like a pavement, and dropped down towards a village on the other side of a small river. The track had been worn into the land here and suddenly they were on a paved stretch of the Roman road, about a hundred yards long. It was hard to believe that this surface had been constructed nearly two thousand years ago and was still in excellent condition.

As they forded the river, Ramón speculated that it had only remained in such good shape because there was a sharp turn before the ascent on the other side. The villagers must have built a bridge upstream, to give farm vehicles another way across.

They entered Undués de Lerda by a long paved alleyway with a dilapidated signpost which confirmed that they were on the Via Romana.

It was a friendly village, so remote from other habitations it seemed to be 'in the middle of nowhere', as Anamar's mother would have said. There was a tiny bar where they had a simple lunch before they set off into the hottest part of the day.

An hour's easy walking in the heat brought them to the frontier between Aragon and Navarre, marked by a single stone. After another hour, beyond a group of monastic buildings, there was a treat for Anamar, the fairy tale castle of Javier. As a child she had been fascinated by castles, but in Ireland all those she had seen were in ruins. Javier was in the process of being restored but it was a magnificent structure, church and fortress linked together, standing as one on a little knoll, commanding a spectacular view of the surrounding countryside.

Ramón had been here before. On two Sundays in March thousands of people gathered here, he explained, for a pilgrimage, called Javierada. His father had brought him as a boy. He had passed this way, too, on his journey to Santiago. The castle dated back to the 11th century. Francisco Javier, known in English as St Francis Xavier, had been born here in 1506. Having been a founder-member of the Jesuits, he had established a base in Goa for the missionary work of the Church in the East and became known as 'the Apostle of Indies'. He was the patron saint of Navarre.

Ramón talked to the workmen and they were allowed inside the church to see a magnificent 13th century crucifix above the altar. Anamar could easily imagine pilgrims staying at Javier Castle on their way to Santiago, hundreds of years ago. In France she had been delighted to find so many traces of the pilgrimage. But since Jaca, she had been astounded by the magnificent buildings, the art and the artifacts of the Church and the wealth and power that these represented over the past millennium.

For someone like herself, who had accepted her religion as an unavoidable part of life, she was staggered by the living history of the Church in Spain. But she had a feeling that, the further she travelled, the closer the link between the mystical pilgrimage to Santiago and the visible presence of the Church.

They stayed the night in Sanguesa in a tiny hotel. In the morning she passed a church which, in spite of all the wonders of art in carved stone she had seen so far, made her stop and marvel. The doorway was Romanesque, Ramón said, the three long, thin figures on one side of the door arch were Marys, on the other side was a hanged Judas.

But such a profusion of figures - Anamar counted fourteen above the doorway and seventeen more in a panel above. And all so skilfully worked together in one stunning artifact.

For the next two days they walked apart. Usually Anamar would be in front but sometimes Ramón would take the lead and she would let him stride ahead until he was out of sight. There was no rift between them, it was only that each needed time with his or her thoughts.

Anamar felt that Ramón seemed preoccupied in the evenings. It was not unusual for him to make telephone calls, there were business matters he needed to attend to. It was some time since they had discussed how far he would go with her. She suspected now that it would not be much further.

On the second day the route was longer. It was hot in the afternoon and there was no shade. They found themselves on a track where the soft rocks had been ground to a white powder. It covered Ramón's boots. It lodged between Anamar's toes. The reflected light was almost unbearable. At last they came out on a road and she washed her feet in a small stream. For the first time the way seemed endless that afternoon. They took to walking together and, although few words were exchanged, they were both glad of the company.

Ramón was scanning the countryside to the left of the road. Then Anamar saw what he was looking for. In open country, with a range of low hills some distance behind and no other buildings anywhere near, stood a chapel.

'Eunate,' said Ramón, 'It's a Basque name meaning, "a hundred doors". They say it was built by the Knights Templar when they came to this part of Navarre to protect the pilgrims in the 12th century.'

The chapel was octagonal, with a wall of arches like an un-roofed cloister around it. The tower had a pointed top and two arches, in one of which a bell was suspended.

'They say the Templars used this design to remind them of the Holy Sepulchre, in Jerusalem, which their order had been formed to defend from the Moors.'

There were strange, disturbing carvings on the capitals of the pillars, a bird with a serpent's tail and a human face, a pattern of circles and stars, gargoyles with grotesque heads, bulging eyes. Inside, Eunate was a cool, peaceful haven from the fierce heat of the day. Anamar sat down on the hard stone and it was a more comfortable seat than she would ever have imagined.

A little further their route joined the main road from Pamplona. This was the place Anamar remembered Ramón telling her about at Mont L'ours. Here the four main medieval pilgrim roads from northern and eastern Europe became one, the Camino, the road of the Franks or foreigners. They were on the outskirts of Puente la Reina.

The new main road skirted the much older buildings and they crossed it to a narrow street which led into the heart of the town. Ramón insisted that they keep going past the square and towards the river. Two young girls and a boy were bringing cattle in from the fields, the way Maureen, Eamon and Anamar would have done when they were that age. The cows had crossed the bridge and were ambling towards Ramón and Anamar when they suddenly turned through an open doorway and into a dwelling. The byres must have been at the back, but the cows were using the same entrance as the humans.

Ramón led the way on to the bridge and stopped in the middle.

'This is as far as we go to-day,' he said, as Anamar remembered him talking about this bridge in Mont L'ours, 'To-morrow you will cross the Puente la Reina, the point of no return on the Road to Santiago.'

THE QUEEN'S BRIDGE

Ramón found rooms at the small fonda in the main square and Anamar was sure he was known to the woman who received them. Her room was on the third floor and looked out across the ancient roof-tops. She wrote up her notes, rested with her feet up on the bed and went out on her own to explore the village before Mass.

She came out of a narrow street and on to the new bridge, the perfect place from which to see the old bridge, which had given the town its name. It was one of the most beautiful sights Anamar had ever seen. There were six arches of golden stone, with arched windows in the pillars of each arch. Ramón had said it was over nine hundred years old, built for the pilgrims by the Queen of Navarre. It was hard to believe that such an elegant structure could have lasted so long.

At dinner Ramón was very quiet, as if there was something on his mind. They ate simply at the fonda and went to bed early.

The village was quiet in the morning when they left over the old bridge. Anamar felt that sense of walking through the past again, with every step on its stones. The track wandered through vineyards, along a river and across low hills towards the town of Estella. She had expected to stay the night there, but they arrived in the town in the early afternoon and had lunch in a bar beside the river.

The man who served them knew that they were bound for Santiago. In France, hardly anyone appeared to have understood the significance of the scallop shell on her rucksack. Once they had passed Jaca, however, nearly everyone they met assumed they were pilgrims and accepted them without the least surprise.

Ramón kept looking at his watch. He seemed anxious to be on the way. Leaving the town they passed three men sitting under a tree and one of them called out in French, asking if they were on the Road to Santiago. It was Anamar's first sight of fellow pilgrims and she wished them a good Camino.

An hour later, Ramón stopped and told Anamar that they were near his parents' home. He wanted her to meet his mother and father and stay for a night or two. This was as far as he would go, he said. He would remain with his parents for a while and let her go on. He was sure she would appreciate travelling on her own.

So this was what had been bothering him. Of course she would like to meet his parents, she said. It would be great to sleep in the same bed for a couple of nights.

They turned right into a side road which led towards a range of hills to the North. Now that Ramón had said his piece, he seemed more relaxed, much happier in himself. He laughed and talked about his parents and their home. He had wanted it to be a surprise for Anamar and had been telephoning to let them know when they would arrive.

A large black saloon car came down the road towards them and stopped, as Ramón had arranged. The driver was about Ramón's own age and delighted to see him. He opened and held the door for Anamar, turned the car and headed back towards the hills. They crossed a ridge and entered an enclosed valley through a gorge. The valley opened out in its middle reaches and narrowed again at the top where a river cascaded down from the hills. The upper slopes on either side were forested. There were crops and pastures at the lower end and extensive vineyards beside a small village.

At the head of the valley a large house sat on its own, overlooking the countryside. It was still half a mile away, but one look from Ramón and Anamar knew this was his home. It was set back on a large raised level about three feet high, with a stone retaining wall and steps. The house itself was as large as an Irish mansion but built in traditional Spanish style, of stone and timber. The roof was of large slates. A wooden balcony ran the full width of the house on the first floor, supported by massive wooden pillars. There was a spacious verandah on either side of the front door, shaded by the balcony.

Well back from the house, and in the same style, there were extensive outbuildings which later proved to be stables, stores and staff quarters. The surrounding grounds were planted with low pines, flowering shrubs and fruit trees.

Don Henriques Barriano, Marqués de Barra and the Marquésa, Doña Marie Mont L'ours Barriano were waiting for them at the head of the stone steps. Don Henriques was a smaller, slighter version of Ramón. Doña Marie was a beautiful woman in her sixties. Living in Spain for so many years could not conceal the fact that she had been born French. She was French by her manner, her clothes, her speech. Deirdre would have said, 'this woman has style!'

Ramón greeted and embraced his parents and introduced them to Anamar. Not sure what she should do, she almost curtsied, as she had seen on the films. It was a great relief when they shook hands with her.

Inside there was a huge cool room on three levels. The roof beams and rails between the levels were of dark wood, the wall panels a much lighter shade. The floor was stone-tiled with large rugs like Oriental carpets. On the rough stone walls there were wrought iron lamps and candle holders painted black. On low tables there was silver and copper ware, ceramics in beautiful designs, elegant flower arrangements.

A row of men and women servants was standing, waiting to greet them. Ramón was obviously a favourite of the staff but there was great interest in this young woman he had brought to meet his parents. Anamar was taken to her room by two of the girls who were astonished to find that she had no luggage except the little rucksack.

The room had its own bathroom, the most luxurious Anamar had ever seen. The wall tiles depicted scenes from Spanish life, dancers, men on horseback, bulls running, cathedrals, medieval bridges. The floor and working surfaces were white marble. There was a French-style bidet between the wash hand basin and the toilet. There was a separate shower as well as a huge bath. There were towels and a bathrobe in dark blue, towelling slippers and an array of toiletries, which Deirdre Ryan might have appreciated but which were well beyond Anamar's experience. The Barrianos were accustomed to treating their guests well.

When she came downstairs, Ramón's parents were having coffee on a shaded balcony on the north side of the house. They looked so happy, now that their son was back. They both spoke English as well as he did, his father's accent Spanish, his mother's French. They were giving Anamar credit for bringing him here. Although like Ramón in his looks, his father was a much more extrovert character and set out to put Anamar at her ease.

His wife was thrilled to have her son home for a few days, but she was pleased to have the company of this young woman, too. She encouraged the men to talk to each other so that she could have Anamar on her own. Doña Marie was enjoying herself but after an hour she insisted that Anamar should have time to rest in her room.

It was cool and calm there, with an outlook to a skyline of blue hills. Anamar took off her sandals and skirt and fell asleep on the bed. It was nearly two hours later when she wakened with a jolt and, for a moment, wondered where she was.

By the time she had soaked in the bath, dressed and was on her way down to meet the others, it was after eight. Guessing that she was hungry, Ramón smiled and told her that, as a special treat for the pilgrims, dinner would be early, at nine o'clock. He was right. She was famished. At home she was used to eating very much earlier. In the winter, tea, High Tea, the hotels would have called it, was at half past five and in summer an hour later. Even in France, dinner was usually available at seven or eight at the latest. It was difficult adjusting to meal-times in Spain.

She and Ramón walked through the gardens around the house. The evening heat was pleasant, the insects and some of the birds were still hard at work. The light breeze was warm but comfortably so, the air perfumed by the herbs of the mountain.

The four of them dined in the grand manner, with four staff serving the wine and food. The polished table was laden with silver candlesticks and cutlery, cut-glass jugs and glasses, exquisite china serving dishes, white linen napkins. Doña Marie was obviously in charge. The staff served or cleared at the nod of her head. Don Henriques' approval was sought before the wines were served, but it was a formality. He had total confidence in every bottle.

Anamar's only experience of dinner parties had been at Deirdre Ryan's and, although Deirdre's food and wine were always of the very best, her occasions were informal. Important though they were, at Deirdre's, eating and drinking must always take second place to conversation.

Here, with Ramón and his parents, and although they were all trying to put her at her ease, Anamar was so nervous she hardly knew what she was eating. She was completely overawed by the formality of the occasion. Doña Marie sensed her guest's discomfort. She had planned this dinner to welcome the pilgrims but could see now that Anamar was not enjoying herself.

Ramón was concerned, too. He became much more talkative than Anamar had ever known him to be. He told the story of how she had come to Mont L'ours, how he had become worried by the prospect of her travelling alone, how he had followed her on her walk, seeing himself as her guardian, while she had felt herself pursued by a Phantom Stalker.

His account of how he had been ambushed by Raoul and Paul in the Pyrenees was hilarious, and his father began to laugh so much he spilled his wine on the table. The servants, waiting for the next nod from Doña Marie, had great difficulty keeping their faces straight as they wiped up the mess.

It was some relief for Anamar when they left the table and went out to sit on the verandah. The view was down the valley and across the low, hazy hills at its foot. Doña Marie sat between Anamar and the men and gently encouraged her to talk. Why had she decided to make a pilgrimage to a shrine in Spain? Were there not famous shrines in Ireland or England? Why did she want to go alone?

When Anamar mentioned her parish pilgrimages to Lourdes, Doña Marie sat forward in her seat and placed a hand on her arm.

'The Blessed Virgin heard my prayers.' she said, 'I went to Lourdes first, three months before Ramón was born. I was ill and depressed. The Holy Mother of God made the birth a joy and she has been my protector since then. But I have never been back to her shrine.'

Anamar jumped to her feet in embarrassment. She had forgotten the holy water from Lourdes. She ran inside to fetch it and came back down to the verandah holding it out to Doña Marie.

'I brought you a little gift,' she said shyly, 'Ramón told me about your pilgrimage to Lourdes and, when I was there two weeks ago, I brought you some water from the spring. It has been blessed.'

Doña Marie took the bottle and held it to her chest. She kissed Anamar on both cheeks, so overcome she could barely find the words to thank her. Anamar tried to help by talking about her rendezvous with Paul and Raoul for the climb across the Pyrenees. Don Henriques, who had been wondering if this beautiful girl was capable of speech, now found himself captivated, as she told the story of the two young men who had incurred her wrath.

'They were dressed like pantomime pilgrims, strutting around as if they owned the town' Anamar said, standing up to demonstrate, 'Bushy beards, cloaks, pilgrims' hats and staffs, the whole thing. I was so mad I nearly devoured them. But then I thought, sure they're only young students, life to them is just about having a bit of fun. What would they know about pilgrimage?'

They all laughed, so she told them about her ride on the motorised cycle around Lourdes and how Paul and Raoul had competed for her attention like school-boys.

Don Henriques was still laughing. Doña Marie clapped her hands, her admiration for Anamar growing by the minute.

'Bravo! Bravo!' she cried, 'Parisians will always get it wrong.'

Anamar came down for breakfast early next morning to find Ramón and his parents sitting at a table on the verandah. Doña Marie gave Anamar a small glass bottle with a ceramic stopper, held in place with a sprung wire collar.

'I was deeply moved when you gave me the Lourdes water,' she said kindly, 'But I thought it best not to take it all. You may have need of some yourself on your journey.'

Anamar was touched by the gesture. There was a long way to go and she could do with all the help she could get.

She and Doña Marie spent an hour talking quietly together. The older woman felt herself energised by this adventurous young woman. She should go back to Lourdes herself, she decided. It was possible she could persuade her husband to accompany her. Perhaps not, he might be a reluctant pilgrim. Much better to find a friend to go with.

She asked Anamar about the West of Ireland. She and Don Henriques had enjoyed a few nights in Dublin on one of their many visits to England but she felt a gallic bond with the Irish and longed to go to the mystical West.

Anamar spent the rest of the morning with Ramón wandering through the fields, vineyards and orchards of the estate. It was obvious that he loved his home here in Navarre, but Anamar could never see him moving from his village of Mont L'ours-les-Cascades in Ariège, to come back here to live.

In the afternoon she had a luxurious siesta stretched out full-length on her bed. It might be a long time until the next opportunity for a day's rest. Later, in the cool of the afternoon, she walked with Ramón again, this time following the river up through the hills behind the house.

When Anamar came down to dinner, Doña Marie had arranged for a different kind of meal to be served to put her at her ease. The table was laid for four on the verandah, two men were cooking on the embers of a fire set in an outdoor fireplace. The smell of roasting lamb was in the air.

There was a great array of Spanish tapas and French hors d'oeuvres - snails in garlic butter, thin sticks of carrot, cauliflower florets, asparagus and celery all prepared as cruditées to be eaten with a choice of mayonnaise. Anamar reckoned there must have been twenty dishes - tiny hard boiled eggs in an onion sauce, a tomato salad dressed with what she called scallions, black and green olives, shrimps in oil and garlic, sweet peppers, different varieties of the garlic sausage called chorizo, little wedges of goat's cheese, mushrooms in white wine sauce. It was just the first course, but looked like a banquet.

It was a wonderful way to start a meal, finding out what was in each dish, tasting, discussing which they liked best. Doña Marie was in her element. She had set the menu and supervised the preparation, now her young guest was enjoying herself.

Don Henriques was delighted when Anamar asked him about the wines. He told her that his vineyards were between Navarre, one of the country's best wine regions and Rioja, the most famous of them all. Although most of the wine produced at his bodega in the village was red, he also made a small amount of white wine and was experimenting with a few bottles of rosado.

They sipped a red which had the smell of ripe fruit and he explained that they grew the traditional Tempranillo grape. In his bodega they used the Rioja method which allowed the wine to age for years in American oak barrels, which gave it a sweet tang of vanilla. His father's wine had soared in popularity in the late nineteenth century when the Bordeaux vines had been destroyed by mildew and disease.

'One man's disaster is another man's blessing.' Don Henriques glanced at his wife, 'For once it was the turn of the French to come to us for good wine.'

Doña Marie looked at Anamar and shrugged her shoulders, 'Sometimes he forgets that I was born and bred French, that our family spans the Pyrenees. I need to remind him that he must take no pleasure from the ill fortunes of France.'

Don Henriques smiled and held up an open hand, palm outwards, in the ancient Roman salute which showed that the hand held no weapon.

'Our wine had always been good, but in their time of trouble, the French wine makers helped us make it great.'

His wife rose from her chair and embraced him without a word and Anamar could guess that Don Henriques was not in the habit of excusing what he had said so gracefully.

The tapas dishes were cleared and a whole leg of lamb brought to the table on a huge wooden platter. One of the servants carved and the meat was served on its own with bowls of garlic mayonnaise.

The dessert was French-style open fruit tarts and cream. Don Henriques whispered to one of his men and a bottle of cold rosado was brought to the table. It was the most delicious wine Anamar had ever tasted, fresh, fragrant, with that faint scent of vanilla again.

The aroma of the lamb roasted with rosemary and the taste of wine in its own vineyard would haunt Anamar on many of the long days ahead.

They moved to the verandah at the other side of the front door and sat on easy chairs at a low table, looking out over the valley as evening quickly changed to night. Anamar smiled to herself. Everything was so different here, the weather, the landscape, the people, the custom of eating in the middle of the night and, of course, the language. It was not just that the words were different, it was the way they were said in Spanish. One moment the tone was sonorous, dramatic, then the words would race together like water in a mountain torrent.

Doña Marie encouraged Anamar to talk about her home in Donegal. But as she began to speak, a sharp ache of homesickness left her speechless for a few seconds. It was quickly gone, there was such happiness here. But she knew that the further she travelled the sharper these pangs might be.

She told them about the Blue Stack Mountains and the lakes of Eske and Belshade. She described her home in Granny Mac's wee cottage, her job in the town in F.B.O'Boyle's shop, her former teacher, now her friend Deirdre Ryan. Ramón was fascinated by the story of the trip back home from Lourdes the previous year when Deirdre had come to meet her in her sports' car.

Doña Marie was delighted to see her young guest enjoying herself so much on this evening. It was not just the informality of the meal. She and Don Henriques had been concerned when Ramón had telephoned to say he was bringing a girl they didn't know. But once she had relaxed in their company, Anamar was an ideal guest. It was the happiest evening she and her husband had shared for years.

They were all up for breakfast at seven on the verandah. Doña Marie and Don Henriques were sad she was going and invited her to return for a longer visit. Ramón drove her down to the road and the point where they had left the route to Santiago. They hardly spoke until he stopped the car.

'This time, I won't be your Phantom Stalker,' he said, 'But only if you promise that we'll meet again.'

'I will, if you will,' Anamar said with a laugh, chanting a little rhyme from her childhood. 'If you will, so will I.' And Ramón's serious look turned to a smile.

That ache of loneliness was back, but this time it was not homesickness. She had become used to being with Ramón, to having him as a companion. Now she would be on her own again. There was a twinge of apprehension and they embraced in a way neither would have been able to accept when they had parted before, after the first day of her walk.

She strode away quickly. Looking back, she could see Ramón waiting at the car until she turned a corner and was out of sight. It was sunny and bright but there were puffs of white cloud high in the sky and a gentle, cool breeze which made for the most pleasant of walking.

In less than three hours she was through Los Arcos, feeling she was travelling better than ever. The town was busy, motor-cars, horse-drawn wagons, pack mules and pedestrians all trying to claim right-of-way. Torres del Rio was another two and a half hours further on and she ate in a bar near an impressive octagonal church. Ramón's notes said it was called after the Holy Sepulchre and that it was one of the wonders of the Camino, but she had too much on her mind to take much notice of religious architecture.

The afternoon was hot. It was only ten kilometres to Viana, but it took over two hours and the walking was as hard as it had been the day she had staggered into Jaca. Having started out so confidently, it was a salutary lesson. She worked out the distance and reckoned she had walked over twenty miles.

The town was empty in the middle of the afternoon but Anamar found a room at a small fonda and had a long rest in bed before going out in the evening to find a meal.

Next morning she left early for Logroño and it was exciting to stroll into such a modern city. There were old buildings amongst the new, fountains, workmen and traders, smartly dressed people on business or at their leisure. It was strange to see here all the horse traffic of the villages amongst the gardens, shops, bars and cafés of the city. She found the way to the main post office to see if there were any letters for her at the Poste Restante.

The girl smiled and produced three. Raoul and Paul recounted their adventures in the Ordesa Canyon and back across the Pyrenees. They described a wonderful evening in Paris with Father Brian, Danny from Tipperary and Henri. They had been the stars of the show, regaling their friends with the tale of how they had rescued her from the Phantom Stalker, who proved to be her friend and mentor, Ramón.

Hank's letter was long and so open about his feelings, she began to realise that, like herself, he found it hard to wear his heart on his sleeve. She stopped after the first page and decided to keep it as a treat for later.

As she would have expected, Deirdre's was short and came to the point right away. Could she come out to meet Anamar near the end of the journey and walk with her for a few days? It would mean a drive through England, a boat from Southampton to Bilbao on the North coast of Spain and a drive to a rendezvous which they could arrange by telephone. Her car could be left at an hotel while she walked with Anamar and she could go back by taxi to collect it later. The letter ended ....

'Give me a ring and tell me what you think. The school is closed for the summer holidays and I can leave anytime.

'With my love and best wishes, Deirdre'

Anamar sat down on a seat in the post office and read the whole letter again. They had discussed a plan like this some time before she had left, but no definite arrangements had been made. Now it seemed like a wonderful idea. She took out her maps and studied the route.

There was a row of telephone booths for trunk calls and Anamar booked a call to Deirdre in Donegal Town. It was great to hear her voice. There were a few crackles on the line but they could understand each other perfectly.

Anamar explained that she should reach the city of Leon in about two weeks time and could choose a town for the rendezvous a few days further on. She would ring again from Burgos in five days time and agree the date and the place. Deirdre was delighted. She already had the details of the sailings to England and Spain. She was dying to see her, she said, it wasn't fair that Anamar was meeting all these interesting men and her stuck in Donegal for the summer.

By the time she reached Navarette it had been another long day, but the letters and the telephone call and, most of all, the prospect of meeting Deirdre in three weeks time had made the kilometres fly. Her room above a small restaurant was clean and comfortable. She washed and lay down on the bed to read Hank's letter properly and to enjoy the day dreams of a long siesta.

It was easy to tell from his letter that he was missing her. Everything he mentioned - his studies, his visits to Donegal, the fishing expeditions with Doctor Corr, the meetings with their mutual friends - always came back to her. If he had been able to talk to her like this in Donegal, there might have been an understanding between them before she left.

At home, it was well known that Irishmen expected their girl friends to know what they were thinking, and would only put their thoughts into words if under the strongest pressure. But Hank was different. Face to face he seemed to find it impossible to reveal his feelings, and Anamar had decided that she would take nothing for granted.

She read the letter three times and drifted off to sleep wondering if she was the one who was making it difficult.

It was a long hot day on the way towards Santo Domingo de la Calzada but a break in Nájera, after the first three hours of walking, gave her renewed strength. This old town of Nájera was another leap back in time to an ancient Spain. There were arcades and monastic buildings which looked as old as the Camino itself. People recognised her as a pilgrim, as their ancestors must have done for centuries, and smiled as she passed.

The path climbed steeply out of the village to a grove of trees and Anamar settled down to a steady pace, slower than before because of the heat. She had a coffee in a bar at Azorfa and filled her water bottles at a tap within the fountain. She found she could still walk in the hottest part of the day by keeping the pace slow, drinking plenty of water and resting frequently in the shade.

On a short, steep hill open to the sweltering heat of the afternoon sun, she day-dreamed as she walked, wondering if the journey was real or simply a trick of the mind. After the first day from Mont L'ours she had been on her own for two weeks and that had really happened, but what of the time since she entered Poudri's Inn on the Col du Tourmalet?

The horror of the attack had gone. Her memories of Raoul and Paul were no longer blighted by their clowning in pilgrims' garb. The travelling with Ramón and the stay at his parents home, all that seemed so improbable now that she was on her own again. Would anyone believe her when she went back to Donegal?

Across a ridge, Santo Domingo appeared below, but the more she walked the further away it seemed to be. She had barely been able to keep her face straight when Ramón had told her so seriously about this trick of the light. He was right, Santo Domingo did seem to keep its distance. How could she tell them this story when she went home? They would think the heat had affected her mind. She laughed out loud and was glad no one was about to hear her.

A long narrow street took her to the cathedral and the abrupt change from the heat and glare of the afternoon sun, to the cool and dim light of the interior affected her perception of the whole day. She sat beside one of the great pillars and felt her mind and body ease. So much prayer was a hasty gabble but now she could let herself sit on this wooden pew without wanting or needing to move. It was a prayer in itself to be here.

She sat for over an hour in the cathedral, unaware of the passage of time. In her whole life, she had never been so free of tension, never felt so close to God.

Ramón had told her the story of the monk, Santo Domingo. As a young man he had been turned down by the holy orders and settled here to help the pilgrims. He had constructed a causeway across a marsh, made a road and a bridge over the river Oja, built a church, a hostel and a hospital. Nine hundred years later the town bore his name and the pilgrims still honoured his achievements.

She remembered, too, Ramón telling her about the famous miracle which had happened here. A young man, travelling with his parents, had spurned a local girl. In revenge, she had planted jewels in his bed and cried that she had been robbed. The young man was summarily tried, found guilty and put to death. That evening as the dignitaries were at dinner, the boy's parents burst into the room to say that St James had restored their son to life. The Mayor had laughed and was saying that the boy was as dead as the roasted fowl he was about to carve, when it rose from the plate and flew around the room.

Before she left the cathedral Anamar found the famous Gothic chicken coop of elegantly carved wood, perched high on a back wall. In it a cock and a hen cackled and crowed, still commemorating the miracle.

That night she stayed with the nuns at Hospederia Santa Teresita. It was really a home for the elderly but a few rooms were kept for pilgrims. Anamar felt herself warmly welcomed, not only by the nuns but by the residents of the home as well. Although the cooking was simple and the portions small, the food was good and the cost of dinner, bed and breakfast the cheapest yet.

Next morning she smiled to herself when she discovered that a second cup of tea had to be paid for. Her mother would have said that it was typical of nuns to look for every penny they could get. Everything was so much cheaper here than at home but there was far less money than in Donegal. She quietly gave a donation to one of the nuns as she left.

The previous day had involved a long walk in extreme heat, but this next one on the way to Belorado was much shorter, much cooler. There were even a few light showers. At first, Anamar delighted in the cool drops on her face but the rain turned the dust to mud, thick, sticky, gluey mud. Her father would have called it glar. It clung to her sandals, making them even bigger and heavier until they felt like snow-shoes. The rain ceased and the sun dried the mud to dust again. It might be hot, but at least it made it easier for the feet and legs.

The inn was closed in Belorado, which was a pity. Anamar felt this would have been a pleasant place to spend the night. There seemed to be far more young people of her own age than in previous towns and she had been looking forward to an early finish.

Two hours later she reached Villafranca de Montes de Oca and found a room at a road-side bar. It was a busy, friendly place and she ate in the bar amongst the lorry drivers and carters. She was the only woman present but no one else seemed to notice. It was in complete contrast to the previous night with the nuns. The helpings were huge. Her wine bottle was replenished each time she filled her glass. The banter amongst the men, the shouted orders to the bar, raised a crescendo of noise which banished the loneliness of this time of the day.

She went to bed at ten and luckily her room was at the back. She could still hear the sound of the bar doing good business but it was muffled and lulled her to sleep.

Anamar promised herself a short day across a range of hills to San Juan de Ortega. The track was deserted and the route difficult to find. She saw no one on the way. There was no sign of habitation or roads and at times she wondered if she was on the right track. But, before the end of the day it became, in a strange way which she could not explain even to herself, a mystical journey with a life of its own.

Earlier in the walk, she had realised that her purpose was not to reach the end but to make the journey. Now, she felt herself much more aware of the sounds and smells of the countryside through which she was passing. She could feel the land through her feet, the sun baking hot on her shoulders, the soothing sip of water from her canteen, the reassuring grip of her hand on her staff.

There had been times before when she had felt at the mercy of the elements and her own frailty. Not any longer. This was her kind of country. This was her journey and she would accept it as it was. She was beginning to understand why she was here, but how could she have explained her feeling to her friends, had they been with her?

In the early afternoon she followed an avenue of trees down to a tiny hamlet. She seemed to know it already. This was one of the places on the whole Camino which had inspired Ramón most. Here, he had told her, he had made his peace with God for his part in the Civil War.

'Something happens at San Juan de Ortega,' he had said quietly.

When she reached the village, the track led directly to a square bounded by a low wall on one side. A huge church at the end was attached to a row of monastic buildings on the other side. There was no sign of life, nor of any other habitations, as if the place was deserted.

Anamar stood in the hot sunshine and felt lost. She wanted to stay here but every door was closed. She tried the church door again but it was locked. A little ledge at the portal allowed her to sit in the shade. It was good to rest. Her water bottle was almost empty but she took a few sips and saved the rest. Her day's journey might not be over.

Across the square a door opened noisily and a priest emerged, walking directly towards her.

'I saw you from the window of the refugio,' he said cheerily in Spanish. 'You are my first pilgrim for three days. Let me show you to your room.'

It was a small dormitory, empty but for eight beds and a table, but it was cool and clean and such a relief for Anamar to have found a bed for the night. By this stage of the journey, the priorities had established themselves. During the day she would carry enough water for four hours walking in the heat, and so always had to be on the lookout to refill her water bottles for the afternoon stretch.

At the end of the day, her first task was to find a bed for the night, food could wait. If it was scarce or unavailable, she always had a few emergency rations in her rucksack - at worst, the dried end of a loaf of bread which only the foolish would discard before more was available.

There was only a handful of people at evening Mass, mainly elderly women who made Anamar feel welcome amongst them. At one stage the priest spoke directly to her in English.

'Peregrinos come here from many countries,' he said, speaking quietly but with an intensity which silenced every sound but his own voice. 'The Camino is for all the world. But the important thing is to be a pilgrim and don't deny it. We must change ourselves if we are to change the world.'

A silent woman served the meal that evening. Soup was followed by a mutton stew with bread and wine. The priest came to join her after the soup, glad of the company, wanting to speak in English, anxious to tell her tales of San Juan de Ortega. He was small, bright-eyed, elderly, but every movement as quick as a bird.

San Juan had been born in the 11th century, he said, and had become a helper to Santo Domingo. He had made a pilgrimage to Jerusalem before settling here and had built a sanctuary amongst the nettles. After his death, miracles were attributed to him and he became the Saint and Protector of children. Queen Isabella, the Catholic Monarch, came here to pray for a son, and arranged for the rebuilding of the church of San Nicolás when her prayers were answered.

They talked for two hours about Anamar's own pilgrimage. When it was time for the priest to leave he smiled broadly.

'One more story,' he said, delighted to have saved it to the end.

'By the 13th century, thousands of pilgrims were coming here from many countries. They arrived through the day and night. A young Irish couple came with their seven-year-old son, who had been born without the power of speech. When they entered the church, some local women were throwing fruit on the tomb of the saint. Suddenly the child spoke. He asked for an apple to eat.'

The priest sat back in his chair and looked at Anamar.

'Many women still come here, like Queen Isabella before them, to pray that they will conceive.' His eyes twinkled. 'I hope that your pilgrimage here will ensure that you conceive too, but in your case, Senorita, let us also pray, Not yet, Lord, not yet!'

They both laughed and he hopped and trotted to the door like a naughty school-boy. Without looking around, he waved good-night with a hand above his shoulder. Anamar would remember the stories of the priest of St John amongst the Nettles.

THE GYPSY MINSTRELS

Anamar had left a donation the previous evening and was about to go at seven next morning when the priest arrived to say good-by. He was still smiling and, for a moment, pretended he was coming with her. Then he laughed. It was just his little joke, he said, and blessed her and her pilgrimage before she set out.

A good track led to a narrow road and on to the main road to Burgos. After the empty landscape of the previous day, Anamar could hardy believe the amount of traffic. Every half-hour she must have been passed by at least one lorry or a horse-drawn cart or a pack mule. But there was so much on her mind she hardly noticed.

The outskirts of Burgos were uninviting, the buildings drab and dilapidated, the streets uncared-for. Then she saw the spires of the cathedral against the sky. They were magnificent, ornately carved spikes of stone pointing to the heavens. They drew her on into the heart of the old city and she found a room in a fonda beside the church of San Nicolás. There was so much to see she washed and went straight out into the streets without her usual siesta. The outskirts had been empty, but here, in the late afternoon, the centre was thronged with people. The life of Burgos was being lived in its city streets.

Her first task was to find the Post Office and the telephone booths for trunk calls. There were no letters for her at the Poste Restante and that was a disappointment. She went to the telephone counter and booked a trunk call to Deirdre in Donegal. She was so excited it seemed to take ages to get a connection. Then her telephone booth number was called and Deirdre was holding on to speak to her.

The line fizzled and crackled, but they managed to arrange to meet in thirteen days time, on the afternoon of the 28th July, at the small town of Villafranca del Bierzo. Anamar would ring again from Leon just before Deirdre left on her long journey. She paid for the call at the counter and left in high excitement.

After half an hour in the cathedral she was unable to settle herself, or relate the interior to other cathedrals she had visited. She failed to find a quiet place to pray. Inside, the space seemed taken up by a building within a building, with access limited to clerics.

It seemed much more appropriate for her to go to evening Mass at the church of San Nicolás. There, the priest had spotted the stranger and he came to greet her at the end. He was Irish and introduced himself when he realised that she was Irish too.

'I'm Father O'Hagen,' he said tersely, 'I saw you earlier with your back-pack. I take it you're a pilgrim on the road to Santiago. Tell me about your travels.' It was more of a command than a request.

He was tall and dark, with high, narrow shoulders held in a tension he was unable to release. His face was set in a serious look. The worry lines were etched so deeply, he was probably ten years younger than he looked. He had claimed Anamar for the Church with his first few words and followed up with a litany of questions, asking where she had been, whom she had met, how often she had been to Mass, why she was travelling alone. It was as if he felt pilgrims needed strict supervision. The travelling life on the road might have given them an inappropriate degree of freedom of thought and action, might have encouraged them to take their duties and observances lightly. But not here in Burgos. Not in his fiefdom.

Anamar had been used to deciding for herself how far she walked, where she stayed, where and when she went to Mass, whether she went at all or not. But she tried her best not to react against this priest. He sounded unfriendly, but he was only doing his job as he saw it, and within his own ability so to do. But it was a struggle for her. She had met Father Brian in Paris and Father O'Hagen was a very different man-of-the-cloth. She could not help feeling that, by the way he asked his questions, he was devaluing her pilgrimage. She decided that it was time to take the initiative.

'It's very good of you to take such an interest in my pilgrimage, Father,' she said brightly, 'But that's enough about me. I was hoping you would be able to advise me how to get to Santo Domingo de Silos. A Spanish friend has been telling me I must see the abbey and hear the Gregorian chant. I gather it's about sixty kilometres off my route, but is there a bus service?'

Father O'Hagen looked at her for a few moments without speaking. He was not comfortable with the way this young woman had taken over the conversation. He gave her a long, not entirely approving look, as if he was ill at ease with one so adventurous.

'Come back here before noon to-morrow,' he said finally, 'We will go to the market and I will get you a lift on one of the lorries which bring vegetables in from the country. They return home after noon. You could stay over in Santo Domingo and come back here with them the following morning.'

Had he been Father Brian she would have given him a hug. Instead, she thanked him with a word and a smile that seemed to make him more uncomfortable than ever.

Next day at noon, Father O'Hagen was even grumpier than before. He led her to the markets' area with hardly a word, except to say she should eat and stay at the Bodega del Camino. He pointed at two young men beside a lorry and left without introductions or good-bye. The men were expecting her and spoke with a courtesy which belied their ragged appearance. Their lorry was ancient but, once out of the city, they made good time, bumping along deserted, unsurfaced roads. They reached Santo Domingo in an hour and a half.

When they stopped at the Bodega and arranged to pick her up next morning at five, she insisted that they take some pesetas for the ride. The priest had obviously told them not to accept any money.

'I won't tell Father O'Hagen, if you don't,' she whispered and made the men laugh.

The bodega was old, built of stone, with huge wooden beams supporting the first storey. It was run by an old man and two girls who might have been his grand-daughters. His son, who owned the bodega, was away for a few days, the old man explained. He and the girls welcomed Anamar, telling her the monastery would be open to visitors at four o'clock and she could hear the monks singing at Vesperas that evening.

Anamar spent the afternoon wandering round the village and sitting in the cool and quiet of the church. At four she went to the monastery and was shown around by a young and very serious monk, who told her that the abbey was una posada del alma, an inn of the soul. The tour was long and Anamar felt weary under the weight of dates and events, but her guide had saved the best to the last. They entered the cloisters. This was why Ramón had been so insistent she must see the abbey as well as hear the chant.

The young monk might have led this tour many times before but, as they walked where monks had walked for centuries, he glowed with excitement as he explained that the cloisters had been designed to celebrate pilgrimage. The carving was superb.

'Like your journey to Santiago,' he said suddenly, as he drew Anamar's attention to a figure of Christ as a pilgrim. Anamar wondered how he knew.

'Every step we take here beneath these stones,' he was pointing at the magnificent Romanesque pillars and arches, his voice quivering with conviction, 'Like every step you take on the Camino, is another step on the pilgrimage of life.'

At Vespers, and in contrast to the early evening heat outside, the church was cold. Anamar shivered and folded her arms across her chest to keep the heat in. A river of sound like a mountain stream flowed from the monks' stalls. Without understanding a single word, the chant led Anamar back through the ages to the ancient practice of her religion.

She was aware of the vigour rising within her, not the physical strength which made her want to get up and walk on, nor the mental power to solve the problems of the world. This was the energy of the spirit. No matter how hard the road would be, she decided, she could do it.

When she came down for dinner the bodega was busy. Six or seven local men sat around a table near the bar, playing cards, drinking red wine, eating thin slices of cured ham. A group of ten adults and children had come by car to hear the monks at Vespers. They were not staying at the bodega, but had decided to eat here before going back to Burgos.

Three handsome young men sat on stools beside the unlit fire, quietly playing and singing Spanish songs. Two had guitars and the third a small drum which he held between his knees and played with his fingers.

The guitar players were young, maybe sixteen or seventeen years of age. They took their lead from the drummer, who was a little older, perhaps twenty, his rhythms dominating all, until he began to sing. Then his voice took over with a haunting gypsy air. Anamar was sure they were Romanies, real gypsies, as her mother called the Romanies. They sometimes came to Donegal, with their dark curly hair and bright eyes. As a child Anamar was never allowed to speak to them. In Ireland, they were a people apart.

Here they were part of the throng, entertaining the guests. Every so often the old man or one of the girls would bring them wine.

Anamar's table was at the other side of the empty fireplace. Although everyone else in the room appeared to be listening, she was the only one giving them her full attention. She took her time over her meal, clapping at the end of each song, and that encouraged the others to do so too.

When one of the girls brought in the meal for the boys, the only free seats were at Anamar's table and she motioned to them to sit with her. They thanked her for her applause. The drummer introduced himself as Javier and the boys as Alfonso and Diego. They were Juglares, Javier said with a brilliant smile. They sang of love and death, of miracles and wars, of good times and bad, the whole history of Spain was in their songs. In France they were called Jongleurs, he said, and there were special laws to protect them.

The boys went back to their places and sang, but Javier stayed beside Anamar, his drum between his knees. In the pauses between songs he talked to her, wanting to hear about her journey. She found herself fascinated by their travelling lives as troubadours. When Javier played, his fingers flew over the skin of the drum like a concert pianist's across the key-board. He showed Anamar his hands. The palms were small, the fingers long and muscular, unable to be still, moving to rhythms only he could hear.

As they talked during the next pause, Anamar's hand was resting palm downwards on the bench beside her and Javier gently took it in his own. If the boys noticed, they gave no sign and no one else could see. She turned her hand palm upwards and returned the gentle grip, as soft as an embrace.

The boys' questions were about her walk and how she had carried her belongings. She went to her room and proudly brought down her one item of luggage and her staff. She explained the purpose of the scallop shell which hung on the back of her sack. She showed them the ex-army water bottle and the leather bottle Ramón had given her.

Diego wanted to switch on her torch to examine the maps, although Anamar was not sure any of them could read. Her picture in her pass-port made them laugh. It made her look like a prisoner, Diego said, although she was very beautiful, he added quickly. Even the stamps on her letters were of great interest to them. She opened out the First Aid wallet and was thrilled that they were so fascinated with her things.

She showed them her silver chain and told them how she had been given the silver cross by Father Brian and his friends in Paris and the silver scallop shell by Ramón. Alfonso wanted to try the chain on his own neck and he wore it for a few moments before placing it on top of her neatly folded spare shirt.

The local men left and the family group were in animated discussion about the visits they would make in Burgos next day. The boys' songs became quieter and the pauses for talk longer. Each time he stopped playing, Javier took Anamar's hand again, but more confidently now.

He sang a song about the moon, his eyes fixed on Anamar. Towards its end he looked as if he might cry. To hide his emotion he stood up, set his drum on the table and went to the door to look at the night sky. Anamar joined him in the doorway, feeling so happy here with her new friends.

Then she realised that the landscape was lit by the moon, like it had been the night she had fled from Poudri on the Col du Tourmalet. She smiled broadly. It was such a contrast to this idyllic evening that she began to laugh and then had to tell Javier about her narrow escape.

Javier put his arm around her and kissed her gently on the lips. As she turned towards him, she heard a noise behind her like the leg of a stool being skraked over a stone floor. She stepped back and turned to see that the place beside the fire was empty. Alfonso and Deigo were gone. So were their guitars.

Her bag and Javier's drum were no longer on the table. She looked towards Javier in the doorway, but he was no longer there. Three strides took her out of the bodega, but the square was empty. He was nowhere to be seen.

Anamar felt faint and staggered to the nearest bench. She hugged her body, willing herself not to be physically sick. Every few seconds a great sob shook her whole body. Some of the family group looked over and, presuming a lovers' tiff, decided not to intervene. One of the serving girls came in. When she saw Anamar's ashen face she called to the old man and the other girl.

They were distraught when Anamar told them that the boys had left, taking her bag with her money purse and all her possessions. With his son away, the old man said, he could do nothing. There was no police post within forty kilometres. The boys would have run off into the hills under cover of darkness.

As usual, Anamar had paid for the room and the meal when she had arrived, knowing she would be leaving at five the next morning. The old man wanted to refund her money but she refused the kind offer, making no mention that her purse had only contained her daily cash. The rest of her money was tucked into the secret pocket on the inside of the waist band of her skirt. Apart from the clothes she wore, it was all she had left.

Some things she could buy in Burgos, like water bottles, clothes and the torch. The contents of her First Aid kit might be harder to find, but what about the maps Ramón had made for her? They were irreplaceable. And her note-book, which she had been trying to write up every evening. And her letters. And her pass-port. What would happen if she was stopped by the police and asked to produce it?

Then she noticed that her stick was missing, and her sun hat with the big brim, and the light, waterproof cape Ramón had given her. She was certain she could not buy anything like it in the city.

But worst of all was the thought that her chain with the silver scallop shell and cross had been stolen by young men she had thought were her friends. And the Rosary beads which Madame Mons had give her, they were gone too. She felt stupid to have shown them all her things so proudly.

The girls made her coffee and comforted her until the family group left for Burgos. Anamar went to her own room, sat down on the bed and began to sob. How could Javier have done something like this to her? She had shown him nothing but friendship and he had tricked her in the most cruel way. She had trusted him and he had let her down. That was far worse than losing her things, even her silver cross and scallop shell, even the Rosary beads. She cried for half an hour or more and lay back on the bed, exhausted.

She must have dozed for a while, waking with a start every few minutes, hoping that what had happened had been a bad dream. The horror of it was not fading as the night wore on, so she washed her face in the bowl on the dresser and went to sit at the window.

Suddenly she thought of her friends and what they would have done. Deirdre would never have let it happen in the first place but, if it had, she would have devised a cunning plan which would have involved both the police and a few local people, who would have been well rewarded for information. Celestine from St Girons would have followed a similar course, but would have borrowed a knife from the old man in the bodega, for the eventual meeting with the miscreants.

Had Ramón still been with her, he would have telephoned his father, who would have arrived a few hours later with a group of his men. They would have taken the law into their own hands.

She had no idea what Hank would have done, nor what he would say when she told him. Maggie and her girl friends at home would tease her unmercifully if they found out, telling her that she should have know better than to trust a man. Men were only after one thing, though in Javier's case it wasn't what Maggie would have had in mind.

She found herself trying to smile. Moonlight was meant to be romantic, but Poudri's advances and Javier's duplicity were hardly the stuff of a young girl's dreams. She lit a candle. looked at her watch and almost laughed aloud. She still had the watch. Thank God she hadn't been playing the part of the great story teller, taking it off to show the inscription and telling them the tale of how it had been a present when her Grannie Mac had sold a clutch of turkey eggs.

A similar thought crossed her mind when she took off her sandals to get into bed. Lucky again! Suppose she had taken off the sandals to show the boys how good they were for walking. Had she done so, she could have been heading back to Burgos in her bare feet.

There was no possibility that she would sleep, but a couple of hours rest in bed would be a help. To hell with Javier, Alfonso and Diego, she said to herself, as she lay down. I'll buy a few things in Burgos and head on along the Road to Santiago with a lighter pack and a watchful eye on handsome young men.

She was up at half past four, forgetting that there was nothing to pack and and no bag to pack it in. She slipped out of the bodega before five as the lorry arrived to pick her up. The driver and his helper had already heard about the robbery. They were annoyed that it had happened in their village. The boys were strangers, they said, no one had ever seen them before.

They arrived in Burgos after half past six and Anamar went straight to Mass. When it was over, she waited for Father O'Hagen and told him the story. It was hard to tell if his angry look was for the dishonesty of the boys or her stupidity. He had no words of comfort, but interrogated her about what had happened and the items stolen.

'Come back for evening Mass,' he said sternly, 'We will speak again.'

Anamar spent the day replacing her things. First, she looked for a bag and managed to get one with shoulder straps like an army haversack. It was easy to find a clothes shop and she bought a light cardigan, a pair of socks and a spare blouse. She chose some underwear, very different from the items she sold in F.B.O'Boyle's, but very serviceable. The two leather water bottles she found hanging outside a shop selling all sorts of tools and materials. The owner kindly rinsed them out with a mixture of vinegar and wine to make sure they were clean.

In a Farmacia she purchased small bandages, a tin of antiseptic cream and adhesive tape, just like the zinc oxide tape she had bought at home. This would be her new First Aid kit and she kept the items together in a brown paper bag. She failed to find a torch, so she bought a candle and a box of matches. The ponchos for sale were made of wool and too heavy to carry, so she bought a large black umbrella and planned to attach two cords to one side of her pack to carry it furled, when not in use.

She finished by buying a little food for the next day's walk and sat down in a café. This shopping was exhausting work for a girl who hadn't shopped properly for weeks.

After evening Mass, Anamar waited for Father O'Hagen inside the door of the church. From beneath a fold in his cassock he produced her pass-port and Rosary beads and set them on the ledge around the baptismal font, without a word. It was obvious that he wanted neither questions about how they had been obtained, nor thanks.

'Take them,' he said gruffly. 'Inside it you will find a list of the towns and villages on the Camino between here and Leon. You will need to know the names, now you have lost your map. I suggest you say nothing to the police about the theft, and leave Burgos in the morning. Trying to find the guilty men will only waste time and divert you from your pilgrimage.'

He blessed her and her pilgrimage, turned on his heel and walked back down the church. Anamar picked up her pass-port and went out into the sunshine of the street.

She left the city before seven next morning. Nearly two hours later she reached Tardajos, the first name on Father O'Hagen's list, and turned off the road on a track which climbed towards the second name, Rabé de las Calzadas. There, her route followed a path across the Meseta, and she walked on in a dream state, trying not to think of the boys and the cunning way they had tricked her.

Now she remembered. While she had been talking to the boys in Spanish, they had exchanged words with each other in another language which she assumed must have been the Romany tongue. That must have been how they set up the robbery. The shame of it. Javier had held her hand, beckoned her to the door, drawn her into an embrace, only to steal her belongings. If they had asked her, she would have given them money, maybe even disclosing her secret pocket in so doing, and that might have enabled them to steal her money too.

She really would have to stop thinking about the whole episode, she decided. It was more unnerving than Poudri's violent attack.

On the great, lonely plateau of the Meseta, it was exciting to be away from roads, to be on the Camino, so little changed from centuries past. The views were immense, huge expanses of the most wonderful, wild country. The flowers were dominated by red poppies, swaying and dancing in the air. For the next two hours, this landscape was empty of people or animals. But the birds and butterflies kept her company. She filled her water bottles at Hornillos del Camino and pressed on. Two hours more and she passed through Hontanos and had a long rest in the shade of the church.

The afternoon was hot and a man told her it was yet another two hours to Castrojeriz. In the morning, a stage of this length always passed quickly, but in the heat of the afternoon it dragged on. At one point the route passed under the arch of a ruined monastery which had been built across the Camino. A sign said it was the Convento San Anton, .

Castrojeriz was long and narrow, built around the lower slopes of a steep hill. Anamar was looking for an inn, when a woman showed her the way to a convent nearby. The sisters were Poor Clares and, although it was a closed house, they had a few guest bedrooms outside the restricted area, run by a local woman.

Anamar spent the evening alone in the guest area but, after a simple meal, she was allowed to speak to the sisters through a wooden grill. The young nuns were very shy, then they all began to question her about her pilgrimage, two or three of them speaking at a time, until an older sister gently indicated that they should be talking much more quietly.

She lay awake for a long time, thinking of the lives these nuns would lead. Every day there would be long hours of prayer and contemplation, work and worship. She wondered how they could bear to cut themselves off from the world, associating only with their sister nuns. But then they had taken their vows. They were Brides of Christ and all seemed to be so happy. It had been a joy to meet them, even though they were separated by the bars.

The church was as cold as winter at Mass next morning, but the singing of the nuns was sublime. Afterwards Anamar had breakfast in the day room and again the young nuns chatted happily with her through the grill. The Mother Superior had a gift for her, a Tau cross in the shape of a capital 'T'. She explained that, since the days when the order had been in residence in the now ruined Convento San Anton, it had been their practice to present pilgrims with a Tau cross, to keep them safe to Santiago.

They had little pastries for sale and Anamar realised that the name meant, 'the fist of St Anthony'. They were little rolls of pastry, filled with confectioner's custard. Anamar bought three, two of which she wrapped up with her food later and ate the third. It was delicious.

On the other side of the grill, a very young nun put a finger through the bars. Anamar touched it with one of hers for a moment. No one else noticed and the young nun smiled.

Anamar had lost some of her most useful possessions, but their place had been taken by new gifts - the touch of a finger, the Tau cross, even the awkward helpfulness of Father O'Hagen had been exactly what was needed in Burgos.

The day's walk started with a stiff climb back up on to the Meseta. On the track there were slivers of stone as transparent as glass and black rocks polished by the feet of thousands of pilgrims. In the afternoon she crossed a river and found a bed in Boadillo del Camino, yet another village whose claim to be on the road to Santiago was verified by its name. She found a room there at the hospederia and marvelled at the huge stone cross with scallop shells amongst its carvings.

After the very long day from Burgos to Castrojeriz, this shorter stage allowed her to recover and to get back into her stride. Her bag was lighter. She laughed to herself and thanked the Romany boys for lightening her load.

For three days she strode out across the plains, through towns on Father O'Hagen's list, like Carrion de los Condes, Ledigos and Sahagun. The weather was hot and getting hotter by the day. There was little shade, but a chance to refill the water bottles in every village. In tiny hamlets there were impressive ruins. In small towns there were substantial churches with carved stone panels and wonderful portals. She had been off roads since shortly after leaving Burgos and outside the villages the landscape was empty.

Occasionally she would meet a shepherd and would stop for a chat. They too had their large umbrellas, as cover in the rain and as shade from the sun. One old man was very interested in how she had attached hers to the side of her pack when not in use. She was delighted to show him how she had made two sets of holes on one side of the pack, one set above the other, and threaded pieces of twine through the holes. The twine could then be used to tie the umbrella to the bag in a vertical position.

He was impressed and patted her shoulder. He would do the same, he said, if he ever had to carry a pack.

It was the hottest day so far as she passed over a low range of hills, crossed a railway line and entered the small village of El Burgo Ranero. There were huge storks' nests on the highest roofs, but their occupants were the only sign of life in El Burgo.

Anamar stood in a narrow band of shade beside a building. There was nowhere to go, nowhere to sit, no one to ask. She waited in the shadow, glad only that there was no point in moving, not in this heat, not in this closed and silent place.

The houses were the same faded red colour as the earth, but then they were built of mud bricks or plastered with dried mud. It looked as though El Burgo Ranero had been by-passed by time and prosperity, and was slipping back into the landscape. Only the storks looked as if they had found good fortune here.

She nearly missed a movement further down the street. A tiny man, dressed in black, staying in the same band of shadow as herself, moved silently from one house to another a few doors away, and slipped inside.

'Senor! Senor!' Anamar was amazed to hear herself shouting. His head peeped out from the doorway.

'Senor, por favour,' she said, walking towards him. When she reached the doorway and he was able to see her properly, the little man startled back at the sight of this foreign woman, in his village, at a time of the day when all decent people were asleep.

Anamar looked past him. There was a bar counter and a burly bar man inside. Was it a mirage? There was no sign outside but this was definitely a bar. But why would they need a sign? The locals were bound to know about the bar and no traveller would think of stopping here on his way across the plain unless he knew the place.

The little man grinned when he saw the look of sheer relief in Anamar's eyes and stepped back, waving her inside with a sweep of his hand like a matador's pass. Anamar knew exactly what she would ask for. There would be no point ordering something ice-cold and fancy, not here in El Burgo.

'Tinto y gaseosa, por favour,' she said without a pause and the bar man smiled broadly. It was always a pleasure to serve a stranger who asked for something he could provide. He set a large tumbler on the counter and began to pour red wine into it.

Anamar stopped him with a wave and a laugh.

'Un poco de vino, senor,' she said, 'Y mucho gaseosa!' and the men began to laugh as the glass was filled with lemonade.

She asked the little man if he would like to join her for a drink. He ordered the same and expressed his thanks effusively. They sat down and clinked glasses. Ramón had told her that, if in doubt, this mixture of a little red wine in a glass filled up with the traditional Spanish lemonade, gaseosa, was always the best drink to order, safer than the local water, always available. Here in El Burgo, it was not ice-cold but pleasantly cool.

The bar man's wife came in from the back, and Anamar was soon shown to a room which was so cool and quiet she fell asleep as soon as she had washed and lain down to rest.

It was less than forty kilometres to the city of Leon, but so hot Anamar decided to break her journey in Mansilla de las Mulas and do it in two days. The first of these was across the rolling plains on a track paved with dark brown cobbles and only one patch of shade the whole way. The second day was better walking, with stretches on the road and on paths, and occasionally in blissful shade.

Having been on her own for so long, it was exciting to enter a new city and, as she walked the streets into the heart of Leon, Anamar was in awe of its size and sophistication. It was in such stark contrast to the primitive villages she had been passing through for the past week.

She came upon the magnificent facade of a huge, ancient building, set well back from the road, in a most commanding position. A smartly-dressed man told her that it was the Monastery and Pilgrim Hostal of San Marcos. He smiled and gently shook his head, as if he had recognised that she was a pilgrim looking for a place to stay, but felt he should indicate that this particular accommodation might not be what she was looking for.

Anamar smiled too. He needn't be concerned, she said to herself. She would much rather have a room in a small family-run fonda. And it was easy to find one in the old part of the city. As soon as she had settled in, she went to see what Ramón had called, 'the Cathedral of Light'. When he had been telling her about the sights of the Camino in Mont L'ours, he had said that this was the the most beautiful structure of all, the finest monument to faith he had ever seen.

Outside, it looked immense, yet elegant, the impressive stone carving so intricate it seemed as delicate as filigree silver. But if the exterior was striking, it was the interior which made true sense of Ramón's admiration. The stained glass windows were so large and numerous, it seemed hardly possible that the stone structure could be strong enough to hold the roof in place.

Ramón was right again. The bright sunshine of the afternoon in Spain was filtered by the stained glass and flooded the building with light. This was a working church and worshippers came quietly to pray, and left again without a word. Anamar lit two candles and left some coins in the box. The seating area was small and she found a place on her own. Prayer had never been easier. She felt she could talk directly to God, not asking for big favours for herself, but remembering her friends, putting her thoughts into silent words, praying for the repose of her mother's soul.

Over an hour later she left the cathedral, feeling restored in body, mind and spirit. She had reached the end of Father O'Hagen's list of places on the Camino, her only guide since Javier and his friends had stolen the maps Ramón had made for her. She found a bookshop and bought a road map. It would have to do. The direct way to Santiago looked fairly obvious. In every village and town she would ask about the old route of the Camino. It would be even more of an adventure without the list.

From here it should take her six days to reach Villafranca del Bierzo, she reckoned, where she had arranged to meet Deirdre. She could hardly wait. It would be wonderful to have some company again. She would ring Deirdre in the morning just to confirm the details.

BREAD AND WINE IN O CEBREIRO

On the way out of Leon next morning the city was at its best. Beside the river, a tree-lined promenade set an elegant tone to the place. Now Anamar saw the old and the new quarters of the city fitting happily together. There were circular plazas with great fountains spouting water aloft in such volumes that it fell with a dull thump, and surged over the inner parapets in huge waves.

She had only been here overnight, but Leon had made a deep impression on Anamar. The three great forces of Spain, as Ramón had described them, the Church, the Monarchy and the Army, were still in power here, although the Monarchy, for the time being, was represented by a self-appointed dictator, rather than following the royal succession. Alongside its great history, its religious traditions and all the evidence of their significance in massive constructions of stone, it was also a flourishing modern centre of commerce. This was old Spain and new Spain trying to find their place in the modern world.

Outside the city Anamar found herself walking quickly, as if she was in a hurry to reach the rendezvous with Deirdre. But that was still five days away. It was barely believable that she had been on the journey now for forty-two days, most of those on her own. But then, if she did think of the incidents of the past six weeks, some seemed to have happened in the distant past. The robbery by Javier and his friends had taken place only a week ago, but she had come so far since then, it might have been a bad memory from a previous life.

Virgen del Camino was a friendly village and a young woman dressed in black gave her directions to Hospital de Orbigo where she intended to spend the night. When they parted, the woman shouted after her that the fonda on the way into the village had good, cheap rooms and meals.

Next day it was a much shorter walk and the high temperatures of a few days past had dropped. Anamar smiled to herself, thinking that, at home, it would have been called the hottest day of the summer. But here, because she was acclimatised now to the fierce heat of inland Spain, it felt pleasantly warm.

In the early afternoon she crossed the railway line and a Roman bridge and strolled into Astorga. The streets were silent, deserted at this time of day and she decided to explore the town before finding a place to stay.

She turned a corner and was astounded to come upon the most bizarre building she had ever seen. It was directly opposite an impressive cathedral, but that served only to emphasise its strangeness. Ramón had prepared her for a shock when he had told her about this famous Bishop's Palace, but she stood and gaped at it in open-mouthed amazement. It had been designed and built, he had told her, by Antonio Gaudi at the end of the 19th century, and was regarded as one of Gaudi's greatest achievements.

As she stared, Anamar was aware that there was something familiar about this building. Then she remembered. It was like the fairy tale castles in Hollywood films. Maybe the artists who designed the sets for movies knew about Gaudi's masterpiece. One thing was certain. Once seen, the Bishop's Palace in Astorga would never be forgotten.

The way out of town was on a road above the main settlement and Anamar found a room at a small hotel. The serious young barman guessed she was a pilgrim. He said his name was José and he had made the pilgrimage to Santiago by bus. Although her route would be different, he could tell her about the next three stages.

The first was very long, he said, at least forty kilometres to Molinaseca. It was not possible to shorten the stage as there was nowhere to stay in the mountains. It would take her eleven hours. José marked the route on her map.

'But why have you no scallop shell,' he asked anxiously, 'You must know that it is the badge of the pilgrim.'

Anamar smiled wanly. Without explaining about the robbery, she simply said it had been stolen from her near Burgos. The barman asked her to wait for a moment and went through the door to the kitchens. Five minutes later he was back with a scallop shell, still wet from being scrubbed clean. He produced a pocket knife, opened a blade with a sharp point and began to bore a hole in the shell. He found a piece of string under the counter, threaded it through the hole and, with a little bow, presented Anamar with a new pilgrim's badge.

Although he had still been on duty when Anamar went to bed the previous evening, her new friend was behind the bar again when she came down for breakfast at six-thirty next morning. She had already paid for her room and evening meal but her friend would take no money for the coffee, bread and buns she had for breakfast.

As she left, he came to the door with her to point the way and give her one more present. The previous evening he had told her about Astorga's famous mantecadas. They were delicious little butter cakes made to a traditional recipe and their popularity was one of the reasons for Astorga's prosperity.

José gave her a small cardboard box of mantecadas and wished her a good journey. Anamar felt a little guilty at accepting this young man's friendship, without even offering him her name in response.

'I'm Anamar, and I'm from Ireland', she said, as she shook hands with him.

'I will remember,' said José in his quiet, serious way, 'I will remember the Irish Pilgrim.'

It was seven as she left Astorga and began the long climb across a range of mountains, the crest of which seemed such a long way away. The summits were on a distant horizon, flecked with patches of snow. In a small clump of trees she found a stick. Since the robbery she had not thought of replacing the one stolen by Javier and his friends, but José had told her she must have a good pilgrim's staff. There were unfriendly dogs in the villages and wild dogs in the mountains.

Steady walking on a country road through small villages brought her to Rabanal del Camino four hours later. José was right, some of the dogs barked at the stranger but Anamar was a country girl, used to country dogs. She brandished her stick, made sure she did not look them directly in the eye and strode on. There were no name plates for villages here, but it was easy to ask.

'Como se llama esto pueblo?' she would say, and repeated the name until she had the right pronunciation. She entered Rabanal by a cobbled street with an open drain down the middle.

The morning was cool and this was the most beautiful part of the Camino since she had crossed the Pyrenees. From a distance, the landscape was like a higher version of the West of Ireland, although up close the plants and bushes were different. But the broom was in bloom and her spirits soared.

An hour and a half later she came to a village falling into ruin. There was all the evidence of a once prosperous settlement, with a large cobbled square and dilapidated buildings which had been fine houses in their day. The few people she met were friendly but resigned. As had often happened in Donegal, when the people began to drift away, the fate of the place as a deserted village was already sealed.

A steady climb led to a cairn of stones and an iron cross. Anamar reckoned she must be half way across the mountains, but the clouds quickly disappeared and the full heat of the sun began to bake the mountainside. Her appetite had gone but she finished the water in one of her leather bottles. The only shade was behind a small bush, but it was so prickly and uncomfortable there, she walked on.

There was another pass to climb, but at last she could see the plains on the other side of the range. The relief of going downhill encouraged her to stroll. It was still a long way, too far to try to go quickly. Two hours later she was able to fill her water bottles at the tiny village of El Acebo and after another hour reached the bigger village of Regio de Ambros where there was a tiny bar in the main street.

At home, Anamar would never have entered a bar on her own, but here it was needs must. She ordered the tinto y gaseosa and again it drew smiles of appreciation from the barman and his wife. This young pilgrim, they reckoned, knew what she was about. They told her it was only five kilometres to Molinaseca where she hoped to spend the night. But this was to prove the hardest stretch of all. The descent was in a gorge with paved sections, which were surely Roman. It was a stunning trek down to the river and out of the mountains but, in the blazing afternoon sun, Anamar was exhausted, more tired than ever she had been in her life.

It was not just the length of the walk and the thousands of feet of ascent. In Molinaseca they told her she had walked forty-two kilometres, over twenty-six miles. The real difficulty had been coping with the extreme temperature. Talking about it later to Deirdre, Anamar said that, if it hadn't been for the beauty of the last stretch in the gorge, she would not have been able to finish the stage that day.

Wearily she crossed a narrow stone bridge into Molinaseca and was directed to an inn on the far river bank. Her mother would have called it rough and ready, but it was a haven after her long trek. It was run by a family, father, mother, daughter and two sons. They knew she had walked the whole way from Astorga and gave her as friendly a welcome as any of the inns so far.

They served meals and drinks but had no guest accommodation. However, there was a spare bed in the daughter's room and Anamar was delighted. She would have slept on the bar floor rather than walk any further. After a cold water wash and a rest in bed, she was amazed to feel so well recovered. The family took it in turns to ask her questions, speaking slowly to help her understand, teaching her new words. They were fascinated by her pilgrimage, amazed she was doing it on her own.

It was Anamar's first really happy evening since leaving the home of Ramón's parents. They boys were busy in the bar. Father grilled lamb chops on an open fire. Mother and daughter sliced the bread in great hunks with a huge knife, made the salads, filled the wine and water jugs, cut the cheese. They told each new arrival that Anamar was an Irish pilgrim on the way to Santiago, that she had walked from Astorga that day, that she was meeting a woman friend from Ireland in Villafranca.

They laughed and joked with her, mother offering her the choice of her sons in marriage, daughter saying that, if Anamar hadn't been meeting a friend, she would have gone with her the rest of the way.

Anamar left late the next morning. It was only a short distance to Ponferrada and felt like a rest day. It was a sad parting from this happy family. She was just a stranger passing through, but they had made it a memorable stop. She would love to come back here and stay for a time. The streets of Ponferrada were quiet in the early afternoon. She found a room at a fonda and explored the old part of the town.

The Templar castle had been one of their most important fortifications in North-Western Spain. The order had been formed to protect pilgrims in the Holy Land and, when they had extended their operations to the Camino de Santiago in the 12th century, their stronghold at Ponferrada became a massive symbol of their wealth, power and sense of purpose.

Having paid the night before, Anamar left the town at six in the morning. She had coffee and bread at the only bar open and was aware that she was walking too quickly. This was the day she was due to meet Deirdre at Villafranca and she could hardly wait. There was so much to talk about. Deirdre would be amazed at her adventures. Maybe she would bring some letters. She would certainty have all the news from home.

Fortunately, it was cloudy and cool and the going easy. Villafranca was at the base of a deep gorge and just off the main road. As soon as she turned into a little square beside the river, there it was, Deirdre's little car. It was a Riley open-top tourer, painted a shade of green which Deirdre liked to call British Racing Green, just to tease some of her Irish Nationalist friends.

It was parked outside the Hostal Puente Neuve and, as Anamar entered through the stone arch which led to its courtyard, she heard the sound of feet on stone stairs. Deirdre must have been watching for her at an upstairs window. Now she appeared in the doorway.

Anamar ran across the courtyard and hugged her friend. It was three months since she had left Donegal and they were delighted to see each other.

'You look great,' Deirdre said, holding her at arm's length, pleased to see Anamar so fit and well, 'Mind you, I think you've lost weight. You haven't been feeding yourself properly. We'll have to do something about that in the next few days, we can't have you going home like a bag of bones.'

She talked on, asking Anamar questions about the walk and how she was feeling, relating the news from home, telling her that she had a room booked for the pair of them, hardly letting her young friend get a word in.

'But I have two surprises for you,' she said, 'Hold on a minute.' She was carrying a leather handbag with a shoulder strap and opened it to produce a letter.

'It's from your lovely boss, F.B.O'Boyle. He says it's too important to trust to the post.'

Anamar took the letter, wondering if she should open it now or wait until she was on her own.

'Just a minute,' said Deirdre, 'Before you get involved with your correspondence, I have another surprise for you.'

She led the way through to the main room of the hostal, which was both bar and restaurant. A man was sitting on the other side of the room looking out of a window. His back was to the door. He stood up as he heard them enter and turned around.

It was Hank.

Anamar was stunned, struck speechless at the sight of him. She looked at Deirdre, who was smiling broadly. She looked back at Hank and he was smiling too.

'It's Hank,' she said, as if she was convincing herself, 'What in God's name are you doing here?' It sounded unwelcoming, although it was not meant it to be so.

He looked embarrassed as he came towards her. They hugged and kissed each other on both cheeks, as if they were uncomfortable in the presence of a third party.

'Don't mind me,' said Deirdre, 'I'll find the staff and order coffee.'

Hank explained that when Deirdre had arranged to come to meet Anamar, she had asked him if he would like to travel with her. He was familiar with car mechanics. It was a long journey through England and across the mountains of Northern Spain. Lectures at Queen's were over and he was free for the rest of the summer. He hoped she didn't mind.

'You won't have heard, but the United States is now at war in Korea.' he said grimly, 'The first major battle was a disaster. The North Korean tanks massacred a US infantry company. I was an infantryman myself. It took me back to the beach at St Tropez and to the state I was in when you met me first. It was Deirdre's idea to get me away from it all.'

Deirdre came back with a young woman carrying the coffee tray.

'And that's the last we're going to talk about war for the next couple of weeks,' she said firmly, 'This walk will give us all enough to think about without worrying about power politics and the conflict between Communism and Capitalism.'

They spent the afternoon talking, at least Deirdre and Anamar did. Hank was happy to speak only when spoken to. Deirdre quickly covered the news from home, and wanted to know about Anamar's time in Paris and her visit to the village near St. Tropez. Anamar had them both laughing when she told them about Father Brian and his friends, and how she had made the shorts for Roger, the Englishman, at the youth hostel in the South of France.

She had written to Hank about her trip to the beach with Yvette, where he had been wounded in the war.

'But I didn't tell you about her baby,' Anamar said gently, 'And Yvette never mentioned him in those letters to her GI which were never answered.'

Hank held his head in his hands for a few moments, and the others said nothing. He looked up.

'When you met me first,' he said to Anamar, ' I could think about nobody's troubles but my own. Now, I may be in the wilds of Spain with two mad Irish women, but I'm here with my friends.'

They explored Villafranca, admiring its manorial houses with their wrought-iron balconies and ancient coats of arms. In a bar on the main street, Anamar introduced them to her version of tinto y gaseosa and they approved.

At the end of the afternoon, Deirdre insisted that Anamar go to bed for a rest. She and Hank would find out about the next day's route and they would have time to talk again at dinner.

Anamar was glad of the rest. It was not just the morning's walk, she was not used to having such long, animated conversations with friends she hadn't met for months. As she took off her skirt to lie down, she found the letter from F.B. O'Boyle in the pocket. In one way, she was curious to see what he had to say, but in another, she was dreading what she might read.

After the surprise of finding that Hank had arrived with Deirdre, she felt it might be better not to take the chance of another shock that evening, and left the letter propped up on a chest of drawers to be read in the morning.

The evening meal was the same good, simple fare Anamar had been enjoying nearly every day, but this time it tasted even better. She was in the company of her friends.

Deirdre questioned her closely about her time in Mont L'ours-les-Cascades and at Ramón's home in Navarre. She and Hank were intrigued by the two very different dinners arranged by Ramón's mother, the formal banquet and the meal on the patio, designed to put her at her ease.

'That French woman was giving you the once over,' Deirdre said knowingly. 'She thinks it's time that son of hers was married and she sees you as the very woman. If you go back to see her, I'm coming too. It's time I ran my eye over both her and her son.'

After dinner they moved to easy chairs, and Anamar told them about Poudri and Javier. She made light of the attack and chase by the man in the chef's hat on the Col du Tourmalet. She told them almost the whole story of being robbed by the Romany troubadours. She was near to tears at the end but then felt much better. It was a help to be able to talk to friends. Deirdre and Hank knew that there was much more to tell, but asked no questions.

They walked the streets of Villafranca in the starlight, arm in arm, Anamar in the middle. From what they had been able to find out, the next day's walk sounded long and arduous. The first section was through the famous Valcarce Gorge, then they would leave the road and follow an ancient track which climbed steeply for thousands of feet to the village of O Cebreiro.

Anamar couldn't wait to do a stage with her friends. It would be so different to writing about it in letters, or trying to explain it to others when she got home.

Anamar's bed was comfortable and she wakened at six next morning. Deirdre was still asleep, so she drew back the curtains and decided it was time for F.B.O'Boyle's letter.

It was on the shop's notepaper and in F.B's. usual style.

O'BOYLE'S HABERDASHERY   DONEGAL TOWN
                                           Sole Proprietor Mr F.B.O'Boyle

Dear Anamar,

I hope you are well and finding grace with every step of your Pilgrimage.

When last I wrote to you, it was to apologise for the embarrassment of a proposal of marriage, which was made in too hasty a fashion. The deeply spiritual experience of our being on the Parish Pilgrimage to Lourdes together, caused me to presume too much. However, that letter also resulted in the happy circumstance of you returning to work at the shop as my senior assistant. That led, as I predicted, to a most significant improvement in business.

This letter is by way of a new proposal of marriage, in my opinion, a more reasoned and dignified proposition. I hope that when you read it you will feel that you are now able to become my wife.

It is appropriate that you should be aware of my prospects. You will, of course, know the value of the business as a going concern and I would be prepared to make you a full partner. Our notepaper would state this for all the world to see - Proprietors Mr F.B. and Mrs Anamar O'Boyle.

Recently I let go a farm on the outskirts of the town, and the proceeds are now safely in the bank. Investments which my mother, God rest her soul, shrewdly made in the thirties, have prospered. She also left me a number of properties in the district, which are currently rented to responsible tenants.

If you feel my present accommodation unsatisfactory, I would be prepared to consider renovating another property or even building a new house.

I list these assets and prospects in confidence and in no spirit of vain self-esteem, but to illustrate to you that, in terms of capital and income, they should be able to take care of all our reasonable needs.

You may have surmised that I feel holiday travel is somewhat self-indulgent, but I greatly admire your devotion to pilgrimage. Indeed, Father Brogan was just saying to some of us the other day, that you are an example to us all. If you have plans for future pilgrimages, say to Rome or Fatima or even the Holy Land itself, I would be prepared to join you, and would feel that the costs would be within our means on a basis of one per year.

I thought I should mention, too, that Father Brogan is privy to my aspirations and has assured me that the match would be in both our interests.

I have also been encouraged to write to you now, because of the course of events at home. Since your American friend came on the scene, I have been reluctant to press my suit, although I am sure there was nothing untoward between you. However, and as you will have heard, he and Miss Deirdre Ryan have become closely involved with each other and thus, as we might say, this has left the way clear for me.

It is tempting for me to press for an early reply but, bearing in mind the consequences of my previous haste, I am happy to await a response at your convenience, either by letter or in person on your return.

I hope and pray that you will consider my proposal favourably and will consent to become my wife.

Yours truly,

F.B.O'Boyle

High Class Clothing Accessories Stylish Tailoring Dressmaking
Dress and Suit Materials Artistic Millinery Modern Designs
Quality and Value Assured

Anamar had to read it again. When Deirdre had given her the letter, she had been expecting some sort of a proposal, but not in these terms. But when she read that Hank and Deirdre 'have become so closely involved with each other', what did he mean?

Deirdre stirred and sat up in bed.

'I see you eventually got round to F.B.' she said sleepily.

Anamar said nothing. She took the letter over to her friend and went back to her bed. Deirdre began to read it aloud. She was an accomplished mimic and delivered the words in a convincing imitation of F.B.'s precise, serious manner of speaking and in his genteel version of the Donegal accent. She did not notice Anamar's unease or her pale colour.

She began to smile when she came to the list of F.B.'s assets. At his promise of a new house, if required, she laughed.

'And not a word about himself as a fine looking man in his prime, a pillar of the church, a great catch for any decent young woman.'

Then she read of Father Brogan's approval of the match and she shook her head in glee.

'He's called on the full power of the church to bless the match and offered you free world travel to boot, provided he's allowed to come too. You are some lucky woman.'

But as Deirdre came to the news about Hank and herself, her speech slowed. She dropped her imitation of F.B., then suddenly stopped.

'Oh my God! The rat even used me to deliver the letter.' Deirdre was devastated. She sounded confused. Anamar had never seen her looking so bewildered and unhappy. She rose from the bed holding out the letter to Anamar, then seemed to change her mind and headed for the door. Still in her nightdress, she went down the corridor to Hank's room and knocked.

The door closed behind her and Anamar sat still on her bed hugging her knees to her chest. It seemed longer, but a little over five minutes later, Deirdre came back to the room with Hank. He was fully dressed and looked shocked. Deirdre pulled on a dressing gown and they both sat down on her bed.

'We were going to tell you,' Deirdre said quietly, she was embarrassed but knew it was up to her to try to explain. 'When you left for Paris we were drawn together, Hank and I. We began to see each other at week-ends, in Donegal or Belfast. Before either of us realised what was happening, we were more than just good friends.'

'I'm sorry Anamar, we didn't think it was something we could write to you about.' Hank was doing his best.

Anamar had been listening intently and feeling disoriented by this turn of events. Suddenly she was aware of a sensation of relief. She found herself surprised, not annoyed. There had been times when she and Hank could have been much closer, but it had never really happened. They had been very good friends but no more. She could no more have married him than she could have walked down the aisle with F.B.O'Boyle. It was a shock to find that Deirdre, who had always kept the Donegal men at arm's length, had taken to her own American boy-friend, as the others called him in Donegal.

She had been worried about her friendship with Hank, hoping at times that he was not reading too much into it. There were other times when she would have liked to be much closer to him, but that was hardly a good basis for a long-term relationship. It had been so confusing. Now it was solved without anyone being hurt. She hoped it would work out for them and, from her own point of view, as F.B. had put it, it left the way clear for her.

She got up and went to look out of the window. They all knew it was her turn to say something, but she wasn't ready yet. In a way she could hardly believe her luck. She was very fond of Hank and had felt a special bond with him since the time they had met in Lourdes. He had taken her to climb the big mountains, in spite of being in the depths of suicidal depression. She had helped him rise above his illness by encouraging him to see beyond himself. They had become close friends, but she hadn't realised she had been so worried about the future of their relationship.

Much as she liked and admired Hank, she was not in love with him. Deirdre would be much better able to cope with his mood swings. The problem had solved itself.

She turned towards them.

'Don't look so glum,' she said cheerily, 'You'd think Hank and I had been engaged and he was now leaving me in the lurch. You're as bad as the rest of the crowd. You thought we were a couple.'

She was laughing at them, so relieved she could have hugged them both.

'And what about this proposal from F.B.? Are you telling me that I should jump at the chance of such a good match. Next year the four of us could head off to Rome and get the Holy Father's blessings on both the unions.'

Deirdre and Hank smiled at each other. They could share Anamar's relief. She got up and embraced them both. She was pleased for Hank but she held Deirdre tighter still, delighted that her friend had found a man she could love.

At breakfast they shared the kind of happiness Anamar had been anticipating for days as she walked towards the rendezvous. Hank and Deirdre arranged for the car to be left in an empty stable until they would return for it. They agreed that they would walk separately or together, as the mood took them, each travelling at his or her own speed but would meet at prearranged stopping places.

Hank went ahead and left Anamar and Deirdre to walk together. They had made it clear that they had a great deal to talk about which was no concern of his.

'Tell me about your handsome gypsy,' Deirdre had just been waiting for this moment.

'Do you remember the verse we use to recite from Flecker's Hassan,

"We who with songs beguile your pilgrimage ....
Who sing to find your hearts we know not why,"

You and I never thought then we'd be pilgrims together, but I want to know about this troubadour who found your heart with his songs.'

Before Anamar had left home, she and Deirdre could never have talked like this except in jest, but now she was able to tell her about Javier. She described the haunting tunes and rhythms of his drum, the way they held hands, how she had gone to him as he stood at the door in the moonlight. She mentioned the kiss which allowed Alfonso and Diego to escape and Javier to disappear from the doorway like a magician's trick.

Deirdre put her arm around her and they walked on without a word. There was little traffic on the road, mainly lorries and carts. It began to rain and they shared the shelter of Anamar's umbrella. The gorge was damp and foreboding and Anamar was glad she was not alone. She had travelled enough on her own. Now that the situation between her and Hank had been resolved, it gave her a sense of freedom. She felt sure she would enjoy his company more, now she was no longer expected to be his prospective fiancée. These next few days would be very different from the three weeks she had walked by herself from the home of Ramón's parents.

Hank was waiting for them at a café and petrol station, where the Camino de Santiago branched off from the road. The proprietor had been describing their route in detail and had recommended that they stay together for the steep climb to O Cebreiro. They would be passing through remote villages, he said, on a track which was hundreds of years old.

They had coffee with him, for which he would take no payment. An hour later they stopped to have lunch. Deirdre was carrying a small, light rucksack. Hank's was bigger and looked heavier. They produced fruit, cheese, cured ham and tomatoes and had a real picnic on the banks of a river. Hank spoke Spanish quite well and Deirdre could make herself understood. They stopped in villages to talk to the local people more frequently than Anamar had done on her own.

They passed through Vega de Valcarce and Herrerias, entered a deep wooded glen and began to climb steeply on the ancient road. It was more than a narrow track, and In parts still paved with cut stones. The clouds cleared and it became very hot, even in the partial shade of the bushes lining the way.

It was hard going, but in La Faba they were able to refill their water bottles and found the villagers helpful. The route steepened and they climbed slowly, resting frequently in the intense heat. If they had found conditions primitive in la Faba, Laguna de Castilla was like a village from the previous century.

Anamar was aware that farming at home was far less modern than she had seen passing through England and France. She had known before she started her pilgrimage that Northern Spain was one of the poorest regions in Europe.

Since crossing the Pyrenees this had been confirmed, although there were occasional prosperous estates like that of Ramón's parents. But these villages in the Valcarce were the most primitive of all. Farm implements were mainly of wood. There were ox carts, wooden ploughs and massive wooden yokes for oxen.

Nearly all the houses had large conical thatched roofs, low stone walls and no windows. Deirdre knew they were called pallozas, she had been reading about this Celtic region of Spain since she had arranged to join Anamar on the Camino. Another circular thatched construction, this time with slatted wooden walls, was perched on pillars three feet high, with large circular caps like huge stone mushrooms. She recognised them from book illustrations as granaries, called horreos, used for storing maize for the cattle. The mushroom-like caps were to keep the rats out. Hank and Anamar were impressed. The people spoke Gallego rather than Castillian Spanish and it made them sound shy or surly, it was hard to decide which.

Above this hamlet the track came out on the open mountain. A staggering view was revealed of an immense panorama of peaks, woods and valleys cut deeply into the terrain. It was an awe-inspiring landscape.

They rested on a height to look back down the way they had climbed. For their first day, Deirdre and Hank were going well. It was only what Anamar would have expected. She knew that they were strong walkers.

Both wore light leather boots with cleated rubber soles of a type which had been developed during the war for Commandos, and were interested to hear how her sandals had worn over the weeks of walking. Anamar was pleased with them. They had been very comfortable but were now showing wear and she was hoping they would last out to the end of the trip.

The last section into the village was almost flat and their spirits were high when they saw the first of the dwellings. O Cebreiro was perched on the pass between the provinces of Galicia and Castile y Leon. The houses were the same pallozas as they had seen on the way up. There were high stone walls as if the village had been fortified, and behind one of these they found the famous church. The door lay open. The walls were damp. There was a large hole in the roof. The rain and snow were slowly destroying the interior. The church was falling into ruins.

They sat down on a stone ledge at the back and Anamar told them one of Ramón's stories about the Miracle of O Cebreiro. In the 14th century the priest had become disappointed by the tiny number who came to evening Mass. One winter's night, with deep snow on the ground, only one old farmer presented himself for the sacrament. As he served the Host, the priest muttered that only a fool would come out on a night like this for a crust of bread and a sip of wine. And at that moment the bread and the wine were transubstantiated. The story had been told by returning pilgrims and the fame of O Cebreiro had spread throughout Christendom. A beautiful chalice commemorated the miracle, some said it was the Holy Grail brought here by the Knights Templar.

Deirdre rose and crossed to the dry wall. She called the others over and there it was, in an niche, the magnificent golden chalice.

A villager told them that there was no shop, or bar or any house where they could have a cooked meal. He showed them the old Hospederia beside the church which was also in ruins and took them to a palloza which was used by pilgrims as a refuge. It was empty except for a few benches, a table and bags filled with straw as mattresses, but there were no blankets. There was no point in lighting a fire for, although there was a fireplace, there was no chimney. The smoke must escape through the door.

Hank and Deirdre went off around the village on scouting expeditions. He came back with some bread and milk, while she had managed to borrow three blankets. They set the food out on the table. There were two apples, one large tomato and, of course, the milk and bread.

There were no windows and the only light entered through the door. Anamar produced her candle and its soft glow lit the whole room. They were in the process of making their meagre rations into a meal when the door opened and a priest came in to meet them. He had heard they were in the village, he said, and he had brought them a present, a jug of red wine, so sharp it set their teeth on edge.

When he heard that they knew the story of the Chalice, he mentioned another miracle. It had happened in the 16th century, he said, when an ancient statue of the Virgin had inclined its head after an important event. He blessed all three of them before he left, much to Hank's bemusement, and paused on the way out to tell them that Mass was at seven next morning.

They put the three straw mattresses together for warmth, took off their footwear, put on all their spare clothes and wrapped themselves in the blankets. It was so cold and uncomfortable, there was much more conversation than sleep. Each time Anamar dozed off she would waken, shaking violently with the cold.

Deirdre began to scratch and they were soon all itching, as the fleas had a banquet. Deirdre cursed them quietly. Anamar swore herself to silence. Hank remarked, after a prolonged period of scratching, that according to Hilaire Belloc, the fleas had teased in the High Pyrenees, but here in Galicia, the fleas didn't tease, they tortured.

END AND BEGINNING IN SANTIAGO

They were all up and ready to go at half past six, but Anamar felt they should wait for Mass at seven, as the priest had given them a special invitation. Hank came with them but stayed in his seat when the others went forward to the altar. They shivered and scratched in the church but were out and walking in half an hour.

Breakfast was the remains of the bread, washed down with water, and they ate and drank on the move. It had been too cold to wash in the village but after two hours they had warmed up and stopped at a stream. A flea inspection was the first priority. They checked each other's hair, as Deirdre said, 'like a family of baboons, proving Darwin was right'. Every garment was examined, inside and out. Anamar demonstrated her mother's way of catching fleas by embedding them in a bar of wet soap. Hank kept a tally.

'Deirdre three, Anamar two, Hank two,' he announced and a few seconds later, 'Correction, Deirdre six, Anamar four, Hank two. They obviously find you two sweeter than me. I have to admire their taste.' Hank was enjoying himself, and they let him have his fun. It was good to see him in such great form.

Anamar's hair was short and easy to wash but Deirdre's was longer and she needed help. They set out again with their little towels tied across their packs to dry.

There was a short, steep climb to the pass of Alto de Poio and, to their great delight, the small bar at the highest point was open. They had coffee, mantecadas buns and cheese and were able to buy garlic sausage and bread for later.

After the long ascent of the previous day, they took their time on the descent to the valley floor. The path led through beautiful countryside, through acres of yellow broom in full bloom, across streams on rickety bridges, through woods and friendly villages. Eventually the track brought them down an alleyway and out on to the main street of Tricastela.

Anamar left the others resting on a log in the village square and went in search of rooms. When she returned, they could tell by the look on her face that she had succeeded, but she had a surprise for them when they climbed the stairs of a nearby bar.

She had booked two rooms. One was tiny and had a single bed. The other was much bigger with one double bed. She let them lead the way and when they reached the landing, the door of her little room was open so that they could see her pack on the bed she had booked for herself.

At that moment Anamar fully understood her sense of relief when she had discovered that Hank and Deirdre were more than just good friends. Of course it had taken her by surprise when she had first read F.B's letter, but it was easy now to understand why she had not been angry or jealous. Hank had been her first serious boy-friend, but she had been drawn to him by compassion, not the passion of love.

She was unpacking when she heard someone behind her. Deirdre was standing in the doorway,

'I'm trying to decide whether you're an angel or a divil,' she said, trying not to laugh. 'But you can be sure of one thing, my girl. If this ever gets back to Donegal Town, you'll be guilty by association and your chance of getting your hooks into F.B.O'Boyle in holy matrimony will be gone for ever.'

Anamar got up to give her a hug,

'Don't forget to let me know when you've established whether I'm a divil or an angel.' she said coyly, 'But whichever it is, you won't have to look far to find the one who taught me all I know.'

The next day's route to Sarria brought them through a string of tiny, picturesque villages, linked by leafy lanes, well away from roads. it was like travelling through a different country. There were traces of the Romans - a bridge and a house with a wall curved to a bend in the track. Little way-side shrines were decorated with recently cut flowers. Towards the end of the day, Hank turned to Anamar,

'Do you remember the time we climbed in the Enchanted Mountains?' he said quietly, 'When you and the peaks put a spell on me which began to free me from the demons of depression.'

Anamar remembered it well. It had been the happiest time of her life. They had been closer amongst the high peaks than at any time since.

'We should call these the Enchanted Lanes,' Hank said quietly.

It took only five hours to Sarria and it was quite a sizable town. They found a simple fonda and this time Deirdre and Hank took the larger room and Anamar the smaller one, as if this was their usual arrangement.

The size of the dining room showed that this fonda's reputation was for food, not accommodation. It was huge, barn-like, with low beams and an interior wooden balcony reached by a short flight of stairs. The tables were long, bare wooden benches with stools for seats. Hanging from hooks there were hams, bunches of onions and garlic, and two great barrels of wine on trestles, spigots at just the right height.

When they came down to eat the room was full of local people, mostly men, but space had been kept for them at the end of one of the tables. The customers were friendly and it was obvious that the pilgrims were not being treated as passing strangers but as honoured guests.

There must have been ten young men and women serving the forty-odd diners. The wine jugs were filled and refilled as necessary. There were carafes of water and dishes of black and green olives. A huge loaf of local bread was placed at the end of each table with a knife like a small sword to slice it.

The tureens were refilled until no more soup was needed. This was the broth of caldo gallego, the speciality of Galicia. Deirdre asked the serving woman how it was made. It was cooked for a long time, she said, then served in two parts. First the soup, then the stew of pork pieces, turnip tops, potatoes and white beans. The woman laughed,

'It is the best food for pilgrims, the journey feeds the soul but the body needs caldo gallego.'

Without exchanging more than a few words with the other customers, Deirdre and Hank, and even Anamar, who had been on the road for so long, felt so much at ease in this room.

'Why is it a surprise that the food and and wine taste so good here?' Deirdre was not expecting an answer. 'But then haven't I always said that a good meal needs good company.'

Deirdre took the proprietor to one side as they left the room to praise him and his staff, and he went straight back into the dining room to share the compliments with his customers.

Hank reckoned that it would take five or six hours to reach Portomarin and, next morning, they decided that for this day only, each would walk on his or her own the whole way, leaving at fifteen-minute intervals. Anamar would go first and Hank last. Deirdre expressed some reservations but said she would wait for Hank in one of the villages, if she felt need of company.

It was a bright, clear day with high fleecy clouds and a light breeze which kept it pleasantly cool for walking. Like the previous day the route was through leafy lanes and on hill tracks, away from the road. There were so many hamlets, they seemed to pass through at least one in every mile. The people she met waited for Anamar to speak first, and then responded in very friendly fashion.

It puzzled Anamar that she should be enjoying the freedom of being on her own, when it had been so good to have Deirdre and Hank for company for the past few days. After two hours she realised she had been busy with her thoughts and the pace was too fast. It was time for a rest.

Now the end of the Camino was near, each stage was distinctly different. On this day there were ancient oak woods, and fields enclosed with upright slate walls. At times she had to climb the bank at one side to let the shepherd leading his sheep pass, or to make way for a pack mule or an ox cart.

In one place, where the track was the bed of a stream for half a mile, a raised pavement of flat stones, two feet wide and about the same height above the surface of the water, had been built for those on foot. Obviously carts and animals followed the stream bed but people could keep their feet dry. It had to be a Roman construction but still in good condition after centuries of use.

The horreos, the granaries of Galicia, were built of wood, oblong-shaped, with slated roofs, raised on stone pillars and with mushroom-like stone caps to keep the rats out. As she wound her way through these stone-built Celtic villages, Anamar had the most profound sense of being connected with all the pilgrims who had travelled this Camino for a thousand years. She realised that it was only now she felt herself fall into the role of the traditional pilgrim.

Even though it was only twenty miles from home in Ireland, she had never been on pilgrimage to Saint Patrick's Purgatory on Station Island in Lough Derg. A childhood friend of her mother's, who was a frequent pilgrim, had sometimes come to visit and Anamar had been fascinated by her stories of Lough Derg.

A pilgrimage usually lasted three days. Pilgrims fasted from midnight on the night before they arrived until midnight on the day they left. They arrived by rowing boat, and had to go barefoot for the whole visit. They were required to perform nine stations of the Cross and must stay awake for a twenty-four hour vigil. They were not allowed to bring musical instruments or cameras or any food or drink, except water. They were required to sleep in cold draughty dormitories and to endure the vicious bites of tiny midges which congregated in dense clouds, even in the day rooms and dormitories.

It was a time for prayer and penance, with suffering as the key to grace. Her own pilgrimage to Santiago seemed so different. Of course, it was very much longer, but then it was a journey of the spirit. There was the extreme physical effort of walking for so many days but, for her, there had been no deliberate mortification of the flesh as there was on the Lough Derg pilgrimage.

Anamar's moments of enlightenment on the Camino had come through the inspiration of the experience, not the suffering. When she prayed, it felt as if she was talking to God as a friend, not as a task-master. But how would she explain the experience when she went back home? Would no one understand, least of all Father Brogan? Would Deirdre and Hank be the only ones with whom she could discuss the journey?

In the afternoon she came over a rise and saw a town in the floor of the valley, built around a bridge over a great river. She waited for Deirdre and they walked down together. Hank joined them at the bridge and they found rooms in a house near the beautiful church of San Nicolás.

Next morning after Mass the priest was keen to talk. Pilgrims always brought the most interesting news, he said, laughing, keeping them entertained for twenty minutes. He invited them to stay with him the next time they came on the Camino,

'Pilgrims always come back, but don't leave it too long,' he said as they were leaving, 'The authorities will build a dam here in the next ten years and the whole village will be moved, stone by stone, to a new site high above the water. God alone knows what they will have done with me by then.'

They climbed out of the valley and stayed together for the next two stages to Arzua, staying a night in Palas de Rei on the way. Reminiscing about this part of the walk months later, all three agreed that it had been one of the happiest times of their lives. These were the enchanted lanes again, leading to tiny villages hiding away from roads.

They could only find one room in Palas de Rei with one double bed and Hank had to sleep on the floor. The weather stayed fine but the heat made the going hard. There was shade in the lanes and a breeze every time they climbed across a rise. The eucalyptus trees filtered the light and their scent made the walk through these woods idyllic.

Some of the little schools in remote areas were the only ugly buildings, square-set, concrete constructions, built to some plan devised by an authority in a distant city, without any concession to the traditional style of Galicia. There were more traces of Roman road and bridges, some restored - but not all well done. There were scallop shell motifs, and sometimes the dagger-shaped cross or sword of Santiago, painted blood red. They appeared on churches, village walls, fountains, on the roofs of horreos, decorating small shrines, as if this route only existed as the Road to Santiago. Next day they climbed a steep short hill and walked down the long, afternoon road into the sun.

Arzua was as pleasant a small town as they could have hoped for. There was a wide main street, shops, bars and three fondas. The first no longer let rooms, it was open only for meals. The second was dingy and dilapidated. The third was just outside the town and looked newly opened.

The proprietor and his wife were delighted to see them. The rooms were large and comfortable, but the shared bathroom was the owners' pride and joy. The walls were tiled with small white tiles, the floor with smooth slabs of dark blue slate. There was a porcelain wash hand basin, a big bath, a shower and the luxury of a sit down lavatory bowl. Deirdre announced that she intended to spend most of their stay in the bathroom and they could allocate the bedrooms as they wished.

They left Arzua in the rain on their second last day, through the farmland and rolling countryside of Galicia. It was like a wet morning at home, with no one out and about unless they had need to be. Anamar led the way on her own and, after a short time together, Hank let Deirdre walk on and followed a distance behind. Although the gaps between them were never more than half a mile, they were out of sight of each other for most of the morning. It was nearly a week since they had met at Villafranca and each felt the need for time without talk.

After two and a half hours in the rain, Anamar stopped to wait for the others at a bar. Deirdre took off her waterproof jacket in the doorway. Like Anamar she was wearing a skirt, very comfortable for walking in the heat but on this day the bottom of it was saturated. Hank pulled off his cape with a flourish and gave it a shake. He was dry except for the bottoms of his trousers. Because there had been no wind, Anamar's umbrella had probably given the best protection of all.

They spent a long time over coffee, talking quietly. On a walk like this there was time for conversation as well as silence. It was easy to speak about the inner thoughts in a way which would be well-nigh impossible at home. They could share their feelings and ideas, trusting the others to understand, leaving a topic and taking it up again later that evening or next day.

Over the second cup of coffee they agreed that the experience of the pilgrimage had made them all more sensitive. High and low points were so much more pronounced. A light-hearted moment could give great joy, but they were all vulnerable to the sad or cruel thought, the effect of which could be devastating.

On the previous day, Hank had been descending steps through dense undergrowth when he felt himself step on something soft. He had managed to lift his foot away without putting his full weight on it. Five or six steps later he had realised that it must have been a frog and had gone back to see what had happened. There was no sign of it on the step or in the surrounding undergrowth.

'Ok! Ok! It was only a frog,' he said, slightly embarrassed, 'And no he-man worth the name would give it a second thought. But I was glad I hadn't killed it.'

It was much better, Anamar said, now she was no longer alone. They could share the fun or the distressing thoughts. The time on her own had given her inner strength. She felt resilient now to the chance misfortune. When she had been by herself the silence had given her time to think about her beliefs. When she had met Raoul and Paul, she had enjoyed the company. Her time with Ramón had given her confidence. But now she was beginning to understand her pilgrimage.

Deirdre had been very quiet. She told them a story she had come across when she was reading about the Camino.

'Although it all happened a very long time ago I feel so bad about it,' she said quietly, looking at Anamar, 'I was dreading you would mention it when you were telling us about the Bishop's Palace in Astorga. You might not have noticed it when you were there but, opposite the palace and beside the Cathedral, is a cell, called Emparedadas, where once loose-living women were incarcerated. They were walled in their prison, with the only opening a small iron-barred window through which passing pilgrims could give them food and water.'

She sighed and took hold of Anamar's hand.

'I'm ashamed to say that when I read this in the comfort of my own home, I saw it as just another bizarre custom of the past. But it has been haunting me on this walk. To think of those women incarcerated for life, uncared for, living in their own filth, dependent on the whim of passing pilgrims for food and water. Man's inhumanity to his fellow men has ony been matched by his inhumanity to women.'

Deirdre's head went down and her shoulders shook. No one said a word but Anamar put an arm around her. In a few moments Deirdre looked up, wiping her eyes with a handkerchief.

'Maybe telling you the story will exorcise it from my mind. But that's enough trauma for one day,' she said, 'Let's get on the road again. You can tell us about the phantom stalker who chased you around the Pyrenees.'

Outside, the rain was over, the heat of the sun was drying the road, wisps of mist rising from the wet surface.

Anamar built the story up over the next few miles, the shock of hearing the stranger behind her in the mountain forest, the tramp of his footsteps on the road, the smell of his pipe tobacco, the sight of him far below when she crossed a pass. She explained her plan to shake him off by pretending to stay in a village, then moving on in the evening, and how she had found herself in Poudri's inn on the col.

'Out of the frying pan and into the fire,' said Deirdre and Anamar tried to ignore her.

She decided that this was not the time to tell them the full story of Poudri's attack and her night flight down the mountain.

'Then when I was crossing the high Pyrenean pass into Spain with Paul and Raoul,' she said, 'They came up with this hare-brained plan to ambush the stalker.'

'I didn't want to have anything to do with it. But they leapt out on this poor man from behind a boulder. Raoul was hauling and pulling at him like a drunken sailor. Paul was punching him like an angry leprehchaun and I had to separate the three of them before he did them both an injury.' Anamar was acting out the fight as they walked along and Hank and Deirdre were laughing, enjoying the story.

'And as soon as I saw the man's face, I was mortified. It was Ramón. He had been following me for days to keep an eye on me, and the only time I needed him I managed to give him the slip.'

'And you're telling us that even that débacle didn't put him off,' said Deirdre, arching her eyebrows. 'A clear case of blind love and devotion if ever I saw it. I'll need to meet this fellow to see if he's suitable.'

In the afternoon they climbed a hill with the sunshine filtering through the grey-green leaves of a eucalyptus forest. The smell was like a balm for the spirit. Very little was said. They had been talking for a week and were content to be quiet.

Anamar could not help but notice that Hank was a changed man. He had always looked physically strong, determined in his movements. Now there was something more. There was an air of self-confidence, the self-assurance of a man at ease with the world. For the first time since she had met him in the bookshop in Lourdes, he was truly happy.

It was hard to find rooms in Lavacolla, the village where pilgrims traditionally washed before the last stage into Santiago. They were about to walk on when Deirdre asked an old lady, and she led them with tiny, frail steps to her home on the edge of the village. Her girls were gone, she said, and they could have their room.

In the morning, Deirdre and Anamar were waiting for Hank. He was taking much longer than usual to get ready. He was always ready first, standing at the door, rucksack on his back. Deirdre went upstairs to investigate.

'You'll never believe it,' she said to Anamar when she came back, 'He's had blisters for the past two days and is so embarrassed he's been treating them when we weren't looking. Isn't it the price of him. The expert walker finds he's human after all.'

Hank appeared behind her, treading carefully, looking mortified now his secret was out.

'I could have told you before you set out,' Deirdre said grandly, 'It was certain sure St James would find a way of reminding a heretic like yourself which was the true faith.'

Anamar gave Hank a sympathetic look and offered him sticking plasters. She could tell that Deirdre would never let him forget the time he had blisters on the Santiago walk.

'I'm only surprised,' she said to Deirdre eventually, 'That Santiago hasn't got around to you yet. Never mind, there's still a wee way to go. I'm sure you'll be on his list.

They left Lavacolla, passed the bandstand, and climbed steadily on the road. It was hot early, and a relief to turn off towards the crest of a hill at Monte del Gozo, where pilgrims traditionally had their first sight of Santiago de Compostela.

Half an hour later, they were in the streets of the city, finding their own way without asking for help. Modern streets led to ancient passage ways and little squares. Deirdre saw them first, twin spires that could only be the Cathedral. For the first time that day they were silent, walking straight on, side by side, past the massive walls of church premises. A flight of steps led down, under the shadow of an arch and out into a patch of sunlight in the great square.

It was the Plaza del Obradoiro. To their right was the magnificent facade of a pilgrim hospital built by Ferdinand and Isabella, Los Reys Católicos, and now an elegant hotel. They turned around and faced the Cathedral, still in shadow. It towered above the square, its stones far darker than Anamar had imagined, its presence more foreboding. The cloud moved on and the cathedral shared their sunshine, its stone now pale golden, intricately sculpted, its look still ominous from this distance but far less threatening.

There were very few people in the square, some climbing the cathedral steps, others strolling in groups. Anamar, Deirdre and Hank embraced in a little ring, arms around shoulders. They thanked each other for the companionship of the Camino.

They broke up smiling. Now that her long journey was finished, Anamar felt a strange sense of loss. She had been on the Road to Santiago for almost eight weeks. There was no sensation of achievement in terms of distance travelled, but there was fulfilment and gratitude for the experience. She was sure she was now a different person. This was the climax of the most important event in her life thus far. She was certain that the Camino would affect her entire future.

She told the others that she was going into the cathedral to thank St James for a safe pilgrimage.

'I'll come too,' said Deirdre, 'If I'm to say all the prayers I need to say, I'd better get started.'

Neither of them asked Hank to join them in case he felt it was an invitation he should not refuse.

'This is the famous Portal of Glory,' Deirdre announced, 'There's a pillar here called the Tree of Jesse. You place your hand in the holes worn deep into the rock by the fingers of pilgrims over hundreds of years. She and Anamar joined the small queue waiting their turn to do so, and neither noticed that Hank had joined the line as well, four or five places behind them.

The cathedral was over half full, and they gathered from a Spanish woman that High Mass was about to begin in a few minutes time, at noon. They sat down near the back and neither was surprised when Hank slipped in beside them.

Deirdre leaned across Anamar to speak to him,

'Tell me if this isn't a fair question,' she whispered, 'But what's a Protestant from the Bible-Belt of the good old USA doing in a Roman Catholic Cathedral in Spain?'

Hank smiled.

'Beg pardon ma'am,' he said, 'But this pilgrimage was rolling long before the Reformation. When this place was built, we were all part of the same church. I reckon you could say even we Methodists own part of it.' He was smiling as he nodded at the vast interior of the cathedral.

Anamar stuffed a finger knuckle in her mouth to stop herself from laughing, the way she, Maureen and Maggie used to do when they were having a fit of the giggles at Mass.

Before the Sacrament, four robed men hoisted a huge, smoking censer high in the nave.

'It's called the botafumeiro,' Deirdre whispered, 'The fumes from the burning incense are meant to disguise the smell of the pilgrims.'

The men swung the censer in great arcs, lengthening the swing until the crowds gasped as it dipped low above their heads.

When the censer had been returned to rest, a procession of men and women in traditional dress came down the aisle, the women in black skirts and beautifully embroidered bodices, with long aprons, little hats and elaborate jewellery. The men wore black jackets and breeches with knee boots and black big-brimmed hats.

They carried loaves of bread and baskets of fruit and vegetables to present to a welcoming party of three priests, waiting at one side of the altar. Some of the young men bore poles with signs showing the names of their villages.

'The Maragatos from Astorga and its villages,' said the woman next to Deirdre, 'This is their annual pilgrimage.'

When the people moved forward for the Sacrament, Deirdre and Anamar waited until the first had been served. A well-dressed couple stood up near the front and filed forward to take their turn. Anamar was startled by a feeling of familiarity although she could see only their backs. She restrained Deirdre for a few moments and clutched her hand when the couple turned away from the priest.

'It's Ramón and his mother,' she whispered in her ear.

As she and Deirdre returned from the altar rails, Ramón and his mother saw her. They were sitting at the end of a row and she paused when she reached them.

'You're a day early,' said Ramón quietly, with a smile.

'Welcome to Santiago,' said his mother, Doña Marie.

When they sat down, Deirdre was now the one in the middle and she was able to tell Hank what had happened.

'This isn't just a happy coincidence,' she declared to the both of them, 'He had it all worked out, knowing when you'd be arriving here almost to the day. No wonder you were so happy when I took this American off your hands.'

They met outside the Portal of Glory and Anamar did the introductions.

'Please, please,' said Doña Marie to Deirdre and Hank, 'I hope we will become good friends. I have heard so much about you. But although we are in Spain, no titles please, you must call me Marie.' They had to step to one side to let the procession of Maragatos out of the Cathedral door.

One of the signs on the poles held by the boys said, 'Anamar, the Irish Pilgrim,' and Deirdre spotted it first. The young man holding it aloft had been asked by José, the Hostal barman in Astorga, to carry it around Santiago until he found Anamar and could give her an envelope.

The letter had been painstakingly written in English, congratulating her on the completion of her pilgrimage and stating that they were now brother and sister in Santiago.

Anamar tore a page from her notebook and wrote José a note which she sealed and gave to the young man, without letting any of the others see what she had written. Doña Marie suggested coffee and they found a café in a little street across the square.

Before they sat down, Doña Marie, reached across and picked a speck from Deirdre's blouse. It was a flea and she cracked it between the nails of her thumb and ring finger. Later Anamar would say that anyone else would have been mortified, but not Deirdre.

'I see you have a great skill for the killing of fleas, which has been perfected by frequent practice,' she said quickly and Doña Marie laughed.

'Better dead than biting,' she said and linked her arm through Deirdre's.

They booked into the small hotel in which Ramón and Marie were staying and agreed to meet for dinner at eight. Anamar and Ramón strolled the arcaded streets of the old part of the city, and Doña Marie went to visit the cathedral museum. Hank and Deirdre disappeared into the narrow alleyways on their own.

That evening Ramón insisted that he would host the meal. He had been to one of the restaurants and booked a table. The wines were Galician, the red vintage, the white well chilled. The array of tapas was of local specialities, served in earthenware bowls and Doña Marie explained what was on offer.

The main course was a huge silver platter of scallops. They were served in their shells in Galician style, with a butter sauce flavoured with minced shallots, lemon juice, black pepper and parsley. The cheese came next, in the Spanish way and then a large almond tart decorated with icing sugar in the spectacular dagger-like shape of the cross of Santiago.

Hank surprised even himself by leading the conversation. He told them about his blisters, as if his reputation as a mountaineer would never recover. He described the meal of bread and the Priest's sharp wine at O Cebreiro. He had them all scratching when he talked about the fleas that tortured in high Galicia.

He pretended that Deirdre was so fussy about her hair she wore a night cap in bed. He told the others that he had secretly christened Anamar the Angel of the Camino and Deirdre, the Santiago Sorceress. He described how he had entertained himself by making up stories about the adventures of the Angel and the Sorceress, when they were too busy chatting to notice him.

Doña Marie loved this company. These young people made her feel youthful too. She decided that she would do much more entertaining at home. She would look up old friends. She would invite these two Irish women and their American friend to come to stay. There would be dinner parties and a fiesta for the villagers. The servants had enjoyed the break in their routine when Anamar had stayed with them.

And if their friends could not come to them, she and the Don Henriques would go visiting. They would travel the world. Her husband would be hard to persuade, but if he would not go with her, she would go alone. Anamar and Deirdre were an inspiration. If they could do it, so could she.

They spent two glorious days in Santiago in the sunshine, with only an occasional downpour to remind them that Galicia was as wet as Ireland. All five of them packed into Ramón's car for the drive back to Villafranca to collect Deirdre's car. For the next stage Hank travelled with Deirdre to share the driving and Anamar stayed with Ramón and Doña Marie. They spent a happy last night together in Burgos, in the luxury of the Mesón El Cid Hotel beside the cathedral, dining well and walking arm and arm in the starlight through the deserted streets.

In the morning they brought the luggage out to the cars. This was where their ways parted. The road to Bilbao and the boat to England branched to the left outside the city, while Ramón's parents home lay straight ahead.

'Yesterday in the car,' Anamar said, looking at Deirdre and Hank, 'When Doña Marie asked me if I would like to go back home with them for a few days, Ramón suggested that the three of us should go on to Mont L'ours-les-Cascades and stay with him for a while.'

Deirdre's look showed not the least surprise.

'I asked for time to think it over last night,' Anamar was finding it hard to tell them but she knew Deirdre would understand. 'It's a very kind invitation and I've accepted.'

Deirdre hugged her tightly and they kissed on both cheeks. Anamar embraced Hank and produced five scallop shells from a paper bag.

'After the meal in Santiago, I went back to the restaurant and collected one for each of us,' she said, 'They'll remind us of our time together on the Camino.'

Hank and Deirdre said their good byes and left first. The car stopped a few yards away and Deirdre beckoned Anamar towards her.

'And what do I say to the lovely F.B.O'Boyle?' she said.

Anamar produced a letter from her pocket.

'I almost forgot to give you this for him,' she said, 'You could always invite him to be best man at your wedding. But well dare you tie the knot until I get back.'

It was remarkable for a woman who found it hard to cry, but there was a tear in Deirdre's eye as they drove off. It was a tear of joy for her friend, the Irish Pilgrim.